I0681550

THE GOLDEN PICKLES OF HOLLOW FIELDS

Hector L. Bones

The Bones Family

CONTENTS

EPILOGUE

AFTERWORD

Library of Congress Control Number:

Book Cover by Hector L. Bones

Illustrations by Hector L. Bones

1st edition 2025

DEDICATION

I dedicate this book to my beautiful wife **Debbie N. Bones**, who has been a great support and source of inspiration. She is the most brilliant person I know to which I can count to bounce off ideas and helping me through but also helps me keep on track and complete our projects in life.

Without you **Debbie** my love I would never have got the courage to get this book out.

I also dedicate this book to my children who inspired me to put my ideas on paper and bring them to life. Thanks **Aerith Nyomi, Alisher Krystal and Aiden Kalel**, for being great kids and an infinite source of inspiration.

INTRODUCTION

A Note Before You Enter Hollow Fields

Small towns collect stories the way old houses collect dust.

Some are the friendly kind—the football legend who never quite left the field, the diner pie that "saved a marriage," the shortcut road you're not supposed to drive after midnight. Others are quieter, half-whispered, wrapped up in warnings that sound like jokes until you notice nobody's laughing.

Hollow Fields is one of those towns.

On the surface, it has everything a place like this should: a farmer's market, a field that goes on longer than it should, a long memory. And for more than a century, it had a strange little specialty—Golden Pickles in squat glass jars, sold on a predictable schedule to anyone willing to make the trip.

That's the tourist version.

The version this book cares about starts underneath that. It starts where a bargain was made with the land itself, where a town learned to live with a curse it didn't fully understand, and where "tradition" stopped meaning recipes and parades and started meaning something much colder.

At the center of it all is a small circle of friends who don't agree on much except this: the official story doesn't make sense. One of them is better with soil than people. One sees the world through a lens. One speaks fluent data. One knows all the angles because he's spent too long running them. They are not heroes on purpose. They're just the ones who were standing closest when the wrong truths started to crack.

In Hollow Fields, the supernatural isn't a doorway to power so much as a machine that's been running too long. Guardian and monster aren't clean categories. The things in the trees know exactly how to use your empathy against you. And sometimes the price for breaking a curse isn't paid in blood on an altar, but in the shape of the life you'll never get to live.

This story is about Golden Pickles and ghost stories and creatures at the edge of the field—but it's also about grief, and what it means to choose responsibility when every easy option is right there within reach. It asks what we owe to the people who came before us, what we owe to each other, and what happens when someone finally decides that "the way it's always been" isn't good enough anymore.

You don't need a map to start. The rules of Hollow Fields will unfold as you go. Trust the land, just enough. Trust the people, cautiously. And pay attention to what happens at the boundary—where the town ends, where the field begins, and where one person's choice might change the shape of everything.

Thank you for picking up The Golden Pickles of Hollow Fields. When you're ready, step over the line with them.

Just remember: in this town, even the smallest jar on the market table might be part of a much bigger bargain.

PROLOGUE

Josh checked the motion sensor for the third time, then caught himself reaching for it a fourth. The battery indicator still glowed 94%. He tapped the equipment case. "Should I swap it for the 97% one? Dad always said use your best tools first, but Grandpa said—"

"You're spiraling." Emily didn't look up from her notebook, pencil scratching observations about the empty market spread before them.

"I'm preparing." Josh shoved his hands in his pockets to stop the fidgeting. "There's a difference."

"Mm-hmm." Emily's pencil kept moving. "How many times have you checked that sensor?"

A grin tugged at Josh's mouth despite the three AM jitters. "Okay. Maybe a little spiraling."

He settled next to Tyler, who was hunched over his laptop monitoring the camera feeds. The market stretched ahead of them, bathed in the pale glow of security lights—empty stalls with canvas tarps snapping in the breeze, vendor trucks parked in neat rows, everything quiet and normal. Exactly how a farmers' market should look at three in the morning.

Too normal.

Josh pulled out the hand-drawn map his grandfather had sketched forty years ago, the edges worn soft from handling. Same layout. Same vendor positions. Like the place was frozen in time. The Golden Pickles legend had been part of his life since Grandpa first told him the story—one of those family tales that got passed down not because anyone believed it, but because it was interesting. A farmer who appeared four times a year selling impossible pickles, then vanished. Everyone had theories. Nobody had proof.

Until tonight.

"Tell me again why we're doing this?" Mike's voice cut through the quiet. He was leaning against Emily's van, arms crossed, though his eyes tracked the market perimeter with military precision. Old habits from his brief stint in ROTC before he'd dropped out.

"Because it's impossible," Josh said, which was reason enough for him.

"That's not a real answer."

"Sure it is." Josh traced the vendor positions on his map. "Four times a year, same spot, pickles that glow like someone stuffed sunlight in a jar. People taste them and can't describe the flavor. Try to resell them and they vanish. That's not just weird—that's a pattern weird. And patterns can be figured out."

Olivia lowered her camera long enough to glance at them. "Your grandfather tried figuring it out. He came back with nothing."

"He came back with questions." Josh folded the map carefully. "There's a difference. And Mom dropped it when she took over his research position. But I think—" He paused, trying to name the feeling that had been building since childhood, listening to Grandpa's stories in that worn armchair, pipe smoke curling toward the ceiling. "I think this is the kind of thing worth finishing."

"Worth staying up all night for?" Mike asked.

"Worth figuring out." Josh pulled out his phone, checked the time again. Three seventeen. Market opened at six. The farmer—if legend held—would appear just before dawn. "The pickles are just the start. The real mystery is how. How does he arrive without anyone seeing? How does he set up in minutes? How does he always sell out? Those are engineering problems. Dad could solve engineering problems."

"Your dad fixes tractors," Emily pointed out.

"Yeah, and tractors are machines with patterns. This is just..." Josh gestured at the market. "A pattern we haven't cracked yet."

Tyler suddenly straightened, fingers flying across his keyboard. "Motion sensor just pinged."

Everyone tensed.

"Which one?" Josh was already moving, pulling up the feed on his own phone.

"East entrance." Tyler's voice had taken on that clipped precision it got when he was focused. "Something tripped it. Small signature. Could be an animal, could be—wait. It stopped. Not moving anymore."

Josh scanned the camera feeds. Nothing visible. Just empty asphalt and canvas tarps. "Show me the thermal."

"Already on it." Tyler pulled up another window. "There. Faint heat signature near the oak tree. Stationary now."

"That's weird." Emily had moved closer, peering over Tyler's shoulder. She pointed at the screen. "Look at the heat pattern. That's not an animal. Too concentrated. Too steady."

"Maybe someone else is staking out the farmer?" Olivia suggested, camera already raised.

"At three AM?" Mike's hand had drifted to the tactical flashlight on his belt. "Who camps out for pickles?"

"Us," Josh and Emily said simultaneously, then exchanged a grin. They'd been pulling this kind of thing since they were kids, following Grandpa's research around Emily's family farm.

Tyler's fingers kept moving. "Heat signature's fading. Like it's... cooling down? That doesn't make sense. Unless—"

The laptop screen flickered. Once. Twice. Then went black.

"What did you do?" Mike asked.

"Nothing. I didn't—" Tyler hammered keys. "Battery's fine. Connection's solid. The whole system just stopped." He looked up, confusion clear on his face. "That's not possible. I've got redundancies on the redundancies."

"Maybe it overheated?" Olivia offered, though her tone suggested she didn't believe it.

"In October? At three AM?" Tyler was already pulling cables, checking connections. "No. Something actively killed the feed."

A cold prickle ran down Josh's spine—not fear, exactly, but that feeling he got when a puzzle suddenly showed more pieces than he'd expected. "All the cameras?"

"All of them." Tyler pulled up his phone, tried to ping the motion sensors manually. "I'm getting nothing. It's like the whole network just... disappeared."

Josh walked to the edge of their makeshift camp, staring at the market. Still empty. Still quiet. The tarps still snapped in the breeze. But something felt different now. Like the air had changed temperature, or the shadows had shifted angles.

"We should check it out," he said.

"Or," Mike countered, "we should acknowledge that having all our equipment simultaneously fail is a really good sign to pack it up."

"We can't pack up. We've been planning this for weeks." Josh looked back at his friends. Emily was watching him with that expression she got— the one that said she could see him working through the problem, see the gears turning. "This is exactly what Grandpa described. Equipment failing. Heat signatures vanishing. That's how the farmer disappears. Whatever we're seeing, this is it. This is the mechanism."

"Or it's just a technical glitch," Emily said, but her voice had lost its certainty. She'd seen the heat signature too. Watched it fade.

"Tech doesn't glitch in patterns." Tyler had stopped trying to revive the system and was now staring at his dark screens. "Simultaneous failure across independent systems? Statistically, that's—" He paused, doing math in his head. "That's basically impossible."

"Impossible is kind of the theme tonight," Olivia murmured, her camera pointed at the market though she wasn't taking pictures. Just looking. Recording in her own way.

Josh made a decision. "I'm going to check the perimeter. See if I can spot what triggered the sensor."

"Josh—" Emily started.

"I won't go far. Just a quick walk around. Dad always said when something breaks, you learn more from investigating the break than if it worked perfectly." He was already moving, pulling on his jacket. "Plus, we've got flashlights. Five of us. It's not like I'm going alone into the woods."

"That's exactly what people say right before they go alone into the woods," Mike pointed out.

"Then come with me." Josh looked at Mike, then the others. "All of us. Five minute perimeter check. See if we can find what spooked the sensors."

Emily stood, slinging her notebook into her bag. "Five minutes. Then we reassess."

"Thank you." Josh felt the familiar pressure ease slightly—the one that whispered you can't let them down, you have to make this worth it. They'd all given up their Friday night for this. Skipped parties, ignored homework, sat in a cold parking lot at three AM because he'd convinced them the Golden Pickles were worth investigating. He had to deliver something.

They moved as a group, Mike instinctively taking point, flashlight sweeping the path ahead. Tyler stayed close to the middle, still trying to revive the system on his phone. Olivia captured everything with her camera, though she'd switched to low-light mode—the flash would ruin their night vision. Emily walked beside Josh, and he was grateful for her solid presence, the way she'd been there for every one of his weird fixations since they were seven.

The market felt different up close. Not threatening, exactly, but aware. Like walking through a room and knowing someone was watching even though you couldn't see them.

"There." Mike's flashlight caught something near the oak tree Tyler had identified. "What is that?"

They approached carefully. On the ground, near the tree's massive roots, were footprints. Just a few, pressed into the soft dirt from yesterday's rain. But they didn't look right. Too large. Too deep. And the tread pattern was weird—smooth in some places, ridged in others, like someone had been wearing boots from three different manufacturers at once.

Josh knelt, studying them. "These are fresh. Look at the edges—still sharp. Rain was yesterday afternoon, so these were made sometime between then and now."

"Big guy," Mike observed. "Size fourteen, at least."

"And walking carefully." Emily pointed at the spacing. "Look how even they are. Deliberate steps, not rushed."

Olivia crouched, getting shots from multiple angles. "Whoever it was, they were watching the market. See how the prints face the vendor area? They stood here for a while."

Tyler had finally abandoned his phone and was examining the tree trunk. "Look at this." He touched something on the bark—a small mark, carved shallow. Not natural. "Is this a symbol?"

Josh leaned closer. It was simple, just a few lines intersecting, but it had been cut recently. The wood was still pale. "Could be a surveyor's mark. Or —"

A sound cut through the quiet. Distant but distinct: the rumble of an engine.

They all froze.

"It's not even four AM," Emily whispered. "Vendors don't arrive until five thirty."

The engine sound grew closer, coming from the west entrance—the one they hadn't been watching because their cameras had failed. An old truck, by the sound of it. Something that shouldn't still be running but somehow was, engine knocking like a heartbeat.

"Move," Mike said quietly. "Back to the van. Now."

They didn't run—that would draw attention—but they moved quickly, keeping low, using the vendor stalls as cover. Josh's mind raced, trying to fit this new piece into the puzzle. The footprints, the symbol, the failed equipment, now this. It was all connected. Had to be.

They reached their camp just as headlights swept across the market entrance. An ancient pickup rolled in, paint job so faded the color was impossible to determine, Michigan plates that looked older than Josh's parents. It moved slowly, deliberately, toward the exact spot where legend said the Golden Pickles vendor always set up.

"That's him," Josh breathed. "That's actually him."

Tyler had his camera app open, recording everything even though the system was still down. Mike positioned himself between the truck and their group, instinct taking over. Olivia's camera clicked steadily, capturing the moment. Emily had her notebook out, pen moving.

The truck parked. Engine shut off. For a long moment, nothing happened.

Then the driver's door opened.

Josh couldn't see the figure clearly—the headlights were behind him, casting his face in shadow—but he was tall, wearing overalls and a straw hat that looked like it belonged in a different decade. He moved around to the truck bed, started pulling out crates with an efficiency that suggested he'd done this a thousand times before.

"He's setting up," Emily murmured. "It's four AM and he's just... setting up like it's normal."

"Where did he come from?" Mike asked. "We were watching the roads. All of them."

"Doesn't matter." Josh was fixated on the figure. This was real. After all Grandpa's stories, after forty years of legends and rumors and failed attempts, this was real. "We're watching it happen."

The farmer worked in silence, assembling his stall with practiced movements. Every action precise. No wasted energy. Within minutes— impossibly fast minutes—he had a full vendor setup: table, canopy, price signs, and several crates that presumably held the pickles themselves.

Then he stopped. Just stopped, standing behind his completed stall, motionless.

Waiting for dawn.

Josh's heart hammered against his ribs. They'd done it. They'd caught the farmer arriving. This was the evidence they needed, the first real piece of the puzzle—

The farmer turned. Looked directly at their hiding spot.

Josh felt his breath catch. Beside him, Emily went very still. Tyler's phone camera was still recording, but his hand had stopped moving.

The farmer raised one hand. Not a wave. Not a threat. Just... an acknowledgment. I see you.

Then he turned back to his stall, face hidden again, and resumed his vigil.

"Did that just—" Mike started.

"Yeah," Emily said quietly. "He knows we're here."

Olivia lowered her camera slowly. "I've seen a lot of strange things. But that—"

"That's impossible," Tyler finished. "We're fifty yards away. In shadow. With the headlights facing away. There's no way he could see us."

But he had. Josh was certain of it. The farmer knew they were watching. Had maybe known the whole time. This wasn't just a man selling unusual pickles. This was something else. Something that followed different rules.

"So," Mike said after a long pause. "What now?"

Josh stared at the distant figure, mind racing through possibilities. They could leave. Pack up, go home, call this a successful night because they'd caught the farmer arriving on film. Or—

"We wait," Josh decided. "Watch him until the market opens. See what happens with the pickles. Maybe approach him, ask questions."

"Josh—" Emily's voice carried a warning.

"I know. I know it's weird. But look at him." Josh gestured at the figure. "He's just standing there. Not hiding. Not threatening. Just... waiting. Maybe he wants us to watch. Maybe that's why he acknowledged us."

"Or maybe," Mike countered, "he was warning us to leave."

"Only one way to find out." Josh settled in, determination overriding the small voice that whispered this was bigger than he'd expected. They'd come too far to back down now. The farmer was real. The legend had substance. Everything Grandpa had wondered about, everything Mom had dismissed —it was all right there, waiting to be understood.

He pulled out his phone, started taking notes. Time: 4:03 AM. Location: west vendor lot, position 17. Farmer arrived in truck (make/model unclear, Michigan plates), set up in approximately seven minutes. Observed us, acknowledged our presence. Currently standing motionless behind completed stall.

Emily was writing too, creating her own record. Tyler had switched to his backup phone, getting footage from a different angle. Olivia moved slowly around their perimeter, capturing the scene from multiple perspectives. Mike stayed on alert, keeping watch not just on the farmer but on the entire market, the woods beyond, the roads leading in.

Dawn crept closer. The sky lightened from black to deep blue to grey. Other vendors would arrive soon, unaware of the vigil that had started hours earlier. The farmer stood motionless, a sentinel waiting for something only he could sense.

And Josh watched, his grandfather's map heavy in his pocket, his father's advice echoing in his mind—when something breaks, investigate the break—and felt the shape of the mystery shifting. The Golden Pickles had been the surface. The farmer was another layer. But beneath it all, Josh could sense something else. Some larger pattern he hadn't seen yet.

"Whatever this is," he said quietly to Emily, "we're going to figure it out."

She glanced at him, and in her expression he saw concern mixed with that familiar determination she got when they were kids, following one of his schemes. "That's what worries me," she said. "You always do."

The sun touched the horizon.

And the farmer, for the first time in over an hour, moved.

He reached into one of the crates and pulled out a jar. Even from their distance, they could see the golden glow. Not reflected light from the dawn. Not a trick of perception. The pickles inside truly glowed, as if lit from within, casting a soft radiance that made the morning shadows seem darker by comparison.

The farmer placed the jar on the table. Then another. And another. Ten jars total, arranged in a precise pattern that Josh's pattern-recognition brain immediately tried to map. Two rows of five? No—something more complex. A constellation? A symbol?

"Let me think about it," Josh murmured, his verbal tic emerging as he processed.

Emily touched his arm. "Cars coming. Vendors."

She was right. Headlights appeared on the access road, the first of the early-bird vendors arriving to set up. Within minutes, the market would wake up, and their chance to study the farmer in isolation would end.

"We should approach him now," Josh said. "Before it gets crowded."

"Bad idea," Mike said immediately.

"Worse idea is waiting," Josh countered. "Once other people arrive, we lose our chance. He might leave. Or we get lost in the crowd. This is it."

Tyler looked up from his phone. "Equipment's still dead, by the way. Every sensor. Every camera. Complete blackout."

"Because of him?" Olivia asked.

"Or because of what he represents," Emily suggested, her anthropology training kicking in. "Sometimes the mystery is more important than the explanation."

"Sometimes," Josh agreed, standing up. "But not today."

He started walking toward the farmer's stall before anyone could stop him. Behind him, he heard Emily's quiet "Joshua" (she only used his full name when worried) and Mike's muttered curse. But they followed. Of course they followed. That's what his friends did—they trusted him even when he was probably making a mistake.

The distance felt longer than it should have. Fifty yards became a hundred, became a mile. Josh's footsteps echoed too loud on the asphalt. The glowing jars ahead pulled him forward like a beacon.

The farmer watched him approach. Still no features visible beneath that hat, just shadow and stillness.

Josh stopped ten feet away. Close enough to talk. Far enough to run if needed.

"Hi," he said, and immediately felt stupid. Hi? That's what he led with? But the farmer didn't react, so Josh pressed on. "I'm Josh. These are my friends. We've been researching the Golden Pickles. My grandfather, he tried to find you forty years ago. Never succeeded. I was hoping—"

The farmer raised one hand again. The same gesture from before. But this time, Josh was close enough to see the hand itself—weathered, work-worn, too many lines for the palm to map easily. A farmer's hand. Nothing supernatural about it.

Except.

The edges seemed to blur slightly, like looking at something through heat waves. Like the hand wasn't entirely solid.

"You're not supposed to be here yet," the farmer said.

His voice was rough, gravelly, with an accent Josh couldn't place. Not quite Southern. Not quite Midwest. Something older.

"We're just—" Josh started.

"Not you." The farmer's hand dropped. "This. The market. Dawn hasn't broken. The time is wrong."

Josh glanced at the sky. The sun was just cresting the horizon, first rays painting the clouds orange. "It's dawn right now."

"Is it?" The farmer's head tilted. "Are you certain?"

And Josh, looking at the sky he'd watched lighten for the past hour, suddenly wasn't certain at all. Because the angle seemed wrong. Too low. Too far north. Like he was looking at a sunrise from a different month. Different season.

"What—" Josh's mouth went dry. "What time is it?"

"The wrong time," the farmer repeated. "You came early. Watching. Waiting. You broke the pattern."

"We didn't break anything," Emily said, moving up beside Josh. Her voice had that directness that meant she was fighting fear with logic. "We just wanted to understand. The pickles, the way you appear—"

"Understanding isn't free." The farmer gestured at his stall. "Every answer costs something. Your grandfather knew that. He paid his price."

Josh felt cold. "What price? What did he—"

"His certainty." The farmer's shadow-face seemed to focus on Josh. "He came looking for answers. Left with questions. Never could commit to the real after he'd seen the impossible. Your mother understood. She stopped looking. Kept the real."

"You knew them?" Josh's heart hammered. "You actually—"

"Boy." The farmer's tone sharpened. "You're standing on the edge of something. Your friends too. You can walk away now. Keep the mystery. Or you can stay, watch, learn. And give up the comfort of not knowing."

Behind Josh, he heard Mike mutter something about this being his cue to leave. Tyler's camera had stopped recording—hand probably shaking too much. Olivia's camera shutter had gone silent.

But Emily. Emily stepped forward, chin up. "Show us."

The farmer regarded her for a long moment. Then nodded once.

He reached into a crate and pulled out one of the glowing jars. Held it up to the strengthening dawn light. The pickles inside seemed to pulse with their own rhythm, slow and organic, like breathing.

"One taste," the farmer said. "And you'll understand."

He set the jar on the table between them. An offering. A test. A point of no return.

Josh stared at it. This was what they'd come for. The answer to the mystery. The solution to the puzzle. Everything his grandfather had wondered about, right there in a glowing jar.

But the farmer's words echoed: Every answer costs something.

"Let me think about it," Josh said automatically, his brain trying to process implications, to model outcomes, to find the safe path forward.

"Take your time," the farmer said. "Dawn will wait. It's gotten good at waiting."

And Josh realized with a start that the sun hadn't moved. It was still sitting on the horizon, frozen in that first moment of breaking, casting those orange rays that never shifted angle. Time had stopped. Or maybe paused. Or maybe—

"This isn't possible," Tyler said, voice shaking slightly.

"No," the farmer agreed. "But it's real. That's the first lesson. Impossible and real aren't opposites. They're neighbors."

Josh looked at his friends. Saw Emily's jaw set with determination. Olivia's wide eyes behind her camera. Mike's hand still near his flashlight like it could protect them from whatever this was. Tyler's analytical mind clearly shorting out, trying to find a framework that fit.

They were here because of him. Because he'd convinced them the Golden Pickles were worth investigating. Because he couldn't leave a mystery unsolved.

And now they were standing in a frozen dawn, facing something that shouldn't exist, with a choice that would change everything.

"We should go," Mike said quietly. "Josh, we should go."

"Yeah," Olivia agreed. "This is... this is too much."

Tyler just nodded, speechless for once.

Emily said nothing. Just looked at Josh. Waiting for his call. Because that's what they did—they let him lead, trusted his judgment, followed where he said to go.

The pressure hit Josh's chest like a fist. Don't let them down. Don't disappoint them. Don't make this a mistake.

The farmer waited, patient as stone, offering a glowing jar that held impossible answers.

And Josh—practical, logical, pattern-seeking Josh who'd spent his whole life trying to figure things out—stood on the edge of a decision that felt bigger than Golden Pickles or frozen dawns or family legends.

"If we stay," he said slowly, "if we learn what this is—can we leave? After?"

"Maybe," the farmer said. "Depends what you learn."

"That's not an answer."

"It's the only one I have."

The sun waited on the horizon. The pickles glowed in their jar. His friends stood behind him, scared but present, trusting him to make the right call.

Josh took a breath. Then another. His grandfather's words echoed: Some mysteries are better left unsolved.

But Josh had never believed that.

"Okay," he said. "Show us."

The farmer's hand reached toward the jar.

And the sun, finally, began to rise.

CHAPTER 1: THE OBSESSION BEGINS

THE MORNING AFTER

Josh hadn't slept.

He sat at his apartment's kitchen table, laptop open, the farmer's frozen dawn playing on loop. Tyler had recovered the footage once the sun actually rose—once time started moving again—and now Josh could watch it frame by frame. The moment the farmer reached for the glowing jar. The moment Josh said "Show us." The moment the sun finally, impossibly, continued its climb.

His coffee had gone cold an hour ago. He didn't notice.

"You're still watching it." Emily appeared in the doorway, her own coffee steaming. She'd crashed on his couch after they'd all stumbled back here at seven AM, too wired to go home. "Josh. You need to sleep."

"I need to understand." He rewound fifteen seconds, watched the farmer's hand blur at the edges again. "Look at this. Right here. His hand isn't solid. It's like—"

"Like we saw something impossible and our brains are still trying to process it?" Emily pulled out a chair, sat down with the heaviness of someone who'd been up all night questioning everything she thought she knew. "Yeah. I noticed."

Josh finally looked at her. Really looked. Emily had dark circles under her eyes, her notebook clutched in one hand like a lifeline. "You okay?"

"No." She took a long drink of coffee. "I watched the sun stop moving, Josh. I have notes about it. Timestamps. Tyler's got corroborating footage. And my brain keeps trying to tell me it was a trick, or we were drugged, or —" She stopped, shook her head. "But I know what I saw."

"Evidence-based Emily meets the impossible," Josh said quietly.

"Don't." She pointed at him with her coffee mug. "Don't make this into one of your 'I told you so' moments. You're freaking out as much as I am. You're just hiding it better."

She was right. Josh's hands had been shaking since they got back. Every time he closed his eyes, he saw that dawn locked in place, felt the weight of the farmer's words: Every answer costs something.

His grandfather had lost his certainty after encountering the farmer. His mother had known to stop looking.

And Josh? Josh had said "show us" and dragged four friends across a threshold they couldn't uncross.

"I shouldn't have done it," he said, the words coming out before he could stop them. "I shouldn't have agreed. I should have walked away."

"But you didn't." Emily's voice was matter-of-fact, not accusatory. "Because walking away isn't something you do. Dad's always said you're like Grandpa that way—can't leave a problem unsolved even when you should."

Josh's father and Emily's father were brothers, which made them cousins technically, but they'd grown up next door to each other, close as siblings. Their families had that kind of tangled rural connection where everyone was related somehow and boundaries between households didn't really exist.

"Grandpa stopped," Josh pointed out.

"Grandpa couldn't stop. That's different." Emily leaned back, her coffee forgotten. "Your mom told me once—he'd be in the middle of farm reports and just drift off, staring at nothing. She said he spent twenty years trying to figure out if the farmer was real or if he'd imagined the whole thing. It ate at him until he died."

Josh felt something cold settle in his chest. "And now I'm doing the same thing to myself. To you. To everyone."

"Hey." Emily reached across the table, grabbed his wrist. Her grip was solid, grounding. "Joshua. Look at me."

He did.

"We made the choice together. You said 'show us,' but we stayed. We could have walked away. Mike wanted to. But we stayed." She held his gaze. "So whatever this costs, we pay it together. Got it?"

The pressure in Josh's chest eased slightly. This was why Emily was family—not the cousin connection, but the way she could see him spiraling and pull him back.

"Got it," he said.

"Good." She released his wrist, picked up her coffee again. "Now. What's the plan? Because I know you've got one forming."

Josh did. It had been building since the moment the farmer vanished, since they'd stumbled back to the van in stunned silence, since Tyler had pulled up the footage and confirmed they hadn't collectively hallucinated.

He pulled up a new window on his laptop—the university library database. "We need history. Everything we can find about the farmer, the Golden Pickles, the markets they've appeared at. Grandpa did some research, but he didn't have the internet. We've got access to digitized newspapers, historical societies, genealogy records—"

"You want to track him through time." Emily was already pulling out her own laptop.

"I want to know what he is," Josh corrected. "And why Grandpa's encounter affected him so much. The farmer knew him. Knew Mom. Knew they'd tried to find him." He pulled up an archive search. "That's not random. There's a pattern."

Emily's fingers were already moving across her keyboard. "Anthropology angle. Folklore studies. If this farmer's been around for a century, there'll be cultural artifacts. Stories. Maybe academic papers."

"Tyler can do image analysis," Josh added, his mind racing now, the familiar comfort of problem-solving pushing back the fear. "Compare photos across decades. If it's really the same person—"

"It is." Emily's voice was flat. "We both know it is."

"Yeah." Josh opened another window. "But we need to prove it. Document it. Build the case."

"Why?" Emily looked up from her screen. "Who are we proving it to?"

Josh stopped typing. That was a good question. The farmer existed. They'd seen him. What did proof matter?

"Because," he said slowly, working through it, "if we can document when and where he appears, maybe we can predict when he'll appear next. And next time—"

"Next time you don't say 'show us' without knowing what he's going to show," Emily finished.

"Yeah."

They worked in silence for a few minutes, the only sound their keyboards clicking and the coffee maker gurgling as Emily started a new pot.

Tyler emerged from Josh's bedroom around nine, hair sticking up, still wearing yesterday's clothes. "Coffee?"

"Fresh pot," Emily said without looking up.

Tyler poured himself a mug, shuffled over to look at Josh's screen. "Newspaper archives. You started without me."

"Couldn't sleep," Josh said.

"Yeah, no kidding." Tyler pulled up a chair, set down his coffee, and cracked his knuckles. "Okay. What am I searching for?"

Over the next hour, they built a research plan. Tyler would handle image analysis and digital forensics—trying to prove the photos from different decades showed the same person. Emily would track the cultural angle—folklore, mythology, any academic studies of impossible farmers or cursed pickles. Josh would dig through local history, newspaper accounts, any documented encounters going back as far as he could find.

Mike appeared around ten, looking rough. "You people are insane. You know that, right?"

"Coffee's in the kitchen," Emily said.

"I don't want coffee. I want to know why you're all acting like last night was normal." Mike leaned against the wall, arms crossed. "We saw something impossible. Sun stopped moving. Farmer with blurry hands. Glowing pickles. And now you're... what? Researching it?"

"What else would we do?" Josh asked.

"Not go back." Mike's voice was sharp. "That's what we do. We saw something weird, we acknowledge it was weird, and we walk away before it gets weirder."

"Mike—"

"No, Josh. Listen to me." Mike moved into the room, tension visible in his shoulders. "I did ROTC for a semester. Know what they teach you about situations you don't understand? You retreat. You regroup. You don't charge forward hoping to figure it out."

"This isn't a combat situation," Emily said.

"Isn't it?" Mike looked at her. "That farmer wasn't making an offer. He was making a threat. 'Every answer costs something.' That's not 'hey, let me explain the mystery.' That's 'if you keep looking, something bad happens.'"

Josh felt the cold creep back into his chest. Mike was right. The farmer's words had been a warning.

But—

"My grandfather looked," Josh said quietly. "And yeah, it cost him. But he survived. He lived for forty more years. Raised Mom, worked his research, died of old age in his own bed." He met Mike's eyes. "Whatever the cost is, it's not death. It's something else."

"You don't know that."

"I know he warned us before showing us. That means he wasn't trying to hurt us." Josh was working through it as he spoke, the pattern forming. "And he let us leave. We walked away. If this was some horror movie trap, we'd be stuck there, right? But we're not. We're here. Safe."

"For now," Mike muttered.

The door opened and Olivia stumbled in, camera bag over her shoulder, looking like she'd gotten maybe two hours of sleep. "Please tell me someone made coffee."

"Kitchen," three voices said simultaneously.

Olivia beelined for caffeine while Mike continued his one-man protest. "Look, I get it. You're all fascinated. Mystery to solve. Puzzle to figure out. But sometimes puzzles are dangerous. Sometimes the smart move is walking away."

"Then walk away," Josh said, not unkindly. "Seriously, Mike. If you don't want to be part of this, I get it. No one's forcing you."

Mike stared at him for a long moment. Then sighed, shoulders dropping. "You're going to do this anyway, aren't you? Even if we all leave."

"Probably," Josh admitted.

"Definitely," Emily corrected.

"Okay. Fine." Mike grabbed a chair, spun it around, and sat down. "But we do this smart. No more midnight stakeouts without planning. No more 'show us' without knowing what we're agreeing to. We research, we plan, and we move carefully. Deal?"

Relief flooded Josh's chest. "Deal."

"Also," Mike added, pulling out his phone, "I'm documenting everything. Every weird thing that happens, every decision we make. That way when this inevitably goes sideways, there's a record."

"Fair," Tyler said. He pulled up a shared document. "Everyone gets access. We track everything—sightings, research findings, encounters. Full transparency."

Olivia returned with coffee, took one look at the laptops covering the table, and groaned. "We're doing this. We're actually doing this."

"You can opt out too," Josh offered.

"And miss photographing the impossible?" Olivia pulled up a chair. "Not a chance. Just let me caffeinate first."

They worked through the day, breaking only for food runs and bathroom breaks. Josh's apartment became a research command center, with papers spread across every surface, laptops glowing, and the whiteboard he used for study notes now covered in timelines and connections.

By evening, they had something.

Josh stood at the whiteboard, marker in hand, staring at the timeline they'd built. "Okay. Walk me through it again."

Tyler pulled up his analysis. "I compared seventeen photographs spanning 1923 to last year. Same hat, same posture, same build. But here's the thing—" He overlaid the images. "Facial recognition software can't lock on him. Not because the photos are bad quality. Because his face doesn't have consistent landmarks."

"What does that mean?" Mike asked.

"It means his face changes slightly between photos. Not enough to look like different people. But enough that biometric analysis fails." Tyler zoomed in on one photo, showing the blurred edges Josh had noticed. "It's like he's not entirely... fixed."

"Not fixed," Emily repeated. "Like he's not solid?"

"Like he's not entirely present," Tyler corrected. "Best analogy I can make: he's like a photograph that's slightly out of focus. You can tell what it's supposed to be, but the details are wrong."

Josh wrote on the whiteboard:

FARMER = INCONSISTENT PHYSICAL PRESENCE.

"What did you find?" he asked Emily.

Emily opened her notebook, flipped to marked pages. "Folklore angle. I found references to 'market spirits' in about a dozen cultures. Entities that appear at crossroads or gathering places, offering trades. Always food or goods. Always valuable. Always with a catch."

"Like fairy tales," Olivia said. "Don't eat the fairy food or you can't leave."

"Exactly like that." Emily pulled up her screen, showing academic papers. "But here's the interesting part—these entities are always tied to place, not time. They appear in the same locations across decades. Markets, crossroads, sacred sites."

Josh added to the whiteboard: TIED TO LOCATION.

"But the farmer moves," Mike pointed out. "We found records of him at different markets."

"Different markets, same pattern." Emily pulled up a map on her laptop. "Look. Every market he's appeared at is near a former settlement. Towns that were abandoned or disappeared. This market? Built on the site of a village that was wiped out by fire in 1847."

Josh felt something click into place. "So he's not tied to the market. He's tied to what's under the market."

"Maybe." Emily zoomed in on historical maps. "I found references to a place called Hollow Fields in some of the older documents. Small settlement, established early 1800s. Thriving for a few decades, then just... gone. Disappeared from records around 1850."

"Hollow Fields," Josh repeated, writing it on the board. "Any connection to the pickles?"

"Working on it." Emily pulled up more notes. "But I did find something weird. Several accounts from the 1850s mentioning 'golden cucumbers' that grew in the area. Descriptions match the pickles—glowing, impossible flavor, disappearing when people tried to trade them."

"So the pickles came first," Tyler said. "The farmer came later."

"Or the farmer was always there and people only started noticing him after the town disappeared." Emily closed her laptop. "I need to visit the historical society. Get access to records that aren't digitized. Town meeting minutes, personal journals, anything from Hollow Fields' final years."

Josh nodded, adding HISTORICAL RECORDS to the board. "Olivia, what about your photos?"

Olivia had been quiet, reviewing her camera's memory card. Now she looked up, face troubled. "Something's wrong with them."

"Wrong how?" Josh moved to look over her shoulder.

She pulled up the photos from last night—the ones she'd taken at the market. "Look at the timestamps." She pointed at the metadata. "These three photos? All taken at 4:47 AM. But I took them over the course of fifteen minutes. The camera's timestamp didn't move."

Mike leaned in. "Maybe your camera glitched?"

"I thought so too. But look." Olivia pulled up more photos. "These are from after we left. 6:23 AM. 6:24 AM. 6:25 AM. The timestamp works fine."

"So only the photos taken near the farmer have wrong timestamps," Tyler said slowly.

"Not wrong. Frozen." Olivia's voice had an edge to it that Josh recognized—her artist's instinct recognizing a pattern. "The camera was documenting what we experienced. Time stopped."

Tyler pulled up his own footage. "My cameras showed the same thing. From 4:03 AM to 5:17 AM, the timecode doesn't advance. Then it jumps forward and continues normally."

Josh wrote on the board: TIME MANIPULATION.

"This is insane," Mike muttered. But he was leaning forward now, engaged despite himself.

"Okay." Josh capped the marker, stepped back to look at the full board. "What do we know for certain?"

He pointed at each note as he read them:
- Farmer appears at markets built on disappeared settlements
- Physical presence inconsistent/blurred
- Associated with Hollow Fields settlement (1800s, disappeared 1850s)
- Golden Pickles predate farmer sightings
- Time manipulation documented via multiple sources
- Encounters across 100+ years show no aging

"And," Emily added, "according to folklore patterns, he's offering a trade. Knowledge for... something."

"Something Grandpa lost," Josh said quietly. "His certainty. His ability to be sure about what's real."

The room fell silent.

Finally, Mike spoke. "So what's the plan? We've got research. We've got patterns. What are we actually doing with this?"

Josh had been thinking about that all day. The pressure was building again—the weight of having convinced everyone to stay up all night, having said 'show us' without knowing what it meant, having led them all into something bigger than Golden Pickles.

He couldn't let them down.

"We find Hollow Fields," Josh said. "The actual location. Where the settlement was before it disappeared. If the farmer's tied to that place, that's where we'll find answers."

"And then?" Emily asked.

"Then we figure out what he really wants." Josh met each of their eyes. "Because he's been appearing for over a century, selling pickles, disappearing. That's not random. That's purposeful. And if we can understand the purpose—"

"We can decide if we want to pay the price," Tyler finished.

"Exactly."

Olivia raised her camera. "Everyone good with this? Because once we go looking for a disappeared town tied to an impossible farmer, there's no pretending this is just weird coincidence."

Around the table, his friends exchanged glances. Josh could see the fear, the uncertainty. But also the curiosity. The same thing that had made them stick with him through every weird obsession, every mystery that turned out to be nothing.

Except this one wasn't nothing.

"Let me think about it," Josh started to say automatically, then stopped himself. He'd already thought about it. Had been thinking about it since dawn froze. "Actually, no. I don't need to think about it. I'm going to find Hollow Fields. But I'm not asking you to come with me."

"Too late," Emily said. "We're already part of this."

"I'm just saying—"

"Josh." Mike's voice cut through. "Shut up. We're in. Stop trying to give us an out."

"But—"

"You're doing the thing," Olivia said. "The 'I'll take all the responsibility' thing. Stop it. We're adults. We chose to stay last night. We're choosing to continue."

Tyler nodded. "Besides, you'll just do something stupid if we leave you alone. At least this way we can make sure you don't die."

Josh felt his throat tighten. "I won't let you guys down."

"We know," Emily said softly. "That's why we trust you."

The weight settled onto Josh's shoulders—heavier than before, more real. They trusted him. Which meant he had to be right. Had to make the correct choices. Had to lead them somewhere safe.

Had to solve this.

"Okay," he said, turning back to the board. "Here's how we do this."

THE RESEARCH MONTAGE

The university library became their second home over the next week.

Josh spent hours in the local history section, pulling every book about early settlements in the region. Most were dry accounts of land deals and crop yields, but occasionally he'd find something interesting—a mention of unusual weather patterns, or crops that failed mysteriously, or residents who vanished.

Hollow Fields never appeared by name in the official histories. But he found references to "the hollow place" and "the empty fields" in personal letters from the 1850s. Always vague. Always uneasy.

Emily worked the folklore angle with academic precision, cross-referencing mythology databases and anthropology papers. She found patterns—stories of spirits tied to land, of places that existed between the real and unreal, of thresholds that shouldn't be crossed.

"It's everywhere," she told Josh one evening, spreading papers across their library table. "Every culture has some version. Places that exist in liminal space. The Japanese have their spirit worlds, Celtic mythology has its fairy mounds, Native American traditions speak of thin places where realities touch."

"You think Hollow Fields is one of these thin places?" Josh asked.

"I think something happened there that thinned the barrier." Emily pulled up her notes. "Look at this pattern. Most of these locations are associated with tragedy. Violent death, mass suffering, injustice. The kind of thing that leaves a mark."

Josh thought about the farmer's words: Every answer costs something. "What if Hollow Fields didn't just disappear? What if something pushed it out of normal reality?"

"Like a ghost town that's actually ghostly." Emily marked something in her notebook. "I need to find out what happened there. Why it vanished."

Tyler approached the problem like an engineer, building a database of every farmer sighting they could document. Date, location, witnesses, duration. He created algorithms to predict appearance patterns, though the data was too sparse for reliable forecasting.

"Here's what I've got," he told the group three days in. "The farmer appears quarterly—winter solstice, spring equinox, summer solstice, fall equinox. Always within three days of the actual astronomical event. Always at dawn."

"Seasonal patterns," Mike observed. "Harvest cycle?"

"More like ritual cycle," Emily corrected. "Those dates are significant in dozens of magical traditions. Threshold moments when barriers are thin."

Mike still didn't love the supernatural explanation, but he'd stopped fighting it. Instead, he'd appointed himself the group's safety officer, making them all carry fully charged phones, share their locations, and check in every few hours when they were researching alone.

"Someone needs to be the paranoid one," he said when Josh teased him about it. "And since you're all charging headfirst into folklore horror territory, might as well be me."

Olivia took a different approach. She visited every market where the farmer had been sighted, photographing the locations, talking to longtime vendors, capturing the feel of each place.

"They all have the same energy," she told Josh, showing him her collection. "Like the light sits differently. Shadow angles are wrong. Your eye wants to skip over certain spots."

"That's pretty subjective," Mike pointed out.

"I'm an artist. Subjective is my job." Olivia pulled up a comparison. "But look. This market, this one, this one—all built on former settlement sites. All have this visual quirk where the background seems too far away. Like the space doesn't make sense."

"Liminal spaces," Emily said immediately. "Physical locations that exist between defined areas. They have a disorienting quality because human perception can't quite lock onto them."

By the end of the week, they had assembled a disturbing picture:

The farmer appeared at locations tied to disappeared settlements. His physical form was inconsistent. He manifested at astronomical threshold moments. Time behaved strangely in his presence. And he offered knowledge at a price that cost certainty.

"So basically," Mike said, looking at their compiled research, "we're dealing with something that exists outside normal reality, appears at specific times in specific places, and wants to trade information that will fundamentally change how we perceive the world."

"Yeah," Josh said. "Pretty much."

"Great. Love that for us."

But despite the weirdness—or maybe because of it—Josh felt energized. This was what he'd been searching for his whole life. Not just a mystery to solve, but a real mystery. Something that mattered. Something that had drawn his grandfather and his grandfather's father. The family obsession that Mom had tried to kill by focusing on practical farm research.

Josh was picking up the torch.

He just hoped he wouldn't burn himself carrying it.

THE DISCOVERY

On Friday afternoon, Emily burst into Josh's apartment without knocking. "I found it."

Josh looked up from his laptop, where he'd been mapping geological surveys. Tyler and Mike were at class. Olivia was out photographing another market. Just him and his research.

"Found what?" he asked.

"The historical society finally let me access their restricted archives." Emily dropped her bag, pulled out a leather-bound journal. "Personal diary of a woman named Mary Stanton. Dated 1848 to 1850. She lived in Hollow Fields."

Josh's heart jumped. "You found primary source documents?"

"Better." Emily opened the journal carefully—it was fragile, pages yellowed and brittle. "I found an eyewitness account of what happened."

She laid the journal on the table and they read together.

June 3rd, 1848

The cucumbers have come again. Father says we should be grateful—they sell for twice the price of ordinary crops. But Mother won't let us eat them. She says they taste of wrong things. Dreams of gold and sorrow.

June 20th, 1848

Samuel Brenner ate three of the golden cucumbers and now will eat nothing else. His wife begs him to stop but he only stares at the fields where they grow. Father says it's natural for a farmer to love his crop. I think it's something worse.

August 15th, 1848

The town council has called a meeting. They say the woman on the hill is responsible for the cucumbers. They call her witch and worse. But I've seen her walking the fields, and she only looks sad. Like she knows something terrible we don't.

September 1st, 1848

They burned her today. I couldn't watch but I heard her screaming. She cursed them with her last breath—cursed the council, the town, the land itself. Said we would reap what we sowed. Said the gold would consume us.

September 3rd, 1848

The cucumbers still grow. If anything, there are more of them. They glow at night now, lighting the fields like captured stars. People have started eating them despite Mother's warnings. They say they can't help themselves.

December 10th, 1848

Half the town is in thrall to the cucumbers now. They work the fields day and night, harvesting, eating, planting. The council says this is prosperity. But I see their eyes and know it's something else.

March 21st, 1849

Mother died today. Father says it was the fever but I know better. She refused to eat the cucumbers. Refused to tend the fields. Refused to accept what the town had become. So the town let her starve.

I'm leaving. Taking what I can carry and walking east. I won't let the gold take me too.

May 1st, 1850

I've returned to write this final entry. I don't know why I came back. Maybe to bear witness. Maybe because some part of me is still drawn to the gold.

The town is empty. Or rather—it's full, but the people aren't people anymore. They tend the fields like before, but they don't speak. Don't sleep. They just harvest and plant and consume. Over and over. Trapped in the cycle.

And standing in the market square, I saw him. A farmer I've never seen before, though he wears Father's hat. He's selling the cucumbers to no one —just standing there, waiting.

I think he'll stand there forever.

I'm leaving again. For good this time. Let the gold have Hollow Fields. Let it consume what's left. I won't look back.

The entry ended there. Josh and Emily sat in silence for a long moment.

"So the witch cursed the town," Josh said finally. "And the curse turned the cucumbers from just crops into something else. Something that trapped people."

"And the farmer," Emily added, "is part of the curse. Maybe he was one of the townspeople. Maybe he was the witch's revenge given form. But he's been standing there, selling cursed cucumbers, for over a century."

"The Golden Pickles." Josh felt the pieces clicking together. "They're not pickles. They never were. They're the cursed cucumbers, preserved. Still carrying the same trap."

"And anyone who eats them—"

"Gets drawn in," Josh finished. "That's the cost Grandpa paid. He tasted them. And the taste never left him. The knowledge that they were real, that the farmer was real, that magic was real. It ate at him until he died."

Emily's face was pale. "Josh. We watched the farmer. We saw the pickles. We crossed the threshold."

"But we didn't eat them." Josh gripped the table edge. "That's the difference. We saw, but we didn't consume. There's still a line we haven't crossed."

"Yet," Emily said quietly.

"Yet," Josh agreed.

They stared at the journal, at Mary Stanton's neat handwriting documenting the slow horror of her town's transformation.

"We have to tell the others," Emily said.

"Yeah."

"And then we have to decide—do we keep looking? Because now we know. The farmer's part of a curse. The pickles are a trap. And Hollow Fields is still out there somewhere, full of people who ate the gold and never stopped."

Josh thought about his grandfather, sitting in that armchair, staring at nothing. Thought about his mother, deliberately choosing practical research over mystery. Thought about the farmer's words: Your grandfather knew that. He paid his price.

The obsession had cost Grandpa his certainty.

But walking away now would cost Josh something else. The not-knowing would eat at him worse than any curse.

"Let me think about it," he said, and this time Emily didn't call him on the verbal tic. Just nodded, understanding.

They called the others.

The group gathered at Josh's apartment that evening. Emily had shared photos of the journal entries, so everyone came prepared.

"Okay," Mike said once they'd all read through the account. "Quick vote. Who wants to keep investigating the cursed town full of possessed farmers?"

Nobody raised their hand.

"Good. Glad we're all sane." Mike stood up. "Meeting adjourned. Let's all go back to our normal lives and pretend this never—"

"Sit down," Emily said.

"Emily—"

"Mike. Sit."

He sat.

Emily looked around the table. "We all know we're not walking away. So let's stop pretending and figure out what we're actually going to do."

"Why can't we walk away?" Tyler asked. Not argumentatively. Genuinely curious.

"Because Josh won't," Olivia said simply. "And if Josh goes alone, something bad happens. So we go with him."

Josh started to protest—they didn't have to, he wouldn't blame them, he could do this himself—but Emily's hand landed on his shoulder, stopping him.

"You're doing it again," she said.

"I'm just—"

"Taking all the responsibility. Yeah, we know." She looked at the others. "But here's the thing. Josh is going to find Hollow Fields whether we help or not. Family trait. He can't walk away from this any more than his grandfather could. So our actual choice is: do we let him go alone, or do we go with him?"

Tyler nodded slowly. "When you put it that way..."

"I still think this is a terrible idea," Mike said. "For the record."

"Noted," Emily said.

"But yeah, obviously I'm coming." Mike pulled out his phone. "Someone needs to document when things go wrong. Might as well be me."

Olivia raised her camera. "I'm not missing the chance to photograph a cursed town."

"You're all insane," Tyler muttered. Then sighed. "Fine. I'm in. But I'm bringing every monitoring device I own. If time's going to stop again, I'm measuring it properly this time."

Josh felt the familiar pressure ease and intensify simultaneously. They were staying with him. Which meant he had to keep them safe. Had to make sure whatever price the farmer demanded, they could afford to pay it.

Had to not let them down.

"Okay," he said, forcing his voice steady. "Then here's what we do."

He pulled up a map on his laptop, showing the area where historical records placed Hollow Fields. "The settlement was here, about forty miles north. Built in a valley between two ridges. According to the geological survey, there's still something there—structures, foundations. But it's not marked on any current maps."

"Because it's cursed," Mike said.

"Because it's off the grid," Josh corrected. "State forest now. No roads. We'd have to hike in."

"How long?" Emily asked.

"Maybe six hours from the nearest access point." Josh zoomed in. "We could do it in a day. Hike in, document what we find, hike out."

"Document what, exactly?" Tyler asked.

Josh pulled up the journal photos again. "Mary Stanton says the town was still standing when she left. The people were there, trapped in the harvest cycle. If the curse is still active—and the farmer appearing suggests it is—then Hollow Fields might still exist. Frozen, like that dawn was frozen."

"A ghost town that's actually ghostly," Emily repeated her earlier phrase.

"Yeah."

Olivia leaned forward, studying the map. "When do we go?"

Josh checked dates. "Next equinox is three weeks away. Spring. If the farmer appears at threshold moments, that's when Hollow Fields will be most... accessible."

"Or most dangerous," Mike pointed out.

"Probably both," Josh admitted.

They spent the next hour planning. Supplies, routes, safety protocols. Mike insisted on redundant communication methods and emergency extraction plans. Tyler wanted to bring enough monitoring equipment to outfit a small research station. Olivia carefully selected which cameras to pack. Emily researched protective folklore—salt, iron, running water, all the traditional barriers against supernatural influence.

By midnight, they had a plan. Rough, but functional.

"Three weeks," Josh said as everyone gathered their things to leave. "That gives us time to prepare, to do more research, to—"

"To talk ourselves out of it?" Mike suggested.

"To be ready," Josh corrected.

At the door, Emily pulled him aside. "Joshua. Listen to me."

He listened.

"I know you feel responsible for us. I know you think it's your job to keep everyone safe." Her voice was quiet but firm. "But you need to understand—we're responsible for ourselves. We're choosing this. All of us."

"I know, but—"

"No buts. You're not carrying us. We're all walking together." She squeezed his shoulder. "Don't make yourself a martyr before anything even happens."

"I'm not—"

"You are. You're already planning how to protect us if things go wrong. I can see it in your face." Emily's expression softened. "Just remember— we're here to protect you too."

After they left, Josh sat alone in his apartment, staring at the map. Forty miles north. A disappeared town. A curse that trapped people in golden obsession.

His grandfather's mystery.

His mother's warning.

His choice.

The journal entry echoed in his mind: Let the gold have Hollow Fields. Let it consume what's left. I won't look back.

Mary Stanton had been smart enough to walk away.

Josh checked his calendar, counted the days until the spring equinox.

Twenty-one days until they went to find what was left of Hollow Fields.

He should sleep. Should rest. Should use the three weeks to prepare properly.

Instead, he pulled up the video of the frozen dawn and watched it again.

The farmer's blurred hands reaching for the glowing jar.

The sun locked in place.

The moment Josh said "show us" and crossed a line he couldn't uncross.

Every answer costs something.

Yeah. He was beginning to understand what that meant.

CHAPTER 2:
PREPARATION AND
DOUBT

WEEK ONE: SUPPLIES AND SECOND THOUGHTS

The camping supply store smelled like nylon and rubber, artificial pine scent pumped through the ventilation to make customers think outdoors. Josh stood in the hiking boot aisle, comparing tread patterns and ankle support ratings, when Mike appeared beside him.

"You're overthinking it," Mike said.

"I'm being thorough." Josh picked up another boot, checked the tag. "Dad always said—"

"'Use your best tools first,' yeah, I know." Mike grabbed a pair off the shelf, same brand Josh's dad had recommended years ago. "These. Waterproof, good ankle support, broken in after twenty miles. Done."

Josh looked at his own selection—three different pairs he'd been mentally comparing for ten minutes. "Let me think about—"

"No." Mike took the boots from Josh's hands, put them back, and handed him the pair he'd chosen. "You're spiraling again. These are good boots. Buy them."

Josh took them. Mike was right. He'd been doing this all week—overthinking every piece of equipment, every supply choice, every detail of the plan. Because if something went wrong, if he'd forgotten something important, if someone got hurt—

That would be on him.

"Thanks," Josh said quietly.

They moved to the next aisle—GPS units, emergency beacons, first aid supplies. Mike had a list, systematic and thorough. Former ROTC training showing through.

"Two-way radios with ten-mile range," Mike read off his phone. "Water filtration system. Emergency shelter. Flares. Snake bite kit."

"Snake bite kit?" Josh raised an eyebrow.

"We're hiking into unmarked forest in spring. Snakes wake up hungry." Mike grabbed two kits off the shelf. "Also: bear spray, emergency blankets, fire starters, and these." He held up a package of high-visibility markers. "We mark our trail every fifty yards going in. That way if the impossible happens and we need to run, we can follow markers out."

Josh felt something ease in his chest. Mike was planning for practical dangers—snakes, getting lost, hypothermia. Normal hiking problems. Not cursed towns or time-stopping farmers.

"You think it'll be that simple?" Josh asked. "Normal hiking dangers?"

Mike was quiet for a moment, studying a tactical flashlight. "No," he admitted. "But if I plan for normal problems, at least I'm doing something. Better than sitting around imagining worst-case supernatural scenarios."

"Fair."

They spent another hour loading the cart—more supplies than five people needed for a day hike, but Mike's philosophy was better too much than not enough. At checkout, Josh pulled out his card, but Mike stopped him.

"We split this," Mike said. "Everyone contributes. You're not funding the whole expedition."

"I'm the one who—"

"Josh. Everyone contributes." Mike's voice had that firm edge that meant arguing was pointless. "You want to lead? Fine. But you don't get to pay for everything like it's your personal guilt trip."

Josh put his card away.

Back at the apartment, they spread the supplies across the living room floor. Organized piles: navigation equipment, first aid, emergency gear, camping supplies, food and water.

Emily arrived as they were sorting, took one look at the spread, and whistled. "You planning to survive the apocalypse?"

"Preparing for contingencies," Mike said.

"He's been reading survival forums all week," Josh added.

"Someone has to be paranoid." Mike organized the first aid supplies into categories. "You two are busy researching cursed towns. Tyler's mapping impossible time distortions. Olivia's cataloging liminal spaces. I'm making sure we don't die of exposure or snake bite."

Emily sat on the floor, picked up one of the water filters. "This is good. Practical." She looked at Josh. "How are you doing? Really."

"Fine."

"Joshua."

He sighed. Emily could always tell. "I keep thinking about Mary Stanton's journal. The way she described people getting trapped in the harvest cycle. Eating the golden cucumbers until that's all they could do."

"And you're worried that's what's happening to you," Emily said. Not a question.

"I haven't eaten the pickles," Josh said. "But I can't stop thinking about them. About the farmer. About Hollow Fields. It's like—" He struggled for words. "Like I'm already caught in something."

"That's called obsession," Mike said, not unkindly. "Totally normal when investigating weird mysteries. Doesn't mean you're cursed."

"Grandpa couldn't stop thinking about it either."

"Your grandpa also didn't have four friends keeping him grounded." Emily gestured at the supplies. "We're going in prepared. We're staying together. And if things get weird—weirder—we leave. Simple as that."

"Is it?" Josh asked. "Simple?"

Emily's expression sobered. "No. Probably not. But we pretend it is until proven otherwise."

Tyler arrived an hour later, carrying a duffel bag that clinked ominously.

"Is that all monitoring equipment?" Mike asked.

"And backup equipment." Tyler unzipped the bag, revealing cameras, sensors, recording devices, batteries. "If time stops again, I want redundant documentation. Multiple cameras with independent clocks. Audio recorders. Motion sensors. If reality breaks, I'm measuring how it breaks."

"That's very on-brand for you," Emily observed.

Tyler pulled out his laptop, opened a program showing the valley where Hollow Fields supposedly existed. "I've been analyzing weather patterns, geological surveys, satellite imagery. And I found something weird."

Josh leaned in. "Weird how?"

"The valley." Tyler zoomed in on the topographical map. "Look at the elevation data. It doesn't make sense. The valley floor should be at 800 feet elevation, but the contour lines show impossible angles. Like the land is folded in on itself."

"Surveying error?" Emily suggested.

"Across five different surveys spanning thirty years? All with the same impossible reading?" Tyler shook his head. "And look at this." He pulled up satellite imagery. "Every photo has the same distortion in that exact spot. Like the camera can't quite focus on it."

Olivia would love this, Josh thought. Visual distortions were her specialty.

"So the land is actually weird," Mike said. "Great. Love that."

"It confirms we're looking in the right place," Josh said. "If the valley has measurable distortions, that's where Hollow Fields is. Or was. Or... exists outside normal space."

"All of the above," Tyler muttered, making notes. "I'll bring the GPS, but don't be surprised if it goes haywire when we get close."

By the end of week one, they had supplies, equipment, and a growing sense that they were preparing for something they couldn't possibly prepare for.

WEEK TWO: RESEARCH AND WARNINGS

Emily found Josh in the library on Tuesday, buried in a stack of books about local folklore. She dropped a folder on his table.

"Historical society came through," she said. "Property records for the Hollow Fields area, 1820 to 1860."

Josh opened the folder eagerly. Deeds, tax records, census data—the dry bones of history. But bones could tell stories if you knew how to read them.

"Look at the pattern," Emily said, pointing. "1820, the valley's empty. 1825, first settlers arrive. By 1830, there's a thriving community. Population peaks at 247 people in 1847."

"And then?"

"Then nothing." Emily pulled out the 1850 census. "Not recorded. 1860 census lists the valley as 'uninhabited, unsuitable for settlement.'"

Josh scanned the records. Names appeared, grew, multiplied—and then vanished. The Brenners, the Stantons, the Clarkes. All documented up to 1847. After that, nothing.

"What about death records?" Josh asked. "If the whole town died, there'd be documentation."

"That's the thing." Emily pulled out another document. "No death certificates. No burial records. No documentation of anyone leaving either. They just... stopped existing on paper."

"Like they were erased."

"Or like they left reality." Emily sat down, pulled out her own notes. "I've been cross-referencing with folklore patterns. Towns that vanish always have a trigger—a curse, a violation of natural law, a threshold crossed. For Hollow Fields, I think the trigger was burning the witch."

Josh thought about Mary Stanton's journal. They burned her today. She cursed them with her last breath.

"Eliza Nightshade," Josh said. "That was her name, according to the records?"

"Never officially recorded. But Mary Stanton calls her 'the woman on the hill,' and there's one property listing for a homestead on the ridge overlooking the valley. No name on the deed, just 'widow, tenant farmer.'" Emily pulled up a map. "That property had a note attached: 'Avoid. Bad soil, cursed ground.'"

"Before or after she was burned?"

"Before." Emily met his eyes. "They thought she was cursed before they killed her. Then she made it true."

The implications sat heavy between them.

"So we're hiking into a valley that was cursed by a dying woman, where 247 people vanished from reality, and which literally can't be properly mapped by satellite." Josh laughed, but there was no humor in it. "Why are we doing this again?"

"Because you can't walk away." Emily's voice was gentle. "And because I think she was innocent. The witch. Eliza. I think she was trying to help, and they killed her for it, and her curse was the only power she had left."

Josh looked at the property records, all those names that stopped existing. "You think she regretted it? The curse?"

"Mary Stanton said she looked sad. Walking the fields, knowing something terrible." Emily closed the folder. "I think she tried to warn them. And when they wouldn't listen, when they burned her instead, the curse happened whether she wanted it or not."

"So maybe she's trapped too," Josh said slowly. "Not just the townspeople. The witch herself, bound to the thing she created."

"Maybe." Emily stood, gathered her papers. "Which means maybe she'd help us. If we can find her."

"Or maybe she'd kill us for trespassing."

"There's that too."

That afternoon, Josh got a call from his mother. He'd been avoiding her since the first farmer encounter—hard to explain "I'm investigating a family mystery you deliberately abandoned" over the phone.

But she always knew when something was up.

"You're researching Hollow Fields," she said without preamble.

Josh nearly dropped his phone. "How did you—"

"Emily's mother mentioned she's spending a lot of time at the historical society. And I know you, Josh. You're like Dad. Once you get an idea in your head..." She sighed. "What did you find?"

Josh hesitated. He could lie. Could say it was just academic interest, a history project.

But this was Mom. She'd walked away from the same mystery for a reason.

"We saw the farmer," Josh said. "The one Grandpa talked about. We saw him appear at the market. And time stopped. Literally stopped, Mom. The sun froze."

Silence on the other end.

Then: "I was afraid of that."

"You knew?" Josh's voice rose. "You knew it was real and you didn't tell me?"

"What would I tell you? That your grandfather wasn't crazy, he just saw something impossible that ate away at him until he died? That there's a farmer who sells cursed pickles and traps people in questions they can't answer?" Her voice was sharp. "What good would that do?"

"It would have warned me!"

"Would it? Or would it have made you more curious?" A pause. "Josh. Listen to me. I know you want answers. I know you think you can figure this out where Dad couldn't. But that's exactly what he thought. And it destroyed him."

"He lived for forty more years—"

"He existed for forty more years. There's a difference." Her voice softened. "Baby, I know you're doing this because you love him. Because you want to finish what he started. But some things are better left unfinished."

Josh looked at the equipment spread across his apartment, the maps, the research. "I can't walk away."

"I know." She sounded tired. "You're exactly like him. That's what I was afraid of."

"Mom—"

"Just promise me something. Promise me you won't eat the pickles. No matter what. Promise me you won't taste them."

The intensity in her voice made Josh pause. "Did Grandpa eat them?"

"No. He was smart enough not to. But he wanted to. Every day for the rest of his life, he wanted to. That wanting—that's the trap, Josh. That's what costs you."

After they hung up, Josh sat staring at his phone.

His mother had never told him his grandfather wanted to taste the pickles. Never mentioned that the obsession wasn't just about finding answers—it was about desire. About wanting something he knew would trap him.

Josh thought about the glowing jars in the farmer's stall. About the impossible flavor people described but couldn't replicate.

He didn't want to eat them.

Did he?

WEEK THREE: TRAINING AND OLIVIA'S REVELATION

The final week, they trained.

Mike insisted on it—practice hikes, navigation drills, emergency protocols. They spent Saturday in the state forest, hiking ten miles with full packs, learning to spot trail markers, practicing with the GPS and two-way radios.

"If we get separated," Mike said during their break, "you stay where you are. Don't wander. Use the radio to call for location. If radio's dead, follow marked trail back to last known position."

"This is very 'don't split up in the horror movie,'" Olivia observed.

"That's because not splitting up is smart." Mike checked his compass. "Real danger in forests is getting lost. People panic, wander off trail, get more lost. We stay together, we stay found."

Josh adjusted his pack, testing the weight distribution. Everything felt too real suddenly. They were actually doing this. In six days, they'd hike into a valley that had swallowed a town.

"Hey." Emily appeared beside him. "You're thinking too loud."

"Just wondering if this is smart."

"It's not." Emily shouldered her own pack. "But we're doing it anyway."

They hiked in silence for a while, Tyler periodically checking his equipment, Mike calling out landmarks, Olivia stopping to photograph interesting light angles through the trees.

Normal. This felt normal. Like they were just friends on a hiking trip, not preparing to explore an impossible place.

Josh wanted to hold onto that feeling.

Sunday evening, Olivia invited them all to her apartment—a first. She'd always been private about her space, deflecting invitations with "it's messy" or "my roommate's studying."

But tonight she'd called them specifically. "I need to show you something."

Her apartment was exactly what Josh expected—brick walls, high ceilings, art everywhere. Photographs and paintings and installations that probably cost more than his car. Old money taste without being ostentatious.

"Okay," Olivia said once they'd all arrived. "I haven't been fully honest about why I'm interested in the farmer."

Emily leaned forward. "You said you'd seen strange things before."

"I have. But I didn't explain the context." Olivia pulled up her laptop, opened a folder of photographs. "Three years ago, I was part of a paranormal investigation group. We chased ghosts, cryptids, UFOs—all the weird stuff. Most of it was fake. People wanting attention, or tricks of light, or explainable phenomena."

She pulled up a photo—a dark forest, a blur of white movement. "But one case was real."

Tyler squinted at the screen. "What are we looking at?"

"I don't know. That's the problem." Olivia cycled through more photos —the same forest, different angles, that same impossible blur. "We were investigating reports of a creature in the woods. Large, moving fast, aggressive. We thought it was a hoax. But then we found it."

"Found what?" Josh asked.

"Something that shouldn't exist." Olivia's voice had gone flat. "It attacked us. My friend Sarah was badly injured. Broke her arm in three places. We ran. Got out. But Sarah's family sued the investigation group— said we'd endangered her, pushed her into dangerous situations, fabricated evidence."

"Did you?" Mike asked bluntly.

"No. But I couldn't prove what happened because the only evidence I had was these photos, and nobody believed them. They said it was photoshopped. Said we were chasing fake ghosts for attention." Olivia closed the laptop. "The group disbanded. I was ostracized from the paranormal investigation community. And Sarah... Sarah won't talk to me anymore."

The room was quiet.

"That's why you're so matter-of-fact about the farmer," Emily said slowly. "You already know the impossible exists."

"And you know nobody will believe you if you document it," Josh added.

"Yeah." Olivia managed a small smile. "So when you said you were investigating Golden Pickles and mysterious farmers, I thought maybe this time I'd have witnesses. People who would back up what we found."

"We will," Tyler said immediately. "We're all seeing this together."

"And the footage is corrupting anyway," Mike added. "Which is weirdly validating. At least we know we're not making it up."

Olivia relaxed slightly. "I wanted you to know before we go to Hollow Fields. I'm not just here to photograph weird things. I'm here to prove I wasn't lying. About any of it."

Josh understood that need. The same drive that made him research the farmer, dig through archives, refuse to walk away. Proof. Validation. Evidence that what you saw was real.

"We'll find answers," Josh said. "All of us together."

Later, after everyone left, Emily pulled Josh aside.

"You know what Saturday is," she said.

Josh nodded. Spring equinox. The day they'd circled in marker on his calendar.

"We could still back out," Emily offered. "Tell everyone it's too dangerous, too uncertain. No shame in walking away."

Josh looked at the equipment piled in his living room. The maps. The research. Three weeks of preparation.

And thought about his grandfather, sitting in that armchair, staring at nothing. Did I really see it? Was it real?

"I can't walk away," Josh said.

"I know." Emily squeezed his shoulder. "See you Saturday morning."

After she left, Josh pulled up the satellite image of Hollow Fields valley. The distortion. The impossible angles. The place that had swallowed 247 people and maybe, just maybe, still held them.

He thought about his mother's warning: Some things are better left unfinished.

And about Mary Stanton, writing in her journal: I'm leaving again. For good this time. Let the gold have Hollow Fields.

The smart move was walking away.

But Josh had never been good at smart moves where mysteries were concerned.

He set his alarm for 5 AM Saturday. They'd meet at dawn, drive to the trailhead, hike into the valley. Six hours in, document what they found, six hours out. Home by nightfall.

Simple.

As long as nothing impossible happened.

FRIDAY NIGHT: THE EVE OF DEPARTURE

Josh couldn't sleep.

It was 2 AM, and he was standing in his kitchen making his fourth coffee of the night, when someone knocked.

Emily stood in the hallway in pajamas and a jacket, her own insomnia obvious.

"Can't shut your brain off either?" she asked.

"Come in."

They sat at his kitchen table, the same one where they'd planned the first market stakeout, where they'd researched Hollow Fields, where Mike had spread out emergency supplies.

"I keep thinking about the farmer's warning," Emily said. "Every answer costs something. What if the cost is worse than we expect?"

"Then we pay it," Josh said. "Together."

"But what if we can't? What if the cost is something we don't have?" She wrapped her hands around her coffee mug. "Mary Stanton walked away. She saw the town trapped and she left. We're walking in."

"We're also leaving," Josh pointed out. "In and out. We're not staying."

"She didn't plan to stay either. But she came back one last time to write that final entry. Like the place pulled her." Emily met his eyes. "What if Hollow Fields doesn't let us leave?"

Josh had been avoiding that thought. But now, at 2 AM with dawn approaching, he couldn't ignore it.

"Then we find a way anyway," he said. "Because we have each other, and Grandpa went alone. We have preparation, and Mary Stanton was a kid running from tragedy. We have Mike's tactical planning, Tyler's monitoring equipment, Olivia's experience with the impossible, your research, and my —"

"Stubbornness?" Emily suggested.

"Determination." Josh managed a smile. "We're going in smarter than anyone before us. That has to count for something."

"Or it means we're overconfident."

"Maybe." Josh finished his coffee. "But we're doing it anyway, so might as well be confident."

Emily laughed despite herself. "You're ridiculous."

"You're here at 2 AM with me, so what does that make you?"

"Equally ridiculous." She stood, rinsed her mug. "I should try to sleep. We're supposed to meet in three hours."

"Yeah."

At the door, Emily paused. "Josh. Whatever happens tomorrow—you know it's not your fault, right? We're all choosing this."

"I know," Josh lied.

She saw through it. "Joshua. I mean it. You're not responsible for us."

"I'm the one who said 'show us.'"

"And we're the ones who stayed." She squeezed his arm. "We're a team. Stop trying to carry us."

After she left, Josh tried to sleep but couldn't. Instead, he checked and rechecked his pack. GPS, compass, maps, water, first aid kit, flashlight, batteries, emergency beacon, trail markers.

Everything they'd need for a normal hike.

Nothing that would help if time stopped again, or if the farmer appeared, or if Hollow Fields trapped them like it had trapped the original settlers.

Josh thought about his grandfather one last time. About the question that had eaten at him: Was it real?

Tomorrow, Josh would find out.

And unlike Grandpa, he'd have witnesses. People to confirm what they saw, to validate the impossible, to share the weight of knowledge.

Unless the cost was greater than any of them expected.

Josh set his alarm—though he knew he wouldn't sleep—and lay in bed staring at the ceiling.

Six hours until dawn.

Six hours until they found out what was left of Hollow Fields.

Six hours until everything changed.

CHAPTER 3: INTO HOLLOW FIELDS

THE DRIVE

The van smelled like coffee and nervous sweat.

Josh drove, hands at ten and two like his dad had taught him, focused on the twisting mountain road. Emily rode shotgun with the maps spread across her lap—topographical surveys, historical property boundaries, Tyler's annotated satellite imagery showing the distortion zone.

In the back, Mike had organized their supplies with military precision: first aid kit accessible, emergency beacon within reach, water and food rationed for twenty-four hours despite this being a day hike. Tyler sat surrounded by equipment, triple-checking batteries and connections. Olivia had her camera out, photographing the changing landscape as they climbed.

Nobody had said much since they'd left the city two hours ago.

Josh checked the rearview mirror. Tyler was mouthing words to himself—probably running through equipment protocols. Mike stared out the window, jaw set. Olivia's camera clicked periodically.

"Twenty miles to the turnoff," Emily said, tracing their route. "Then we hike in from there."

"How's everyone doing?" Josh asked, keeping his voice light.

"Fine," Mike said immediately.

"Good," Tyler added.

"Great," Olivia said without looking up from her camera.

Emily gave Josh a look that said they're all lying.

"Okay," Josh tried again. "Real check. How's everyone actually doing?"

Silence.

Then Mike: "I've been mentally running through every survival scenario I can think of. Bear attack, broken ankle, getting lost, hypothermia, snake bite—"

"Mike," Emily said.

"I'm just saying, I've got protocols for all of them." He pulled out a laminated card from his pocket. "See? Emergency procedures. If we get separated, if someone's injured, if we need evac—"

"We're going to be fine," Josh said, with more confidence than he felt.

"You don't know that." Mike's voice was flat. "None of us know that."

Tyler looked up from his equipment. "The probability of normal hiking injury is approximately 2.5%, according to—"

"Tyler, this isn't a normal hike," Olivia said quietly.

That shut everyone up.

Because she was right. They were driving toward a valley that literally distorted on satellite imagery. To investigate a town that had vanished from records in 1850. Following a legend about a witch's curse and golden vegetables that trapped people.

This wasn't normal by any definition.

"Look," Josh said, navigating a tight curve. "I know this is weird. I know we're all scared—"

"I'm not scared," Mike interrupted.

"Terrified, then."

"That's more accurate."

Josh caught Emily's small smile. At least they could still joke. Sort of.

"We've prepared as much as we can," Josh continued. "We have equipment, emergency protocols, each other. We go in, we document what we find, we come out. Six hours max."

"And if it's not that simple?" Olivia asked.

Josh thought about his grandfather. About Mary Stanton's journal. About his mother's warning. About the way the sun had frozen on the horizon.

"Then we adapt," he said. "Like Dad always says—if something breaks, you figure out how to fix it. We'll figure it out."

"Your dad's advice doesn't really apply to cursed towns," Emily pointed out.

"No, but the principle does. Problem solving is problem solving." Josh took the next turn. "We stay together, we think clearly, we don't panic. That's the plan."

"That's not much of a plan," Mike muttered.

"It's what we've got."

They drove in silence for another few minutes before Tyler spoke up.

"I've been thinking about temporal displacement theory," he said.

"Of course you have," Mike said.

"If time actually stopped at the market—which the timestamps suggest —then the valley might exist in a different temporal state. Not frozen, exactly, but... offset. Running parallel to our timeline but not synchronized with it."

"What does that mean practically?" Emily asked.

"It means our watches might not work right. GPS definitely won't. Our sense of how long we've been in there might not match actual elapsed time." Tyler pulled up a program on his laptop. "I've got redundant timekeeping—mechanical watches, atomic clocks, even a sundial compass. If we can compare readings when we come out, we might be able to measure the temporal offset."

"You're treating this like a science experiment," Olivia said.

"That's how I process fear." Tyler's voice was matter-of-fact. "I measure things. Makes them feel manageable."

Josh understood that. His own processing method was problem-solving. Mike's was tactical planning. Olivia's was documenting. Emily's was researching until she understood the pattern.

Different methods, same goal: control something that felt increasingly uncontrollable.

The turnoff appeared suddenly—an unmarked dirt road disappearing into trees. Josh almost missed it, had to brake hard and reverse.

"This is it?" Mike asked, leaning forward.

"According to the property records." Emily checked her maps. "Old logging road, hasn't been maintained since the sixties."

Josh turned onto the dirt road. Immediately, the van started jolting over ruts and rocks. Trees closed in on both sides, branches scraping the windows.

After half a mile, the road became impassable—fallen trees, overgrown brush, the path simply disappearing into forest.

"End of the line," Josh said, putting the van in park.

They sat for a moment, engine ticking as it cooled.

"Last chance to back out," Emily said softly. She wasn't looking at anyone specifically. Maybe talking to herself.

Josh's hand was on the door handle. He thought about all the reasons to drive away. His mother's warning. Mary Stanton's fear. His grandfather's obsession that had cost him certainty.

He opened the door.

"Let's go find Hollow Fields."

THE HIKE IN

The forest felt wrong from the start.

Not obviously wrong—the trees were normal trees, the ground was normal ground, the morning sun filtered through the canopy like it should. But there was something about the quality of the light, the way sounds seemed muffled, that made Josh's skin prickle.

Mike took point, compass in hand, marking their trail every fifty yards with bright orange tags. Josh followed with the maps, then Emily, then Tyler with his equipment, Olivia bringing up the rear and photographing their path.

They hiked in formation, like Mike had drilled them.

"Gradient's off," Emily said after the first mile, checking the topographical map. "We should be descending more steeply. It's too gradual."

"GPS agrees," Tyler added, frowning at his device. "Signal strength is nominal, but the elevation reading doesn't match the terrain. We've descended 200 feet according to GPS, but the compass says 400."

"Which one's wrong?" Mike asked.

"Maybe both," Josh said. "Or maybe the land actually is impossible here, like the satellite imagery suggested."

They kept hiking. The trail—if it could be called that—wound between massive old-growth trees. No clear path, just spaces between trunks wide enough to walk through. Mike's bright orange markers stood out like beacons, reassuring proof they could find their way back.

After two hours, they stopped for water and a quick rest.

"Something's been bothering me," Olivia said, scrolling through her camera's images. "Look at these."

She showed them photos from the hike so far. The forest, the trees, Mike's markers.

"What are we looking at?" Emily asked.

"The light." Olivia zoomed in. "See how the shadows fall? They're consistent in each photo, which means the sun hasn't moved. At all. We've been hiking for two hours, the sun should have shifted position, but the shadows are identical."

Tyler immediately checked his watches. "Mechanical says 9:47. Atomic clock says 9:47. But I started it at 7:30, so two hours seventeen minutes elapsed. My phone says—" He frowned. "7:51."

"Your phone's broken?" Mike suggested.

"I charged it full last night. And look." Tyler held it up. "Full bars. Battery at 96%. GPS working. It's just the time that's wrong."

Josh felt something cold settle in his stomach. "The sun's not moving. Time's running different here."

"Just like at the market," Emily said quietly.

They all remembered. The sun stuck on the horizon. The way everything had felt suspended.

"So we're in it," Mike said. "The temporal whatever. We're already in the effect zone."

"Looks like it." Tyler was taking readings, documenting everything. "My hypothesis is that we passed a threshold sometime in the last hour. Probably gradual, which is why we didn't notice immediately."

"Can we still get out?" Olivia asked.

"Don't know." Tyler didn't look up from his instruments. "The effect might be uni-directional. Or it might be like a gradient—easier to go deeper, harder to go back."

"That's not comforting," Mike said.

"You asked."

Josh looked at the forest around them. Still normal-looking. Still wrong-feeling. They'd known going in that Hollow Fields existed in some kind of temporal distortion. But knowing it intellectually and experiencing it were different things.

"We keep going," Josh said. "We're already in the effect. Might as well find out what's at the center."

"Or we turn back now," Emily suggested. "Before we get any deeper."

"And come all this way for nothing?"

"Better than not coming back at all."

Josh looked at her. Emily's face was set, that combination of fear and stubbornness he'd known since childhood. She'd come this far, but she'd also call him out if he was being stupid.

Was he being stupid?

"Let me think about it," Josh said.

He walked a few steps away, pulling out Mary Stanton's journal—or rather, the photocopies they'd made. He flipped to a marked passage.

The town looked wrong even from a distance. The buildings stood, but they seemed... thin. Like drawings of buildings rather than real structures. I should have left then. But I needed to know.

Mary had kept going. She'd walked into Hollow Fields twice. Seen the impossible. And survived to write about it.

But she'd also written: Let the gold have Hollow Fields. Some places are better left behind.

Josh looked at his friends. Mike checking weapons (bear spray, knife, flashlight). Tyler organizing equipment. Olivia reviewing photos. Emily watching Josh with that expression that meant she'd support whatever he decided but wouldn't pretend she agreed with it.

They'd all chosen to come. But he was the one who'd said "show us" to the farmer. He'd started this.

"We keep going," Josh decided. "But carefully. We mark the trail extra carefully from here. And if anyone wants to turn back, we all turn back. No questions."

"Democracy in action," Mike said dryly.

But they shouldered their packs and kept hiking.

The forest changed gradually. The trees grew taller, their trunks wider. The underbrush thinned out until they were walking through cathedral-like spaces, sunlight (unmoving sunlight, Josh reminded himself) slanting through in golden shafts.

It would have been beautiful if it wasn't so eerie.

"We're getting close," Emily said, checking the maps. "The valley should open up ahead."

Tyler's GPS beeped. "Signal's degrading. I'm getting impossible readings now. It thinks we're in three different locations simultaneously."

"What about your analog compass?" Mike asked.

Tyler checked. "Still works. And it agrees with what the map says—we're headed north-northwest. Just can't trust GPS anymore."

They crested a small rise, and—

"Oh," Olivia breathed.

The valley spread below them.

FIRST SIGHT

Hollow Fields lay in a bowl-shaped valley, exactly where the old property records said it should be. But nothing could have prepared them for actually seeing it.

The town was still there.

Buildings lined dirt streets in a grid pattern. A church stood at the center, its steeple reaching toward the sky. Homes, shops, what looked like a town hall. All of it perfectly preserved, or nearly so. Wooden walls, shingled roofs, glass windows.

It looked like a living town.

Except nothing moved.

No smoke from chimneys. No people in the streets. No animals, no birds, no sound at all. Just structures standing in perfect stillness under that frozen sun.

"It's real," Tyler whispered. "It's actually real."

Josh pulled out binoculars, scanning the town. The buildings looked solid, three-dimensional. Not thin or ghostly like Mary Stanton had described. Maybe the effect changed depending on where you viewed from.

"I can see details," Josh said. "Shutters on the windows. A sign for a general store. Is that a well in the center square?"

"Let me see." Emily took the binoculars. After a long moment: "It looks... normal. Like a preserved historical site. If there weren't temporal distortions and a witch's curse, I'd say it was just an abandoned town that got lucky with decay."

"Nothing about this is lucky," Mike said.

Olivia was already photographing, her camera clicking rapid-fire. "I'm getting clear images. The camera's focusing properly, everything's sharp. Whatever blocks the farmer from being photographed isn't affecting the town."

"Maybe because the town's not actively magical," Tyler suggested. "It's just caught in the effect, not generating it."

"Or maybe it wants to be seen," Emily said quietly.

That thought hung heavy.

"Let's get down there," Josh said. "We can observe from the edge, document what we find, then decide if we want to go into the town proper."

"Wait." Mike held up a hand. "We need a fallback plan. If something goes wrong, if we get separated, what's the rally point?"

"Here," Josh decided. "This ridge. We can see the whole valley from here, and it's the last place we're certain is outside the main effect zone."

"Agreed." Mike pulled out more orange markers, creating a bright reference point. "If anyone gets split off, you come back here. You wait two hours. If no one shows, you hike out and call for help."

"Will phones even work outside?" Olivia asked.

"We'll find out if we need to."

They began their descent into the valley. The slope was steep but manageable, and Mike's trail markers glowed bright against the dimming forest.

Dimming?

Josh looked up. The sunlight was fading, even though the sun itself hadn't moved. Like reality couldn't decide if it was day or dusk.

"Anyone else notice the light?" he asked.

"Yeah," Emily said. "It's getting darker. But there are no shadows changing. The light's just... uniformly decreasing."

Tyler checked his instruments. "Ambient lux levels dropping steadily. But astronomical readings say it's still 9:47 AM. The sun's in the wrong position for this light quality."

"Add it to the list of impossible things," Mike muttered.

They reached the valley floor. The grass here was waist-high, golden brown, swaying slightly despite no wind. Josh pushed through it, the others following in single file.

Up close, the town felt even stranger. The buildings were too still. Too perfect. Like a photograph brought to three dimensions.

They stopped at what would have been the town's edge—a split-rail fence, mostly intact, marking the boundary between wild land and settlement.

"Last chance to stay outside," Emily said.

Josh looked at the town. At the street stretching before them, dirt road lined with buildings. At the church in the distance. At windows that might have reflections or might be empty.

Mary Stanton had walked in twice. She'd seen something in there, something that had terrified her enough to leave forever but had also pulled her back one last time.

What had she seen?

"We go in," Josh said. "But we stay tight. We don't split up. And we leave at the first sign of real danger."

"Define 'real danger,'" Mike said.

"We'll know it when we see it."

"Not comforting."

"I know."

Josh stepped over the fence.

The moment his foot touched the town proper, something shifted. Not dramatically—no flash of light or rush of wind. Just a subtle change in pressure, like his ears popping. The quality of silence changed from forest quiet to something deeper. Heavier.

"Did you feel that?" Olivia asked.

"Yeah." Josh took another step. The ground felt solid. Normal. But there was an awareness now, a sense of being observed.

The others followed him over the fence.

Tyler immediately pulled out instruments, taking readings. "Temporal distortion is significantly stronger here. My atomic clock just jumped forward three hours, then jumped back. My mechanical watch is running backward. Very slowly, but it's definitely going counterclockwise."

"That's not possible," Mike said.

"And yet." Tyler showed him the watch. Sure enough, the second hand was sweeping backward.

They walked down the main street, boots thudding on hard-packed dirt. The buildings rose on either side—a general store, a boarding house, a blacksmith's shop with anvil still visible through the window.

Everything was preserved. Frozen in time.

Josh stopped at the general store, peered through the window. Shelves lined the walls, stocked with goods. Fabric, tools, jars of preserved food. A counter with a cash box. Everything covered in dust but otherwise intact.

"It's like everyone just... left," Olivia said. "Mid-day. They walked away and never came back."

"Or they didn't walk away," Emily said grimly. "Mary's journal said they were trapped."

Josh moved to the next building—a home with a front porch. The door was closed but not locked. He pushed it open carefully.

The interior was dark, but his flashlight revealed a parlor frozen in time. Furniture arranged for conversation. A table set for dinner. Books on shelves. Photographs on the walls.

"Someone lived here," Josh said. "Recently. Or what passed for recently in 1850."

Tyler was photographing everything, making notes. "No decay. That's what's wrong. There should be water damage, rot, mold, insects. This place should be falling apart after 170 years. But it's just... preserved."

"The temporal effect?" Emily suggested.

"Maybe. If time isn't moving normally, maybe decay isn't either."

They moved through the house carefully, not touching anything. Three bedrooms upstairs, all furnished. A kitchen with dishes in the basin. A root cellar with provisions still stocked.

It felt like walking through a museum exhibit, except museum exhibits felt dead. This felt suspended. Waiting.

"I don't like this," Mike said. "It's too intact. Too ready for people to just walk back in and resume their lives."

"Like they're expected to return?" Olivia asked.

"Or like they never really left."

Josh thought about that. The townspeople had vanished from records but maybe not from the town itself. Maybe they were still here, somehow. Trapped in the same temporal distortion that preserved their homes.

They continued down the street, documenting each building. All the same—preserved, waiting, empty.

Until they reached the church.

The building was larger than the others, white-painted wood with a proper steeple. The double doors stood open, as if inviting them in.

"That's ominous," Mike said.

"Maybe it's just open," Josh suggested, but he didn't believe it.

They approached cautiously. The church steps were worn but solid. The interior visible through the open doors was dark.

Josh stepped to the threshold and stopped.

Someone was inside.

Or something that looked like someone.

A figure knelt at the altar, head bowed in prayer. Motionless. A woman, based on the silhouette—long dress, hair pinned up.

"Hello?" Josh called out.

The figure didn't move.

"We should go in," Emily whispered.

"Should we?" Mike countered.

But Josh was already stepping inside.

The interior of the church was simple—wooden pews, a raised altar, windows letting in that strange unchanging light. And the figure, kneeling before the altar.

Josh walked down the center aisle slowly. His footsteps echoed despite the dirt floor.

The woman didn't react to his approach.

"Hello?" Josh said again. "We're not here to hurt anyone. We're just trying to understand what happened."

Nothing.

He was close enough now to see details. Her dress was old-fashioned, homespun fabric in a simple style. Her hands were clasped in prayer. Her head bowed.

But she wasn't moving at all. Not breathing. Not shifting. Perfectly still.

Josh reached out carefully, meaning to tap her shoulder—

"Don't," Emily said sharply.

Josh's hand stopped inches away.

Because now that he was this close, he could see the truth.

The woman wasn't alive. But she wasn't dead either.

She was between states, caught like a photograph. Real but not quite real. There but not quite there.

"She's part of the town," Josh whispered. "Frozen like everything else."

"Then we should leave her alone," Mike said. "Whatever she is, we're not equipped to deal with it."

But Olivia was photographing, fascinated. "Look at her face."

Josh hadn't looked directly at her face. Now he did.

She was young. Maybe early twenties. Peaceful expression. Eyes closed. And on her cheeks—

Tear tracks.

Frozen tears, caught mid-fall.

She'd been crying when time stopped.

"Oh god," Emily breathed. "She's been like this for 170 years. Trapped in the middle of praying, the middle of crying. Aware but unable to move."

"We don't know that she's aware," Tyler said.

"Look at her face. That's suffering."

Josh felt sick. If this woman had been trapped like this since the curse—if all the townspeople had been frozen in whatever they were doing—

That wasn't death. That was worse than death.

"We need to help them," Josh said.

"How?" Mike demanded. "We don't know how to break curses. We barely understand what we're seeing."

"But we can't just leave them."

"We can't do anything for them right now," Emily said gently. "Josh. Look at me. We can't help her yet. We need to understand what happened first."

Josh knew she was right. But looking at that frozen figure, those preserved tears—

"I'm sorry," he whispered to the woman.

She didn't answer. Couldn't answer.

They left the church carefully, respectfully. Outside, the unchanging light felt oppressive. The silence was suffocating.

"There could be hundreds of people like her," Olivia said. "Trapped in houses, in the streets. All frozen mid-moment."

"The monsters," Emily realized. "Mary Stanton's journal talked about people becoming monsters. Maybe that's what happens if the temporal freeze breaks. They've been trapped so long they've become twisted."

"Or maybe the monsters are something else entirely," Tyler suggested. "We don't know enough yet."

They stood in the town square, surrounded by buildings that waited. By lives suspended. By a curse they were only beginning to understand.

"We need more information," Josh said. "The witch. Eliza Nightshade. If she's the one who cast the curse, maybe she's the key to breaking it."

"Where would we even find her?" Mike asked.

"Mary Stanton said she lived on the ridge overlooking the valley." Emily pulled out the historical maps. "There was a homestead marked up there. We could—"

She stopped mid-sentence.

Because the light was changing again.

Not fading this time. Shifting.

The frozen sun was finally moving.

And with it, the shadows in the town began to lengthen. Shift. Change.

"Guys," Tyler said, voice tight. "Time's moving again. The temporal freeze is releasing."

"That's good, right?" Olivia asked.

"For us, maybe." Tyler was watching his instruments. "But for everything that's been frozen—"

The church door slammed shut behind them.

From inside, they heard a sound. A gasp. Like someone taking their first breath after drowning.

Then a scream.

The frozen woman was waking up.

And she was not okay.

The scream came again, raw and terrified. Not one voice—many voices. Rising from the buildings around them like a wave of sound.

People were waking up.

All of them.

"Move," Mike said. Not loud, but commanding. "Back to the ridge. Now."

They ran.

Behind them, the sounds intensified. Screams, cries, confusion. Doors slamming. Glass breaking. The town coming violently to life after 170 years of frozen silence.

Josh risked a glance back.

Figures stumbled from buildings. Men, women, children—all dressed in 1850s fashion, all moving with jerky, unnatural motions. Like puppets whose strings had been cut and were learning to move again.

Some were human-shaped. Others—

Others weren't anymore.

Josh saw a man whose body had twisted, limbs too long, joints bending wrong. A woman whose face had partially melted into something else. A child who flickered between solid and translucent.

The temporal freeze hadn't just preserved them. It had changed them.

"Don't look back!" Emily grabbed Josh's arm, pulled him forward.

They crashed through the golden grass, heading for the valley slope. Behind them, the sounds of the town grew louder. Chaotic. Some of the voices were calling for help. Others just screamed.

Tyler tripped, equipment scattering. Mike grabbed him, hauled him up. "Leave it!"

"I need—"

"LEAVE IT."

They hit the slope and started climbing. The trail they'd marked was clear, but the slope was steep and they were panicking, not hiking efficiently. Josh's lungs burned. His legs screamed.

Keep going keep going keep going—

A figure appeared at the valley's edge below. One of the townspeople— or what they'd become. It looked up at them with eyes that were too bright, too aware.

And smiled.

Not a friendly smile. A hungry one.

"They're following us," Olivia gasped.

More figures emerged from the grass. Moving faster now, more coordinated. They weren't stumbling anymore. They were hunting.

"How much further?" Mike asked, voice strained.

"Two hundred yards to the ridge!" Emily checked behind them. "They're gaining!"

Josh looked back. At least a dozen figures now, climbing with unnatural grace. Their bodies moved wrong but fast. And more were coming from the town.

They weren't going to make it.

"Josh," Mike said. "The bear spray. I have to—"

"No," Josh said. "They're victims. They're people."

"They're FOLLOWING US!"

"There has to be another way." Josh's mind raced. Think think think—

The fence.

When he'd crossed the town's boundary, he'd felt something shift. A threshold. What if that boundary worked both ways?

"The fence line!" Josh shouted. "Get across the fence!"

"What?"

"The town boundary—it's a threshold! Get across it!"

They changed direction, angling toward where the split-rail fence marked the edge of settlement. The figures behind them adjusted course, closing the distance.

Fifty yards.

Thirty yards.

One of the creatures—Josh couldn't think of them as people anymore—was close enough that Josh could hear its breathing. Wet. Wrong.

Twenty yards.

Ten.

Josh hit the fence first, vaulted over.

The pursuing figure slammed into an invisible barrier and ricocheted back like it had hit a wall.

It couldn't cross.

The others made it over—Emily, Tyler, Olivia, Mike—and the pursuing figures all stopped at the fence line. Unable or unwilling to cross.

They stood there, watching. Some still looked mostly human. Others had transformed into something else. But all of them were aware, intelligent, trapped.

"Why can't they cross?" Tyler panted.

"The boundary," Josh said. "Mary Stanton wrote that nothing could leave the town. The curse binds them here."

"So they're prisoners," Olivia said softly. "They woke up after 170 years, and they're still prisoners."

One of the figures—a woman who still looked largely human—stepped closer to the fence. She studied them with sharp, assessing eyes.

"You came from outside," she said. Her voice was hoarse, like she hadn't spoken in years. Which she hadn't. "You don't belong here."

"We're trying to understand what happened," Josh said carefully. "We want to help."

"Help?" The woman laughed, but there was no humor in it. "You want to help us? After everything?"

"We didn't cause this—"

"Your kind did." Her eyes blazed. "The ones who burned her. The ones who cursed us."

"Eliza Nightshade?" Emily asked.

The woman's expression shifted to something complicated. Pain and anger and... fear.

"Don't speak her name," she whispered. "Not here. Not unless you want her attention."

"Where is she?" Josh asked.

"Where she's always been. The hill. Her home." The woman pointed toward the ridge opposite the one they'd descended from. "She watches. Waits. And if you're foolish enough to seek her out, she'll show you what happens to those who disturb the dead."

"Is she dead?" Tyler asked.

"Define dead." The woman smiled bitterly. "She's no more dead than we are. She's just... different."

Other figures were gathering behind her. Silent now. Watching. Waiting.

"You should leave," the woman said. "Before night falls. The sun's moving again, which means the cycle's turning. Night is when the worst of us come out."

"The worst?" Mike asked.

"The ones who changed completely. The ones who aren't people anymore." She looked back at the town, expression haunted. "We try to hold them back, those of us who remain ourselves. But when night comes, they're stronger. And they're hungry."

"Hungry for what?" Josh asked, though he dreaded the answer.

"For life. For warmth. For escape. For everything they lost." The woman's eyes met his. "They can't cross the boundary. But you can. And if you're inside the town when night falls, boundary won't help you."

"Thank you for the warning," Emily said.

"Don't thank me. Just leave. And don't come back." The woman turned away, then paused. "Unless you can actually break the curse. If you can do that... maybe there's hope for us."

She walked back toward the town, the other figures parting to let her through.

The group stood at the fence line, watching them go. Watching them return to their prison.

"We need to get back to the ridge," Mike said. "Now. Before anything else happens."

They climbed in silence, moving quickly but carefully. The forest felt different now—menacing instead of just eerie. Shadows moved at the edges of Josh's vision.

When they reached the ridge overlook, they collapsed, breathing hard.

The town lay below, buildings standing in the failing light. Figures moved through the streets—some human-looking, others not. A community of the trapped and the transformed.

"What do we do?" Olivia asked.

Josh looked at the town. At the ridge opposite where Eliza Nightshade supposedly waited. At his friends, exhausted and scared but still here.

"We find the witch," Josh said. "We learn how to break the curse. And we free them."

"Just like that?" Mike asked.

"No. Not just like that." Josh's hands were shaking. Adrenaline crash. "But we came here to understand. Now we understand part of it. People are trapped in that town. Suffering. We can't just walk away."

"We could," Emily pointed out. "We absolutely could walk away right now."

"Could you?" Josh looked at her. "Knowing they're down there?"

Emily held his gaze for a long moment. Then: "No. I couldn't."

"Neither can I."

Tyler checked his equipment—what was left of it. "If we're really doing this, we need supplies. Better preparation. Maybe research support from outside."

"And we need to talk to Elizabeth," Emily added. "She's a Nightshade descendant. She might know things that aren't in the historical records."

"So we go out," Mike said. "Regroup. Come back prepared."

Josh nodded, but his eyes stayed on the town below. The woman's words echoed: Unless you can actually break the curse. If you can do that... maybe there's hope for us.

His grandfather had spent forty years wondering if what he saw was real.

Josh knew it was real now. And he knew people were suffering.

Grandpa had walked away with questions.

Josh wasn't going to do the same.

"Let's go," he said. "But we're coming back."

They hiked out of Hollow Fields as the strange light dimmed toward something like evening. Mike's orange markers guided them through the forest. Tyler's instruments slowly returned to normal as they left the effect zone.

When they finally reached the van, exhausted and shaken, the dashboard clock read 2:47 PM.

"We were gone seven hours," Mike said. "Felt like three."

"Time distortion," Tyler confirmed, making notes. "Just like I predicted."

They loaded equipment, got in the van, started the long drive home.

Nobody spoke much. There was too much to process.

Josh drove, eyes on the road, but his mind was back in Hollow Fields. In the church with the frozen woman. At the fence watching transformed people who couldn't escape. Standing at the boundary between cursed and free.

He thought about his choice at the market. Show us, he'd said.

The farmer had shown them. More than they'd expected. More than they were ready for.

And now they knew.

The Golden Pickles weren't just mysterious food. They were the lure for a trap that had held for 170 years. The farmer wasn't just selling pickles. He was continuing a curse, bringing victims to feed whatever power sustained Hollow Fields.

They'd found the mystery. Uncovered the secret his grandfather had died wondering about.

And discovered something worse: people were still trapped there. Still suffering. Still waiting for someone to break the curse.

"I'm coming back," Josh said quietly.

"I know," Emily replied. "We all are."

Because that's what happened when you looked into the darkness and found people trapped there.

You didn't walk away.

You figured out how to free them.

CHAPTER 4: THE GHOST TOWN

I hadn't slept. Every time I closed my eyes, I saw the farmer's face in that cabin, heard those words: I am a prisoner, just like the rest of them.

So instead of sleeping, I'd spent the night trying to make it make sense. Drew diagrams connecting the pickles to the farmer to the cabin. Listed every fact we had. Searched through Grandpa's notebooks for anything about cursed farmers or vanishing towns or time that ran wrong. Nothing fit the pattern.

Dad would say: "When the pieces don't fit, you're looking at the wrong puzzle."

Maybe. Or maybe the puzzle was way bigger than I thought.

The sun was just breaking through the trees when the others found me at the forest edge, surrounded by scattered notes and equipment checks. Tyler's motion sensors, recalibrated twice. Emily's evidence folders, reorganized by timeline. Mike's suggested escape routes, mapped and re-mapped. Everything I could control, controlled. Everything I could prepare for, prepared.

Emily stopped a few feet away, arms crossed. Didn't say anything at first. Just looked at me, at the mess of papers and gear, at the circles under my eyes I could feel but couldn't see.

"You've been here all night."

Not a question. She'd known me since we were kids. Could read me like one of Grandpa's old textbooks.

"Had to think about it." I stood, brushing dirt from my jeans. The motion sensors beeped—still functional, still reading normal. Which made yesterday even less normal. "The cabin. The farmer. That stone with the glowing symbols. It's all connected to something bigger."

"Yeah." Mike dropped his pack on the ground with a thud that said he wasn't happy about being up this early. "Connected to us getting the hell out of here."

I met his eyes. "We can't. Not yet."

"Joshua." Emily's full-name voice. The one that meant she was worried and didn't want to show it. "We found a cursed cabin in cursed woods with a farmer who says he's a prisoner. That's where normal people cut their losses and leave."

"Normal people didn't bring their friends here." The guilt sat heavy in my chest, had been sitting there all night. "I did. And I'm not leaving until I know we're not..." I gestured vaguely at the forest behind us. "Trapped. Like he said we might be."

Olivia had her camera out already, checking settings with that focused look she got when she was about to document something. "The woman yesterday. In the cabin. She wasn't threatening us. She was warning us."

"Exactly." I grabbed my pack, felt the weight of Grandpa's journal in the side pocket. "So we need to understand what she was warning us about. We need to know if we're already caught in whatever caught them."

Tyler's laptop showed yesterday's GPS data—the weird fluctuations, the impossible loops where we'd walked straight but the computer said we'd circled. "Tech says we walked in circles for two hours. But we walked straight. I watched the compass the whole time."

"So either the forest is messing with GPS—" I started.

"Or the forest is messing with space itself." Emily's voice was flat, that evidence-based tone she used when the evidence wasn't making sense. "Neither option is good, Josh."

"I know." I checked the motion sensors one more time. Still reading normal. Still giving me that false sense of control. "But Grandpa always said the best way through fear is understanding it. You can't fix what you don't understand. So." I gave myself thirty seconds. Counted it in my head while I looked at everything we knew. The farmer's words. The cabin symbols. The woman's warning. The impossible GPS readings. The way time had felt wrong even though our watches had run fine.

Pattern: everything pointed deeper into the woods.

"We go back," I decided. "But we're smarter this time. No splitting up. We mark our trail—two colors, Mike's and mine, so we can tell if we're looping. Tyler monitors GPS in real-time. First sign things are going wonky again, we follow our marks straight back out."

"And if we can't find our marks?" Mike asked. "What if they disappear like yesterday's did?"

I didn't have an answer for that. Let the silence say it.

Emily sighed, that heavy sigh that meant she knew I wasn't going to change my mind and she was going to come anyway because that's what we did. "This is a terrible idea."

"Yeah." I shouldered my pack, felt the flashlight and rope and first aid kit and all the other things I'd packed that probably wouldn't help against whatever was out there. "But it's the only one I've got. Let me think about it while we walk. Maybe I'll come up with something better."

We both knew I wouldn't. But we both also knew I had to try.

The forest felt different in full daylight. Not safer—just different. Like the wrongness yesterday had been hiding in the shadows, and now we could see the edges of it even in the sun.

I kept checking my compass against Tyler's GPS. Both agreed on direction: northeast. Both had been agreeing yesterday too, right up until they started lying.

"Marking trees every fifty feet," Mike announced, pulling out the fluorescent orange tape from his pack. He'd been a con artist before college, always had an angle, always looking for the exit. Now he was using those instincts to cover our backs. Funny how people grow. He wrapped bright orange around a thick trunk. "Anyone sees these markers going in circles, we abort. No discussion."

"Agreed." I pulled out my own tape—blue, Dad's trick for double-checking patterns when you're working alone. If we ended up looping, we'd see both colors overlapping. I marked a tree a hundred feet from Mike's orange, offset so the pattern would be obvious. "And I'll mark every hundred feet. Different rhythm, different color. Can't miss if we're doubling back."

Tyler walked with his laptop open, eyes flicking between screen and path every few seconds. "Signal strength steady at 78%. Magnetic readings nominal. Barometric pressure holding. Yesterday around this point, same readings went completely haywire. Like we'd walked into a different..." He trailed off, frowning at the screen. "...a different space."

"Except here's just trees." I looked around. Normal forest. Maple, oak, some pine. Birds singing somewhere above us—I could hear them now, clear as anything. "Here" looked exactly like forest should look.

"Too quiet yesterday," I muttered, more to myself.

"What?" Emily was close enough to hear anyway.

"The birds. We didn't hear any yesterday, remember? Not a single one. Now they're everywhere."

She tilted her head, listening. Farm kid habit—she could identify bird species by call, predict weather from their behavior. "You're right. That's robins. Couple of sparrows. Crow in the distance. Normal birds doing normal bird things." Her eyes met mine. "Whatever we walked through yesterday, we're not in it yet."

"Yet," Mike repeated, adding another orange marker. "I love how you said yet. Very reassuring."

Olivia had her camera up, shooting the canopy, the way sunlight filtered through leaves. Professional equipment, expensive glass—she came from old money even if she didn't fit with her family. "Light's different too. Yesterday felt like everything was underwater. Today it's just..." She lowered the camera, looked around. "It's just woods."

"Then we haven't reached the weird part yet." Mike tied off his marker with maybe more force than necessary. "Great. I love waiting for weird."

We walked for another hour. I kept checking the equipment—all normal. Mike's orange tape appeared at regular intervals, cheerful and bright against the gray bark. My blue tape marked the hundreds, a slower rhythm underneath his pattern. Tyler's readings stayed steady, no fluctuations.

Normal walk in normal woods toward something that definitely wasn't normal.

Then my compass needle started spinning.

Just slowly at first. A lazy circle like it was confused. Then faster. Then so fast the needle was just a blur of silver in the center of my palm.

"Tyler." I held up the compass without looking away from it. "Check yours."

Tyler's GPS flickered once. Twice. Then locked on a heading that made no sense—the screen said we were walking west, but the sun was clearly ahead and to the right. North. We were walking north.

"Here we go," Tyler muttered, fingers flying over his keyboard. "Same pattern as yesterday. Magnetic north is rotating relative to true north. GPS thinks we're—" He stopped. Looked up at me. Looked back at the screen. "Josh. According to this, we're three hundred feet above our starting elevation."

I looked around. We hadn't climbed. The path had been level the whole way. Even sloped slightly down at one point.

"The town," Olivia said softly. Her camera was already up, motor drive whirring. "The ghost town. It's close."

"How do you know?" Mike asked.

"The light." She pointed without lowering the camera. "Look at how the sunlight's coming through. It's not quite right anymore. Not underwater, but not quite normal either. Like everything's slightly..." She searched for the word. "Muted. Distant."

Emily saw it too, I could tell by the way she'd gone still. "Fog's coming."

There wasn't any fog. Not yet. But the temperature was dropping, I could feel moisture in the air. The kind of change you learned to read growing up in the country, the shift that meant weather was coming whether you saw it yet or not.

"Check the markers," I said.

Mike turned, counted steps back the way we'd come. Found his orange tape. Counted forward. Found the next one. "Still fifty feet. We're not looping."

"Yet," Emily added quietly.

Tyler's GPS flickered again, the numbers jumping. "We're definitely not where this thinks we are. According to the satellite positioning, we should be standing in the middle of a lake that doesn't exist."

I stopped walking. The others stopped too.

Ahead, through the trees, I could see something that wasn't trees.

Buildings.

"Tell me you see that," Mike said, his voice carefully flat.

"I see it." I pulled out my phone, snapped photos even though I had a feeling they wouldn't develop right. Or would develop too right. Olivia was already shooting, her professional camera rapid-firing that distinctive motorized click-click-click.

Structures. Man-made. Definitely buildings.

And according to Tyler's GPS, they didn't exist.

We moved forward slowly. Not because we'd decided to—I'm not sure any of us made that decision consciously—but because now that we could see them, we had to know.

Had to understand.

The first building resolved out of the trees like something coming into focus. An old house, maybe. Or what was left of one. Sagging roof, broken windows, walls that might've been white once but were gray now with age and neglect.

But that wasn't what made me stop cold.

"How did we miss this?" The question came out quieter than I meant it.

Because we'd been walking between buildings for the last hundred feet without realizing it. There was a structure to my left, half-buried in underbrush, so covered in vines it looked like a hill. Another to my right, trees growing through what used to be its roof. Behind us, I could see now, more buildings. Ahead, more still.

We'd walked right into a town without noticing we were in it.

"That's not possible," Mike said. But his hand was near his belt, where I knew he'd started carrying a knife after yesterday. Old habits. "We would've seen—we were looking—"

"We weren't looking at the right time," Tyler said, staring at his screen. "Or the right... place. Josh, I'm getting zero signal here. Complete dead zone. GPS has no idea where we are anymore. It's like we stepped off the map."

"We're somewhere," Olivia said, camera still working. She'd moved to the nearest building—what might've been a house once, hard to tell now. "Look at the construction. That's timber frame, early nineteenth century. But the nails—" She moved closer, forgetting danger in the puzzle, which was very Olivia. "The nails are wrong. They're twentieth century. And that joint work there, that's not American construction at all. That's European joinery. German, maybe. Or Swiss."

I looked where she was pointing. She was right—I'd helped Dad build enough to recognize the difference. Those joints were mortise-and-tenon, old-world craft, the kind Grandpa used to point out in antique barns. But they were holding together wall studs that were clearly cut by power saw. Recent.

"These buildings don't match," I said slowly. "Not just different eras. They don't match themselves."

"None of them match." Emily had wandered to what might've been a barn, was running her hand along the foundation. "This is farm storage. I can tell by the ventilation placement—you do it specific, this height off ground, this spacing, so the crop can breathe. But it's built into what looks like a residential foundation. That's not how you do it. Ever. You don't want your living space connected to bulk storage because of humidity, pests, temperature control..."

"Who cares how you do it?" Mike was still scanning the perimeter, old con-artist instincts measuring exits. "We've got maybe two hours of daylight left, and we're standing in a dead-zone ghost town. Can we document and leave?"

I wanted to. Every instinct that had kept me alive so far said Mike was right—document, note, leave, come back with help. But Grandpa's voice in my head: When something doesn't make sense, there's information you're missing. Can't solve a puzzle with missing pieces.

"Fifteen minutes," I said. Compromise. "We check the nearest buildings, figure out what this place was, mark our exit route clear, then we leave."

"Why fifteen?" Tyler asked.

"Because in fifteen minutes, the sun will move far enough that we'll know if we're in the same time flow." I pulled out my phone, started photographing. The images looked normal on the screen, but I didn't trust them. "Shadow angles. If the shadows don't move in fifteen minutes—"

"Then we're in whatever time bubble the farmer's in," Emily finished. Her voice was steady, but I saw her hand shake slightly as she pulled out her own phone to photograph the shadow from a broken post.

Time check: 2:47 PM.

We had until 3:02 to figure out where we were.

And what, exactly, we'd walked into.

The nearest building was less a house and more an architectural frankenstein—and yeah, I know that's a weird description, but it fit. One wall looked like it came from the 1800s, hand-hewn logs still showing axe marks. Another wall was clearly 1920s, maybe '30s, machine-cut lumber with factory nails. The roof was wrong for both, too steep for the older section, too shallow for the newer.

"Someone kept repairing it," I murmured, running my hand along a door frame that had been replaced at least three times. Different wood each time. Different nails. Different construction styles, like whoever did the work was from different time periods and didn't realize the methods didn't match. "But they didn't have the right materials. Or didn't know the right way."

"Or they were from different time periods," Emily said quietly.

That stopped me cold. Because once she said it, I couldn't unsee it. The house wasn't just old and patched. It was layered. Bits of different eras stacked on top of each other like someone had been living here continuously for a hundred and fifty years, replacing pieces as they broke, but each generation used whatever was available in their time.

Before I could process that fully, Olivia called from inside the building. "Journal. There's someone's journal in here."

We found her in what might've been a kitchen once, though the stove was rusted through and the walls were more hole than surface. She was photographing a small book on a broken table, the leather cover cracked and peeling.

I picked it up carefully. The cover page read: Mary Stanton, 1892

"Eighteen ninety-two," Tyler said softly. "That's..."

"One hundred and thirty-three years ago." I opened to the first entry. My hands were shaking slightly, had been since the compass started spinning, but I made them steady enough to read.

May 12th, 1892 – The fog has returned, thicker than ever. I fear what it brings. The people of the town grow more restless by the day. They speak of leaving, but none dare venture into the woods. Not after what happened to the Thompsons.

I read it aloud. Emily crowded close, reading over my shoulder. Mike kept watch at the door—I noticed he'd positioned himself where he could see both inside and out. Olivia photographed each page as I turned them.

May 14th, 1892 – The farmer came to town today. He didn't speak, as usual, but his presence brought a chill to the air. The others avoid him, but I can't shake the feeling that he knows something. There's something in his eyes... something ancient.

The handwriting was neat but getting shakier with each entry. I flipped forward.

May 20th, 1892 – The pickles. They say they're cursed. Those who eat them are never the same. But I don't believe it. There has to be an explanation. There has to be...

The entries got more desperate, more fragmented. Whole days skipped. Then weeks. I flipped to the final page.

June 1st, 1892 – The fog has consumed the town. We are trapped. The farmer is gone, but the curse remains. The others have stopped speaking. I don't know how much longer I can stay. The air grows colder by the day. We are not alone here. Something watches from the fog...

The journal ended there. Not completed—abandoned. Mid-thought. Like she'd just stopped writing and never picked it up again.

"She never left," Emily said softly.

"None of them did." I looked up at the building's wrong architecture, the layers of different time periods. "They've been here. For a hundred and thirty-three years. Trapped."

"Check the time," Tyler said suddenly.

I pulled out my phone: 3:04 PM.

We'd been inside for seventeen minutes.

Olivia was already at the door, moving to where we'd marked the shadow before we came in.

It hadn't moved.

At all.

The sun outside had definitely traveled—I could see the angle was different in the trees. But the shadow inside this building, from this post, was exactly where it had been seventeen minutes ago. Exactly the same angle, the same length.

Time had stopped.

"Time's not moving the same here," Tyler said. His voice had gone quiet, almost flat. The tone he used when he was trying to process something his brain was rejecting. "The town's... it's outside normal time flow."

"Like the farmer," I whispered.

From deeper in the town, a sound.

Footsteps.

Slow. Deliberate. Coming closer.

"Out," Mike said. "Now."

But before any of us could move, a figure stepped out of the fog—and there was fog now, thick and white and rolling down the street like something alive—at the far end of what might've been a main road.

It was a woman.

She was dressed in clothes from another century, long skirt, high collar, the kind of thing you saw in history books or those old daguerreotype photos. Her face was pale—not just pale, wrong pale, the color of old paper. Her eyes were hollow, empty, but somehow still focused. Still seeing.

She looked at us. Not through us. At us.

And in that moment, I saw recognition in those hollow eyes. Saw awareness. Saw something that was still, impossibly, a person.

She opened her mouth. Her voice was barely a whisper, but it carried through the dead, unmoving air:

"You shouldn't be here."

My voice came out steadier than I felt. "We're trying to understand. We want to help."

The woman's eyes focused on me, and for a brief moment I saw something human in them. Something desperate. Something that had been suffering for a very, very long time.

"You can't help," she whispered. "You can only leave. Before you're trapped like us."

"Wait." I took a half-step forward. Emily grabbed my arm, but I gently pulled free. "Mary Stanton?"

The woman's hollow eyes widened slightly. Surprise, maybe. Or shock that someone knew her name after all this time.

"We found your journal," I continued, keeping my voice gentle. Like talking to a scared animal, which maybe wasn't far off. "We read about the fog. About being trapped. We want to understand what happened here."

The woman—Mary, if I was right—stood perfectly still for a long moment. When she finally spoke again, each word seemed to cost her effort, like speaking was something she'd almost forgotten how to do.

"The... pickles," she managed. "We ate... the pickles. We thought..." Her voice faded, then came back stronger, clearer, like she was remembering how. "We thought they were blessed. The farmer said they'd protect us. From the plague."

"What plague?" Emily asked, her need for information temporarily overriding her fear.

"1892. Cholera." Mary's form flickered slightly, like a light bulb with a loose connection. "It killed half the state. We were so scared. Then the farmer came with his pickles. Said they'd keep us safe. Keep the sickness away. We believed him."

My mind was racing, connecting pieces. "But they didn't keep you safe."

"They trapped us." Mary's voice cracked. "We couldn't leave. We tried. God knows we tried. But the fog... the fog always brought us back. And the others—the ones who were cruel, who hurt people, who were greedy—they changed. Became something worse. Something that hunts us."

"The creatures," Olivia whispered.

Mary nodded, a jerky movement like she was remembering how bodies were supposed to move. "We hide. Those of us who are just trapped, who didn't do anything wrong. We hide from them. We wait. We hope..." She looked at me with such desperate hope it made my chest hurt.
"Are you here to break the curse?"

"I—" I started, then stopped. Because honestly? I had no idea. "We're trying to understand it first. We didn't even know there was a curse until yesterday."

"You can't help." The sadness in her voice was overwhelming. "No one can help. You can only leave. Before the town traps you too. Before you become like us. Or worse—before you become like them."

"Who's them?" Mike asked, his voice tight.

But Mary was looking behind her now, and the expression on her translucent face was pure terror. "They're coming. The council. They know you're here. They'll try to—"

A bell tolled from somewhere deeper in the town. Deep, resonant, impossible. The kind of sound that shouldn't exist in a place where time had stopped.

Mary's form started to fade, like fog burning off in sunlight. "Run. Please. Don't let yourself become another victim of Hollow Fields. Don't let them—"

"Wait!" I stepped forward, reaching out even though I knew I couldn't touch her. "How do we break the curse? There has to be a way. Tell us how!"

But she was already gone. Completely. Like she'd never been there at all.

For a moment, nobody moved. We just stood there in the dead, silent street, staring at the empty space where a woman who'd been dead for over a century had just warned us to run.

Tyler broke the silence first, staring at his laptop. "Electromagnetic readings just spiked off the charts. Whatever she was—ghost, temporal echo, I don't even know the right word—she was using massive amounts of energy just to manifest. Just to exist long enough to talk to us."

"Did you get footage?" Emily asked Olivia.

Olivia lowered her camera slowly, her face pale. "No. Nothing. Camera shows empty street. Like she wasn't there at all."

"But we all saw her," Mike said.

"We all saw her," I confirmed. I looked down at the journal still clutched in my hands. Mary Stanton's journal. Mary Stanton who'd just appeared as a ghost to warn us. Mary Stanton who'd been here, trapped and suffering, for one hundred and thirty-three years.

The bell tolled again. Closer this time. Heavier. Like whatever was ringing it was getting closer.

"The council," Emily said quietly. "She said the council is coming."

Tyler was already closing his laptop, hands shaking slightly. "We need to leave. Now. The markers—"

"Are gone," Mike finished grimly. "I checked while you were talking to the ghost. Every single marker. Both colors. Orange and blue. It's like they never existed."

My stomach dropped. "The town is keeping us here."

"Like it kept Mary," Olivia said, barely above a whisper. "Like it's kept everyone who came here for over a hundred years."

From the center of the town, more sounds. Footsteps. Multiple sets. Heavy, deliberate. Not trying to hide their approach. And underneath the footsteps, something else. A wet, organic sound. Like something moving that shouldn't be able to move. Like meat sliding against stone.

"The creatures," I whispered.

Tyler snapped his laptop shut completely. "Okay. New plan. We don't need the markers. We use the sun. It's west, we head east. Basic navigation. Simple."

"Except time isn't moving the same here," Emily reminded him. Her voice was remarkably steady considering we were talking about running from creatures in a ghost town. "The sun might not be where we think it is."

"Then we pick a direction and run anyway." Mike was already moving, assessing angles, looking for the clearest path. "Because staying here with whatever is making those sounds? Not an option."

I looked at the journal in my hands. Looked back at where Mary had stood. She'd been desperate. Pleading. Not for herself—for us. She knew what this town did to people. Had lived it—was still living it—for longer than I could comprehend. And she'd used what little power she had left to try to save us from her fate.

"We run," I agreed. "But we remember this place. We remember Mary. We remember all of them. Because..." I met each of their eyes in turn. "Because someone needs to come back here. Someone needs to break this curse."

"That someone doesn't have to be us," Mike said.

I didn't argue. But I was already thinking it might have to be. Because who else knew? Who else would believe? Who else would care enough about a woman who'd been suffering for 133 years to do something about it?

The wet, organic sounds were getting louder. Closer.

"Move," Emily ordered.

We moved.

Behind us, the bell tolled a third time.

And ahead of us, the fog began to rise.

We ran blind for maybe ten minutes, following Emily's sense of direction. On the farm, she could navigate by sun and shadow even when the trails disappeared. Here, with time distorted and fog rising, she was mostly guessing. But it was better than anyone else could do.

The sounds behind us faded slightly, which should've been comforting but somehow wasn't. Like whatever was chasing us knew it didn't need to hurry. Like we were already caught and just didn't know it yet.

We broke through a line of twisted trees and stopped.

The church stood at the top of a low hill—the only hill in the entire town. From here, I could see the full layout of Hollow Fields spread out below us, and it made a horrible kind of sense.

All the buildings, randomly placed, chaotically organized... they all faced the church. Every single structure was oriented toward this central point, even when their doors and windows pointed in other directions. The buildings themselves faced the church like flowers facing the sun.

"It's a spiral," Tyler said, pulling up his dead GPS, using the cached map he'd been making. "Look. If you ignore the paths and just look at building placement. It's a spiral with the church at the center."

He was right. I could see it now from this height. The town wasn't random at all—it was a pattern. A spiral pattern. And the buildings got older the further from the church you went, and newer the closer you got. Like the town had been growing inward, collapsing toward this point over time.

"Or being pulled inward," Olivia said quietly, photographing the layout from our vantage point. For once, her camera was working—the image on her screen showed exactly what we were seeing.

Which somehow made it worse.

I checked my phone: 3:17 PM.

We'd been in the town for thirty minutes total.

It felt like hours.

"We shouldn't go in there," Mike said, staring at the church. "Every single instinct I have is screaming that walking into that building is the worst idea we've ever had."

"Agreed," Emily added. "But we need information. Mary said the council is coming. Town councils met in churches—that's where they kept records, held meetings, made decisions. If there's any record of what actually happened here, it'll be in there."

I was already moving up the hill. Not because I disagreed with Mike— my instincts were screaming too—but because Emily was right. We needed to understand the mechanism. Needed to know what we were dealing with. And understanding meant investigating the center of the spiral.

"Let me think about it," I said, even though I was already walking. Thirty seconds to process. The spiral pattern. The church at the center. Mary's warning about the council. The farmer's words: I am a prisoner. All of it pointed to the church being important. Being the key somehow.

"Josh," Emily called after me. "If we go in there—"

"I know." I didn't stop walking. "But we need to know. We can't break a curse we don't understand."

"Who said anything about breaking it?" Mike muttered, but he followed anyway. Because that's what we did. We followed each other into stupid, dangerous situations because the alternative was letting one person go alone.

The church doors were open. Not broken, not forced—just open. Like someone had unlocked them and left them that way. Waiting.

"I hate this so much," Mike said, but he stepped through the doorway with me.

Inside, the church was wrong in the same way every other building had been wrong. Pews from different eras—some hand-carved from the 1800s, some factory-made from the 1920s, some that looked almost new except for the dust. An altar that had been rebuilt multiple times, layers of different construction styles stacked on top of each other. Windows that didn't match, some original leaded glass, some modern panes, some just boarded up with wood from different decades.

The whole building had been cannibalized and reconstructed over and over again, like people had been living in it and repairing it continuously for a century and a half.

And standing in front of the altar, his back to us, wide-brimmed hat casting his face in shadow, was the farmer.

He didn't turn around. Just stood there, completely still, hands at his sides.

"You're still here," I said, keeping my distance but keeping my voice steady.

"I never left." His voice echoed in the empty space. "I haven't left in 143 years."

"Mary Stanton said 1892," Emily said from beside me, her mind automatically doing the math.

"That's only 133 years."

"For her." The farmer finally turned, and I could see his eyes now—hollow and empty like Mary's had been. "For me, it's been longer. I was the first. Before the plague. Before the pickles were supposed to save anyone. Before any of this."

"Tell us," I said. "Please. Help us understand what happened here."

The farmer looked at me for a long moment. His hollow eyes seemed to see right through me, measuring something. Then he nodded slightly, like he'd made a decision.

"You want to understand? You want to know how a town becomes a prison? How good intentions become curses? How salvation becomes damnation?"

"Yes."

"Then listen carefully." He gestured to the windows. Through the warped glass, I could see the fog was rising faster now, spreading through the streets like water filling a basin. "Because you're running out of time."

He turned back to the altar, and when he spoke again, his voice was different. Not hollow anymore, but heavy. Weighted with more than a century of pain.

"The council built this church in 1849. Five men. They were good men, originally. Wanted to create a perfect community. A place where everyone shared resources, where no one went hungry, where faith and prosperity lived together in harmony."

"What went wrong?" Olivia asked quietly.

"Same thing that always goes wrong. Power." The farmer's voice was bitter now. "The council realized they could control the town through the church. Make all the decisions. Allocate all the resources. Decide who prospered and who didn't. And people let them, because the council framed everything as God's will. Hard to argue with God's will."

"And when the plague came?" Emily prompted.

"1892. Cholera swept through the region, killed thousands. The council saw an opportunity." He turned to face us again. "To consolidate power even more. To make themselves indispensable. They hired me—I was just a traveling farmer back then, not whatever I am now—to create something that would protect the town. Keep people healthy."

"The pickles," I said.

"I used my grandmother's recipes. Old magic, old ways. Things she'd learned from her grandmother, going back generations. Made pickles that would strengthen immunity, fortify the body, keep disease at bay." His form flickered like Mary's had. "And they worked. People ate them and got better. The plague passed over Hollow Fields while towns all around us died."

"But the council wanted more," I guessed.

"They demanded I only sell through them. Only make what they approved. Use the pickles to control who had protection and who didn't."

The farmer's hands clenched into fists at his sides.

"Turn my grandmother's gift into their weapon. I refused."

The silence that followed was heavy.

"So they killed you," Tyler said quietly.

"Burned me. Right out there in the town square." The farmer pointed toward the window.

"Accused me of cursing the town, of bringing the plague in the first place. Said I was a witch who'd tricked them with dark magic. The townspeople believed them. Or were too scared not to believe them. Either way, I burned."

"But you didn't curse the town," I said.

"No. But dying with that accusation, with that injustice..." He looked down at his translucent hands. "The magic in the pickles was real. My grandmother's gift was real. And when I died with that much injustice, with that much anger, the magic... twisted. Changed. The pickles I'd already made, the ones people had already eaten—they became a trap. The magic that was supposed to protect became magic that imprisoned."

"It trapped everyone who'd eaten them," Emily said slowly, understanding dawning.

"And me. Bound me to this place, to this curse I never meant to create." The farmer looked up at us. "And the council—the five men who killed me, who lied about me, who destroyed me to protect their power—the curse recognized them. Knew them. Transformed them into the creatures they'd always been inside. Fed on their greed, their selfishness, their hunger for control, and made it visible."

"The creatures aren't random monsters," I said, pieces clicking together in my head. "They're the council. And anyone like them."

"The council and their descendants. Anyone whose greed resonated with the original sin. The curse feeds on greed, amplifies it, transforms it into something the rest of us can see. A visible corruption." The farmer's voice was barely a whisper now. "The people you call monsters—Mary, the others trapped here—they're innocent. Just victims. The real monsters are the ones who look almost human. Until you see what they've really become."

A bell tolled above us. The church bell, right over our heads, so loud it shook dust from the rafters.

"They're here," the farmer said. "The council. What's left of them. They know you're in their church."

"What do they want?" Mike demanded, his voice tight.

"Same thing they've always wanted. More. More time. More life. More victims to feed on. The curse has kept them alive for over a century, but they need fresh souls to maintain it. Fresh suffering to sustain their immortality." The farmer started to fade, his form becoming translucent. "That's why the pickles kept appearing at the market. The town needs to lure in new victims periodically. Needs fresh souls to replace the ones that finally fade."

"How do we stop them?" I asked urgently. "How do we break the curse?"

But the farmer was almost completely transparent now, his voice barely audible. "The curse can be broken. But not by me. Not by the trapped. Only by someone who sees the injustice clearly. Someone who understands what was done wrong. Someone willing to make it right."

"How?" I practically shouted it. "Tell us how!"

His final words came as barely a whisper, right before he vanished completely:

"Find the witch. Find Eliza. She's the key to everything. She's been the key all along."

Then he was gone.

And from deeper in the church—from below us, beneath the floor—came the sound of many footsteps. Heavy. Wrong. The wet, sliding sound of bodies that didn't move right anymore. Coming up from the basement we hadn't known existed.

Tyler's laptop went completely dead. Not sleeping, not low battery—dead. Screen black, no power, like all the energy had been sucked out of it.

"There's a basement," he whispered, staring at his dead screen. "There's a basement under us and something's coming up."

Mike was already at the door. "Back to the exit. Now."

But when we reached the entrance, the fog had risen to fill the doorway. Not just creeping in—standing there like a solid wall. Thick and white and completely impassable.

"Back door," Emily said, already moving.

We ran to the rear of the church. Same thing. Fog wall. Solid. I reached out to touch it and my hand just... stopped. Like hitting concrete.

The footsteps from below were getting closer. Louder. And with them, voices. Multiple voices, speaking in perfect unison:

"Welcome to Hollow Fields. You'll make fine additions to our congregation. Fresh souls for the harvest. Fresh suffering for the feast."

"Windows," I said, looking up. They were high—maybe twenty feet up—and narrow. Probably wouldn't fit an adult. But they were our only option. "We go up."

"Are you insane?" Mike hissed.

"Olivia, your camera strap." I was already pulling off my belt. "Tyler, your belt. Mike, anything we can tie together. Now!"

They moved fast, years of friendship meaning they trusted me even when I was asking them to do something crazy. Camera strap, two belts, a length of rope from Mike's emergency kit, Emily's backpack straps. We knotted them together, tested the weight. It might hold. Might.

The basement door burst open.

What came through wasn't Mary's gentle tragedy. These were the creatures she'd warned about.

The council members. They wore human faces—mostly—but the faces were wrong. Too smooth. Too perfect. Like masks. And their bodies moved wrong, bent at angles that shouldn't be possible, joints bending backward, arms too long, legs that dragged.

But it was their eyes that were worst. Golden. Glowing. The same color as the Golden Pickles. Like they'd been infected by the same magic that had trapped everyone else, but instead of imprisoning them, it had transformed them into something else. Something that fed on the trapped.

There were five of them. Six. Seven. They kept coming, filling the church, moving with that horrible wrong grace.

"Climb!" I shoved Emily toward the makeshift rope. "Now!"

She grabbed it, pulled herself up. Tyler followed, his lighter frame making it easier. Olivia went next, professional climber from all her documentary work. Mike right behind her.

The creatures were advancing slowly, like they were savoring this. Like they knew there was nowhere to run and wanted to enjoy our fear.

I grabbed the rope, started pulling myself up.

A hand grabbed my ankle. Cold. Dead. Strong.

I looked down. One of the council creatures had reached me, its too-perfect face smiling with too many teeth.

"You cannot leave," it said in a voice that might have once been human but was now something else entirely. "The town requires payment. Fresh souls to replace the old. You volunteered when you walked in. When you trespassed on holy ground."

I kicked. Hard. My boot connected with what might have been a face. The grip loosened just enough.

I pulled myself up, through the window that was definitely too small but I made myself fit anyway, fell onto the church roof outside.

"Go! Move!" I shouted at the others who were waiting for me.

We slid down the roof tiles—steeper than they'd looked from inside—hit the ground hard but running. Behind us, the church bell tolled again. And again. And again. Faster now, urgent, like an alarm.

The fog parted ahead of us, showing a clear path through the trees.

"It's a trap," Mike panted as we ran. "Has to be."

"Do we have a choice?" Emily gasped back.

We didn't.

We ran through the fog passage, every instinct screaming that the trap was about to spring, that the creatures were right behind us, that we'd never make it out.

Instead, we burst out of the treeline into normal forest.

Real forest. Real sunlight. Real birds calling. Real air that didn't taste like time standing still.

I stumbled, caught myself, kept running for another twenty feet before my brain processed that we were out. We were actually out.

Emily pulled out her phone with shaking hands: 3:24 PM.

My watch read: 6:15 PM.

We'd been in Hollow Fields for thirty-seven minutes according to our phones. Three hours according to our watches. According to the sun, which was definitely lower in the sky than it should be. According to the growling in my stomach and the exhaustion in my bones.

Tyler sat down hard on the ground, staring at his dead laptop like it had betrayed him. "What just happened?"

"We found Hollow Fields," Olivia said, still clutching her camera like a lifeline. "The real one. Not the legend. Not the story. The actual, cursed, impossible ghost town."

"And we barely made it out," Mike added, checking himself like he couldn't quite believe all his parts were still attached.

"But we know how to break the curse now," I said, even though my hands were shaking and my voice didn't sound as confident as I was trying to make it. "The farmer told us. We need to find Eliza."

"The witch," Emily said, finally lowering her phone. "He said find the witch. But who is she? The one who cursed him?"

"No." I was seeing the pattern now, the horrible logic of it all. "She's the one who was wrongly accused. Just like the farmer was. The council has been blaming witches and burning people for a hundred and fifty years. Eliza is probably the first one. The original victim. The first person they killed to consolidate their power."

"Then why would she be the key to breaking the curse?" Tyler asked, still staring at his dead equipment.

I looked back at the forest. The fog was still visible just inside the treeline, a wall of white that marked the boundary of Hollow Fields. The town was still there. Still waiting. Still holding Mary Stanton and the farmer and everyone else prisoner.

"Because," I said slowly, working through it out loud, "breaking a curse that was born from injustice means making the injustice right. Means proving the accusation was false. Means clearing her name. The farmer's curse came from dying while being falsely accused. If Eliza was the first—

if she was the original witch they blamed everything on—then her curse is probably the foundation.

The beginning. Break hers, and maybe you break all of them."

"And how exactly do we do that?" Mike asked. "We don't even know who she was, what she was accused of, when she died, anything."

I didn't have an answer. Not yet. But I knew where to start.

"We research. We find out who Eliza was, what happened to her, what she was accused of. We find proof that she was innocent. We clear her name." I looked at each of them. "We make it right."

"Josh." Emily's voice was gentle but firm. "We barely survived that place. Those creatures almost got us. We lost three hours somehow. Tyler's equipment is dead. We don't even know if the footage we took will show anything real. And you want to go back?"

"Not right now," I said. "But eventually? Yeah. Because Mary Stanton has been trapped there for 133 years. The farmer for 143. How many others? How many people have suffered because five greedy men decided to blame a woman for their own evil? How long do we let that keep happening?"

The silence that followed was heavy.

Finally, Olivia spoke. "He's right. Someone has to do something. Someone has to make it right."

"And that someone has to be us?" Mike asked, but his voice had lost its edge. He already knew the answer.

"Who else?" I looked back at the fog wall one more time. "Who else knows? Who else would believe? Who else would care enough to do something about it?"

Emily sighed, that deep sigh that meant she was accepting something she didn't like but couldn't argue against. "Fine. But first we get somewhere safe. We process what just happened. We make sure we're not being followed by time-ghost-council-creatures. And then we figure out how to research a witch who was probably killed a hundred and fifty years ago."

"Deal," I agreed.

We started walking, putting distance between us and the fog wall, between us and Hollow Fields. But I kept looking back. Couldn't help it.

Somewhere in there, Mary Stanton was still trapped. Still suffering. Still waiting for someone to break the curse.

And the farmer's words kept echoing in my head: Only by someone who sees the injustice clearly. Someone willing to make it right.

I saw it. Clearly. Five men had killed innocent people to maintain their power. Had created a curse that had been causing suffering for over a century. Had trapped an entire town in a loop of pain and fear and death that never ended.

That was wrong.

Someone had to make it right.

And looking at my friends—Emily with her need for evidence and truth, Olivia with her drive to document and bear witness, Mike who'd changed from con artist to protector, Tyler who needed logical answers to impossible questions—I realized we might be the only ones who could.

Grandpa had spent forty years wondering about the Golden Pickles. Trying to understand the mystery. Maybe this is what he'd been searching for all along. Not just the mystery of the pickles themselves, but the truth about the injustice that created them.

And maybe now it was my turn to finish what he'd started.

To find Eliza.

To learn her story.

To prove her innocence.

To break the curse.

"Let's go find out who Eliza was," I said.

We walked out of the forest as the sun was setting, our phones showing 3:24 PM but the sky showing early evening. Time was wrong. Everything was wrong.

But we had a direction now. A purpose.

Find the witch.

Prove her innocence.

Break the curse.

Make it right.

Let me think about it, I thought to myself. Let me think about how we're going to do this.

But for the first time since we'd started this investigation, I felt like I wasn't just trying to solve a puzzle anymore.

I was trying to correct an injustice.

And that felt like something worth fighting for.

Something worth risking everything for.

Even if I didn't know yet just how much "everything" would end up meaning.

CHAPTER 5: THE WITCH'S CURSE

I didn't go back to my apartment.

Couldn't. The idea of being in a closed space, with walls and a ceiling and four corners that made sense, felt wrong after Hollow Fields. Like trying to fit a puzzle piece into the wrong spot—technically it might sit there, but you'd know it didn't belong.

So instead I went to the 24-hour diner on the edge of campus, the one that smelled like burnt coffee and had booths with cracked vinyl seats. The kind of place where nobody looked twice at college students who showed up at weird hours with haunted expressions.

My phone said 3:47 AM. My watch said 6:47 PM. I'd reset it three times, but it kept drifting back to evening. Like even the watch knew we'd lost those three hours and was trying to find them again.

Tyler's laptop sat on the table in front of me, still dead. I'd plugged it in, tried different outlets, even pulled the battery and reseated it. Nothing. Whatever had happened in that church, it had killed the thing completely. Drained it of something more than just electricity.

Mary Stanton's journal was next to it. I'd taken it. Probably shouldn't have—it belonged to her, belonged to Hollow Fields—but I couldn't leave it there. Evidence. Proof. Documentation that a woman had suffered in that place for 133 years.

And I'd just walked away.

"You planning to actually drink that, or just stare at it until it evaporates?"

Emily slid into the booth across from me. She looked how I felt—exhausted, wired, like sleep was a foreign concept that happened to other people. Her hair was pulled back in a messy ponytail, and she'd changed out of her forest clothes into jeans and a sweatshirt that said "FARMS FEED AMERICA" across the front. Comfort clothes.

"Didn't know you were coming," I said.

"You texted the group chat that you'd be here." She gestured to my phone. "Two hours ago."

I looked down. Apparently I had. Didn't remember doing it.

"The others?" I asked.

"Mike went home to his family for the weekend. Needs to not be anywhere near this for a bit." Emily flagged down the waitress, ordered coffee. "Tyler's with his mom, trying to explain why his laptop's dead and he looks like he saw a ghost. Olivia's in her darkroom, processing film."

"And you?"

"Couldn't sleep either." She waited until the waitress brought her coffee, took a sip, made a face. "Okay. So. We need to talk about what happened."

"We walked into a ghost town trapped outside of time, talked to a woman who'd been dead for a century, got chased by council members who'd been transformed into creatures by their own greed, and barely escaped." I tapped Mary's journal. "That about cover it?"

"That covers the what." Emily's voice had that edge it got when she was building to something. "I'm asking about the how. And more importantly, the why."

"Why what?"

"Why we're not calling this a win and walking away." She leaned forward. "Josh. We found the town. We documented it—Olivia's got photographs, Tyler got some footage before his equipment died. We found Mary's journal. We have proof that Hollow Fields exists, that the curse is real. Mission accomplished. We can write this up, publish it, let someone else figure out how to break the curse."

I looked at her. Really looked at her. Emily had always been practical, evidence-based, the one who kept the rest of us grounded. And she was right—objectively, we'd accomplished what we set out to do. We'd solved the mystery of the Golden Pickles.

But we hadn't solved the injustice.

"Mary's still there," I said quietly.

"I know."

"She's been there for 133 years. The farmer for 143. How many others? Decades of people, trapped, suffering, because five greedy men killed innocent people and blamed them for their own evil."

"I know," Emily repeated.

"Then you know we can't just walk away."

She sighed, that heavy sigh that meant she'd known I'd say that. "Josh. We barely made it out. We lost three hours somehow. Tyler's equipment is dead. We don't even know if half the footage will show anything real. Those creatures almost caught you. You. The one who always finds a way out. They nearly dragged you into that basement."

The memory of that cold hand on my ankle made me shudder. "But they didn't."

"This time. What about next time?"

"There won't be a next time. Not the same way." I pulled out the notebook I'd started filling at some point—didn't remember when, but the pages were covered in my handwriting. Diagrams. Timelines. Lists.

"Because now we know what we're dealing with. The farmer told us how to break the curse. We just have to figure out who Eliza is, prove she was innocent, clear her name."

Emily looked at the notebook, then at me. "You've been up all night working on this."

"Couldn't sleep."

"Josh." She said my name the way she did when she was worried and trying not to show it. "This isn't just curiosity anymore. This is becoming something else."

"Good." I met her eyes. "It should be something else. Five men murdered innocent people to consolidate power. Created a curse that's been causing suffering for over 150 years. Trapped an entire town in a loop of pain and death. That's not just interesting—that's wrong. Someone has to make it right."

"And that someone has to be you?"

"Who else?" I gestured at the empty diner. "Who else knows the full story? Who else has been there? Who else would care enough to do something about it?"

The silence that followed was heavy.

Finally, Emily said, "Okay."

"Okay?"

"Okay, we figure out who Eliza is. We research her story. We find proof she was innocent." She pointed at me with her coffee cup. "But we do it smart. Methodical. Research first, then action. No running back to Hollow Fields until we actually know what we're doing. Deal?"

Relief flooded through me. "Deal."

"And you get at least four hours of sleep before we start."

"Emily—"

"Four hours, Joshua. Or I walk."

I knew that tone. She wasn't bluffing.

"Fine. Four hours." I checked my phone—the one that said 4:15 AM. "Where do we even start researching a witch who was probably killed 150 years ago?"

"University library opens at eight." Emily drained her coffee. "Historical archives. Local records. Witch trial documentation if it exists. Someone had to record these things."

"And if the records were destroyed? Or never existed?"

She smiled faintly. "Then we get creative. But one step at a time. Let me think about it."

I almost laughed. She'd picked up my phrase.

"Come on." She stood, dropped money on the table for both our coffees. "I'm driving you home. You're sleeping. Then we're going to solve this thing the right way."

"The right way?"

"With research. Evidence. Proof." She picked up Mary's journal, handled it carefully. "We're going to tell Eliza's story. And we're going to make sure people know the truth."

Four hours of sleep turned into six because Emily literally stood outside my apartment until I texted her a photo of me in bed with the lights off. Then she set an alarm on my phone that I couldn't turn off without her password.

I dreamed about Hollow Fields. About Mary Stanton standing in that fog, her hollow eyes pleading. About the farmer in the church, fading away while trying to warn us. About Eliza's statue in the town square, the inscription blaming her for everything.

About cold hands grabbing my ankle.

When the alarm went off at 10:15 AM, I woke up with my heart racing and my sheets soaked with sweat. But at least I'd slept.

The others were already at the library when I arrived—even Mike, who'd apparently cut his family visit short. Tyler had his dead laptop on the table like a deceased pet, was taking it apart with a precision screwdriver set.

"Anything?" I asked.

"Everything's fried." Tyler pointed at internal components I didn't recognize. "Not just the battery. The logic board, the hard drive, even the LED indicators. It's like something sucked all the energy out at once. Electromagnetic pulse, maybe? But localized. Targeted."

"The creatures," Olivia said softly. She had her camera equipment spread out, was reviewing footage on her laptop. "They gave off that golden glow. Same color as the pickles. Maybe they can drain electronics somehow."

"Or time itself did it." Emily had three books open in front of her, was cross-referencing something. "If the town exists outside normal time, maybe modern technology can't handle the paradox. Like trying to run a computer program in the wrong operating system."

Mike just had coffee and looked tired. "Can we please talk about something else? Anything else? My brain can't handle temporal mechanics before noon."

"We're researching Eliza Nightshade," I said, sitting down. "The witch. The one the farmer said is the key to breaking the curse."

"Right. The dead witch we know nothing about except that she got burned and blamed for everything." Mike sipped his coffee. "How exactly do we research someone who probably doesn't exist in any official records?"

"She exists." Emily pushed one of the books toward me. "Or at least, someone exists. Look."

The book was old, leather-bound, titled "Witch Trials and Accusations in Rural America: 1820-1900." Emily had bookmarked a page near the middle.

I read aloud: "1849, Hollow Fields Township. Eliza Nightshade, aged 37, accused of witchcraft and consorting with dark forces. Executed by burning after a trial conducted by the town council. Evidence presented included testimony from five council members who claimed she had cursed the land, causing crop failures and sickness."

"Five council members," Tyler said quietly. "The same ones the farmer mentioned."

"Joseph Simmons, Thomas Bell, Richard Hayes, Edward Clarke, and Charles Morley," I confirmed, pulling out my notebook where I'd written them down. "They accused her, they tried her, they killed her. Then they became the creatures that hunt the trapped residents."

Emily flipped to another bookmarked page. "But here's what's interesting. Look at the dates. Eliza was executed in 1849. The cholera plague that Mary Stanton mentioned? That didn't hit until 1892. Forty-three years later."

I felt something click in my mind. "The farmer said he'd been trapped for 143 years. If he died in 1892—"

"Then Eliza died in 1849," Emily finished. "Which means her curse came first. The farmer's curse is layered on top of hers."

"So breaking Eliza's curse breaks everything," Olivia said, seeing where this was going. "She's the foundation."

"Which means we need to understand what actually happened in 1849." I looked at the book again. "What was she accused of? What were the crop failures and sickness?"

Emily pulled up another page. "According to this, Hollow Fields experienced a drought in 1848. Crops failed for two seasons. People were getting sick—not plague, just general illness from poor nutrition and stress. The council blamed Eliza, said she'd cursed the land because they'd denied her request to purchase certain herbs for her healing work."

"They killed her over herbs?" Mike's voice was sharp with disbelief.

"They killed her over control." I was reading ahead, seeing the pattern. "She was a healer. People came to her for medicine, for help. That meant she had influence, power that didn't come from the council. They couldn't control her, so they eliminated her and blamed her for problems they probably caused themselves."

"Slash and burn agriculture," Emily said, nodding. "If you read between the lines here, it sounds like the council pushed farmers to over-plant in 1847, trying to maximize yields. Which depleted the soil. Which led to crop failure in 1848. Basic agricultural mismanagement, but they couldn't admit that. Needed a scapegoat."

"So they burned a woman alive and blamed her for their incompetence," Olivia said, her voice tight. "And that created the curse."

"Not immediately." Tyler had been reading over Emily's shoulder. "Look at the timeline. Eliza died in 1849. But according to this, Hollow Fields didn't become 'cursed' until later. The actual disappearance of the town isn't documented until the 1850s. A few years of people avoiding the area, weird stories, until eventually the town just... stopped being on maps."

I thought about what the farmer had said. About dying with injustice creating something. About the magic mixing with his death and the council's greed.

"She cursed them as she died," I said slowly. "She cursed the council specifically. Not the whole town—just them. But then when they killed the farmer in 1892, his death layered another curse on top. And that's when everyone got trapped."

"Two curses," Emily said, eyes widening. "One targeting the council. One targeting everyone who'd eaten the pickles. Both born from unjust executions."

"Which means we need to break both." I felt the weight of it settling on me. "Prove Eliza was innocent. Prove the farmer was innocent. Clear both their names."

"How do we prove someone was innocent 175 years ago?" Mike asked. "It's not like we can interview witnesses or check security footage."

"No, but we can find evidence." I was already making lists in my head, prioritizing research paths. "Medical records showing the sickness wasn't supernatural. Agricultural records showing the crop failures were natural. Testimony from people who knew Eliza. Her own words, if she left any. We build a case."

"Like we're defense attorneys for a dead woman," Olivia murmured.

"Exactly." I looked around at them. "Who's in?"

Tyler raised his hand immediately. "I need to know why my laptop died. Plus, systematic research? That's what I do."

Olivia nodded. "I've got all the footage from Hollow Fields. Whatever we find here, I can add visual documentation. Build a complete picture."

Mike sighed. "You know I'm in. Someone needs to make sure you all don't get burned as witches yourselves."

Emily just looked at me. "I'm in. But Joshua? We need to be careful. This obsession you've got—making it right, fixing the injustice—it's good. But don't let it consume you. We saw what happened to Eliza when she tried to fight the council. We saw what happened to the farmer."

"I know." But did I? Because sitting there, looking at the evidence of a woman who'd been murdered for trying to help people, I felt something burning in my chest. Anger. Determination. A need to correct this wrong that felt almost physical.

Someone had to make it right.

And if that someone had to be me, then I'd find a way.

We worked in the library until it closed at midnight, then continued in my apartment. Emily had created a timeline on my wall, using string and index cards to map out every event from Eliza's birth (approximately 1812, based on her age at death) to the present.

Tyler had recovered what data he could from his laptop's hard drive, had it running on a backup computer. The footage from Hollow Fields was corrupted in weird ways—some of it played fine, some showed static, some showed things that hadn't been there when we'd filmed. But enough was intact to prove the town existed.

Olivia had printed photos, had them spread across every available surface. The town square. The church. Mary Stanton's house. And Mary herself—or rather, the empty space where Mary had stood, because just like she'd said, the camera had captured nothing.

Mike was on his laptop, tracking down historical records from nearby towns, looking for anyone who'd mentioned Hollow Fields or Eliza Nightshade in letters or diaries.

And I was reading everything.

Every document Emily found, every book Tyler pulled from digital archives, every newspaper article Mike located. I was looking for one thing: evidence that Eliza Nightshade was innocent.

Around 2 AM, I found it.

"Here." My voice cracked from not using it for an hour. "Listen to this."

The others looked up.

I read from a scanned document Tyler had found in a county historical society database: "Letter from Margaret Hayes to her sister, dated June

1849. 'The trial of Miss Nightshade was a shameful affair. My husband Richard came home that night and wept, said he'd lied to save his position on the council. Said Eliza had done nothing wrong, had only tried to help when the council's foolish planting schemes failed. He said the other council members threatened him, said if he didn't testify against her, they'd accuse his own family. I've never seen him so distraught. He said some sins can never be washed clean.'"

Silence.

"Margaret Hayes," Emily said slowly. "Wife of Richard Hayes. One of the council members."

"And he confessed," Olivia breathed. "Admitted they lied. Admitted Eliza was innocent."

"After they'd already killed her." I felt sick. "He knew she was innocent, testified anyway, then went home and cried about it."

"Did he try to clear her name later?" Tyler asked. "Make it right?"

I scrolled through the rest of the document. "He died in 1851. Two years later. The letter mentions he was 'never the same after the trial, his health failing, his spirit broken.'"

"Guilt," Emily said quietly. "The curse started with the council, but at least one of them had a conscience. For whatever that's worth."

"It's worth evidence." I highlighted the passage, added it to our growing case file. "This proves at least one council member knew Eliza was innocent. Which means the execution was murder, not justice. We have proof."

"One letter proves one council member had regrets," Mike pointed out. "Doesn't prove Eliza was innocent to everyone else."

He was right. We needed more.

We worked through the night, pushing past exhaustion into that weird state where everything feels slightly unreal but your brain is still somehow functioning. By dawn, we had:

- Margaret Hayes's letter (proof of false testimony)
- Agricultural records from 1847-1848 (proving over-planting by council directive)
- Medical records from a traveling doctor who'd passed through in 1848 (showing the illnesses were malnutrition-related, not supernatural)
- Three witness statements from people who'd known Eliza, describing her as a skilled healer
- Documentation of the council purchasing land at below-market prices during the crisis (profiting from disaster)

It was a case. A real case. Proof that Eliza Nightshade had been innocent, that the council had lied, that she'd been murdered to cover up their own incompetence and greed.

"This is it," I said, looking at Emily's timeline on the wall, now filled with evidence. "This is what we need to break her curse."

"But how do we actually break it?" Olivia asked. "Do we go back to Hollow Fields? Perform some kind of ritual? What?"

That's when my apartment door opened without anyone knocking.

We all froze.

A woman stepped in, maybe in her forties, athletic build, sharp eyes that scanned the room with the kind of attention that said she missed nothing. She was carrying a worn leather satchel and had an air of authority that made me think "professor" before she even spoke.

"I'm sorry to intrude," she said, her voice calm but firm. "But I couldn't help overhearing what you're working on." She gestured to my open window, which apparently had let more sound out than I'd thought. "You're researching Eliza Nightshade?"

"Who are you?" Mike was on his feet, positioned between her and the rest of us.

"Elizabeth." She set the satchel down carefully. "Dr. Elizabeth Holloway, folklore and mythology professor. And before you ask how I found you, graduate student gossip is remarkably efficient when a group of undergrads are researching a topic that's consumed my family for generations."

My heart started pounding. "Your family?"

She smiled, but it was sad. "My family has been trying to break the curse of Hollow Fields for over a century. We've gotten close several times. But something always stops us."

She pulled out a worn journal from her satchel—older than Mary's, the leather dark with age.

"This belonged to Sarah Nightshade. Eliza's younger sister." Elizabeth set it on the table. "I'm her descendant. Which makes me, in a strange way, the last living relative of the witch of Hollow Fields."

We all stared at her.

"You're Eliza's—" Emily started.

"Great-great-great-great-granddaughter, more or less. The exact genealogy gets complicated." Elizabeth sat down uninvited, looked at each of us in turn. "I know what you're trying to do. I know because my family has tried the same thing for 175 years. And I need to tell you something before you go any further."

"What?" I asked.

Her expression was grave. "The curse doesn't just trap the people of Hollow Fields. It traps anyone who tries to break it. My family has lost three people over the generations to that town. They went in with good intentions, with proof of Eliza's innocence, determined to make it right. And they never came out."

The room felt colder.

"But we have evidence," I said. "We have proof she was innocent."

"So did they." Elizabeth pulled out another journal. And another. And another. Five journals total, from different eras. "My great-grandmother in 1912. My grandfather in 1948. My mother in 1983. And my aunt in 2007. All of them found evidence. All of them went to Hollow Fields. All of them disappeared."

"Then how are you here?" Tyler asked quietly.

"Because I never went." She looked down at the journals. "I was supposed to go with my aunt in 2007. I was seventeen. But I got sick the day before—just a cold, but enough that she went alone. Said she'd be back by evening. She wasn't." Elizabeth's hands tightened on the journals. "They found her car at the forest edge. Not a trace of her beyond that."

"I'm sorry," Olivia said softly.

"Don't be sorry. Be smart." Elizabeth looked at me. "I've spent eighteen years studying this curse, trying to find a way to break it that doesn't require going back to that town. And I've learned something important. Something my family never understood."

"What?" I leaned forward.

"Proving Eliza's innocence isn't enough." Elizabeth opened Sarah Nightshade's journal. "Because the curse wasn't cast by Eliza herself. According to Sarah, Eliza tried to prevent the curse. She saw what the council's greed was doing to the land, tried to warn them, tried to heal it. They killed her for it. And her death—the injustice of it, the tragedy—created the curse. Not as her revenge. As the land's response to what was done to her."

"The land itself cursed the council," Emily breathed.

"And then the farmer's death layered on top, trapping everyone." Elizabeth nodded. "Which means to break the curse, you don't just need to prove Eliza was innocent. You need to make the land understand that the injustice has been corrected. That the wrong has been righted."

"How?" I asked.

Elizabeth looked at me for a long moment, and something in her eyes made me cold.

"I don't know," she said quietly. "That's what my family never figured out. That's why they all disappeared trying."

She stood, gathering the journals. "I came here to warn you. To tell you that good intentions aren't enough. Evidence isn't enough. Even proof of innocence isn't enough. The curse requires something more. Something none of us have been willing to pay."

She left the journals on the table, headed for the door.

"Wait," I called after her. "You're just going to warn us and leave? You're not going to help?"

She turned back, and her expression was haunted. "I've already lost too much to that place. I won't lose myself too." She paused at the door. "But I'll tell you what I know. What all the journals say. The curse can be broken by someone who understands the injustice and is willing to correct it. But correction requires sacrifice. Something given freely that balances what was taken unjustly."

"What does that mean?" Emily asked.

"I wish I knew." Elizabeth opened the door. "My office hours are Tuesdays and Thursdays, 2-4 PM. If you're determined to pursue this—and I can see that you are—come see me. I'll share everything my family learned. But please, please be careful. Hollow Fields has consumed everyone who's tried to save it."

Then she was gone, leaving us with five journals and more questions than we'd started with.

We sat in silence for a long moment.

Finally, Mike spoke. "So. That was ominous."

"She lost her mother and aunt to that place," Olivia said quietly. "And she's still researching it. Still trying to understand. That's not just academic curiosity."

"That's obsession," Tyler finished. "Just like—"

He stopped, but we all knew what he'd been about to say.

Just like Josh.

Emily was looking at me, concern clear on her face. "Josh. Did you hear what she said? Everyone who's tried to break this curse has disappeared. Including people with way more knowledge and preparation than we have."

"I heard her." I looked at the journals on the table, at the evidence spread across my walls, at Mary Stanton's journal with its desperate, unfinished entries. "But I also heard what the farmer said. And what Mary said. They're trapped. They're suffering. And we're the first people in probably decades who know the full story and have the chance to do something about it."

"At what cost?" Emily's voice was sharp. "Josh, you can't save everyone. Especially not if it means getting yourself trapped in there forever."

"We don't know that would happen—"

"We know four members of Elizabeth's family disappeared trying. Four. That's not a coincidence. That's a pattern."

"Then we'll be smarter. More careful. We'll—"

"You'll what? You'll succeed where generations of Eliza's own bloodline failed? Because you're that special? That chosen?" Emily stood, anger and fear mixing in her voice. "This is exactly what I was worried about. You're so focused on making it right that you're not thinking about the cost. About what happens if you fail. About what happens if you succeed but it requires —"

She stopped. Couldn't say it. But I heard it anyway.

—requires your life.

"We don't know what it requires," I said quietly. "Not yet. But Elizabeth said she'd help us figure it out. We have her family's journals now. We have more information than anyone's had before. We can—"

"Josh." Emily's voice cracked. "Please. Just... please think about this. Really think about it. Because I can't—" She grabbed her jacket. "I need some air."

She left, the door closing harder than necessary behind her.

The others looked at me.

"She's right," Olivia said gently. "You're getting obsessed, Josh. And I get why—what happened to Eliza and the farmer and Mary is horrible, is wrong—but Emily's right. You can't save them if you get trapped yourself."

"I'm not planning to get trapped."

"Neither did Elizabeth's family." Tyler was quiet, but his words hit hard. "They all went in thinking they'd figured it out. Thinking they had the answer. And they all disappeared."

Mike just looked at me. "You're not going to stop, are you?"

"No." I met his eyes. "Would you? If you knew people were suffering, if you had the chance to help them, would you just walk away?"

"Yeah, man. I would." Mike's honesty was brutal. "Because staying alive and keeping my friends alive is more important than saving ghosts from 175 years ago. That's going to sound harsh, but it's true."

"They're not just ghosts." I picked up Mary's journal. "She's a person. A real person who wrote about being scared, about being trapped, about watching her friends change into monsters. She's not ancient history—she's suffering right now. Today. While we sit here debating whether she's worth saving."

The silence that followed was heavy.

Finally, Olivia spoke. "What if we compromise? We take Elizabeth's offer. We study her family's journals. We learn everything they learned, figure out where they went wrong, make a better plan. But we don't rush back to Hollow Fields. We do this smart, methodical, with every advantage we can get. Deal?"

I wanted to argue. Wanted to say that every day we waited was another day Mary spent trapped, another day the farmer suffered. But looking at their faces—at Tyler's worry, Mike's frustration, Olivia's concern—I realized I was pushing too hard. Scaring them.

"Deal," I said. "We research. We learn. We plan. And we don't go back until we actually know what we're doing."

"Good." Olivia stood, started gathering her photos. "Because I'm exhausted, and I'm pretty sure we all need actual sleep before we can think straight."

Tyler and Mike agreed, started packing up.

As they filed out, each of them looked back at me. Like they were worried about what I'd do once they left.

I wanted to be offended. But honestly? I was worried about what I'd do too.

Because even as I'd agreed to wait, to research, to be careful—I'd felt that burning in my chest. That need to make it right. To correct the injustice.

And I was starting to realize that need wasn't just determination.

It was becoming something else.

Something that might not listen to reason or caution or warnings about people who'd disappeared trying the same thing.

Something that whispered in the back of my mind: Someone has to sacrifice something to balance what was taken unjustly.

And I was starting to think that someone might be me.

CHAPTER 6: THE PATTERN OF FAILURES

Elizabeth's office was exactly what you'd expect from a folklore professor who'd spent eighteen years obsessing over one curse: organized chaos with a system only she understood.

Books lined every wall, stacked three deep in places. Old photographs pinned to corkboards showed the same location across different decades—the forest edge where her family members' cars had been found. A large map of the region dominated one wall, marked with colored pins and string connecting various points. And on her desk, arranged in chronological order, sat five leather journals.

"My great-grandmother, 1912." Elizabeth touched the oldest journal. "My grandfather, 1948. My mother, 1983. My aunt, 2007. And..." She pulled out a fifth journal I hadn't seen at my apartment. "Me. 1995, 2003, and 2015."

"Wait," Emily said. "You said you never went to Hollow Fields."

"I didn't. But I tried. Three times." Elizabeth opened the most recent journal, and I recognized her handwriting—but it was dated ten years ago. "I don't remember writing this."

The office felt colder suddenly.

"You don't remember," Tyler repeated slowly, "writing your own journal. From ten years ago."

"No." Elizabeth's voice was steady, but I could see her hands shaking slightly. "I found it last year while organizing my research. Read it cover to cover. It describes my planned expedition to Hollow Fields, my theory about how to break the curse, my determination to succeed where my aunt had failed." She looked up at us. "I have no memory of any of it."

Olivia leaned forward. "Is that possible? Memory loss that complete?"

"Not from any medical condition I know of." Elizabeth pulled out another journal—this one had different handwriting. "This is also mine. From 2003. Same thing. Detailed plans, careful research, absolute confidence." She set both journals on the desk. "And then I found photos. Me, at the forest edge. Me, with equipment. Me, about to enter the woods. I don't remember any of it."

"The pickles," I said quietly, pieces clicking together. "You tasted them."

Elizabeth nodded. "Three times. That I can prove. There might be more attempts I haven't found evidence of yet."

"But the pickles only affect people who go to Hollow Fields," Mike said. "How did you taste them if you never—" He stopped. "Oh."

"I went," Elizabeth said. "Multiple times. Entered the forest. Maybe even made it to the town. But something happened each time that made me taste the pickles, and then..." She snapped her fingers. "Everything gone. Reset. Start the research over from scratch, not knowing I'd already tried."

Emily pulled out her notebook—she'd been documenting everything since we'd gotten back. "So the curse doesn't just trap people who eat the pickles in Hollow Fields. It has a secondary effect: mind-wipe for anyone who tries to break it."

"Specifically for Eliza's descendants." Elizabeth opened her great-grandmother's journal. "Sarah Nightshade—Eliza's sister—wrote about this. She suspected the curse was designed to prevent Eliza's bloodline from ever undoing it. A failsafe. The council knew Eliza had family, knew they might try to clear her name. So the curse targets us specifically."

"That's..." Olivia searched for words. "That's incredibly cruel."

"It's incredibly effective," Elizabeth corrected. "My family has been trying for 113 years. We've gotten close—proof of innocence, understanding of the curse mechanics, even entering Hollow Fields itself. But we can never finish because the moment we do, the memory erases. We start over. Forever."

I picked up the 1912 journal carefully. "Can we read these?"

"That's why I brought you here." Elizabeth gestured to her journals. "You're not descended from Eliza. The curse shouldn't affect you the same way. If anyone can actually break it, it's someone outside the bloodline who still cares enough to try."

"So, no pressure," Mike muttered.

We spread out across Elizabeth's office. She'd brought extra chairs from the classroom next door, and we settled in for what I suspected would be hours of reading.

The journals were heartbreaking.

Elizabeth's great-grandmother, 1912:
"I have found proof that Great-Aunt Eliza was innocent. The council's own records, hidden in the town archives, show they knew the crop failures were due to over-planting. They executed her to maintain power. I will go to Hollow Fields and clear her name. Justice will finally be served."

The entries continued for several weeks—careful documentation, plans, supplies gathered. Then, abruptly, a final entry:

> "Tomorrow I enter the forest. I have everything I need. The truth will set Eliza free. The truth will set us all—"

It ended mid-sentence. The remaining pages were blank.

Tyler looked up from his journal—Elizabeth's grandfather's from 1948. "Same pattern here. Months of research, careful preparation, absolute confidence. Then the final entry: 'Tonight I camp at the forest edge. Tomorrow morning, I enter.' And then nothing."

"Mine too," Olivia said, reading from 1983. "Elizabeth's mother was so methodical. She mapped everything, interviewed locals, even hired a private investigator to document the area. But her last entry says, 'The pickles appeared at the market today, as predicted by the cycle I discovered. This is my sign. I go tomorrow.' Then blank pages."

Emily had Elizabeth's aunt's journal from 2007. She was reading slowly, carefully, and her expression was troubled. "Josh, look at this."

I moved to read over her shoulder.

The aunt—her name was Margaret—had written extensively about the curse mechanics. She'd figured out things we were only just discovering: the two-curse layer (Eliza's and the farmer's), the distinction between trapped innocents and transformed council members, even the time distortion.

But it was her final entries that made my blood run cold.

> "I've studied every attempt by my family. My grandmother, my father, my sister Elizabeth. All failed. All disappeared. But I see the pattern they missed.
>
> The curse requires balance. An injustice created it—Eliza's unjust execution. To break it, the injustice must be corrected. But correction in this case doesn't mean proving innocence. The council will never accept that truth. Correction means replacement.

Someone innocent must willingly take Eliza's place. Someone must choose, freely and with full knowledge, to sacrifice themselves to balance what was taken unjustly.

I think that someone has to be me."

The next page showed a date—June 15, 2007—and a single line:

> "Tomorrow I go to Hollow Fields. If this works, my family will finally be free. If I'm wrong, at least I tried."

Nothing after that.

"She knew," I said quietly. "Your aunt figured it out."

Elizabeth's face was pale. "Figured what out?"

I showed her the entry.

Elizabeth read it, then sat down heavily in her chair. "Sacrifice. She thought breaking the curse required sacrifice."

"And she went anyway," Emily said softly. "Knowing that."

"But she disappeared like the others," Tyler pointed out. "So either she was wrong about the sacrifice, or something else went wrong."

I kept reading Margaret's journal, flipping back through earlier entries. She'd been thorough, systematic. And I found something that made me pause.

"The pickles appear quarterly at the market. Spring, summer, fall, winter. The curse is cyclical. I believe attempts to break it can only succeed during specific windows—possibly only during the season when Eliza was executed. She died in spring 1849. Perhaps the curse can only be broken in spring as well."

"What month is it?" I asked.

"October," Emily said. "Why?"

"Margaret went in June. Summer." I showed them the entry. "She theorized the curse could only be broken in spring. If she was right—"

"Then she would've failed regardless of her willingness to sacrifice," Tyler finished. "Wrong season. Wrong window."

"Which means we have to wait until spring to try," Mike said. "That's six months. We could prepare, really prepare, figure out—"

"No." I was still reading, and I'd found something else. Something that changed everything. "Look. Margaret's research into the quarterly cycle. She tracked disappearances. They align with the pickle appearances."

I spread out her notes—she'd mapped every disappearance in the area for the past century, correlated them with the farmers' market schedule. The pattern was clear: people disappeared in April, July, October, and January. Always within a week of the market.

"October," Olivia breathed. "The market's next week. The cycle is coming around again."

Emily looked at me, and I could see her putting it together. "Josh. If the curse is cyclical, and it's strongest during market week, and we need to attempt to break it during the right season..."

"We have one week," I said. "The October market is in one week. That's our window."

"That's insane," Mike said. "One week to prepare for something that's killed four generations of Elizabeth's family? We need more time. We need better equipment. We need—"

"We need to go next week, or we wait until January." I looked at the journals, at the pattern of failures. "And January isn't spring. Margaret was right—Eliza died in spring. That's when the curse is weakest, when breaking it is possible. But we can't wait until April. People are suffering in Hollow Fields right now. Mary, the farmer, all the trapped residents. Every day we wait is another day they're imprisoned."

"Josh," Emily's voice had that warning tone. "We're not ready. We barely survived last time, and that was just reconnaissance. Actually trying to break the curse?"

"Is why we're here." I stood, feeling that burning in my chest again—that need to make it right. "We have proof of Eliza's innocence. We have Elizabeth's family's research. We know more than anyone's ever known before. We can do this."

"Can you?" Elizabeth's voice cut through my determination. "Or are you just the next person to disappear trying?"

I looked at her—at the haunted expression, at the journals documenting generations of failure.

"I don't know," I admitted. "But I have to try."

"Why?" She leaned forward. "And don't say 'because it's the right thing to do.' Four members of my family said the same thing. They're all gone. So I'm asking you: why are you willing to risk your life for people who've been dead for over a century?"

The office was silent.

"Because they're not dead," I said finally. "Mary Stanton isn't dead. She's trapped. The farmer isn't dead—he's suffering. And they've been suffering for over a hundred years because five greedy men murdered innocent people and blamed them for their own corruption. That's not history. That's ongoing injustice. And if I can stop it, if there's any chance I can make it right, then I have to try."

"Even if it kills you?"

The question hung in the air.

I didn't answer. Couldn't. Because I was starting to suspect that making it right might require exactly that.

Emily must have seen something in my expression because she stood abruptly. "No. Joshua, no. You're not doing this."

"I'm not—"

"You're thinking about it. About Margaret's theory. About sacrifice." She moved between me and the journals. "I can see it in your face. You're already considering it."

"We don't know if that's required—"

"But you suspect it is. And you're already okay with that possibility." Her voice cracked. "You've known me since we were five years old. I can tell when you're lying to yourself. And right now, you're lying when you say you're not already planning to be the one who stays behind."

The others were watching us. Tyler looked worried. Mike looked angry. Olivia had her camera down, for once not documenting.

"I'm not planning anything," I said quietly. "I'm just... thinking through possibilities. That's what I do. Problem-solving."

"This isn't a problem to solve," Emily shot back. "This is your life. Your actual life. And you're treating it like another puzzle, another challenge, another thing to fix."

"Because it is a thing to fix. People are suffering—"

"People who are already dead!"

"They're not—"

"Yes, they are!" Emily's voice rose. "Mary Stanton died in 1892. The farmer died in 1892. They're ghosts, Josh. Spirits. Echoes of people who lived and died a century ago. They're tragic, yes. Their suffering is real, yes. But they're not more important than you. Than us. Than the people who are alive right now and care about you."

"So I should just abandon them? Let them suffer forever because saving them is inconvenient?"

"It's not inconvenient—it's impossible!" She grabbed the journals, held them up. "Four people, Josh. Four people who were smarter than us, better prepared than us, who had a lifetime to plan, and they all failed. All of them. What makes you think you're special enough to succeed where they failed?"

"I don't think I'm special." But even as I said it, I wondered if that was true. Because somewhere deep down, I did think I could do this. Had to do this. "I just think... someone has to try. Someone has to care enough to risk it. And right now, that someone is me."

Emily stared at me for a long moment, then turned to Elizabeth. "Tell him. Tell him what happens to people who care too much about this curse."

Elizabeth looked between us, then down at the journals. "They disappear. Every single one. The ones who care the most, who feel the injustice deepest, who can't let it go—those are the ones the curse takes."

"See?" Emily turned back to me. "The curse targets people like you. People who can't walk away. People who think they have to fix everything, save everyone, make every wrong right. That's not heroic, Josh. That's how you get killed."

"Then what am I supposed to do?" I asked. "We've seen Hollow Fields. We've met Mary, talked to the farmer. We know they're suffering. How do I just... go back to normal life knowing that?"

"I don't know." Emily's voice softened. "But I know dying for them isn't the answer. Because if you die, if we lose you, Mary and the farmer are still trapped, and we've lost the one person who actually gave a damn. How does that help anyone?"

She had a point. Intellectually, I knew she had a point.

But emotionally, viscerally, I couldn't let it go.

"We have a week," I said, trying to steer to safer ground. "Let's use that week to prepare. To learn everything we can from Elizabeth's family. To make a plan that doesn't end with anyone dying. Can we agree on that?"

Emily looked like she wanted to argue more, but finally nodded. "One week. Research and planning only. No rushing into Hollow Fields. No hero complex. Just preparation."

"Deal."

But as she turned away, I caught Elizabeth watching me. She knew. She knew I was already thinking past the planning stage, already considering what Margaret had written.

Someone innocent must willingly take Eliza's place.

We worked through the night again, but this time in Elizabeth's office where she had resources we couldn't access elsewhere. She'd built a database over eighteen years—every scrap of information about Hollow Fields, Eliza Nightshade, the council, and her family's attempts to break the curse.

Tyler was in heaven, cross-referencing data, building timelines, creating maps. "Okay, so look at this. Every disappearance—family and non-family—happens within a quarter mile of this point." He marked a spot on the map. "It's not the town center. It's not the church. It's... somewhere in the forest between the market and the town itself."

"The threshold," Elizabeth said. "That's what my mother called it. The point where you cross from the normal world into Hollow Fields proper. Time distorts there. Electronics fail. The curse is strongest."

"So if we're going to break the curse, we need to get past the threshold," Olivia said. She had Elizabeth's photographs spread out, was comparing images from different decades. "Look—same trees, same configuration, but the light is different in each photo. Like time of day shifts when you're at that spot."

Emily was still working on the timeline, but now she was tracking something else: the pattern of Elizabeth's mind-wipes. "You said you found evidence of three attempts. 1995, 2003, 2015. That's eight years, then twelve years. The gap is increasing."

"The curse is learning," Elizabeth said quietly. "First time I tried, I forgot immediately. Second time, I stayed interested in the topic for a few years before the compulsion faded. Third time, I've been researching for ten years straight. The curse is getting better at keeping me invested without letting me actually break it."

"That's..." Tyler stopped. "That's actually terrifying. It's adaptive. It's not just a static spell—it's evolving."

"Which means our approach needs to account for that," I said, making notes. "We can't just follow Elizabeth's family's methods. The curse has adapted to those. We need something new."

Mike, who'd been quiet for a while, spoke up. "What if we're overthinking this? Margaret's journal said the curse requires willing sacrifice. Balance for injustice. What if the answer is simpler than we think? What if someone just needs to... volunteer? To say 'I'll take her place' and mean it?"

"And die," Emily added sharply. "Let's not gloss over that part. You're talking about someone volunteering to die."

"I'm talking about what the curse might require," Mike said. "I'm not saying we should do it. I'm saying we need to understand the terms."

"The terms," I said slowly, "might not be literal death."

Everyone looked at me.

"Think about it. Eliza was executed unjustly. Burned alive as a scapegoat for the council's crimes. The injustice wasn't just that she died—it was that she died being blamed for things she didn't do. Her name was destroyed. Her reputation. Her legacy. She died with everyone believing she was a witch who cursed the land."

"So correcting the injustice means clearing her name," Tyler said, catching on. "Which we have evidence to do."

"But her family has tried that for generations," Olivia pointed out. "They had evidence too. It didn't work."

"Because they couldn't complete the ritual," I said. "They'd get to Hollow Fields, start the process, but then the mind-wipe would trigger. They'd taste the pickles and forget. They never finished."

"So we need someone who can complete the ritual without tasting the pickles," Emily said. "How?"

I pulled up Margaret's research again. "She tracked the pickle appearances. They manifest at the market, but they also appear in Hollow Fields itself. Specifically, they appear to people who are close to breaking the curse. It's how the curse protects itself—offers the pickles, person tastes them, memory wipes, attempt fails."

"So the curse uses the pickles as a defensive mechanism," Tyler said. "Anyone gets too close to breaking it, the pickles appear and stop them."

"Which means we need to know how to recognize that moment," I said. "The moment when the pickles would appear. And we need to be ready to resist."

"How do you resist magical pickles that appear specifically to tempt you?" Mike asked. "That's like saying 'just don't be cursed.' It's not that simple."

He was right. And I didn't have an answer.

We worked until dawn, until Elizabeth gently suggested we get some sleep because we weren't processing information anymore, just staring at pages.

As we gathered our things to leave, Elizabeth pulled me aside.

"I saw your face when you read Margaret's journal," she said quietly. "When she wrote about willing sacrifice."

"I'm not—"

"Don't lie to me. I've lost too many people to this curse to accept comforting lies." She looked tired, older than her years. "I saw the same expression on my aunt's face the night before she went to Hollow Fields. The same determination. The same acceptance."

"I haven't accepted anything," I said.

"Maybe not consciously. But part of you is already considering it. Already running through scenarios where you're the one who stays behind." She put a hand on my arm. "I need you to understand something. My aunt thought her sacrifice would free my family. She was wrong. She disappeared, and we're still trapped. Still researching. Still trying. Her death —if she is dead—changed nothing."

"Then maybe she didn't do it right," I said. "Maybe—"

"Maybe you're not listening." Elizabeth's voice was sharp now. "I'm telling you that voluntary sacrifice didn't work. My aunt tried it. She's gone. The curse remains. So whatever you're planning, whatever you're thinking, remember that. Remember that dying for this curse doesn't break it. It just adds another name to the list of people it's consumed."

"I hear you," I said.

"But you don't believe me." She let go of my arm. "Just... be careful. Please. Your friends need you alive. And frankly, if you die trying to break this curse, I'll have to live with one more person's death on my conscience. I already have four. I don't want a fifth."

I nodded, not trusting myself to speak.

As I walked out to meet the others, I felt the weight of Elizabeth's journals in my backpack. I'd borrowed them with permission, promising to return them safely.

But I'd also slipped Margaret's journal into my bag when no one was looking.

I needed to read it again. Alone. Without Emily watching my reactions, without Tyler analyzing my logic, without Mike questioning my sanity.

Because Margaret had figured something out. Something that had made her willing to go to Hollow Fields alone, knowing she might not come back.

And I needed to know what that something was.

Even if—especially if—it confirmed what I was starting to suspect.

That breaking the curse might require exactly what Emily feared most.

CHAPTER 7: THE WEEK OF PREPARATION

MONDAY

I didn't sleep Sunday night.

Told myself I would. Emily had made me promise—four hours minimum, she'd said, or she'd physically drag me to bed. But after she left, after everyone left, I sat at my desk with Margaret's journal open and couldn't stop reading.

"The curse requires balance. An injustice created it—Eliza's unjust execution. To break it, the injustice must be corrected. But correction doesn't mean proving innocence. Correction means replacement."

I'd read that line fifty times. Maybe a hundred. Each time, it settled deeper into my chest, heavy and cold and undeniable.

Someone innocent must willingly take Eliza's place.

My phone buzzed. Emily: Did you sleep?

Me: Yes (lie)

Emily: Liar. Get coffee. Library at 10. We're making a plan.

I looked at the journal, at Margaret's handwriting getting shakier toward the end of her entries, and closed it carefully. Slipped it into my backpack under my textbooks where no one would see.

Someone had to take Eliza's place.

I just hadn't told anyone yet that I suspected who.

The library study room felt smaller with all six of us crammed in. Elizabeth had brought her laptop, Tyler had his backup computer (still mourning his dead one), and Emily had created what she called "The Plan Board"—a huge piece of poster board with the next seven days mapped out in her careful handwriting.

"We have six days," Emily said, tapping Monday on her timeline. "The market is Sunday. According to Elizabeth's research, the October market is when the curse is most active. That's our window."

"To do what, exactly?" Mike asked. He'd gotten maybe three hours of sleep based on the bags under his eyes. "We going back to Hollow Fields? Because last time nearly killed us, and we didn't even make it to the center of town."

"We have to go back," I said quietly. Everyone looked at me. "We have proof of Eliza's innocence now. We know what the council did. We can break the curse, but we have to do it at the source."

"The church," Olivia said, flipping through her photos. "That's where the farmer was. That's where everything seems to center."

Elizabeth pulled up a satellite image on her laptop—or tried to. The area where Hollow Fields should be was just pixelated blur, like the satellites couldn't process it. "My family tried to map it for generations. Technology fails there. GPS, cameras, phones—everything goes dead past the threshold."

"The threshold," Tyler repeated. "That's the point where time started acting weird, right? Where my laptop died?"

"Where everything dies," Elizabeth corrected. "Electronics, battery power, even mechanical watches. The closer you get to the town center, the worse it gets. By the time you reach the church, you're operating completely blind."

"So we need backups for the backups," Tyler said, already making notes. "Analog equipment. Old-school cameras. Mechanical watches. Paper maps."

"And we need to mark our trail better," Mike added. "Last time, all our markers disappeared. Both colors. We need something the town can't erase."

Emily wrote EQUIPMENT GATHERING on her board under Monday and Tuesday. "Tyler, you're in charge of tech. Mike, you handle trail marking—whatever you think will actually work. Olivia, you make sure we have documentation methods that don't rely on batteries."

"What about me?" I asked.

Emily's eyes met mine, and I saw the worry there. "You research. You've got Elizabeth's family journals. You find out what they all missed—why they failed when they tried to break the curse."

"That's the critical question," Elizabeth said. "My great-grandmother had proof of innocence. My grandfather had proof of innocence. My mother, my aunt—they all had evidence. They all understood the curse mechanics. But they all failed. Something else is required beyond knowledge and proof."

Sacrifice, I thought but didn't say. That's what Margaret figured out.

"Then we figure out what that something is," Emily said. "We have six days. Let's use them."

TUESDAY

Tyler dragged me to three different camera stores and a pawn shop that smelled like mothballs and regret.

"Okay, check this out." He held up what looked like a camera from the 1960s. "Fully mechanical. No batteries, no electronics. Just optics and chemistry. If anything can photograph Hollow Fields, this can."

"Does it work?"

"I'll test it." He bought four of them, plus twenty rolls of film. The clerk looked at us like we were time travelers.

We hit an outdoor supply store next. Tyler filled a cart with stuff I'd only seen in my dad's old camping gear: compass that used actual magnetism, mechanical altimeter, wind-up watches, even a sextant.

"Little overkill, don't you think?" I said, looking at the sextant.

"Your watch kept jumping to 6:47 PM. Mine stopped entirely. Mike's ran backwards." Tyler's voice was tight, that edge that meant he was barely holding it together. "If we can't trust time, we can't trust direction, we can't trust location. We need every analog backup I can find."

"Hey." I caught his arm. "We're going to be okay."

He looked at me, and I saw the fear he was trying to hide behind efficiency. "You don't know that."

"No," I admitted. "But we're doing everything we can to make sure. That counts for something."

Tyler nodded, didn't look convinced, but added the sextant to the cart anyway.

While Tyler shopped, I went back to my apartment and opened Margaret's journal again.

She'd dated every entry, tracked her preparation methodically. It was like reading my own planning process, except she'd been forty-seven years old with a PhD in folklore and I was twenty-one with a history degree I hadn't finished yet.

But we thought the same way. Same pattern recognition. Same systematic approach.

Same determination.

June 10, 2007: I've mapped every attempt by my family. The failures all share common elements: they went in without understanding the full cost. They thought proof would be enough. Knowledge would be enough. But the curse doesn't care about logic. It cares about balance.

June 12, 2007: I've been studying sacrificial magic across cultures. The principle is consistent: to break a curse born from innocent blood unjustly spilled, innocent blood must be justly given. Voluntarily. With full understanding of the cost.

June 14, 2007: I'm going tomorrow. I've told no one—my sister Elizabeth would try to stop me. But if I'm right, this will free my family from generations of attempting and failing. Someone has to be willing to stay. Someone has to choose to take Eliza's place. I think that someone is me.

My phone buzzed. Emily: Where are you? You said you'd help with research.

I closed the journal. My hands were shaking.

Me: On my way

I wasn't ready to tell them yet. Wasn't sure how to tell them. "Hey guys, I think breaking the curse requires me to die in Hollow Fields, but don't worry about it" wasn't a conversation I knew how to start.

Let me think about it.

WEDNESDAY

Mike showed up at my apartment at 6 AM with a duffel bag and a grin that meant trouble.

"Okay, so I got thinking about the markers disappearing," he said, dumping the bag on my floor. "Both colors, right? Red and blue. Gone. So I figured, what if we're thinking about it wrong?"

"What do you mean?"

He pulled out a container of white powder. "Marking the path means something the town recognizes as intrusive. But what if we marked it as part of the landscape?"

"Mike, that's—is that flour?"

"Flour, chalk dust, limestone powder." He grinned. "Stuff that looks natural, that could've been there for years. We drop it in patterns only we recognize. Subtle. The town might not even notice we're marking trail."

"That's actually smart," I admitted.

"Don't sound so surprised." But he was pleased. "Also got us these." He pulled out five whistles on lanyards. "Old-school. No batteries. We get separated, we can signal each other. Different pattern for each person."

He handed me one. I turned it over—plain metal, probably cost two dollars.

"Thanks," I said.

Mike studied me. "You okay? You look like you haven't slept in days."

"I'm fine."

"That's what people say right before they do something stupid." He wasn't joking anymore. "Josh, man. Whatever you're planning, whatever you're thinking... we're in this together, yeah? You don't have to carry it alone."

I wanted to tell him. Wanted to show him Margaret's journal, wanted to say I think I know what it takes to break the curse, and I think it's going to cost me everything.

Instead I said, "I know. We're a team."

"Good." He slung his bag over his shoulder. "Because you trying to be a hero and getting yourself killed? That's the one thing I can't negotiate our way out of."

After he left, I sat on my floor with the whistle in my hand and wondered how many of us would actually make it back to use them.

THURSDAY

Elizabeth called a meeting in her office. When we arrived, she'd laid out all five family journals in chronological order.

"I want you to see something," she said. "Tyler, can you pull up that pattern analysis you were working on?"

Tyler opened his laptop. He'd created a timeline of every Nightshade family attempt to break the curse, color-coded by person, with notes about what they'd tried and when they'd disappeared.

"Look at the intervals," Elizabeth said. "My great-grandmother: disappeared in spring 1912. My grandfather: disappeared in spring 1948. My mother: disappeared in spring 1983. My aunt: disappeared in summer 2007."

"The intervals are changing," Emily said, seeing it. "Thirty-six years, thirty-five years, twenty-four years. It's accelerating."

"And the season changed," Olivia added. "Your aunt went in summer, not spring."

Elizabeth nodded. "The curse is adapting. Learning. Each generation, it gets better at stopping us. My aunt thought she'd figured out the sacrifice requirement. She went in fully prepared to give her life if necessary." She touched the 2007 journal. "But she went in summer. Margaret theorized the curse could only be broken in spring, when Eliza died. But what if she was wrong? What if the curse wants us to think that, to keep us waiting for the right season?"

"So we don't know when the window actually is," Tyler said.

"We know the market cycle correlates with power spikes," I said, thinking about Margaret's notes. "October market is in four days. If the curse is most active then, maybe that's also when it's most vulnerable."

"Or most dangerous," Mike pointed out.

"Both," Elizabeth said. "My family has always tried in April—spring equinox, anniversary of Eliza's death. None succeeded. Maybe October is different. Maybe that's why the curse pushed Margaret to go in June—to keep her from the October window."

"So we're guessing," Emily said flatly. "We're gambling that October might work better than April even though we have no evidence."

"We have negative evidence," I said. "We know April hasn't worked for 113 years. We know summer didn't work. October is the only season no one's tried."

"Because no one lived long enough to try multiple seasons," Emily shot back. "Josh, this isn't—we can't just—" She stopped, frustrated. "You're gambling with our lives based on a guess."

"It's not a guess. It's elimination. We know what doesn't work. This is what's left."

"Or it doesn't work either and we're all—" She caught herself. "I need some air."

She left. The others looked between me and the door.

"I'll go," Olivia said, following Emily out.

The silence that followed was heavy.

"She's scared," Mike said quietly. "We all are. But Emily's scared specifically of losing you. You two have been friends since you were kids. She's processing that you might not come back."

"We're all coming back," I said.

Elizabeth looked at me with those haunted eyes that had seen too much loss. "That's what my aunt said."

FRIDAY

I found Emily in the library, the table around her covered in medical texts.

"What are you doing?" I asked.

"Research." She didn't look up. "Hypothermia, exposure, trauma. If we're going into a town where time doesn't work right, where electronics fail, where people disappear—I want to know how to keep people alive."

I sat down across from her. "Emily."

"Don't." Her voice was sharp. "Don't tell me it's going to be fine. Don't tell me we're all coming back. I've been reading Elizabeth's family journals. I've been looking at the pattern. And I see what you see, Josh. I see what you're not saying."

My stomach dropped. "What am I not saying?"

"That you think you know what it takes. That you've figured out what Margaret figured out. That you're reading her journal every night—yes, I noticed it in your bag—and you're preparing yourself for something you're not telling us about."

"Emily—"

"Are you planning to die in Hollow Fields?" Her voice cracked. "Because that's what it sounds like. That's what it looks like. And I need you to tell me I'm wrong. I need you to promise me you're not going in there planning to sacrifice yourself."

I opened my mouth. Closed it.

Couldn't lie to her. Couldn't tell the truth either.

"I'm planning to break the curse," I said finally. "Whatever that takes."

"That's not a no."

"That's the only answer I have."

She stared at me, and I saw something break in her expression. "You're really going to do it. You're really going to—" She stood up abruptly, gathering her books. "I can't. I can't watch you do this to yourself. To us."

"Where are you going?"

"To figure out how to keep you alive even if you're determined to die."

She left me sitting there, surrounded by her medical textbooks, wondering if I was making the biggest mistake of my life.

Or if the mistake was thinking I had any other choice.

SATURDAY

We met one final time in my apartment. Tomorrow morning, we'd drive to the forest edge. Tomorrow afternoon, we'd enter Hollow Fields for the second time.

This time, we were prepared. Tyler had equipment staged. Mike had marking materials ready. Olivia had three different types of cameras. Emily had a first aid kit that could handle anything short of major surgery.

And I had Margaret's journal in my backpack, the weight of it constant.

"Everyone clear on the plan?" Emily asked. She'd printed maps, marked routes, created contingencies. "We enter at the threshold Tyler identified. We mark trail every fifty feet—Mike's system. We stay together. No splitting up. No hero bs."

That last part was directed at me.

"We get to the church," she continued. "Josh presents the evidence of Eliza's innocence. We perform whatever ritual is needed to clear her name. We document everything. Then we leave. Together. All of us."

"All of us," Olivia repeated.

"All of us," Tyler agreed.

Mike looked at me. "Right, Josh? All of us come back?"

I met his eyes. Couldn't bring myself to lie.

"That's the plan," I said instead.

It wasn't the same as a promise, and Mike knew it. But he nodded anyway.

"Okay then," Elizabeth said. She'd insisted on coming to this final meeting even though she couldn't go with us. "You have everything my family ever learned. You have better equipment than anyone's ever had. You have each other." She looked at each of us. "My aunt went alone. My mother went alone. My grandfather went alone. That might be why they failed. You're going as a team."

"Strength in numbers," Tyler said.

"Or," Elizabeth said quietly, "one of you comes back to tell what happened to the others. That's the dark possibility none of you want to consider."

The room went silent.

"If something goes wrong," she continued, "if you have to make hard choices—remember that the curse wants you to fail. It's designed to stop people from breaking it. Everything that happens in there will be trying to separate you, to make you doubt, to make you afraid. Don't let it."

"We won't," I said.

Elizabeth looked at me. "Josh. Can I talk to you privately?"

The others filed out, giving us space. When the door closed, Elizabeth's expression shifted from professional to haunted.

"I know what you're planning," she said.

"You don't—"

"I found my aunt's letter. The one she left for me before she went to Hollow Fields. She never mailed it, but I found it years later in her desk." Elizabeth pulled out a folded paper. "I want you to read it."

She handed it to me. The paper was old, yellowed at the edges. Margaret's handwriting.

Dearest Elizabeth,

If you're reading this, I didn't come back. And I need you to understand why I went anyway.

I figured out what the curse requires. Willing sacrifice. Someone innocent choosing to take Eliza's place. To stay in Hollow Fields so others can go free. I know you'll think I'm being dramatic, but I'm not. I've studied this for decades. I'm certain.

I'm going because I'm older. Because I've lived a full life. Because our family has suffered for generations and someone has to end it. I chose it to be me.

But Elizabeth, if I'm wrong—if I fail—I need you to promise me something. Don't let the next person who figures this out make the same choice I'm making. Don't let them think their life is worth less than breaking a century-old curse. Don't let them sacrifice themselves for ghosts.

I know I'm doing exactly what I'm telling you to prevent. I know I'm being a hypocrite. But I'm forty-seven and I've spent my whole life on this curse. I'm ready for it to be over, one way or another.

But the next person who tries? They'll probably be younger. They'll have their whole life ahead of them. They'll think they're being heroic.

Don't let them make my mistake.

I love you.

Margaret

I read it twice. My hands were shaking.

"She wrote this the night before she disappeared," Elizabeth said. "She was planning to sacrifice herself. She went in knowing she might not come back."

"But she didn't succeed," I said. "She disappeared, and the curse remained."

"Yes. Which means either she was wrong about what the curse requires, or she didn't manage to complete the sacrifice. Either way—" Elizabeth's voice cracked. "She died for nothing. And I can see you making the same calculation she did. I can see you thinking 'I'm the one who should stay behind.'"

"I'm not—"

"Don't lie to me, Josh. I've watched too many people disappear into that town. I can recognize the signs. The way you look at your friends. The way you're memorizing their faces. The way you keep deflecting when Emily asks you to promise you're all coming back."

I couldn't answer.

"Margaret was wrong," Elizabeth said. "Maybe the curse doesn't require sacrifice. Maybe it requires something else entirely. Maybe her willingness to die wasn't enough because death isn't what the curse wants. We don't know. But I need you to promise me you won't assume martyrdom is the answer."

"I can't promise that."

"Then promise me you'll consider other options first. Promise me you won't jump to sacrifice unless you've exhausted every alternative." She gripped my shoulders. "You're twenty-one years old. You have your whole life ahead of you. Don't throw it away on a guess."

"It's not a guess," I said quietly. "It's the only thing that makes sense. Eliza died unjustly. To balance that, someone has to die justly. Willingly. Someone who knows what they're doing and chooses it anyway."

"And you think that someone is you."

"I think if it has to be someone, it should be someone who understands why it matters. Someone who sees the injustice clearly enough to correct it."

"That's what Margaret thought too." Elizabeth's eyes were wet. "And she's gone. And nothing changed."

"Then maybe she didn't do it right. Maybe I need to do it differently."

"Or maybe you both need to stay alive and find another way." She let go of my shoulders. "Just... think about it. Please. Tonight. Before you go in tomorrow. Really think about whether dying for this curse is the answer, or whether there's something else you haven't considered yet."

"I will," I said.

She studied my face. "You're lying."

"No. I will think about it." That was true. I'd been thinking about nothing else for days. "But I'm also going tomorrow. With or without answers. Because Mary Stanton has been trapped for 133 years, and I can't walk away from that."

"Even if it kills you."

"Even then."

Elizabeth handed me Margaret's letter. "Keep this. Read it again before you go in. And remember—she thought she was making the right choice too."

That night, I sat in my apartment with all the lights off, Margaret's journal open, her letter next to it, and tried to think of any alternative.

Any way to break the curse that didn't require someone staying behind.

Any way to correct the injustice without equivalent sacrifice.

But every path I followed led back to the same conclusion: someone innocent had to choose to take Eliza's place. Had to willingly stay in Hollow Fields. Had to understand the cost and accept it anyway.

And if that was true, it should be me.

Because I'd brought my friends here. I'd convinced them to investigate. I'd pushed us deeper into this mystery until we were in too far to stop.

Because I understood the injustice in a way that felt personal, visceral. Eliza had been trying to heal the land and they'd killed her for it. That wrong needed correction, and I was the one who felt it most deeply.

Because I'd read Margaret's letter, and Elizabeth's plea, and I knew everyone would try to stop me if they knew what I was thinking.

So I wouldn't tell them.

I'd go to Hollow Fields. I'd present evidence of Eliza's innocence. I'd do everything I could to break the curse the normal way.

But if—when—it required more than that, I'd be ready.

I'd be the one who stayed.

My phone lit up. Emily: See you at 7 AM. Van's packed. Are you okay?

Me: Fine. See you in the morning.

Another lie to add to the collection.

I looked at my friends' names in my phone contacts. Thought about Emily's medical textbooks. Tyler's cameras. Olivia's determination to document truth. Mike's whistles that were supposed to bring us back together if we got separated.

They were all planning to come home.

I was planning to make sure they did.

Even if I didn't.

Let me think about it one more time, I told myself, knowing I'd already made the decision. Knowing I'd made it the moment I read Margaret's journal. Knowing I'd probably made it when I first saw Mary Stanton's hollow eyes and realized she'd been suffering for over a century.

Someone had to make it right.

And I was starting to accept that someone was me.

Outside my window, dawn was still hours away. But I could already feel tomorrow coming.

Feel Hollow Fields waiting.

Feel the weight of the choice I'd already made pressing against my chest like a physical thing.

Tomorrow, we'd go back.

Tomorrow, I'd do whatever it took to free them.

Whatever it took.

Even if my friends never forgave me for it.

CHAPTER 8: CROSSING THE THRESHOLD

SUNDAY - 6:47 AM

Emily's knock came exactly at seven, three sharp raps that meant she was already annoyed.

I opened the door. She stood there with two travel mugs of coffee, her expression somewhere between concerned friend and disappointed parent.

"You didn't sleep," she said. Not a question.

"I slept some." Lie. I'd been reading Margaret's journal until 4 AM, then staring at my ceiling until Emily's knock.

She handed me a coffee. "Liar. But at least you're dressed."

The van was parked at the curb, Tyler already in the driver's seat running pre-departure checks. Mike sat in the back organizing equipment. Olivia was on the sidewalk with her camera, taking what she called "before" photos of all of us.

"Documentation," she said when she caught me looking. "In case we need to prove we were okay before we went in."

"Cheerful," Mike called from the van.

"Realistic," Olivia corrected.

I loaded my backpack—Margaret's journal hidden at the bottom under spare batteries and protein bars. Emily watched me, and I could feel her trying to read my expression, trying to figure out if I'd changed my mind about whatever she thought I was planning.

I hadn't.

Tyler leaned out the driver's window. "GPS is set. Three hours to the forest edge by normal roads. Then we're on our own—my backup GPS might work for a while past that, but once we hit the threshold..." He shrugged.

"Then we use landmarks," I said. "And Mike's trail markers."

"And we stay together," Emily added, looking directly at me. "Right?"

"Right," I agreed.

Tyler started the engine. The sound of it—normal, mechanical, reliable —felt like the last connection to the world we knew. Once we crossed into Hollow Fields proper, nothing would work the way it should.

Olivia took one last photo of the van, of all of us standing around it, then climbed in.

We were really doing this.

8:15 AM - THE HIGHWAY

For the first hour, it felt like a normal road trip. Tyler had music playing quietly. Mike was going through equipment, doing inventory out loud. Olivia watched the landscape through the window, occasionally taking photos.

Emily sat beside me in the middle row, her medical kit at her feet, her research notes spread across her lap.

"I mapped every disappearance location I could find," she said quietly, showing me her handwritten chart. "Your grandfather's notes, Elizabeth's family records, newspaper articles going back to 1890. Eighty-three people that we know of. Could be more that weren't reported."

"Eighty-three," I repeated.

"They all entered somewhere along this forest edge." She traced her finger along a red line on her map. "But the exact entry points vary. Like the forest is... permeable in some places, solid in others."

"Or like it chooses who gets in," Olivia said from the front.

"I don't think it chooses," I said. "I think it's always open. We just don't see the opening unless we're looking for it."

"Or unless it wants us to find it," Mike added.

Tyler turned down the music. "Speaking of which—we're twenty miles out from where you guys entered last time. Based on your description and the photos Olivia got before the cameras died, I think I can get us pretty close to that same entry point."

"Why the same spot?" Mike asked.

"Because we know it works," I said. "We got in there before. We made it to town. We know the route, at least partially. Starting somewhere new means learning everything from scratch."

"Makes sense," Emily agreed, though she didn't look happy about any of it.

The highway gave way to smaller roads. Two-lane county routes, then single-lane access roads. The trees got denser, the air through the open windows cooler. Tyler had to slow down as the pavement turned to gravel, then dirt.

"We're close," he said.

10:30 AM - FOREST EDGE

Tyler parked in the same spot we'd used last time—a small clearing where the dirt road ended. The forest stretched out in front of us, dense and dark even in midmorning sun.

I recognized it immediately. Same trees. Same configuration. Even the same fallen log we'd used as a marker.

"This is it," I said.

We unloaded equipment methodically. Tyler distributed the mechanical cameras, showed everyone how to wind them, how to check the film. Mike handed out whistles on lanyards—each person got a different pattern to blow if we got separated.

"Mine's three short," he demonstrated. "Em's is two long. Josh, yours is one long, one short. Olivia, yours is—"

"Let me guess," Olivia said. "Four short?"

"You got it. Tyler's is all-long."

Emily opened her first aid kit one more time, checking supplies. "We have enough for basic trauma, but if anyone gets seriously hurt, we need to get them out immediately. No heroics."

"Define seriously hurt," Mike asked.

"Anything I can't fix with what's in this bag." She zipped it closed. "Which includes most head injuries, major bleeding, broken bones—"

"We get it," Tyler interrupted. "Don't get hurt."

"Don't get separated either," Emily said, her voice firm. "That's rule number one. We stick together. We stay in visual contact. If you can't see at least two other people, you stop and blow your whistle until someone finds you."

We all nodded.

I checked my watch—10:47 AM. Wound it carefully, the way Dad had taught me. Mechanical watches needed regular winding. Something about that felt important, like maintaining a connection to time even as we walked into a place where time didn't work right.

"One more thing," Tyler said. He pulled out a notebook, had us all sign our names and write the current time. "If we all come back but our sense of time is different, at least we have a record of when we left."

Smart. That was Tyler—always thinking about data, documentation, proof.

We signed. I wrote: Josh - Sunday, October 17th, 10:47 AM - Entering Hollow Fields.

Emily wrote underneath mine: Emily - Same date/time - Under protest.

That made me smile despite everything.

"Okay," I said, shouldering my backpack. "Let's go."

10:55 AM - THE WALK BEGINS

The first hundred yards felt normal. Forest floor, fallen leaves, birds in the distance. Sunlight filtering through branches. Our footsteps crunching.

Mike dropped flour every fifty feet, barely-visible white marks that could be mistaken for natural limestone deposits. He made patterns only we'd recognize—three dots in a triangle, four dots in a square, five dots in a pentagon. Simple but effective.

Tyler navigated with his backup GPS at first, calling out coordinates every few minutes. "Still reading. Signal's weak but present. We're... northeast of our starting point, about point-two miles in."

"Matches last time," I said.

Then, at the quarter-mile mark, everything changed.

It wasn't dramatic. No thunder, no sudden darkness. Just... shift.

The air got cooler. The bird sounds stopped. The sunlight, which had been filtering normally through leaves, seemed to come from the wrong angle.

And my watch stopped.

I looked down—the second hand was frozen at 6:47.

"Tyler," I said. "Check your GPS."

He looked at the screen. "It's... it's gone. No satellites. No signal. Like they just disappeared."

Emily pulled out her phone. "Same. No service. Not even emergency only. Just... nothing."

Mike's digital watch was blank. Olivia's phone was dead despite being fully charged this morning.

"This is the threshold," Tyler said quietly. "The point where normal physics stops working."

I wound my watch, set it to what I thought was the right time. Eleven AM, roughly. The second hand started moving again—whether it was accurate or not, at least it was moving.

"Everyone check your mechanical watches," I said.

We synchronized as best we could. All set ours to 11:00 AM. At least we'd be on the same time system, even if it was wrong.

"How far to town from here?" Mike asked.

I thought about our last trip. "Maybe two miles? Hard to say. Distance gets weird here too."

"Then we keep going," Emily said. "But careful. Deliberate. We mark the trail every fifty feet. We check in with each other every five minutes. And if anything feels wrong, we stop and regroup."

"Everything feels wrong," Olivia muttered.

"Wronger," Emily amended.

We pressed forward.

11:30 AM (MAYBE)

Time became unreliable immediately. My watch said we'd been walking for thirty minutes, but it felt like hours. Or maybe fifteen minutes. I couldn't trust my internal sense of it.

The forest changed as we walked. Trees got taller, their bark darker. The undergrowth thinned out until we were walking on almost bare ground. Everything felt slightly wrong—angles that shouldn't work, distances that didn't make sense.

"Josh," Tyler called. "Look at this."

He was kneeling by a tree. Carved into the bark was a symbol—a circle with lines radiating out like a compass rose.

"You recognize this?" he asked.

"No. But look." I pointed further along. Another tree, another symbol. Then another. "Trail markers. Someone else marked the route."

"Your grandfather?" Emily suggested.

"Maybe. Or Elizabeth's family. Or..." I trailed off. "Or the town itself. Leading us in."

"Comforting," Mike said.

But we followed the symbols anyway. They were heading in the same direction we needed to go—toward the center, toward the church, toward whatever waited in Hollow Fields.

12:15 PM (ACCORDING TO MY WATCH)

We found the first building at what my watch said was 12:15, though the light suggested either late afternoon or early morning—I couldn't tell which.

It was a house, or had been. Two-story farmhouse, windows broken, door hanging open. The same decrepit architecture we'd seen last time.

"This is farther in than we got before," I said. "Last time, we barely made it past the first buildings before we had to run."

"So we're already beyond our previous exploration," Emily said. "Which means we don't know what to expect."

"We know the church is at the center," I said. "We head toward that."

"And if we run into..." Olivia paused. "What did we run into last time? The farmer? Mary?"

"Residents," I said. "The people trapped here. They weren't hostile. They were scared. Confused."

"What about the corrupted ones?" Tyler asked. "The council members Elizabeth talked about?"

"We haven't seen them yet," I said. "And maybe we won't. Maybe they only appear at certain times. During the lottery cycle, or during the market, or—"

A sound cut me off.

Footsteps.

We froze.

The footsteps were slow, deliberate, coming from around the side of the farmhouse. The crunch of gravel, the shuffle of feet.

Then a figure emerged.

It was a man, middle-aged, wearing clothes from maybe the 1940s. His face was pale, his eyes unfocused. He walked right past us like we weren't there, heading down what must have once been a street.

"Did he..." Mike whispered. "Did he see us?"

"I don't think so," Olivia said. She raised her mechanical camera, snapped a photo. The click of the shutter seemed impossibly loud.

The man didn't react. Just kept walking until he disappeared behind another building.

"The residents," Emily breathed. "We're seeing them in real time."

"Or we're seeing echoes," Tyler said. "Recordings. Moments from the past playing on repeat."

"Does it matter?" I asked. "Either way, they're here. And we need to be careful not to disturb them."

We moved forward more cautiously, staying close together, trying to stay quiet. Every few hundred feet, we'd see another figure. A woman hanging laundry that wasn't there. A child playing with a ball we couldn't see. An old man sitting on a porch that had partially collapsed.

None of them looked at us.

None of them seemed to know we were there.

"This is worse than last time," Emily said quietly. "Last time, Mary saw us. Talked to us. These people are just... gone. Lost in whatever loop they're stuck in."

"Maybe time of day matters," I suggested. "Or maybe we're seeing different layers. Different moments of the curse."

"Or maybe," Olivia said, "we're the ghosts to them. Maybe we're the ones who don't belong."

1:30 PM (MY WATCH)

The church came into view slowly, emerging from the fog like something being born from mist. It was exactly as I remembered—tall, imposing, white paint peeling from wooden walls, steeple leaning slightly to one side.

But something was different.

"There are people," Tyler said.

He was right. The church steps were crowded with figures, maybe thirty or forty of them, all standing still as statues. They faced the church doors, silent and unmoving.

"What are they doing?" Mike asked.

"Waiting," I said.

"For what?"

"For the lottery, maybe," Emily said. "Elizabeth's family journals mentioned that the lottery was performed at the church. Maybe this is... the moment before. The moment when they all gather to see who'll be chosen."

"Then we're seeing a specific time," Tyler said. "A specific moment in the curse's cycle. The October lottery. It's happening now—or it's about to happen."

"How do we know when 'now' is for them?" Olivia asked.

Good question. My watch said 1:30 PM on a Sunday in October 2025. But for the people on those steps, it could be any October from the last 143 years.

"We need to get inside," I said. "The church is where the farmer was last time. Where Eliza's journal is probably still hidden. Where we can present the evidence of her innocence."

"Josh," Emily said carefully. "There are forty people between us and that door."

"They didn't see us before. The man walking, the woman with laundry —none of them reacted to us."

"These people are in a crowd. Focused on something. That's different than being alone and oblivious."

"We have to try," I said.

Mike pulled out his whistle. "If something goes wrong, everyone blows pattern. We regroup and run."

We approached slowly, staying together. The crowd didn't move, didn't react. Their faces were blank, expressionless. Some wore clothes from the 1890s. Others from the 1920s, 40s, 60s, 80s. Different eras all standing together, all waiting for the same thing.

The lottery.

I reached the steps first, started climbing. The figures didn't part, so I moved between them, careful not to touch. Emily followed close behind, then the others.

The church doors were open.

Inside, the air was colder. Rows of pews stretched toward an altar at the far end. And standing at the altar, his back to us, was the farmer.

He wore his familiar straw hat, faded overalls. He stood perfectly still, facing something on the altar we couldn't see from this angle.

"That's him," Emily whispered. "The one from the market. From before."

"Should we..." Tyler trailed off. "Should we talk to him?"

Before I could answer, the farmer spoke without turning around.

"You came back."

His voice was rough, tired. The voice of someone who'd been speaking the same words for over a century.

"You all come back," he continued. "Different faces. Same questions. Looking for the same answers."

"We know about Eliza," I said. "We know she was innocent. We know the council killed her unjustly."

"Everyone knows," the farmer said. "Eventually. The knowledge doesn't free us."

"Then what does?"

Finally, he turned.

His face was weathered, lined with more than just age. His eyes were hollow, seeing something beyond us.

"Someone has to choose," he said. "Someone always has to choose."

"Choose what?" Emily asked.

The farmer's eyes found me, locked onto mine like he could see straight through to the journal hidden in my backpack.

"You already know," he said to me specifically. "You've read her words. Margaret's words. Eliza's words. You know what the curse requires."

My heart pounded.

"Someone innocent," I said quietly. "Someone who understands the injustice. Someone willing to stay."

Emily's hand grabbed my arm, tight enough to hurt.

The farmer nodded slowly. "October's a powerful time. When the veil is thin. When choices made carry more weight." He looked at all of us now. "But choosing doesn't mean understanding. Margaret chose. Still failed. Others chose before her. All failed."

"Why?" I asked. "If they were willing, if they understood, why did they fail?"

"Because choosing to die isn't the same as choosing to live," the farmer said. "Eliza didn't choose death. They forced it on her. To balance that wrong, someone must choose to live here. Forever. Awake. Aware. Holding the curse at bay not through death, but through eternal vigilance."

The silence that followed was crushing.

Not death.

Worse than death.

Living here, in this town where time didn't work, where reality bent, where residents walked in loops forever. Living here conscious, aware, unable to leave, holding back the corruption through sheer will.

Forever.

"That's—" Emily's voice broke. "That's impossible. No one could—"

"Eliza did," the farmer said. "For six years. From when the council first tried to corrupt the land until they killed her. She held the magic pure through her will alone. When she died, that's when the curse took hold. Because there was no one left to guard against it."

He turned back to the altar.

"The town will tell you who's capable," he said. "The magic will know. And when it knows, you'll know. You'll feel it calling to you specifically. Asking if you're willing."

"Has it called to you?" I asked.

"Every day," he said. "For 143 years. But I'm not the one. Never was. Just a witness. Just someone who stays to tell the story when people like you find your way here."

He gestured to the altar. On it sat a book—old, leather-bound, familiar.

"That's Eliza's journal," I breathed.

"Full version," the farmer said. "Everything she learned about the magic, the curse, how to hold it. Everything you'll need to know if you choose to take her place."

I stepped forward, reached for the journal.

Emily grabbed my wrist. "Josh, no. Don't even—we're not—you're not —"

"I'm just looking," I said.

But we both knew that was a lie.

I opened the journal. Eliza's handwriting filled the pages, neat and precise at first, getting shakier toward the end as she grew weaker, as the council closed in.

The final entry was dated April 1849:

They're coming for me tonight. I can hear them gathering outside. They believe I cursed the land because I wouldn't let them corrupt it. They'll burn me as a witch, and the magic will have no guardian. The curse will take hold because there will be no one left to resist it.

I tried. God knows I tried. Six years of holding the magic pure while they bled it dark. Six years of fighting alone.

I'm so tired.

If anyone finds this, if anyone understands what I tried to do—the magic needs a guardian. Someone strong enough to stand against corruption. Someone willing to give everything to keep the land pure.

I failed. Perhaps you won't.

I closed the journal, my hands shaking.

The farmer's voice came from behind me: "She's waiting to know. The magic. It's asking you right now: are you capable? Are you willing?"

"Josh," Emily said, her voice desperate. "We're leaving. All of us. Right now."

But I couldn't move. Because the farmer was right.

I could feel it.

The magic, reaching out, testing me, asking a question I wasn't ready to answer.

Are you willing?

"We need to go," Mike said, backing toward the door. "This is—we shouldn't be here."

"Josh," Olivia added. "Come on."

But the magic kept asking, kept probing, kept waiting for an answer.

And somewhere deep inside, in a place I hadn't wanted to acknowledge, I realized I'd known what it would ask since I first read Margaret's journal.

I'd just been hoping I was wrong.

"Josh!" Emily pulled on my arm. "JOSHUA. We're leaving. Now."

The use of my full name—the serious one—broke through.

I let her pull me away from the altar, away from Eliza's journal, away from the farmer who watched us go with those hollow, knowing eyes.

We backed out of the church, down the steps, past the crowd that still stood frozen, through the streets where residents walked their eternal loops.

We didn't stop until we reached the tree line, until my watch showed 4:30 PM (though I had no idea if that was accurate), until we could see the forest edge ahead.

And even then, even after we'd crossed the threshold, after our phones blinked back to life and Tyler's GPS found satellites again, after we piled into the van and Tyler started driving back toward civilization—

Even then, I could still feel it.

The magic, asking its question.

Are you willing?

And the answer, the one I'd been avoiding, the one I hadn't told anyone
—

Maybe.

Maybe I was.

CHAPTER 9: THE WEIGHT OF KNOWING

MONDAY - 8:30 AM

I didn't go to class.

Couldn't sit in a lecture hall and pretend to care about historical agricultural patterns when I'd spent Sunday walking through a town where time didn't work, talking to a man who'd been dead for 143 years, feeling magic ask me a question I still didn't know how to answer.

Are you willing?

My phone buzzed. Emily: Where are you? You missed comparative history.

Me: Apartment. Not feeling great.

Emily: BS. I'm coming over.

I started to type a response, then stopped. Let her come. Maybe talking about it would help. Maybe saying it out loud would make it feel less overwhelming.

Or maybe it would make it more real.

She showed up twenty minutes later with coffee and the expression I'd learned to dread—the one that meant she'd figured something out and wasn't going to let it go.

"You felt it," she said, not a question. She set the coffee on my desk and sat on my bed, watching me with those eyes that had known me since I was five. "In the church. When the farmer was talking. You felt something."

"Emily—"

"Don't." Her voice was sharp. "Don't deflect. Don't give me the 'let me think about it' line. I watched your face, Josh. I saw the way you looked at Eliza's journal. The way you couldn't move when the farmer asked if you were willing. Something happened to you in there."

I wrapped my hands around the coffee cup she'd brought. Still hot. Probably from the campus shop. Normal coffee, normal Monday morning. Except nothing about Monday felt normal anymore.

"The magic is alive," I said finally. "You felt it too. We all did."

"That's not what I'm asking about."

"I know."

She waited. Emily was good at waiting. Patient in ways that made you want to fill the silence just to make it stop pressing against you.

"It asked me something," I admitted. "The magic. In the church. It was like... probing. Testing. Trying to figure out if I was capable of something."

"Capable of what?"

"I don't know."

"Joshua."

There it was. Full name. Serious mode.

"I don't know," I repeated, and that was mostly true. I knew what the magic wanted—eternal vigilance, someone willing to stay and guard like Eliza had. But I didn't know what that actually meant in practice. Didn't know if I could do it. Didn't know if I was willing.

Are you willing?

"The farmer said Margaret failed," Emily said, her voice careful. "Said she chose death but that wasn't enough. That the curse needs someone to choose life. To stay. Forever."

"I know."

"And you're thinking about it."

"Emily—"

"You're thinking about volunteering. About being the one who stays." She stood up, pacing my small apartment. "I can see it in your face. The way you've been since we left. You're already planning it, aren't you? Already figuring out how to be the one who doesn't come back."

"I'm not—"

"Don't lie to me." She stopped in front of me. "We've known each other seventeen years. I know when you're lying. And I know when you're trying to talk yourself into something you think is noble but is actually just you being unable to walk away from a problem."

"It's not about being noble—"

"Then what's it about? Why are you so determined to be the one who fixes this?"

Because I brought us here. Because I convinced you all to investigate. Because I'm the one who felt the magic asking, which means I'm the one it wants. Because if someone has to stay, it should be me.

I didn't say any of that.

"I'm just trying to understand what it takes," I said instead. "That's all. Research. Learning. Same thing we've been doing this whole time."

She stared at me, and I saw the moment she decided to let it go. Not because she believed me, but because pushing harder wouldn't get her anywhere.

"Fine," she said. "Then let's research together. Because if we're figuring this out, we're doing it as a group. All of us. Not you alone in your apartment reading Margaret's journal at 3 AM."

My stomach dropped. "How did you—"

"Your light was on last night when I drove past at midnight. And at two. And at four when I couldn't sleep and drove past again." She crossed her arms. "Don't insult me by pretending you're not obsessing over this."

She was right. After we'd gotten back Sunday evening, after Tyler had dropped everyone off, I'd pulled out Margaret's journal and read it cover to cover three more times. Looking for something I'd missed. Some clue about what "choosing to live" meant versus "choosing to die."

Margaret had gone in willing to sacrifice herself. Willing to die. She'd been certain that's what it took.

But she'd failed.

The farmer had been clear: choosing death wasn't enough. The curse needed someone willing to live there. Forever. Conscious. Aware. Holding the magic back through active will, not through martyrdom.

That was so much worse than dying.

"Group meeting," Emily said. "Noon. Elizabeth's office. Everyone's coming. We're going to talk about what we learned yesterday and figure out what it means. Together."

"Okay."

"And Josh?" She paused at my door. "Whatever you're planning—whatever you think you have to do—remember that we're in this together. You're not alone. You don't have to carry it all yourself."

After she left, I sat with my coffee growing cold and thought about what "together" meant when only one person could be the guardian.

NOON - ELIZABETH'S OFFICE

We gathered in the familiar chaos of Elizabeth's office—books stacked everywhere, maps pinned to walls, her family's journals spread across every surface.

Elizabeth looked tired. More tired than I'd seen her. The kind of tired that came from watching people walk toward the same fate her family had faced for generations.

"Tell me everything," she said.

We did. Tyler described the threshold crossing, the technology failures. Olivia showed her photos from the mechanical cameras—most showed empty spaces where spirits should have been, but a few captured ghostly outlines. Mike talked about the residents we'd seen, walking their loops.

And I told her about the church. About the farmer. About what he'd said about choosing life versus choosing death.

Elizabeth listened without interrupting. When I finished, she was quiet for a long moment.

"My aunt wrote something similar," she said finally, pulling out one of her family journals. "In her last entries. She said the curse needed a guardian, not a martyr. But she went anyway, thinking she understood. Thinking her willingness would be enough."

"But it wasn't," Emily said.

"No. Because willingness isn't the same as capability." Elizabeth looked at me. "The magic doesn't just need someone willing. It needs someone capable. Someone strong enough to hold the corruption back indefinitely. Someone who can maintain that vigilance not for days or weeks, but for decades. Centuries, potentially."

"That's impossible," Mike said. "No one could—"

"Eliza did," I said quietly. "For six years. While the council tried to corrupt the land, she held the magic pure. Alone. For six years."

"And it killed her," Emily pointed out. "The strain of it, the isolation—that's what made her vulnerable to the council. They waited until she was weak enough to overcome."

"So the magic needs someone strong enough to do what Eliza did," Tyler said, thinking through the logic. "But indefinitely. Forever. Without breaking."

"Without dying," Olivia added. "Because if the guardian dies, the curse returns. It all starts over."

"Which means the guardian has to be immortal," Mike said. "Or at least not age. Otherwise it's just delayed failure."

We all looked at Elizabeth.

"Does the magic make you immortal?" I asked. "If you become the guardian, do you stop aging?"

"I don't know," Elizabeth admitted. "My family's research suggests yes—that becoming guardian transforms you somehow. Makes you part of the land itself. But no one's succeeded in becoming guardian, so we have no proof."

"Eliza aged normally," Emily said. "She was thirty-seven when she died. If she'd been immortal guardian for six years before that, she would've been thirty-one forever."

"But she wasn't guardian officially," I said, thinking it through. "She was holding the magic back, but she hadn't accepted the role permanently. Maybe there's a difference between temporary resistance and permanent guardianship."

"That's a lot of maybes," Mike said. "A lot of guessing."

"It's all guessing," Emily said flatly. "We're trying to figure out rules for magic based on one person's fragmentary journal and a ghost's cryptic warnings. We don't actually know anything."

"We know the curse exists," Olivia said. "We know people are trapped. We know something went wrong with Margaret and Elizabeth's family. Those aren't guesses."

"But how to fix it is," Emily insisted. "And we're sitting here talking about permanent guardianship and immortality like those are normal options when we don't even know if they're real."

"Then we need more information," I said. "We need Eliza's full journal. The one the farmer showed us in the church. That has everything—her techniques, her knowledge, what worked and what didn't."

"You want to go back," Elizabeth said.

"We have to. If we're going to understand this, we need to read what Eliza wrote. All of it."

"Josh," Emily's voice had warning in it. "Going back means crossing the threshold again. Means putting ourselves back in range of the magic. If it's looking for a guardian, if it's testing for capability, you're giving it another chance to claim one of us."

"I know."

"And you're okay with that."

"I'm okay with getting answers."

She stared at me, and I could see her working through it—trying to figure out if I was being practical Josh (gather information, solve the problem) or martyr Josh (sacrifice yourself to fix everything).

I wasn't sure which one I was being anymore either.

"We all go," Mike said suddenly. "If we're doing this, we do it together. Full team. No one goes in alone."

"Agreed," Tyler said.

Olivia nodded. "Documentation. We need more photos, more evidence. If Josh is right and we need Eliza's journal, then we get it and document everything."

Emily looked at each of us, then at me. "Vote. Who thinks we should go back?"

Mike raised his hand. Tyler followed. Olivia raised hers after a moment's hesitation.

Emily didn't raise hers.

"Em," I said quietly.

"I'm not voting no," she said. "I'm abstaining. Because I think you're all making this decision based on Josh's determination to find a solution, and I think Josh is making decisions based on what the magic asked him in that church. And I think we're all pretending that's not what's happening."

The silence that followed was heavy.

"But," Emily continued, "I'm not going to let you go back alone. So if you're going, I'm going. Not because I think it's smart. Because I'm not letting my best friend walk into that place without someone who'll drag him back out if necessary."

"Em—"

"Don't." She stood up. "If we're doing this, we do it right. We plan. We prepare. We go in with better equipment, better understanding, and an actual exit strategy. Not just 'get the journal and hope the magic doesn't claim us.'"

"Agreed," I said.

"And Josh?" She looked directly at me. "If the magic asks you that question again—if you feel it probing, testing, asking if you're willing—you tell us. Immediately. Before you make any decisions. Because this isn't just about you anymore. Whatever happens in Hollow Fields happens to all of us."

I nodded, knowing it was a promise I might not be able to keep.

6:00 PM - MY APARTMENT

We'd spent the afternoon planning. Equipment lists, route mapping, timing. Tyler wanted to try entering at dusk instead of morning, see if time of day affected the threshold. Mike suggested we bring actual rope, tie ourselves together so we couldn't get separated.

Now they were all gone, and I sat alone with Margaret's journal open to her final entry.

Someone has to choose. Someone has to be willing to stay.

My phone buzzed. Text from an unknown number.

This is Elizabeth. I got your number from Emily. I need to talk to you privately. Can you come to my office? Now?

I grabbed my jacket and headed out.

6:45 PM - ELIZABETH'S OFFICE

She was waiting with two cups of tea and the expression of someone about to deliver bad news.

"Sit," she said.

I sat.

"The magic asked you specifically," she said without preamble. "In the church. You felt it reaching out, asking if you were capable. Testing you."

"How did you—"

"Because it did the same thing to my aunt. She told me about it in her letter. The one I showed you." Elizabeth pushed one of the tea cups toward me. "The magic identifies candidates. People who might be strong enough, determined enough, to be guardians. It doesn't ask everyone. It only asks people it thinks might actually succeed."

My stomach tightened. "What are you saying?"

"I'm saying the magic chose you. Specifically. Out of your whole group, it asked you. Which means it sees something in you—some quality or capability—that makes you a viable candidate for guardianship."

"That doesn't mean I have to accept."

"No. But it means if someone from your group becomes guardian, it'll probably be you. The magic has already marked you."

I wrapped my hands around the warm tea cup, let the heat ground me. "Margaret was marked too, wasn't she?"

"Yes. And she went in anyway. Went in willing to become guardian. Went in thinking her willingness and capability would be enough." Elizabeth's eyes were sad. "But she didn't understand what 'choosing to live' meant. None of my family understood. They thought it meant accepting immortality, accepting the role. They didn't understand it meant giving up everything else."

"What do you mean?"

"Being guardian isn't like being alive and also guarding the town," Elizabeth said carefully. "It's becoming part of the land. Merging with it. You don't get to leave. You don't get to interact with the living. You don't get relationships, experiences, growth. You become a consciousness bound to the magic, aware but not participating. Forever."

The tea suddenly tasted bitter.

"So when the farmer said choosing to live, he meant—"

"He meant existing. Conscious existence. But not living in any meaningful human sense." Elizabeth leaned forward. "That's why Margaret failed. She went in willing to die for the cause, which is heroic. But the curse doesn't want heroic death. It wants eternal, conscious sacrifice. And when she understood what that actually meant, she couldn't accept it. So the magic rejected her."

"But if she couldn't accept it, and she was willing, then who could?"

"Someone who doesn't go in seeing it as sacrifice. Someone who goes in seeing it as purpose. As calling." Elizabeth's eyes held mine. "Someone who's been searching for where they belong their whole life and recognizes guardianship as the answer."

My throat felt tight.

"Josh," she said gently. "I'm not telling you this to encourage you. I'm telling you this because you need to understand what you'd be choosing. My aunt thought she understood. She was wrong. And it killed her. Or trapped her. We don't know which, because she never came back."

"But if I'm marked," I said slowly. "If the magic chose me, and I don't accept, then—"

"Then you don't become guardian. Someone else might. Or no one. The curse continues. People stay trapped." She set down her tea. "But you live your life. You go back to school. You have a future. You don't give up everything for a town full of ghosts."

I thought about Mary Stanton. Thought about the farmer. Thought about the residents walking their endless loops, trapped for over a century.

"How long?" I asked.

"How long what?"

"How long do I have to decide? If the magic marked me, if we go back and get Eliza's journal, how long before I have to give an answer?"

Elizabeth's expression became very sad. "Based on my family's experiences? Once you return to Hollow Fields knowing what you know, having been marked, the magic will ask again. More insistently. And if you don't answer, it will start affecting you. Dreams. Compulsions. The sense of being called. It won't force you, but it will make staying away very difficult."

"So I'm already committed."

"No. You can still walk away. It'll be hard, but possible. The farther you get from Hollow Fields physically, the weaker the pull becomes. You could transfer schools. Move to another state. Build a life somewhere the magic can't reach you."

"And leave them all trapped."

"Yes."

I stood up, walked to her window. Campus was visible below, students heading to dinner, to library, to normal Monday night activities. A world I'd been part of just yesterday but that already felt impossibly distant.

"If I became guardian," I said, not looking at her. "Would I be conscious? Aware? Would I know what was happening?"

"Based on Eliza's journal fragments, yes. You'd be aware. That's the point—active vigilance requires consciousness. You'd know you were there. Know what you were doing. Know what you gave up."

"Forever."

"Forever."

I closed my eyes. Thought about my mom's face when I told her I wasn't coming home for Thanksgiving. Thought about Emily's expression when she realized what I was planning. Thought about never finishing my degree, never traveling anywhere, never falling in love or having kids or doing any of the thousand things I'd vaguely assumed I'd do someday.

Thought about spending eternity as a consciousness bound to a cursed town, holding back corruption, watching seasons change and people try to break in, knowing I'd never leave, never age, never die, never be free.

That's what "choosing to live" meant.

And the magic wanted to know: Are you willing?

"Thank you for telling me," I said, turning back to Elizabeth. "I need to think about it."

"Take your time. But Josh?" She stood. "Remember that you're twenty-one years old. You have your whole life ahead of you. The magic is asking if you'll give that up. Make sure your answer is really yours, not just you trying to fix a problem because you can't walk away from people who need help."

10:30 PM - MY APARTMENT

I pulled out my phone, typed a text to Emily: You're right. I'm thinking about it. About volunteering. About being guardian.

Stared at it for five minutes.

Deleted it.

Typed instead: Can't sleep. Want to get coffee?

She responded immediately: Yes. Twenty minutes. The place that's open late.

We met at the 24-hour diner near campus. She looked as exhausted as I felt.

"You talked to Elizabeth alone," she said as soon as we sat down. "I saw your car at her building."

"She wanted to explain what guardianship actually means."

"And?"

I told her. All of it. The marking, the call, the eternal conscious existence bound to the land. The fact that Margaret had failed because she couldn't accept what it actually meant.

Emily listened without interrupting, her coffee growing cold as I talked.

When I finished, she was quiet for a long time.

"So you'd be conscious," she said finally. "Aware. Knowing what you gave up. Forever."

"Yeah."

"And you're considering it."

"I don't know."

"Yes, you do." She looked directly at me. "I can see it in your face. You're already trying to convince yourself it's worth it. That saving them is worth never having a life."

"Em—"

"No, listen. Because I need to say this and you need to hear it." She leaned forward. "You're my best friend. You've been my best friend since we were five years old. I know you, Josh. I know that you can't walk away when people need help. I know that you feel responsible because you brought us all here. I know you think the fact that the magic chose you means you're supposed to accept."

"It chose me for a reason—"

"Because you're incapable of walking away," Emily interrupted. "That's why it chose you. Not because you're special or powerful or the only one who can do this. Because you're the one who can't say no. And the magic is exploiting that."

"That's not—"

"It is." Her voice cracked. "You would give up everything—your entire life, your entire future—because you think that's what being a good person means. But Josh, there's a difference between being good and being self-destructive. And I'm watching you slide toward self-destruction while convincing yourself it's noble."

I didn't know what to say.

"I can't stop you," she continued. "If you decide to do this, if you decide to become guardian, I can't physically prevent it. But I need you to know—I need you to understand—that if you make that choice, you're not just giving up your life. You're taking something from all of us too. From your mom. From your friends. From everyone who cares about you."

"I know."

"Do you? Because right now, you seem pretty focused on the people you'd be saving and not very focused on the people you'd be leaving behind."

She wasn't wrong.

I'd been thinking about Mary, about the farmer, about the residents trapped in Hollow Fields. I'd been thinking about justice, about making things right, about correcting a 176-year-old wrong.

I hadn't been thinking much about what it would do to my mom to lose her only child. What it would do to Emily to lose her best friend. What it would mean for Tyler, Mike, and Olivia, who'd trusted me to lead them safely through this.

"I'm not making any decisions tonight," I said quietly. "I just wanted you to know what Elizabeth told me. Because you asked me to tell you if the magic asked me anything else. And this felt like something you should know."

Emily nodded, wiping her eyes quickly. "Thank you for telling me."

"Em, I promise—whatever I decide, I'll talk to you first. I won't just disappear. I won't make that choice without at least saying goodbye."

"That's not comforting."

"I know."

We sat there until the diner closed at midnight, not saying much, just being together. Because maybe this was one of a finite number of times we'd get to do this.

And maybe I needed to pay attention to that.

Maybe what the magic was asking wasn't just "Are you willing to stay?"

Maybe it was also asking: "Are you willing to leave everything else behind?"

And I still didn't know the answer.

CHAPTER 10: THE CALLING

TUESDAY - 3:47 AM

I woke up in the church.

Not dreaming about the church—actually there. Cold stone floor beneath me, smell of old wood and decay, straw hat hanging from the altar rail where the farmer had left it.

My heart slammed against my ribs. I was in my apartment. I'd fallen asleep at my desk reading Eliza's journal fragments. I was not in Hollow Fields. I could not be in Hollow Fields.

But the church felt solid. Real. The chill in the air bit through my t-shirt.

Are you willing?

The voice wasn't sound. It was sensation—magic pressing against my consciousness like a question written directly on my thoughts.

I tried to move, couldn't. Tried to speak, couldn't. Just stood there (when had I stood up?) facing the altar where Eliza's full journal waited.

You know what I need. You know what I am asking.

"I'm not ready," I managed to say.

Time is not infinite. The corruption grows. Without guardian, without vigilance, the curse strengthens. How long will you make them wait?

"I don't know if I can do what she did. Six years alone, holding back the council—"

She was not alone. She had purpose. She had calling. You search for where you belong. I am showing you.

The journal on the altar started glowing, pages turning on their own. I couldn't read the words, but I felt them—knowledge pouring into my consciousness. How to merge with land. How to maintain vigilance. How to become guardian.

How to give up everything else.

"JOSH!"

Emily's voice, distant but real. The church flickered.

"JOSH, WAKE UP!"

I gasped awake at my desk, Emily shaking my shoulder, her face pale and scared in the dim light of my apartment.

"You were talking," she said. "You were saying 'I'm not ready' over and over, and you wouldn't wake up."

I looked down. My hands were gripping the edges of my desk hard enough to leave marks. Margaret's journal was open in front of me, but I'd been asleep. Couldn't have been reading it.

"What time is it?" My voice came out rough.

"Almost 4 AM. I couldn't sleep, was driving past, saw your light still on." She pulled up my desk chair, sat down. "Josh, what's happening to you?"

"Bad dream."

"Don't." Her voice was sharp. "You were sleep-talking about not being ready, about holding back corruption, about six years. Those aren't random nightmare words. That's you processing what Elizabeth told you about Eliza."

I rubbed my face, trying to clear my head. The church had felt so real. I could still feel cold stone under my feet.

"It's calling you, isn't it?" Emily said quietly. "The magic. Like Elizabeth warned. It's starting."

"It was just a dream—"

"Joshua." Full name. "If this is starting, if the magic is reaching out to you even here, even this far from Hollow Fields, we need to know. We need to understand what we're dealing with."

I met her eyes. Saw fear there, mixed with determination.

"I dreamed I was in the church," I admitted. "It felt real. The magic was asking me again—are you willing. Showing me what guardianship means. Teaching me."

"Teaching you?" Her face went even paler. "What do you mean teaching you?"

"How to do it. How to merge with the land, maintain vigilance, become guardian. Like it was..." I struggled for words. "Like downloading information directly into my head."

Emily stood up fast enough to knock the chair over. "We're not going back. If the magic is already reaching you here, already trying to prepare you, then we absolutely cannot go back to Hollow Fields. It'll be even stronger there."

"We need Eliza's full journal—"

"We need to keep you away from that town before it claims you." She started pacing my small apartment. "This is exactly what Elizabeth warned about. The calling. The compulsions. You're already being pulled in."

"Em—"

"No. Listen to me. Your grandfather spent forty years researching the Golden Pickles and never once went to Hollow Fields. He understood there were some mysteries you don't try to solve because solving them costs too much. Maybe it's time we learned that lesson."

I wanted to argue. Wanted to point out that walking away meant Mary and the farmer and all the residents stayed trapped forever. But I could still feel the ghost sensation of cold stone beneath my feet, still hear the magic's voice in my head.

Are you willing?

"Let me think about it," I said.

"That's what you always say when you've already decided."

She wasn't wrong.

TUESDAY - 11:00 AM - LIBRARY

I skipped morning classes again. Couldn't focus. Every time I closed my eyes, I saw the church. Felt the magic probing, asking, teaching.

Tyler found me in the library stacks, surrounded by books on folklore, mythology, anything I could find about magical guardianship in other cultures.

"You look terrible," he said, sitting across from me.

"Didn't sleep much."

"Emily texted the group. Said you had a nightmare about Hollow Fields. Said the magic is already reaching for you." He pushed his laptop around so I could see the screen. "I've been researching all morning. Time dilation, spatial distortion, reality anchoring. Trying to understand what we're actually dealing with."

"Any luck?"

"Lots of theoretical physics that might apply if magic follows any natural laws, which it probably doesn't." He pulled up files. "But I found something interesting. Historical accounts of people who claimed to be called by specific places. Spiritually bound to locations. Most were dismissed as mentally ill, but the patterns match what Elizabeth described."

He showed me case studies. People who reported dreams about places they'd never been. Compulsions to travel to specific sites. Sensation of being taught information while sleeping.

"How many of them went?" I asked.

"Most. Nearly all." Tyler met my eyes. "And none came back the same. Some never came back at all. Josh, if this is what's happening to you—if the magic is already calling you—the historical precedent isn't good."

"I know."

"Do you? Because you're sitting here researching guardianship like you're planning to accept. Emily's freaking out. Mike wants to organize some kind of intervention. And you're just... researching. Like this is another puzzle to solve."

"Because it is a puzzle. There are people trapped in that town, Tyler. Real people who've been suffering for over a century. I can't just walk away because the solution is hard."

"The solution is you giving up your entire life. Forever. That's not hard, Josh. That's impossible."

"Eliza did it for six years—"

"And it killed her. They burned her alive because six years of that vigilance broke her down until she was vulnerable." Tyler leaned forward. "I know you feel responsible. I know you're the one the magic chose. But choosing you doesn't mean you have to say yes. You're allowed to walk away."

"Am I?" I closed the book I'd been reading. "Because the magic disagrees. It's calling me, Tyler. Even here, even this far from Hollow

Fields, I can feel it. And it's getting stronger."

"Then we keep you away. Transfer schools. Move to another state. Whatever it takes."

"For how long? The rest of my life?" I shook my head. "That's not living. That's running."

"Running is better than sacrificing yourself."

"Is it?"

Tyler didn't have an answer for that.

TUESDAY - 4:00 PM - OLIVIA'S APARTMENT

Mike had called an "emergency group meeting" at Olivia's place. When I arrived, everyone was already there, looking at me like I was a bomb that might go off.

"Intervention time," Mike announced. "Josh, sit."

I sat.

Mike paced in front of me like a lawyer delivering closing arguments. "Okay. Here's what we know. One: magic is calling you specifically. Two: Elizabeth said this would happen and get worse. Three: you're already having magic dreams where it's teaching you how to become guardian. Four: you're researching guardianship instead of ways to avoid it. Five: you've got that look on your face—the determined problem-solver look that means you've already decided but haven't told us yet."

"I haven't decided anything—"

"BS." Mike stopped pacing. "I've known you three months, and even I can tell when you're lying. These guys have known you for years. You're not fooling anyone."

Emily was sitting on Olivia's couch, arms crossed. "Mike's right. You're already planning it. Already figuring out how to be the one who stays."

"I'm considering options—"

"You're convincing yourself it's noble," Olivia interrupted. Her camera sat on the table, for once not in her hands. "I've been thinking about what Elizabeth said. About the magic identifying people who can't walk away. You know what that sounds like to me? Exploitation. The magic finds someone with hero complex and exploits that to get what it wants."

"It's not exploitation if the cause is real," I said. "Those people are actually trapped. Mary, the farmer, the residents—they're suffering. That's not manipulation; that's reality."

"But why does it have to be you?" Tyler asked. "Why can't it be someone else? Why can't we find another solution?"

"Because the magic chose me. It's marked me. I'm the one it's calling."

"So un-mark yourself," Mike said. "Tell it no. Walk away. Let it find someone else."

"There might not be someone else. What if I'm the only person in position to do this? What if walking away means they stay trapped forever?"

"Then they stay trapped," Emily said flatly. "I know that sounds cruel. I know it sounds selfish. But Josh, they're already dead. They've been dead for over a century. You're alive. You have a future. And I am not going to watch you throw that away for people who are already gone."

"They're not gone. They're trapped."

"THEY'RE GHOSTS." Emily stood up, voice rising. "You're talking about sacrificing your life—your entire life, everything you could be, everything you could do—for ghosts. For memories. For a town that's been abandoned for 176 years."

"They were people. They are people. Just because they're dead doesn't mean they don't matter."

"Of course they matter. But they don't matter more than you."

The silence after that was heavy.

"Look," Mike said, his voice gentler. "We get it. We understand feeling responsible. But there's a difference between trying to help and lighting yourself on fire to keep others warm. This isn't help. This is self-destruction dressed up as heroism."

"You don't understand—"

"Then explain it," Olivia said. "Explain to us why becoming guardian—giving up everything, existing forever as consciousness bound to cursed land—why that's better than living your life."

I tried to find words. Tried to articulate what I'd been feeling since the farmer asked if I was willing. The sense that this was what I'd been searching for. The purpose I'd been looking for since realizing I was stuck between rural and city, between grandfather's history and mother's science, between wanting to belong somewhere and never quite fitting in.

"Because maybe this is where I belong," I said finally. "Maybe this is what I'm supposed to do."

"You're twenty-one years old," Emily said, her voice breaking. "You don't know what you're supposed to do. Nobody knows at twenty-one. That's not belonging; that's latching onto first thing that makes you feel needed."

"It's more than that—"

"Is it? Because from where I'm sitting, you've been searching for purpose your whole life. And now magic literally hands you one—become eternal guardian, save trapped souls, be hero of story—and you're ready to jump at it without considering that maybe, just maybe, it's too good to be true."

"You think the magic is lying?"

"I think the magic doesn't care about your well-being. I think it needs guardian and you're vulnerable to manipulation because you've been looking for calling." She moved closer. "Josh, please. Please think about this more. Don't make this decision based on three days of magic dreams and sense of purpose. Give it time. Think about what you'd be giving up."

I looked around the room. At Emily's desperate expression. At Mike trying to find angle to negotiate my survival. At Tyler analyzing problem like equation to solve. At Olivia watching everything through eyes that had seen too much paranormal tragedy already.

They all cared. They were all trying to save me.

But none of them felt what I felt. The calling. The certainty that this mattered in ways I couldn't quite articulate.

"I won't make any decisions without telling you first," I said. "I promise. But we still need to go back for Eliza's journal. We need to understand what guardianship actually entails before deciding anything."

"Josh—"

"We need the information, Em. Even if I decide to walk away, we should understand what we're walking away from. That's just practical."

She didn't like it, but she couldn't argue with the logic.

"Friday," Tyler said. "We go Friday. That gives us three more days to prepare, research, and make sure everyone's on same page."

"And Josh?" Mike fixed me with serious look. "If the magic calls you again between now and Friday, you tell us immediately. No hiding it. No pretending you're fine. We need to know what we're dealing with."

"Agreed."

They didn't trust my agreement—I could see it in their faces. But they accepted it because there wasn't another option.

WEDNESDAY - 2:17 AM

The calling came again.

I was in bed this time, actually trying to sleep. But sleep became the church became standing at altar became magic flowing through my consciousness like cold water.

You know what I need.

"I'm not ready."

You do not have infinite time. The corruption strengthens. I weakened with each year after Eliza's death. The council's greed fed darkness. Now the barrier is thin. Without guardian, it will break entirely.

"What happens if it breaks?"

Hollow Fields becomes nexus of corruption. The magic that should flow naturally becomes poisoned. It will spread beyond the town. Beyond the forest. Into the land you call normal. Reality will warp. Time will fracture. And there will be no way to contain it.

"You're trying to scare me."

I am telling you truth. You have until October market. Three weeks. If guardian is not chosen by then, the barrier fails.

"Three weeks? That's—that's not enough time to—"

To decide? You have already decided. You resist naming it, but you know. You felt it when you first heard Mary's story. Felt it when you discovered Margaret's journal. Felt it when the farmer asked if you were willing. You know what justice requires.

"Justice requires me giving up everything?"

Justice requires someone stand in place of the one who was wronged. Eliza held this land for six years alone. She deserves rest. She deserves someone to take the burden. You understand this.

"Understanding doesn't make it easier."

Nothing worthwhile is easy.

I wanted to argue. Wanted to rage against magic that could ask this of someone. But deep down, beneath the fear and resistance, I knew it was right.

I had felt it. That pull. That sense of rightness when the magic first asked. Like tumbler clicking into place in lock I'd been trying to open my whole life.

Three weeks, the magic repeated. Choose.

I woke up shaking, 4:23 AM on my clock, text from Emily already waiting: Did it happen again?

Me: How did you know?

Emily: Because I'm watching your apartment. Your light came on. You've been standing at your window for five minutes.

I looked down. I was at window. No memory of getting out of bed.

My phone buzzed. Emily: I'm coming up.

She sat with me until dawn, neither of us sleeping, just being present while I processed what the magic had told me.

"Three weeks," she said finally. "Until October market."

"Yeah."

"That's the deadline. If you don't choose by then, the barrier fails and corruption spreads."

"That's what it said."

"Could be lying."

"Could be." I pulled my knees up to my chest. "But I don't think it is."

Emily was quiet for long time. When she spoke again, her voice was small, defeated. "You're going to do it, aren't you? You're going to say yes."

"I don't know."

"Josh."

"I don't know," I repeated, and that was honest. Part of me wanted to say yes immediately—to accept the calling, embrace the purpose, become the guardian the land needed. But another part—the part that loved my mom, loved Emily, loved the life I'd barely started living—wanted to run as far and fast as possible.

"I have three weeks to decide," I said. "Let me use them."

"Okay." She leaned her head against my shoulder. "But I'm not leaving you alone anymore. If magic is calling you at night, teaching you, pushing you toward decision, then you need someone here to anchor you to this world. To remind you what you'd be giving up."

"Em—"

"I'm not asking permission. I'm telling you. Until we figure this out, you're not alone."

And true to her word, she stayed.

We sat there watching sun rise over campus, over normal world where people went to classes and worried about exams and didn't feel magical lands calling them toward impossible choices.

A world I might only have three more weeks to belong to.

THURSDAY - 11:00 AM - ELIZABETH'S OFFICE

I needed to understand the timeline. Needed to know if magic was telling truth about three-week deadline.

Elizabeth listened to my dream account without interrupting. When I finished, she pulled out her family journals, flipping through them quickly.

"My grandfather wrote about this," she said, finding the passage. "The October market. He called it 'the thinning.' Every October, the barrier between Hollow Fields and normal reality weakens. That's when the Golden Pickles appear most reliably. When the farmer can cross over most easily."

"Why October?"

"Samhain. Halloween. The old celebration of boundary between living and dead becoming permeable. The magic follows ancient patterns." She showed me her grandfather's notes. "He theorized that major changes to guardianship could only happen during thinning periods. When barrier is already weak, transition is possible. Other times, it's locked."

"So the magic wasn't lying. Three weeks really is deadline."

"For accepting guardianship, yes. For the barrier failing..." She hesitated. "That's harder to verify. But based on my family's research, there's truth to it. The longer the land goes without guardian, the more corruption seeps through. Eventually, it will become unstoppable."

"How long is eventually?"

"We don't know. Could be years. Could be months. Could be weeks." She met my eyes. "But Josh, you can't make this decision based on fear that barrier might fail. The magic is using urgency to pressure you. That doesn't mean you have to accept."

"But if I don't, and people die because corruption spreads—"

"Then that's the magic's fault, not yours. You didn't create this situation. You're not responsible for fixing it."

"Aren't I? I'm the one it chose. I'm the one it's calling. Doesn't that make me responsible?"

Elizabeth sighed. "My aunt asked the same question. Right before she went to Hollow Fields for the last time." She closed the journals. "I can't tell you what to choose. But I can tell you this: whatever you decide, make sure it's really your choice. Not the magic's. Not guilt's. Not your friends'. Yours."

"How do I know the difference?"

"If you're choosing because you can't live with yourself otherwise, that's guilt. If you're choosing because magic is calling, that's compulsion. But if you're choosing because—after considering everything—this is what you genuinely want to do with your life, even knowing the cost... that's choice."

I thought about that as I left her office. Thought about it all through Thursday afternoon and evening.

Was I choosing guardianship because I wanted to? Or because I couldn't live with walking away?

And did the distinction even matter?

THURSDAY - 11:47 PM - MY APARTMENT

Emily was crashed on my couch, textbooks scattered around her. She'd moved in basically. Slept here, studied here, watched me constantly for signs magic was calling again.

It hadn't. Not since Wednesday night's warning about three weeks.

But I could feel it. Constant presence now, like background hum. Always there. Always waiting.

I pulled out my phone, started typing text to my mom: I need to tell you something important.

Stared at it for five minutes.

Deleted it.

Started again: I love you. I'm sorry.

Deleted that too.

What could I possibly say? "Hey Mom, might be giving up my life to become eternal magical guardian of cursed town. Just FYI."

She'd drive up here immediately. Try to talk me out of it. And the worst part was, she'd probably succeed. Because hearing my mom cry would break my resolve faster than any argument Emily could make.

So I didn't text her.

Didn't call.

Just sat there holding phone, thinking about how many conversations I might only have three more weeks to have. How many sunrises. How many normal moments.

"You're spiraling again," Emily said from the couch without opening her eyes.

"How did you—"

"I can hear you thinking from here. It's loud." She sat up, rubbing her face. "What time is it?"

"Almost midnight."

"Can't sleep?"

"No."

She moved to sit next to me on the floor, back against my bed. For a while, neither of us spoke.

"When I was eight," Emily said finally, "I broke my arm falling out of the barn loft. Compound fracture. Bone sticking out. Dad drove me to hospital, but I wouldn't let them set it until you got there. Do you remember that?"

I nodded. I remembered Emily's dad calling my house, my mom driving me to the hospital, Emily white-faced in ER bed but refusing treatment until I arrived.

"You held my other hand while they set the bone," Emily continued. "Told me stories about your grandfather's research. Distracted me from pain. You were eight years old and you were the only person who could make me feel safe enough to let them hurt me to fix me."

"Em—"

"I'm not telling you this to manipulate you. I'm telling you so you understand." She looked at me. "You've been the person I trust most in the world since I was eight years old. Since before I even knew what trust meant. And now I have to watch you consider giving that up. Giving us up. And I can't—" Her voice broke. "I can't make you stay if you've decided to go. But I need you to know what you'd be taking from me."

I didn't have words.

"Three weeks," she whispered. "We have three weeks. So before you make your decision, before you say yes to the magic, I need you to really be here. Present. Not half-gone already, not distracted by calling. I need you to really look at what you'd be leaving. Can you do that?"

"Yeah," I managed. "I can do that."

"Good." She wiped her eyes. "Because Friday we're going back to Hollow Fields to get that journal. And I need to know you're making this decision with full information. Not just what magic is showing you in dreams."

"I will be. I promise."

She nodded, then pulled me into hug that felt like goodbye already.

And maybe it was.

CHAPTER 11: THE SECOND CROSSING

FRIDAY - 6:58 AM

Emily knocked on my door at exactly 7 AM, three sharp raps that had become ritual over the past week.

"I'm awake," I called out. I'd been awake since 3 AM, actually, staring at ceiling and feeling the magic hum beneath my consciousness like distant music.

Three weeks. Choose.

She came in without waiting for invitation. She'd been doing that for days now—camping on my couch, monitoring me, watching for signs the magic was calling again. She brought coffee, set it on my desk with the kind of careful precision that meant she'd barely slept either.

"You feel it right now, don't you?" she asked. Not accusation. Just tired observation.

I nodded. No point lying. "It's stronger today. Knows we're going back."

"And?"

"And I can handle it."

"Joshua."

"I can," I insisted. "We need that journal. We need to understand what Eliza learned, what worked, what didn't. This is just information gathering."

"Information gathering that requires going back to a place that's actively trying to claim you as permanent resident." She sat on my bed, pulled her knees up. "We could send someone else. Mike and Tyler could go, get the journal, bring it back—"

"The magic marked me specifically. If we send someone else, it might not let them take the journal. Or worse—might mark them too."

"So you're saying you HAVE to be the one to go."

"I'm saying I'm already connected. Using that connection makes sense."

She stared at me, trying to read whether I was being logical Josh (assess risks, mitigate them) or martyr Josh (find excuses to throw self at danger).

I wasn't sure which one I was being anymore either.

"The others are already at the van," she said finally. "Tyler loaded all the equipment last night. Mike's got the rope system ready. Olivia's bringing both mechanical and digital cameras. We're as prepared as we're going to be."

"Okay." I grabbed my backpack—already packed with Margaret's journal, notebook, flashlight, protein bars. Normal gear for abnormal trip.

Emily caught my wrist as I reached for the door. "Josh. If the magic calls you while we're in there—if you feel it pulling you toward acceptance —you tell me. Immediately. Before you make any decisions. You promised."

"I know. I will."

She held my wrist a moment longer, then let go. "Okay. Let's get your information."

7:15 AM - THE VAN

Mike was doing equipment inventory when we arrived. Tyler sat in driver's seat running pre-departure checks. Olivia was arranging her cameras with the kind of focus that meant she was anxious and channeling it into preparation.

"Everyone slept great, I'm sure," Mike said dryly when he saw us. "We all look well-rested and ready for fun field trip."

"Speak for yourself," Tyler muttered, checking the GPS one more time even though it would stop working at the threshold. "I got maybe three hours."

"I didn't sleep at all," Olivia admitted. "Kept thinking about... what if we get stuck? What if time slips again and we can't find our way back?"

"We have better equipment this time," Tyler said, trying for reassuring. "Mechanical watches synchronized, compasses, those flour trail markers Mike made—"

"And rope," Mike added, holding up thick climbing rope. "We're literally tying ourselves together. Buddy system on steroids."

He started threading rope through everyone's belt loops, creating a linked chain with about fifteen feet of slack between each person. Josh at front, Emily behind him, then Olivia, Tyler, and Mike at rear.

"If anyone gets separated or time slips, we'll still be physically connected," Mike explained. "Can't lose each other if we're literally tied together."

"Unless the rope breaks," Olivia said.

"Thank you for that positive contribution," Mike replied.

Emily finished checking her medical kit, then pulled out printed paper—chart she'd made. "Timeline. We enter at threshold around 10 AM. Travel approximately two miles to church. Retrieve journal. Exit immediately. Total time in Hollow Fields: two hours maximum. If we're not back to threshold by noon, we abort and return next weekend."

"What if the church isn't where we remember?" Tyler asked. "Last time, things shifted around us. Buildings weren't always in same spots."

"Then we follow the trail markers from last time," Josh said. "The symbols carved in trees. Those guided us in before."

Everyone looked at me, and I realized I'd barely spoken since arriving. Normally I'd be the one running through the plan, checking details, making sure everyone understood the route.

But I couldn't focus. The magic was so loud now, like orchestra tuning up before performance. Not quite calling yet—just warming up. Letting me know it was ready whenever I was.

Are you willing?

"Josh?" Emily's hand on my shoulder brought me back. "You okay?"

"Fine. Just... thinking about route."

She didn't believe me. None of them did. But we were out of time for doubts.

"Let's go," Tyler said, starting the engine.

9:47 AM - APPROACHING THRESHOLD

The drive felt longer this time. Maybe because we all knew what waited at the end. Maybe because with each mile closer, the magic got louder in my head.

Not words anymore. Just presence. Constant awareness that something was waiting for me, had been waiting for me, would keep waiting as long as necessary.

Emily sat next to me in middle row, fingers laced through mine. Grounding me. Keeping me connected to present, to group, to choice not to answer the magic's question.

"I can feel it," I said quietly. "Even here, even this far out. It's like... like standing next to amplifier that's turned on but no music playing yet. Just the hum. The potential."

"We can turn around," Emily said. "We can turn around right now and drive back to campus and forget we ever heard about Golden Pickles."

"No we can't."

"Josh—"

"We can't," I repeated. "Even if we wanted to. Even if I wanted to. The magic has marked me, Em. It's not going to forget just because I drive away. Eventually, I'll have to answer. The only question is whether I answer with information or without it."

She was quiet for long moment. "So this was always inevitable."

"Maybe. I don't know. But I'd rather face it knowing what I'm actually choosing."

Tyler pulled into the same clearing as before—fallen log marker, dense tree line, exact spot where technology started failing. We all checked our phones: full signal, full charge, perfect normal function.

"Enjoy it while it lasts," Mike said. "In about fifty yards, we enter the dead zone."

We climbed out, Tyler distributing mechanical watches. Everyone synchronized to 10:00 AM exactly.

Mike checked the rope connecting us all, made sure it wouldn't snag or tangle. "Remember: if you feel time slipping, call out. If you see something that shouldn't be there, call out. If Josh starts walking toward magic with glazed eyes and talking about eternal vigilance, definitely call out."

"Not funny," Emily said.

"Little bit funny," Mike replied. But his eyes were serious when they met mine. "We're watching you, man. The second you start looking hypnotized, we're yanking you back out. Physically if necessary."

"Understood."

Olivia took starting photo—all five of us standing at threshold, roped together, mechanical watches showing 10:00 AM, last moment of normal reality.

"Okay," I said. "Let's get the journal."

10:12 AM (PROBABLY) - INTO HOLLOW FIELDS

The threshold crossing was worse this time.

Last visit, the shift had been gradual—slow dimming of bird sounds, subtle cooling of air, gentle time distortion. This time, it felt like walking through membrane. Like reality resisted our entry.

At exactly 10:04 (by my watch), my phone died. Not low battery gradually declining—just instant black screen. Tyler's GPS went dark same moment. Mike's digital watch blank.

"Threshold," Tyler confirmed unnecessarily. "We're in."

But I'd felt it before the technology failed. Felt the magic notice my return. Felt it recognize me.

You came back.

Not quite words. More like welcoming warmth spreading through my chest.

"Josh?" Emily's hand tightened on mine. "Your expression just changed."

"It knows I'm here."

"Define 'knows,'" Mike said, his voice careful.

"Like... recognition. Acknowledgment. Awareness." I tried to articulate what I was feeling. "Last time, the magic was examining me, testing me, asking if I was capable. This time, it already knows the answer. It's just... waiting for me to acknowledge it too."

"That's not ominous at all," Olivia muttered, raising her mechanical camera and winding it. Click. "For the record: 10:06 AM, approximately one hundred yards past threshold, Josh reports magic is 'waiting for him.'"

"You're documenting this?" Tyler asked.

"Someone has to. If Josh gets magic-claimed, at least we'll have timeline of how it happened."

"Also not helping," Emily said.

We continued walking, following the trail markers from last visit—carved symbols in tree bark, flour patterns Mike had left, signs pointing toward church.

The forest felt different. Last time, it had been eerie but navigable. This time, it felt aware. Like every tree was watching. Every shadow was listening. The magic wasn't just in the land anymore—it was in the air, in the light, in the space between moments.

At 10:19 (by Tyler's watch, though it felt like we'd been walking hours), the first building appeared: the farmhouse from last time. Same broken windows, same sagging porch. But now there was someone on the porch.

The farmer.

He sat in rocking chair that hadn't been there before, hat pulled low, perfectly still. Watching us approach.

We stopped at property line.

"Do we..." Olivia began.

"He's waiting for us," I said. "Specifically for me."

Emily's grip on my hand became painful. "We don't have to talk to him. We can go around, head straight for church—"

"He has information. We need it."

"Josh—"

But I was already walking forward, rope pulling taut between us until the others had to follow or cut me loose.

The farmer didn't move as I approached. Didn't speak. Just sat there, ageless eyes tracking my movement.

"We came back for the journal," I said when I reached the porch steps.

"I know." His voice was exactly as I remembered—rough, weary, impossibly old. "Magic told me. Told me you'd return. Told me you were beginning to accept."

"I haven't accepted anything. I'm gathering information."

"Information is acceptance's first step." He gestured to empty chair next to him. "Sit."

Emily pulled at the rope. "Josh, we don't have time—"

"Sit," the farmer repeated. "I have things to tell you. Things magic can't teach in dreams."

I hesitated, feeling magic's pull like warm current, feeling Emily's fear through rope connecting us, feeling the weight of choice pressing down.

Then I climbed the porch steps and sat.

10:23 AM - THE FARMER'S WARNING

For a long moment, neither of us spoke. The others stayed at property line, tethered to me by rope, watching tensely.

"You're feeling it now," the farmer said finally. "Not just questions anymore. Calling. Compulsion. The certainty that this is what you're meant to do."

"Yes."

"That's how it starts. How it started for me." He pulled off his hat, and for the first time I saw his face fully. Young. Couldn't be more than thirty, though his eyes looked ancient. "I was twenty-three when I accepted. Thought I was saving the town. Thought I understood what eternal vigilance meant."

"You were guardian?"

"Before Eliza. I was the first." He turned the hat in his hands. "The magic chose me because I couldn't walk away from people who needed help. Sound familiar?"

My throat felt tight.

"I accepted because the town was suffering. Plague, crop failure, corruption starting to seep in from old council magic. I thought: someone has to stand against it. Someone has to protect these people. And the magic said: yes. You. Be guardian. And I said yes."

"But you failed," I said. "The council corrupted the land anyway."

"Because I didn't understand what I'd agreed to." He put the hat back on. "I thought being guardian meant living in the town and protecting it. Like a sheriff. But that's not what it means. Being guardian means merging with the land. Becoming part of the magic itself. And when you do that... you stop being human in any meaningful way."

He stood up, moved to porch edge. "I couldn't eat. Couldn't sleep. Couldn't talk to people I was supposed to be protecting because I couldn't interact with them anymore. I was consciousness bound to land, aware but separate. Like watching life through window you can't open."

"Eliza did it for six years—"

"Eliza had no choice. She accepted when I failed, when council was already corrupting everything. She held them back because someone had to. But it destroyed her. Slowly, completely, until she was more magic than woman. And when they finally killed her body, her consciousness stayed trapped because she'd merged too deeply."

He turned back to me. "That's what you're considering. Not death. Worse. Eternal awareness without participation. Forever."

"Then why does the magic keep asking? If it's that terrible, why would it want someone to accept?"

"Because the land needs guardian. Magic can't protect itself. It needs consciousness, will, determination to hold back corruption. Without guardian, Hollow Fields becomes nexus of wrong. And corruption spreads."

"So someone has to do it."

"Yes. But it doesn't have to be you." He sat back down. "You're young. Twenty-one? You have entire life ahead of you. The magic is exploiting your sense of justice, your inability to walk away from injustice. But choosing to be guardian isn't justice. It's self-destruction."

"What about the people trapped here? What about Mary, what about the residents? Don't they deserve justice?"

"They're already dead. They've been dead longer than you've been alive. Giving up your life for theirs doesn't bring them back. It just adds you to the list of victims."

I wanted to argue. Wanted to point out that Eliza deserved rest, that the residents deserved freedom, that someone had to make things right.

But the farmer was watching me with eyes that had seen this exact argument too many times.

"You'll choose anyway," he said quietly. "That's why magic marked you. Because you're incapable of walking away. But I want you to understand what you're choosing. Not the noble sacrifice story you're telling yourself. The reality. The endless, conscious awareness without end. Forever."

He stood up. "Journal's still in the church. Take it. Read what Eliza wrote. Maybe her words will reach you in ways mine can't."

He walked inside his farmhouse, door closing with quiet finality.

I sat there, rope connecting me to Emily and the others, feeling magic's presence surrounding me like patient fog.

Three weeks. Choose.

Emily pulled the rope. "Josh. We need to go."

I stood up, walked back down porch steps. My friends' faces were mixture of fear, concern, determination.

"What did he tell you?" Mike asked as we resumed walking toward church.

"The truth," I said. "What being guardian actually means."

"And?" Emily's voice was tight.

"And we still need the journal."

10:51 AM - THE CHURCH

The church stood exactly where we remembered: white paint peeling, steeple leaning, doors slightly ajar. But this time, as we approached, I could feel it like gravitational pull. The magic was strongest here. This was the heart of whatever decision I'd eventually make.

"Everyone ready?" Mike asked, checking rope connections one more time.

We were as ready as we'd ever be.

I pushed the church doors open.

Inside, everything was as I remembered: broken pews, dusty floor, altar at far end. And on the altar, exactly where it had been before: Eliza's journal. Leather-bound, worn, filled with her handwriting and knowledge.

But this time, standing in front of the altar, was a figure.

Not the farmer. A woman.

Tall, dark hair, eyes that burned with intensity that made my breath catch. She wore simple dress from 1840s, and even though she was translucent—clearly spirit rather than solid person—her presence filled the church.

"Eliza," I whispered.

She nodded. "Joshua. You returned."

Behind me, I felt the others tense. Emily's hand found mine again.

"I came for your journal."

"I know. I've been waiting." She moved aside, gesturing to the journal. "Everything I learned is in there. Every technique for maintaining vigilance, every method for holding back corruption, every price I paid for this power. Take it. Learn from my mistakes."

I started to move forward, but she raised her hand.

"But first, you must understand something. I chose this because I had no alternative. The council had already poisoned the land. My family was threatened. People I loved were suffering. I chose to be guardian because every other choice had been taken from me."

She looked directly at me. "You still have choices. You still have life. Taking my journal is taking first step toward the path I walked. And that path ends only one way: with you becoming what I became. Consciousness without body. Awareness without life. Forever."

"The farmer said the same thing."

"Because he knows. Because I know. Because everyone who has ever considered guardianship eventually learns: this is not noble sacrifice. This is willing damnation." Her expression softened. "I see so much of myself in you. The determination. The sense of justice. The inability to accept that some wrongs cannot be fixed. That's why the magic chose you."

"Then you think I should refuse."

"I think..." She paused, and for first time looked uncertain. "I think you should understand what you're choosing before you choose it. My journal will tell you everything. But it will also make the calling stronger. Knowledge is weight. Once you understand fully what guardianship requires, the magic will expect answer."

"I'll give it one."

"In three weeks. At October market. When the barrier is thinnest." She stepped back. "Take the journal, Joshua. Learn what I learned. Just remember: some knowledge cannot be unlearned. And some questions, once answered, change you forever."

She faded then, dissolving into the dim light of the church, leaving only the journal on the altar.

I approached slowly, rope connecting me to my friends, feeling like every step was choice. Turn back now, walk away, keep the ignorance that allows normalcy.

Or take the journal, learn the truth, and know exactly what price the magic would ask.

My hand touched leather binding.

The magic surged through me like electric current, not painful but overwhelming. Information flooding my consciousness: techniques for merging with land, methods for maintaining vigilance, ways to extend consciousness beyond body.

Everything Eliza had learned. Everything I'd need to become guardian.

I gasped, nearly dropping the journal, but Emily was there, her arms around me, anchoring me.

"Josh! What's happening?"

"The journal—it's teaching me—showing me—"

"Put it down! Josh, put it down!"

But I couldn't. The knowledge was pouring in too fast: six years of Eliza's experience compressed into seconds, her memories becoming my memories, her techniques becoming my understanding.

How to merge.
How to protect.
How to endure.
How to sacrifice everything.

Are you willing?

The magic asked again, but this time with weight of full understanding behind it. This time knowing exactly what I'd be accepting.

"JOSH!"

Emily's voice broke through. Mike grabbed my shoulders. Tyler and Olivia were pulling the rope, trying to drag me back from altar.

I blinked, and suddenly I was on church floor, journal clutched against my chest, my friends surrounding me.

"How long?" I managed to ask.

"Thirty seconds," Tyler said, his voice shaking. "You touched it and just froze. Staring at nothing. We thought we'd lost you."

I looked down at the journal in my hands. Innocent-looking leather book that contained everything I needed to know.

And everything I wished I could unknow.

"We have what we came for," I said. My voice didn't sound like my own. "Let's go home."

11:34 AM - RETURNING TO THRESHOLD

The walk back felt longer. Or maybe shorter. Time was unreliable here even with mechanical watches.

I walked in daze, journal in backpack, Eliza's knowledge still echoing through my consciousness. I understood now. Fully. Completely. What being guardian meant.

The farmer was right. It was worse than death.

But I also understood why someone had to do it. Why the corruption would spread without active resistance. Why the magic needed conscious will fighting against the darkness.

Someone had to be guardian.

The question was whether that someone had to be me.

"Josh." Emily walked beside me, hand gripping mine. "Whatever happened in that church—whatever the journal showed you—you don't have to carry it alone. We're here. We're with you."

"I know."

"And you don't have to decide right now. We have three weeks. We can study the journal together, figure out if there's another way, find alternative —"

"There isn't."

She stopped walking, pulling me to halt through rope. The others stopped too.

"What do you mean there isn't?"

I turned to face her. "The journal taught me everything Eliza knew. Everything she tried. Every possible alternative she explored. There is no other way, Em. Someone has to be guardian. It's the only thing that works."

"Then we find someone else. We search for volunteers, we advertise, we find some other person who's willing—"

"The magic chose me. It marked me. It won't accept random volunteer. It needs someone specifically connected to this situation. Someone who understands the injustice. Someone who can't walk away."

"So you're saying you're going to accept." Her voice was breaking.

"I'm saying I understand what the choice is now. Really understand. And I have three weeks to decide if I can live with making it."

"You mean three weeks to decide if you can live with not making it," Mike said quietly. "Because we all know which way you're leaning, man. We can see it."

They were right. They could see it. Because the magic had shown me everything, and knowing everything made walking away so much harder.

"Let's just get back to campus," I said. "Study the journal. Make informed decision."

We walked the rest of the way in silence, crossed back through threshold at 11:52 AM (by our watches, though by Tyler's phone it was 2:47 PM—time slip of nearly three hours).

Climbed into van. Tyler drove.

I sat in back with journal in my lap and Eliza's knowledge in my head and three weeks to decide if I could refuse what I now fully understood.

The magic was quiet as we drove away.

But I could still feel it. Patient. Waiting.

It knew I'd be back.

CHAPTER 12: THE WEIGHT OF KNOWLEDGE

FRIDAY - 5:23 PM

We sat in my apartment, Eliza's journal on the coffee table between us like unexploded bomb.

Nobody wanted to touch it first.

Tyler had made coffee. Emily had ordered pizza. Olivia was arranging her cameras—the photos from today's trip, mechanical and careful. Mike paced, checking his phone, then checking it again even though he knew there were no messages.

All of us avoiding the journal.

"Someone should read it," Mike said finally.

"Josh already did," Emily replied. Her voice was flat. "In the church. It downloaded into his brain or whatever. Right, Josh?"

I nodded. "I have... I have Eliza's knowledge. Her techniques. Her understanding of how the merger works."

"So you don't need to read it again."

"No. But you do. If we're going to find alternative, you need to understand what she tried. What failed."

Olivia reached for it first. Opened to random page, started reading aloud:

> Day 847: The merger deepens. I can feel roots of oak tree on north boundary. Can sense rabbit warren beneath church. The land's awareness spreads through me like water through cloth. I am becoming less Elizabeth, more Hollow Fields.
>
> The technique for maintaining separation: focus on single memory. One moment of pure humanity. Hold it like anchor. I choose: my daughter's laugh. The sound of her joy. If I lose that, I lose myself entirely.

Olivia's voice cracked. She closed the journal. "That's... that's what it's like?"

"That's year two," I said quietly. "She lasted six years total. By year four, she couldn't remember her daughter's name."

Emily pulled the journal toward her, flipped pages. Read silently for several minutes. When she looked up, her face was pale.

"This isn't a manual for being guardian. This is a suicide note written over six years."

"It's documentation," I corrected. "Of process. Of what works and what doesn't."

"Josh." She stared at me. "Listen to what you just said. 'What works.' You're already thinking about how to do it, not whether to do it."

I couldn't meet her eyes.

Tyler took the journal next, scanning technical sections. "She tried fourteen different approaches to maintaining consciousness while merged. Only one worked longer than eighteen months." He looked up. "And even that one failed eventually. She just... dissolved. Became the land completely."

"That's why October market matters," I said. "She writes that the thinning periods—the quarterly markets—were only times she could manifest physically. Rest of the time, she was just... awareness. Consciousness spread across the land."

"Shoot," Mike said softly.

We sat in silence. Pizza arrived. Nobody ate.

Finally, Emily spoke. "Okay. Here's what we do. We spend this weekend analyzing every page. Every technique she tried. Every alternative she considered. We find the one she missed. The approach that works."

"Em—"

"No. We have two weeks and six days until deadline. We are not spending that time accepting the inevitable. We're spending it finding another way."

She opened her laptop. "I'm making spreadsheet. Every technique Eliza tried, why it failed, what we could modify. Mike, you research guardianship across cultures—see if anyone else solved this differently. Tyler, analyze the magic mechanics—find technical weakness we can exploit. Olivia, document everything—we need timeline of Josh's psychological state."

"What's Josh doing?" Mike asked.

Emily looked at me. "Josh is going to help us research. Right?"

I should have said yes. Should have thrown myself into finding alternatives. Should have joined their desperate hope that there was another way.

But Eliza's knowledge was in my head now. I'd seen every path she'd tried. Every alternative she'd explored. Every dead end she'd hit.

There wasn't another way.

"Right," I lied. "I'll help research."

SATURDAY - 2:17 AM

I couldn't sleep.

Eliza's techniques kept cycling through my consciousness. How to initiate merger. How to extend awareness across land. How to maintain identity core while dispersing into magic.

I got up, went to desk. Opened notebook.

Started writing what I understood. Not for them—for me. To organize what Eliza had taught me. To prepare for what I knew was coming.

The First Step: Willing Acceptance

Must approach merger without reservation. Magic reads intention. If any part of consciousness is resistant, merger fails or becomes unstable. Complete acceptance required.

Eliza's mistake: She accepted out of desperation. Fear-driven choice. Magic sensed the fear, made merger painful.

Better approach: Accept from genuine calling. From sense that this is where you belong. Magic responds to authentic choice.

I heard footsteps in hallway. My door opened.

Emily stood there in sleep clothes, her face exhausted. "You're researching."

"Couldn't sleep."

She came in, closed door. Looked at what I was writing. Her expression crumbled.

"Those are merger techniques."

"Em—"

"You said you'd help us find alternatives." Her voice broke. "You promised you'd research with us. But you're not looking for another way. You're practicing for the one way."

"I'm keeping notes. Understanding process. That's not the same as—"

"Stop lying to me!" Her voice rose, then dropped to whisper. "Josh. Please. Stop lying."

I set down pen. "Okay. You want truth? Eliza tried everything. Everything we're going to spend this weekend researching—she already tried it. It's all in her journal. Fourteen different approaches. Seven different alternatives. Twenty-three variations of technique. All failed."

"Then we find the twenty-fourth—"

"There isn't one." I looked at her. "The magic requires conscious guardian. Living will actively resisting corruption. That's not negotiable. And it specifically needs someone connected to this situation. Someone who understands the injustice. Someone the magic has marked."

"So find someone else it can mark. Advertise online. Find volunteers—"

"It chose me, Em. I felt it. In the church, when the journal transferred knowledge. The magic recognized me as match. That's not arbitrary. That's specific."

She sat on my bed, pulled knees to chest. "So you've decided. You're going to accept."

"I haven't decided. I'm just... preparing for possibility."

"That's the same thing." Tears on her face now. "You're already halfway gone. You're pulling away from us, from life, from everything normal. You're becoming guardian before you've even made the choice."

"I'm studying. That's not the same as accepting."

"Isn't it?" She looked at my notebook. "What was your plan? Spend two weeks secretly preparing, then announce on October market day that you're staying? Just disappear into the magic without letting us say goodbye?"

"I don't know. I haven't thought that far—"

"Because you can't think that far. Because thinking about what your choice does to us makes it too hard to choose." She wiped her eyes. "Let me make it harder, then. Let me tell you what happens if you become guardian."

"Em—"

"Your mom loses her only son. The kid who was supposed to carry on your grandfather's legacy. She'll blame herself for not seeing the signs. For not stopping you."

"She'll understand—"

"She won't. Nobody understands willing martyrdom. We just feel abandoned." Emily's voice was shaking. "And your friends—Mike, Tyler, Olivia, me—we'll spend rest of our lives wondering if we could have stopped you. If we'd been better friends, paid more attention, said the right thing at the right moment, would you have chosen to live?"

"That's not fair—"

"None of this is fair! That's the point!" She stood up. "You think you're being noble. Taking on burden nobody else can carry. But Josh, you're just running away. From life that's complicated and difficult and doesn't have clear purpose. The magic offered you meaning, and you grabbed it because it's easier than figuring out normal life."

"That's not true."

"Isn't it? You've spent your whole life searching for where you belong. For what you're meant to do. And first thing that offers you clear answer, you jump at it. Never mind that the answer is 'dissolve yourself into magic forever.'"

I didn't respond. Couldn't.

Because she was partly right.

"I'm going back to sleep," she said. "Or trying to. You should too. Because tomorrow, we're researching alternatives. All of us. Together. And you're going to actually participate. Not just pretend while secretly planning your exit strategy."

She left.

I sat at desk, looking at notebook full of merger techniques, feeling weight of her words.

Was she right? Was I running toward purpose instead of running toward life?

Or was I finally finding place I belonged, even if that place wasn't alive?

I didn't know anymore.

SATURDAY - 9:00 AM

Emily woke everyone early. We gathered in library study room she'd reserved, spreading out with laptops, books, printouts of Eliza's journal sections.

She'd made detailed spreadsheet overnight. Columns for: Technique, Duration Successful, Reason for Failure, Possible Modification.

"Okay," she said, voice determined. "We have fourteen documented approaches Eliza tried. Let's analyze each one. Find the variable she missed."

Technique 1: Partial Merger (Eliza's first attempt)
- Tried to merge with only part of consciousness
- Duration: 3 months
- Failure: Magic rejected partial commitment. Merger unstable. Physical body weakened rapidly.

"What if," Tyler suggested, "modern technology allows monitoring that she didn't have? Medical support, life support systems—"

"Magic actively resists technology," I said. "My phone died at the threshold. Your GPS stopped working. Life support wouldn't function in

Hollow Fields."

Emily wrote: Technology incompatible. Cannot modify.

Technique 2: Rotating Guardians (Eliza's third attempt)
- Tried to share burden with another volunteer
- Duration: 8 months
- Failure: Magic needs single consistent consciousness. Split attention weakened protection. Corruption began spreading.

"Multiple guardians taking shifts?" Mike proposed.

"Magic doesn't work in shifts," I replied. "Needs constant vigilance. One consciousness, always present, always aware."

Emily wrote: Cannot be divided.

We went through all fourteen techniques.

Every one: failed.

Every modification we proposed: already tried by Eliza or impossible due to magic's nature.

By 2 PM, Emily's spreadsheet was full of dead ends.

"There has to be something," she insisted. "Some approach that works."

"There is," I said quietly. "Complete merger. Full acceptance. Authentic choice driven by genuine calling rather than fear or obligation. That's the one approach that lasted longest for Eliza—five years before deterioration."

"Five years until she dissolved completely," Emily countered. "That's not success. That's slow death."

"It's five years of protection. Five years the corruption didn't spread. Five years the residents had peace."

"And then what? After five years, guardian dissolves and corruption comes back? So someone else has to become guardian? It's just endless cycle of sacrifice."

She was right again.

The magic needed guardian. Guardian eventually dissolved. New guardian required. Forever.

"Maybe that's the point," Mike said slowly. "Maybe it's not supposed to have permanent solution. Maybe the magic needs guardian precisely because the corruption is permanent threat. Like... like maintenance. Someone always has to be doing it."

"That's horrifying," Olivia said.

"Yeah," Mike agreed. "But it might be true."

We sat in silence.

Finally, Tyler spoke. "I researched guardianship in other cultures. Found seventeen different traditions worldwide. Guardians of sacred sites, protectors of magical locations, consciousness bound to land."

He pulled up his notes. "Every single one: same pattern. Guardian merges with land. Lasts years or decades. Eventually dissolves. New guardian needed. Continuous cycle."

"So this isn't unique to Hollow Fields," Emily said.

"No. It's apparently universal magical principle. Some places need conscious protection. That protection requires sacrifice. There's no hack. No technical solution. Just... acceptance."

Another silence.

"We should eat," Olivia said finally. "Can't research on empty stomachs."

We left library, went to campus café. Ordered food nobody wanted.

Emily kept checking her spreadsheet, looking for variable she'd missed. Mike scrolled through guardian traditions, searching for exception. Tyler analyzed magic mechanics, hunting for weakness.

I watched them research. Watched them fight. Watched them desperately search for answer I already knew didn't exist.

And I felt something settle in my chest. Heavy, but also oddly peaceful.

They were fighting because they loved me.

But I was going to lose this fight because I loved them.

Someone had to be guardian. The magic wouldn't accept random volunteer. It had chosen me specifically.

So the question wasn't whether someone would be guardian.

The question was whether I'd let that someone be me, or spend two weeks watching them torture themselves searching for alternative that didn't exist.

SATURDAY - 8:45 PM

We returned to my apartment. Exhausted. Frustrated. No closer to alternative.

Emily's spreadsheet: sixteen techniques analyzed, zero modifications viable.

Mike's research: thirty-two guardian traditions found, zero exceptions to sacrifice requirement.

Tyler's analysis: magic mechanics dependent on conscious will, no technical workaround possible.

Olivia's documentation: forty-seven photos of Josh looking increasingly accepting, increasingly distant.

"We'll start again tomorrow," Emily said, voice hollow. "Find the thing we're missing."

But she knew. They all knew.

There wasn't anything we were missing.

After they left, I opened Eliza's journal again. Read the final entries.

> Day 2,104 (Year 6): I can no longer maintain the memory. Sarah's laugh has faded. I tried to hold it, anchor to it, but consciousness is too dispersed now. I am more Hollow Fields than Eliza.
> The magic is gentle about it. Doesn't force dissolution. Simply... accepts my spreading awareness. Welcomes it. Like coming home.

> If anyone reads this: Do not mourn. I chose this. And for six years, I protected people I loved. That was worth the price.

> Final note: The calling will come to someone else eventually. When it does, tell them: This is not death. This is transformation. And some transformations are necessary.

I closed the journal.

Sat in dark apartment.

Made decision I'd been circling since Friday afternoon.

I would become guardian.

Not because I wanted to disappear. Not because life was too hard to face. Not because I was running from difficulty.

But because someone had to do it, and the magic had chosen me, and I couldn't live with myself if I walked away and let corruption spread.

That was the truth Emily couldn't see.

I wasn't running from life. I was running toward purpose. Even if that purpose required sacrificing everything else.

Two weeks and five days until October market.

Two weeks and five days to say goodbye without saying goodbye.

Two weeks and five days to be present with friends who didn't know they were losing me.

I could do that.

I could give them that.

SUNDAY - 10:00 AM

Emily knocked at 7 AM again.

This time, I was ready. Showered, dressed, coffee made.

"You look better," she said cautiously.

"Slept," I lied. "Feel clearer."

"Good. Because we're doing this again. All day. Until we find answer."

"Okay."

We gathered at library. Repeated Saturday's process. Analyzing techniques, proposing modifications, hitting dead ends.

But this time, I participated fully. Asked questions. Proposed theories. Engaged.

Not because I thought we'd find alternative.

But because Emily needed to see me trying. Needed to believe I was fighting alongside them.

If I was going to leave them, I could at least let them believe I considered every option first.

At 3 PM, Mike found something.

"Wait. Look at this." He pulled up research on Irish guardian traditions. "The Tuath Dé guardians. They weren't permanent. They served seven-year terms, then were replaced."

"How?" Tyler asked.

"Says here the outgoing guardian trained replacement. Transferred knowledge. Then... left."

"Left how?" Emily demanded.

Mike scanned further. "Doesn't specify. Just says 'returned to mortal life' after term ended."

Hope flared in Emily's eyes. "So it IS possible. Guardian doesn't have to be permanent."

"Maybe," Tyler said carefully. "But we don't know if Hollow Fields magic works the same way. Different land, different magic, different rules."

"But we could try," Emily pressed. "We could propose term limit to the magic. Seven years of service, then Josh returns. That's fair. That's reasonable."

I opened my mouth to explain why it wouldn't work—that Eliza's journal mentioned term attempts, that Hollow Fields magic was different, that consciousness merger wasn't negotiable once begun.

But Emily looked so hopeful.

"We could propose it," I said instead. "When we go back next weekend. Present it as option."

"Yes!" She grabbed her laptop. "Okay, I'm drafting proposal. Seven-year term. Conditions for service. Method of replacement. We present this to the magic as formal offer."

She typed frantically.

Mike and Tyler exchanged glance. They knew—like I knew—that it wouldn't work.

But they let her hope.

Because hope was all she had left.

SUNDAY - 11:30 PM

Everyone had gone home. Emily back to her apartment, finally, after three days of watching me constantly.

I sat alone with Eliza's journal.

Reread the section on term limits.

> Attempted to negotiate seven-year service with magic. Magic did not respond to negotiation. Merger is not contract. It is transformation. Once begun, cannot be reversed. Consciousness that spreads across land cannot be gathered back into single body. Would be like trying to un-pour water.

I closed the journal.

Emily's proposal wouldn't work.

But I'd let her present it anyway. Let her feel like she'd tried every option. Let her believe I'd considered every alternative.

Then, when magic rejected it, when we were out of options and out of time, I'd accept.

And maybe—if I framed it right—she'd understand.

Or maybe she'd hate me forever.

Either way, the residents would be free. Eliza would rest. Corruption would be contained.

That had to be enough.

MONDAY - 7:15 AM

Emily texted: One week until next weekend trip. Two weeks until October market. We're getting closer to answer. I can feel it.

I replied: Yeah. Getting closer.

Which was true.

Just not in the way she meant.

CHAPTER 13: THE FIRST MANIFESTATION

MONDAY, OCTOBER 14TH - 11:47 AM

Emily's Anthro 401 lecture got cancelled.

She texted Josh she'd be back early, got no response, and used her key to let herself into his apartment at 11:47 AM instead of the expected 2 PM.

The living room was empty. Josh's bedroom door was closed.

Emily set her backpack down quietly, about to call out, when she heard it.

Josh's voice. Talking to himself. Low, focused, like when he worked through complex problems.

"—feeling the connection. Grounding consciousness to earth. Like Eliza's journal described. Step 4 is—"

Emily's hand froze on her phone.

Step 4.

She moved toward the bedroom door. It was cracked open slightly. Through the gap, she could see Josh kneeling on the floor, both hands pressed flat against the hardwood.

And his hands were sinking.

Not breaking through. Not cracking the wood. Sinking. Like the floor was water and his hands were passing through the surface, submerging knuckle-deep into solid oak.

Emily's breath caught.

Josh's eyes were closed, face serene with concentration. "Anchor consciousness here. Feel the foundation beneath. The earth below the foundation. The network of—"

His hands sank deeper. Wrist-deep now.

"—spreading awareness through root systems. Sensing the—"

Emily shoved the door open. "What tha' are you doing?"

Josh's eyes snapped open. His hands jerked back—pulled free of the floor with a sound like suction breaking. He scrambled backward, breathing hard.

"Emily. I—you're not supposed to be back yet."

"My class got cancelled." She stared at the floor where his hands had been. The wood looked normal. Undisturbed. Like it had never been violated. "Josh. Your hands were in the floor."

"I can explain—"

"How long?" Her voice was sharp. Direct. "How long have you been practicing merger techniques?"

Josh's face went carefully neutral. The expression he used when he was about to lie and knew she'd catch him.

"Joshua Bennett," Emily said, using his full name. "How. Long."

He held her gaze for a long moment. Then his shoulders sagged.

"Since Saturday night."

The words hit like a physical blow.

"Saturday," Emily repeated. "Three days ago. When we were all researching alternatives, you were already—" She couldn't finish.

"I'm sorry."

"You LET US." Her voice was rising. "You let us spend sixteen hours researching solutions you already knew wouldn't work. You let me—" She stopped. Started again. "When did you decide?"

Josh looked away. "Saturday night. After we went through Eliza's journal. I realized there was no other way. The Steps were clear. Someone had to merge, and I was—"

"The only one stupid enough to volunteer," Emily finished. "Jesus, Josh."

"It's not stupid. It's necessary."

"Don't." She held up a hand. "Don't you dare make this sound noble. You made this decision three days ago and didn't tell anyone. You've been practicing becoming land while we've been desperately trying to save you."

"I needed to be sure—"

"Of what? That you could go through with it? That the process would work?" She moved closer. "Or that we'd waste enough time on alternatives that by the time we figured out what you were doing, it would be too late to stop you?"

Josh flinched. Direct hit.

"Emergency group meeting," Emily said, pulling out her phone. "Now. Everyone gets here by two PM or I'm telling them you've started the merger process without permission."

"Em—"

"Two PM, Josh. You owe them the truth."

She turned and walked out, leaving Josh kneeling on the floor where his hands had violated reality itself.

Behind her, she could have sworn she heard the floorboards creak. Like the wood was settling back into place after being disturbed.

Like the earth beneath was waking up.

MONDAY, OCTOBER 14TH - 2:17 PM

They gathered in Josh's living room. Mike arrived first, confused by the urgent summons. Tyler came with his laptop bag, sensing this was documentation-worthy. Olivia showed up last, camera already around her neck, intuition telling her to record.

Josh stood near the window. Emily sat on the couch, arms crossed. The others arranged themselves between, sensing the tension.

"So," Mike said, breaking the silence. "Who wants to tell us why we're here?"

Emily looked at Josh. "Go ahead. Tell them."

Josh took a breath. "I've started the preparation process. For the merger."

The room went still.

"What preparation process?" Tyler asked carefully.

"Steps 1 through 6. They have to be completed before Step 7—the core marker planting. I've been practicing since Saturday night."

"Saturday," Mike repeated. "While we were researching alternatives."

"Yes."

"While we were trying to find ways to save you."

"Yes."

Mike stood abruptly. "You let us spend sixteen hours researching. Knowing it was pointless. Knowing you'd already decided."

"I needed to be certain there were no alternatives," Josh said. "And there aren't. The journal is explicit. Someone has to merge, and I'm—"

"You're what?" Olivia's voice was quiet. "The chosen one? The martyr? The only person capable of sacrifice?"

"I'm the one who brought us to Hollow Fields," Josh said. "I'm the one who started this investigation. I'm responsible."

"BS," Emily cut in. "We all chose to come. We all investigated together. You don't get to claim sole responsibility so you can play hero."

Tyler had his laptop open, typing rapidly. "What Steps have you completed?"

"Steps 1 through 4. Started Step 5 this morning before Emily arrived."

"And Step 7?"

"Scheduled for Friday morning. Seven days before the October market. That gives the merger process the full week it needs to complete by the deadline."

Tyler's face went pale as he cross-referenced the journal. "That's... Josh, Step 7 is the point of no return. Once you plant the core marker, Steps 8 through 12 happen automatically. You can't stop them."

"I know."

"So you have four days," Tyler continued, voice shaking slightly. "Four days to change your mind. After Friday morning at—" he checked his notes, "—after Friday morning at dawn, you're committed. The process completes whether you want it to or not."

"I know," Josh repeated.

Mike's hands were clenched into fists. "There's always another deal, Josh. There's always an angle. You taught me that. Why aren't you looking for one now?"

"Because there isn't one." Josh's voice was steady. "I've read the journal seventeen times. I've cross-referenced every tradition Emily found. There's no alternative after the October market barrier fails. Someone has to merge. And it can't be—"

He stopped.

"Can't be what?" Olivia asked.

Josh looked at each of them in turn. "Can't be any of you. You all have lives, futures, people who need you. I'm—I'm searching for purpose. This IS my purpose. I can save everyone by doing this."

"By condemning yourself to eternal conscious existence," Emily said flatly. "By becoming land. By stopping being Josh."

"By protecting people. By making sure Hollow Fields never traps anyone again."

"For how long?" Mike demanded. "A year? Ten years? Forever?"

"Forever," Tyler answered, still staring at his screen. "Consciousness merged with land doesn't age, doesn't die, doesn't end. Josh would be aware, sensing everything within Hollow Fields' boundaries, for..." He looked up. "For eternity. Literally."

The weight of that word hung in the room.

Olivia raised her camera, then lowered it. "I can't photograph this. I don't know how to document someone choosing forever."

"Then don't," Josh said. "Just accept that it's necessary."

"It's not necessary," Emily argued. "There have to be alternatives we haven't found yet. We just need more time—"

"We don't HAVE more time," Josh interrupted. "Three weeks until the barrier fails. One week for the merger process itself. That leaves two weeks to find alternatives that don't exist." He moved away from the window. "I've made my decision. Step 7 happens Friday morning. Steps 8 through 12 complete automatically over the following week. By Monday October 21st at dawn, the merger is done."

"And you're gone," Mike said hollowly.

"And Hollow Fields has a guardian," Josh corrected.

Tyler was typing frantically now. "I need full transparency. No more secrets. I need to know every Step, every preparation, every stage of the process. If we're going to watch you do this, I'm documenting everything. Complete record. So if—when—someone else faces this situation, they'll have data."

"Agreed," Josh said.

"I want to photograph you," Olivia added. "Not the process. You. Human Josh. Before Friday. Before you start becoming something else. Will you let me do that?"

Josh nodded. "Yes."

They all looked at Emily.

"I'm never forgiving you for this," she said. "I'm going to help because abandoning you would be worse. But I'm never forgiving the choice. Never."

"I understand."

Mike was pacing now. "I can't—I need to think. I need to process. This is—" He stopped at the door. "I'm leaving. I need time. I'll be back Wednesday after I've... after I've figured out how to watch my friend commit suicide."

"It's not suicide," Josh started.

"It's worse," Mike cut in. "Suicide ends. This doesn't. You're choosing conscious existence forever. That's worse than death."

He left without looking back.

The remaining four sat in heavy silence.

Then Tyler spoke. "I'll stay. Document Steps 5 and 6. Verify the process matches the journal. Make sure you're doing this correctly if you're going to do it at all."

"I'll make dinner," Olivia said quietly. "Take photos. Preserve normal moments before Friday makes normal impossible."

Emily said nothing. Just stared at Josh with an expression that mixed fury and heartbreak in equal measure.

"Thank you," Josh said. "I know this is—"

"Don't," Emily interrupted. "Don't thank us for watching you disappear. Just... don't."

She stood and walked to the window where Josh had been standing earlier. Looked out at the campus, the normal world continuing its normal existence while their friend prepared to stop being human.

"Four days," she said to her reflection in the glass. "We have four days to change your mind or find an alternative. After that, you're committed."

"Em—"

"Four days, Josh. That's the window. So let's not waste it talking. Let's use it."

She turned back to face him, and her expression was determined despite the tears threatening to spill.

"If you're doing this, you're doing it with full understanding of cost. And we're bearing witness. All of us. Together."

Josh nodded. "Together."

But even as he said it, something moved in the corner of the room.

Just a flicker. A shadow where no shadow should be.

Tyler's head snapped toward it. "Did you see—"

"Yeah," Olivia whispered, camera already rising.

The shadow was gone.

But the air where it had been felt cold.

Wrong.

Like something from somewhere else had briefly manifested in Josh's apartment.

Emily looked at Josh, then at the corner. "What was that?"

"I don't know," Josh said, but his voice was uncertain.

Tyler's equipment suddenly beeped. Electromagnetic readings spiking. "This is... Josh, your apartment is showing the same energy patterns as Hollow Fields. How is that possible?"

"I don't know," Josh repeated.

But he did know.

The merger preparation was already creating a breach.

And something from the other side was starting to come through.

MONDAY, OCTOBER 14TH - 7:34 PM

They ordered pizza they barely touched. Olivia photographed the group sitting together—maybe the last normal meal before everything changed. Tyler monitored readings that shouldn't exist in a campus apartment.

And Josh felt it.

The pull of Hollow Fields, stronger than ever. Like the land was recognizing his commitment and reaching back.

Emily checked her watch. "It's getting late. We should—"

All the lights went out.

Not a power outage. The streetlights outside were still on. Just Josh's apartment plunged into darkness.

"Everyone stay calm," Mike said—when had he come back?—his voice tight.

Tyler's laptop screen provided the only illumination. "Electromagnetic interference. Something's disrupting the electrical system locally. Just this apartment."

"Josh?" Olivia's voice from the kitchen. "Where are you?"

"Living room. I'm—"

He stopped.

Because standing in the middle of the room, visible in Tyler's laptop glow, was a figure.

Translucent. Flickering. Like a projection from somewhere else.

It wore clothes from another century. Its face was hollow, eyes empty. And it was staring directly at Josh.

"Everyone see that?" Mike whispered.

"Yeah," Tyler confirmed, hands hovering over his keyboard. "Recording. Whatever this is, I'm getting it."

The figure's mouth moved. No sound came out, but Josh could read the lips.

"Join us."

"No," Josh said aloud. "I'm not—this isn't—"

The figure raised one translucent hand, pointing at Josh.

Then past Josh.

At the others.

"Bring them too."

"What?" Emily moved closer to Josh instinctively. "What does that mean?"

More figures materialized. Three, then five, then a dozen. All translucent. All from wrong time periods. All staring at the group with those hollow eyes.

"The land is waking," they said in unison, voices like wind through empty buildings. "The guardian comes. The barrier thins. Others may join. Others may merge. Become eternal. Become one."

"Get out," Josh said, voice stronger now. "You're not welcome here."

The figures flickered.

"You invited us. Your preparation opened the way. The breach grows wider with each Step. By Friday, we'll be free."

They faded slowly, dissolving into the darkness.

The lights came back on.

Everyone was pressed together in the center of the room, breathing hard.

"What the FUCK was that?" Mike demanded.

Tyler was frantically reviewing his recordings. "I got it. All of it. Visual, audio, electromagnetic readings. This is—Josh, this is proof. Proof that your merger is creating a breach between worlds."

"They said others could join," Olivia whispered. "They said we could merge too."

"No," Emily said immediately. "No. Absolutely not. Whatever they're offering, the answer is no."

Josh felt sick. "I didn't mean to—I was just practicing the Steps. I didn't know it would—"

"You're opening a door," Tyler interrupted, staring at his data. "Every Step you complete, the barrier between here and Hollow Fields gets thinner. By Friday when you plant the core marker, the breach will be—" He looked up, face pale. "Josh, what happens to this apartment when you complete the merger? What happens to campus?"

"I don't know," Josh admitted.

"The journal," Emily said urgently. "Does it say anything about geographical breach? About the land spreading?"

Tyler was already pulling it up. Skimming frantically. "Here. Step 11— final anchoring to land. 'The guardian's consciousness merges completely, stabilizing the barrier and sealing the breach. The land's influence returns to its original boundaries.'"

"So it DOES spread," Mike said. "It spreads until the merger completes. Then it snaps back."

"How far?" Olivia asked.

Tyler kept reading. "Journal doesn't specify. But based on tonight's manifestations appearing here, five miles from Hollow Fields... it could be significant."

Emily looked at Josh. "You're risking campus contamination. You're risking your friends being pulled in. You're risking Hollow Fields spreading to populated areas. And you didn't think to mention this?"

"I didn't know!" Josh protested. "The journal mentions breach but not— not THIS. Not creatures showing up. Not recruitment."

"Recruitment," Mike repeated. "They wanted us to join. Wanted all of us to merge."

"And they'll keep trying," Tyler said, still reviewing data. "As Josh progresses through Steps 5 and 6 this week, the breach will widen. More manifestations. Stronger manifestations. Building to Friday's Step 7 when the barrier is thinnest."

"Then we have four days," Emily said grimly. "Four days to either find an alternative OR help Josh complete Step 7 safely before the breach does permanent damage."

"I vote for finding an alternative," Mike said.

"There isn't one," Josh insisted. "We've been through this."

"Then we go through it again," Emily snapped. "Because option B is watching campus get contaminated by Hollow Fields while creatures try to recruit us into eternal consciousness. I'm not accepting that as inevitable."

A phone buzzed. Tyler's. He checked it, face going white.

"What?" Olivia asked.

"Campus alert. Multiple students reporting 'atmospheric anomalies' tonight. Shadows moving wrong. Voices where no one's present. Cold spots in dorm rooms." He looked up. "It's already spreading. The breach is already wider than we thought."

The group exchanged horrified looks.

"Four days," Emily repeated. "We work together for four days. Josh continues preparation because we can't risk the barrier failing. But we also research alternatives because we can't accept eternal consciousness as the only option. And we stay together because those creatures will try to pick us off individually."

"Agreed," Mike said. "Strength in numbers."

"I'm staying here tonight," Olivia added. "Not going back to my dorm alone after that."

"Same," Tyler said. "I'll monitor readings. Document any additional manifestations."

Emily looked at Josh. "This is happening whether we like it or not. So we're doing it together, with full transparency. No more secrets. No more solo decisions. Clear?"

"Clear," Josh agreed.

But as they settled in for the night—Mike and Tyler taking the couch, Olivia claiming the armchair, Emily spreading out on Josh's bedroom floor —none of them could shake the memory of those hollow eyes.

"Join us."

The offer hanging in the air like a threat.

Or a promise.

TUESDAY, OCTOBER 15TH - 3:23 AM

Emily woke to the sound of whispers.

She lay perfectly still on Josh's bedroom floor, listening. The whispers were coming from everywhere and nowhere. Like the walls themselves were speaking.

"Emily Bennett. Cousin. Friend. Skeptic."

She sat up slowly. Josh was asleep in his bed, breathing evenly. The door to the living room was closed.

"You demand evidence. We provide it. You seek truth. We offer it. Join him. Witness eternity together."

"I'm dreaming," Emily whispered.

"You are awake. As awake as you have ever been. More awake than the sleeping world outside."

A figure materialized at the foot of Josh's bed. Not translucent like the ones from earlier. Solid. Real. Wearing clothes Emily recognized.

Josh's grandfather.

"No," Emily said. "You're not him. He's been dead for eight years."

The figure smiled. Josh's grandfather's smile. "I watched him grow. Taught him to see patterns. He was searching for purpose, and I gave him mystery. Now mystery gives him purpose."

"You're not real."

"I am memory. Memory made manifest. The land remembers everyone who touched it. Everyone who wondered. I am what Josh carries of his grandfather. And when he merges, I will be preserved. Part of him. Part of the land. Forever."

Emily's throat tightened. "That's not comfort. That's horror."

"Is it? To be remembered perfectly? To never fade? Most memories blur with time. Die when carriers die. But land remembers. Land preserves. Josh will carry his grandfather forever. And you could carry Josh."

"No."

"You love him. Sibling love. Lifelong bond. When he merges, that bond severs. Unless you join. Then connection remains. You could speak to him. Know him. Be with him. Not separate. Not grieving. Together."

Emily stood, hands clenched. "Get out of my head."

"We're not in your head. You're in ours. The moment you decided to help Josh, the moment you agreed to stay, you entered our awareness. The land knows you now, Emily Bennett. The land sees your love. The land offers permanence."

"I said GET OUT."

The figure dissolved.

But the whispers remained. Following Emily as she fled Josh's bedroom, stumbling into the living room where Tyler was awake, monitoring equipment.

"You heard them too," Tyler said. It wasn't a question.

Emily nodded, not trusting her voice.

"They offered me data," Tyler said quietly. "Complete understanding of the process. Every technical detail. All the measurements I can't capture with instruments. They said if I merged, I could KNOW. Really know. Not just document from outside but experience from inside."

"What did you say?"

"I said no." Tyler looked at his screens. "But I wanted to say yes. For a second, I wanted it. Complete understanding. No more questions. No more failed equipment. Just... knowing."

Mike sat up on the couch. "They got me too. Showed me infinite deals. Every negotiation I ever lost, replayed with perfect solutions. Showed me becoming a negotiator between worlds. Infinite leverage. Infinite angles. All I had to do was say yes."

Olivia's voice came from the armchair. "They showed me truth. Real paranormal activity. Not distant glimpses but full immersion. Every question I've had since my last group disbanded, answered. All I had to do was merge. Experience directly. Become the documentation."

Emily looked at the three of them. "They're targeting us specifically. Personal temptations based on what we want most."

"It's effective," Mike admitted. "I almost—for a second—I almost called out. Almost agreed."

"So did I," Tyler said.

"Me too," Olivia whispered.

They looked at each other, the reality sinking in.

"They're not going to stop," Emily said. "Josh progresses through Steps 5 and 6 this week, the breach gets wider, the offers get stronger. By Friday, the temptation might be—"

"Irresistible," Mike finished. "We might not be able to say no."

Tyler was typing, documenting. "Then we don't go anywhere alone. We stay together. Watch each other. If someone starts to give in, the others intervene."

"Buddy system," Emily agreed. "No one faces the offers solo."

A noise from Josh's bedroom. They all froze.

Josh appeared in the doorway, face pale. "They're in my head too. Showing me all of you joining. Showing me we'd be together forever. That I wouldn't lose anyone. That the merger wouldn't separate us." His voice cracked. "They made it sound beautiful."

"It's not beautiful," Emily said firmly. "It's a trap. They want multiple guardians. Want all of us bound. That's not saving each other. That's condemning each other."

"I know," Josh said. "But knowing doesn't make the offer less tempting."

They stood in the pre-dawn darkness, surrounded by equipment that couldn't fully measure what was happening, fighting an offer that grew stronger by the hour.

"Four more days until Step 7," Tyler said. "Four more days of this getting worse."

"Then we document everything," Emily said. "Track the pattern. Understand the mechanism. Knowledge is our defense."

"And we stay together," Olivia added. "Witness for each other."

Mike nodded. "Strength in numbers. They can tempt individuals. But five of us watching each other? That's harder."

"Agreed," Josh said. "No one goes anywhere alone. We're a unit until this is done."

But as they settled back into uneasy vigil—none of them willing to sleep again—the whispers continued.

Softer now.

Patient.

Waiting for the moment when defenses weakened.

When temptation outweighed resistance.

When one of them said yes.

TUESDAY, OCTOBER 15TH - 11:17 AM

Classes were optional now.

Not officially. But when three separate professors dismissed students early citing "feeling unwell" and two others never showed up, the unofficial cancellation spread across campus.

Tyler pulled campus security reports. Overnight: forty-three students reported nightmares involving recruitment. Seventeen reported seeing figures in their rooms. Nine reported hearing whispers offering impossible things.

"It's spreading exponentially," Tyler said, showing the data. "Last night was campus-wide. Five miles in every direction from Josh's apartment."

"And it's only Tuesday," Mike said. "We have three more days until Step 7."

Josh was practicing Step 5—emotional severance. His face was carefully neutral as he worked through the meditation, trying to create distance between consciousness and feeling. But Emily could see the strain around his eyes.

"Josh," she said carefully. "What happens if you DON'T complete Step 7 on Friday?"

He opened his eyes. "The barrier fails on November 1st. Without a guardian to stabilize it. Hollow Fields spreads uncontrolled. The breach doesn't close. It expands."

"But what if someone else merges?" Olivia asked. "What if we find another volunteer?"

"Takes eight days," Josh said. "We don't have eight days after the barrier fails. The contamination would be irreversible by then."

Tyler's phone buzzed. Then Olivia's. Then Mike's.

Campus emergency alert.

SEVERE WEATHER ADVISORY: Unusual atmospheric conditions predicted for Wednesday. Students advised to remain indoors. Details to follow.

"Severe weather," Mike read aloud. "In October. With clear skies."

Tyler was already pulling weather data. "No storm system within three hundred miles. No meteorological explanation for this advisory."

"It's not weather," Emily said quietly. "It's the breach. They're coding it as weather because they can't explain the real cause."

Josh's phone showed a different alert. From campus administration.

TO: All students in Patterson Hall (Josh's building)
RE: Temporary relocation

Due to unexpected maintenance requirements, residents of Patterson Hall may request temporary housing reassignment. Contact housing office for details.

"They're trying to evacuate your building," Olivia said, reading over his shoulder. "Without saying why."

"They can't explain why," Tyler said. "So they're calling it maintenance. But look—" He pulled up a campus map, overlaying security reports. "Every manifestation, every report, every anomaly—all within a five-mile radius of this apartment. Command wants people out of the contamination zone without admitting there IS a contamination zone."

Mike looked at Josh. "If you left. If you went somewhere else to complete the merger. Would the breach follow you?"

"Don't know," Josh admitted. "Journal doesn't address it. But consciousness is anchoring here because I'm here. If I moved—"

"The breach moves too," Emily finished. "You're not just opening a door. You ARE the door."

"So we can't evacuate," Olivia said. "Because wherever Josh goes, the problem goes."

"And we can't stop the preparation," Tyler added, "because stopping means the barrier fails on November 1st with no guardian. Campus contamination becomes permanent."

They sat in grim silence, the logic box tightening around them.

"There's no good option," Mike said finally. "Every choice makes things worse."

"There's one option," Josh said quietly. "The one I already chose. Complete Step 7 on Friday. Accept the temporary breach expansion. Trust that Step 11 on Monday stabilizes everything and pulls the contamination back."

"Temporary," Emily repeated. "You're betting that eight days of expanding breach will be reversible."

"The journal says—"

"The journal was written by someone who SUCCEEDED," Emily interrupted. "We don't have journals from the people who FAILED. We don't know if the contamination is actually reversible or if that's just what Eliza believed."

Tyler was typing. "Running probability models. If the breach expands at current rate through Friday, peaks during the weekend, stabilizes Monday... the contamination radius would be approximately—" He stopped. Looked up. "Thirty miles. Maybe more."

"Thirty MILES?" Mike stood abruptly. "Josh, that's not just campus. That's the whole city. That's hundreds of thousands of people exposed to recruitment offers, manifestations, reality breakdown—"

"For four days," Josh said. "Friday through Monday. Four days of breach, then it stabilizes and pulls back."

"IF it pulls back," Emily said. "IF the journal is right. IF nothing goes wrong. That's a lot of ifs to bet an entire city on."

Josh's hands were shaking. "Then what do you want me to do? Stop preparing? Let the barrier fail on November 1st and make it permanent? At least my way, there's a chance—"

"At least your way, you're committed by Friday," Emily shot back. "Step 7 is irreversible. After that, you CAN'T stop even if we find an alternative. Even if the breach becomes catastrophic. Even if—"

She stopped.

Because standing in the corner of the room was a figure.

Solid. Clear. Wearing clothes from the 1800s.

"You argue," the figure said. Its voice was hollow, echoing. "You debate. You search for better options. But there are no better options. There is only acceptance. Or there is catastrophe."

"Who are you?" Josh demanded.

"I was the guardian before Eliza. I merged in 1847. I know what waits. I know the cost." The figure moved closer. "And I know that hesitation does not prevent catastrophe. It only delays the choice until choice becomes impossible."

"You're trying to rush us," Emily said. "Make us commit before we've exhausted alternatives."

"There ARE no alternatives. The magic demands a guardian. The barrier requires anchoring. The land needs consciousness. These facts do not change because you wish them to."

Mike stood. "Then prove it. Show us what happens if Josh doesn't merge. Let us see the future where he walks away."

The figure was silent for a long moment.

Then it gestured.

The apartment dissolved.

They stood in the same location, but campus was transformed. Buildings crumbling. Vegetation wild, overtaking pavement. And everywhere— EVERYWHERE—translucent figures wandering. Students who'd said yes to recruitment. Merged but imperfectly. Trapped between human and land. Conscious but fragmented.

"This is November 15th," the figure said. "Two weeks after the barrier failed. This is what happens when there is no guardian. When the breach expands unchecked. When offers are accepted by desperate people seeking escape."

They watched in horror as a translucent student walked through a wall, barely aware of the physical world. Watched as another stood motionless, staring at nothing, consciousness diffused too far to maintain coherent thought.

"They merged seeking connection," the figure continued. "But without proper anchoring, without the Steps, they became lost. Neither human nor land. Aware but ungrounded. Suffering but unable to die."

"Stop," Olivia whispered. "Please stop."

The vision dissolved. They were back in the apartment.

The figure looked at Josh. "You know what you must do. You have always known. The only question is whether you act with time to prepare, or whether you wait until desperation forces imperfect merger on someone less ready."

It faded.

Leaving them standing in the restored apartment, the vision's implications hanging heavy.

"Okay," Mike said finally. "Okay. That was—that was effective manipulation. Show us the worst possible outcome, imply Josh's way is the only alternative. Classic scare tactic."

"Except it might be true," Tyler said quietly. "My projections show similar results if the barrier fails without a guardian. Not exactly that, but... similar. Contamination spreading. People attempting merger without preparation. Failure cascade."

Emily looked at Josh. "You saw the same thing we saw."

Josh nodded. "Yeah."

"And you still think Friday is the right choice."

"I think Friday is the ONLY choice," Josh said. "And I think every hour we delay is an hour the breach expands further before I can stabilize it."

"Then we have three days," Emily said. "Three days to verify there really are no alternatives. Three days to prepare for what Friday means. And three days to accept that we're going to watch you become something else."

She looked around at the others. "Anyone leaving?"

No one moved.

"Then we stay," Emily said. "Together. Whatever comes."

"Whatever comes," they echoed.

But outside the window, the afternoon sky was darkening.

Not with clouds.

With something else.

Something wrong.

And on campus, students were beginning to notice.

Beginning to ask questions administrators couldn't answer.

Beginning to feel the pull of offers they didn't understand.

The breach was widening.

And they had seventy-two hours until it became irreversible.

WEDNESDAY, OCTOBER 16TH - 6:47 AM

The fog shouldn't exist.

Emily woke to the sound of campus emergency sirens. She stumbled to the window and stopped.

Fog.

Thick, rolling fog that obscured buildings twenty feet away. Fog that moved wrong—not drifting but flowing, purposeful, searching.

And inside the fog, shapes moved.

Not quite human. Not quite anything else.

"Josh," she said, not taking her eyes off the window. "Josh, wake up."

He appeared beside her, Tyler and Mike and Olivia joining a moment later.

They stared down at campus transformed.

The fog was everywhere. Covering everything. And the shapes inside it were becoming clearer.

Creatures.

No longer translucent. No longer flickering.

Solid. Real. Walking through campus like they belonged there.

"Step 5," Josh whispered. "I completed Step 5 last night. Emotional severance. The journal said it would strengthen the breach but not—not like this."

Tyler's equipment was screaming. Readings off every scale. "The barrier isn't just thin. It's permeable. Hollow Fields is bleeding through."

On campus, students emerged from dorms, phones out, recording the impossible fog. Some were filming the shapes. Others were backing away. A few stood motionless, staring at the creatures with expressions of recognition.

"They're seeing recruitment offers," Olivia said. "Look—that girl there. She's listening to something. And that guy—he's reaching toward a creature like—"

"Like he's about to say yes," Mike finished.

Emily grabbed her phone. "We need to warn people. Tell them not to engage. Not to listen."

"Tell them what?" Josh asked. "Don't listen to the centuries-old creatures offering everything you want most? Don't accept eternal consciousness? They won't understand. They can't understand. Not without context."

"Then we give them context," Emily said. "Tyler, can you upload your documentation? Make it public?"

"Already doing it," Tyler said, typing frantically. "Creating repository. Uploading every recording, every reading, every piece of evidence. If people are going to face this, they need information."

A knock at the door.

They froze.

The knock came again. Polite. Patient.

Josh moved to answer, but Mike blocked him. "Let me check first."

He looked through the peephole, then stepped back, face pale.

"It's one of them," he said. "A creature. Standing in the hallway. Just... waiting."

"Don't open it," Olivia said immediately.

Another knock.

Then a voice. Clear. Human. Familiar.

"Joshua. We need to speak with you. Regarding Friday's Step 7. There are... complications."

Josh recognized the voice. His history professor. Dr. Morrison. Who'd died three years ago.

"Josh, no," Emily warned.

But Josh was already opening the door.

Dr. Morrison stood in the hallway. Looking exactly as Josh remembered. Except for the eyes. The eyes were wrong. Too aware. Too ancient.

"Thank you for answering," Dr. Morrison said. "May I come in? We have much to discuss. And very little time before the fog brings others who will be... less reasonable."

Josh looked back at his friends. Then at Dr. Morrison.

"Come in," he said.

And stepped aside to let the creature enter his apartment.

Behind it, the fog in the hallway swirled.

Waiting.

Hungry.

Reaching.

CHAPTER 14:
CREATURES IN THE FOG

WEDNESDAY, OCTOBER 16TH - 6:52 AM

Dr. Morrison stood in Josh's living room, looking exactly as he had three years ago before the heart attack. Tweed jacket with elbow patches. Wire-rimmed glasses. The same patient expression he'd worn when students struggled with complex historical analysis.

Except his eyes held centuries.

"You're not Dr. Morrison," Josh said.

"I am and I'm not," the figure replied. "I'm what the land preserved of him. He visited Hollow Fields twice in the 1980s. Researching local folklore for a paper he never finished. The land remembers him. When you opened the breach, those memories became... accessible."

Emily had her phone out, recording. "What do you want?"

"To warn you." Dr. Morrison—the thing wearing his form—moved to the window. The fog outside was thickening. "Friday's Step 7. You're planning to plant the core marker at dawn. 7:23 AM, according to optimal magical timing."

"Yes," Josh said carefully.

"You'll fail."

The word dropped like a stone.

Tyler looked up from his laptop. "Explain."

"The breach is wider than historical precedent. When previous guardians reached Step 7, the contamination radius was perhaps a mile. Manageable. Containable." Dr. Morrison gestured at the fog-shrouded campus. "This is five miles on Wednesday. By Friday, it will be fifteen. Maybe twenty. And everything within that radius will experience the overlap."

"Overlap?" Olivia asked.

"The moment of core marker planting. When consciousness anchors to land. For approximately seventeen minutes, the barrier dissolves completely. This world and Hollow Fields occupy the same space. Previous guardians did this in isolated areas. You're doing it in the center of a populated campus."

Mike's face went pale. "Seventeen minutes of complete overlap. With thousands of students in range. What happens to them?"

"They experience Hollow Fields directly. See the cursed town. Encounter its inhabitants. Face recruitment offers at maximum intensity." Dr. Morrison's borrowed face showed something like sympathy. "Most will resist. But some won't. And those who say yes during the overlap—their merger won't be anchored like Joshua's. They'll become lost. Fragmented. Like the vision you were shown yesterday."

"Then we evacuate campus," Emily said immediately. "Get everyone out by Friday morning."

"You have forty-eight hours to evacuate fifteen thousand students without causing panic or explaining why." Dr. Morrison shook his head. "And evacuation won't help. The overlap follows Joshua. Wherever he plants the marker, the breach opens. Move him to the woods? You just expand contamination to wildlife and hikers. Move him to the city? You expose hundreds of thousands."

Josh felt sick. "So what do I do?"

"Complete Step 7 as planned. Accept the cost. Seventeen minutes of overlap is survivable. Permanent barrier failure is not." Dr. Morrison moved toward the door. "I came to ensure you understood the stakes. And to ask that you prepare your friends. Because they'll experience the overlap too. They'll see what you're becoming. And some of them may not survive the seeing."

"Wait," Josh said. "What does that mean?"

But Dr. Morrison was already fading, becoming translucent.

"The land is waking, Joshua. And when it fully opens its eyes, not everyone can bear the sight."

He dissolved completely.

Leaving them standing in the apartment while outside, the fog grew thicker.

And the shapes inside it grew bolder.

WEDNESDAY, OCTOBER 16TH - 9:34 AM

Classes were officially cancelled.

The administration tried to frame it as a precautionary measure due to "atmospheric anomalies," but students weren't stupid. They could see the creatures walking through fog. Hear the whispers promising impossible things. Feel reality bending around them.

Tyler's uploaded documentation had three thousand views in two hours. Six thousand by lunch. Students were sharing it, trying to understand what was happening.

Some of the comments made Josh's stomach turn.

"I heard the offer. It sounded beautiful. Should I say yes?"

"My roommate walked into the fog an hour ago. She hasn't come back. She's just standing there, listening to something."

"The creature looks like my dead brother. It knows things only he would know. How is that possible?"

Tyler was monitoring campus security feeds. "Seventeen students have approached creatures in the last three hours. Fourteen returned to their dorms. Three are still standing in the fog. Just... listening."

"Someone needs to pull them out," Mike said.

"I tried." Tyler's voice was hollow. "Sent message to campus security. They responded that they're 'monitoring the situation' but not intervening unless students are in 'immediate physical danger.'"

"Listening to recruitment offers IS immediate danger," Emily snapped.

"They don't understand that," Olivia said quietly. She had her camera out, photographing the fog through the window. "To them, it's just students standing outside. They can't see what we see. Can't hear what we hear."

Josh moved to the window. In the fog below, he could make out shapes. More creatures than before. Dozens. Maybe hundreds. And among them, students. Some backing away. Others moving closer. One girl had her hand extended, almost touching a translucent figure.

"I'm going down there," Josh said.

"No," Emily said immediately. "You go out there, every creature will target you. You're the one completing the merger. They want you specifically."

"Then they'll get me. But maybe I can pull those students back first."

"Josh—"

"Emily, I'm the reason this is happening. My preparation opened the breach. Those students are in danger because of MY choice. I have to at least try."

Mike stood. "Then I'm coming too. You go out there alone, you'll be swarmed."

"Same," Tyler said. "Someone needs to document."

Olivia was already checking her camera. "And someone needs to record for the students who can't see what's really happening."

Emily looked at all of them. Then nodded. "Fine. But we stay together. Formation. Don't let creatures separate us."

They headed down.

WEDNESDAY, OCTOBER 16TH - 9:47 AM

The fog was worse up close.

It moved like liquid, flowing around buildings, seeping under doors. And it was cold—not weather cold, but wrong cold. The cold of something that had never been alive.

The creatures noticed them immediately.

A woman in Victorian dress turned, her hollow eyes focusing on Josh. "The guardian comes. The one who opens. The one who anchors."

More creatures converged. A man in colonial clothing. A child from the 1920s. A teenager in 1960s attire. All translucent. All ancient. All staring.

"We're just here for the students," Mike said, voice steady despite the fear. "The living ones. They need to go inside."

"Why?" asked the Victorian woman. "Inside is separation. Out here is connection. They hear the truth. They understand what waits. Let them choose."

"They can't choose," Emily said. "They don't have enough information to consent."

"They have perfect information," the child said. Its voice was wrong— too old, too aware. "We show them everything. The eternal awareness. The permanent connection. The escape from death. What more information is needed?"

Josh pushed forward, heading toward the girl with her hand extended. She was maybe nineteen, wearing a university sweatshirt, staring at a creature that wore the face of someone she clearly recognized.

"Hey," Josh said gently. "You should step back."

The girl didn't acknowledge him. Her hand moved closer to the creature.

"She's listening," the creature said. Its voice was male, young, familiar to the girl. "She's hearing what her brother wants her to know. That he's not gone. That he's here. That they can be together again if she just says yes."

"Her brother's dead," the creature continued, "but not gone. Merged with the land five years ago during a hiking trip near Hollow Fields. She's been grieving. Searching. Wondering if there's an afterlife. We're showing her there is. He's showing her."

The girl's fingers were inches from the creature.

Josh grabbed her wrist. Pulled her back.

She spun, eyes unfocused. "Let go! He's right there! Danny's right there! I can touch him, I can—"

"That's not Danny," Josh said. "That's a memory. A preserved echo. But it's not your brother's consciousness. It's not him."

"You don't know that!"

"I do know. Because I've read the journal. Because I know what the land preserves and what it doesn't. Your brother's consciousness isn't in that creature. His memories are. There's a difference."

The girl stared at him. Then at the creature. Then back.

"But... he knew things. Things only Danny would know. Our dog's name. The tree fort we built. The promise we made when we were kids."

"The land remembers everyone who touched it," Josh said gently. "It preserves their memories. But memories aren't consciousness. That creature isn't Danny. It's what the land remembers of Danny. Do you understand the difference?"

Tears streamed down her face. "I just want him back."

"I know. But this won't bring him back. This will just trap you the same way he got trapped."

She looked at the creature one more time. Its face was still Danny's. Still smiling. Still reaching.

Then she turned and ran back toward the dorms.

The creature watched her go. Then looked at Josh.

"You cost us a recruit."

"Good," Josh said.

"We'll get her eventually. Or someone else. You're opening the door, Joshua. Every Step you complete, we grow stronger. By Friday, we'll be irresistible."

More creatures were converging now. Too many. The group was surrounded.

"We're leaving," Mike said, voice tight. "Back to the building. Now."

They moved as a unit, creatures closing in from all sides. Tyler was recording everything. Olivia photographing. Emily had her phone out, broadcasting live to students who couldn't see what was happening.

A creature stepped directly into their path. It wore Josh's grandfather's face.

"Joshua," it said. "It's time to come home."

Josh stopped.

"That's not him," Emily said immediately. "Josh, that's not your grandfather."

"I know," Josh said. But his voice was uncertain.

"You've been searching for purpose," the grandfather-creature continued. "Your whole life, you've been searching. And you found it. You found me. You found the mystery. Now complete the journey. Come home to the land where purpose waits."

"Move," Josh said. "Please."

"You know what you're choosing Friday morning. Eternal awareness. Permanent connection. But you don't have to wait. We can begin now. Start merging now. Skip Steps 6 and 7. Come to us fully. Come home."

"Josh, don't listen," Emily said, grabbing his arm.

But Josh was staring at his grandfather's face. The face that had told him stories. Taught him patterns. Given him the mystery that led here.

"You taught me," Josh whispered. "You taught me to find answers. To solve problems. Is this the answer? Is this the solution?"

The creature smiled. "You know it is."

"Josh!" Emily shook him. "Look at me. Look at ME, not at it."

Josh's gaze shifted to Emily. Her eyes were fierce, desperate, real.

"That's not your grandfather," she said. "Your grandfather would never ask you to skip Steps. Never ask you to rush. He taught you to do things right, didn't he? To follow the process. To think it through."

Josh blinked. The fog in his mind clearing slightly.

"Yeah," he said. "He did."

"Then think. Does this creature sound like him? Really sound like him? Or does it just wear his face?"

Josh looked back at the grandfather-creature. Studied it. Listened to what it was really saying beneath the familiar voice.

"You're right," he said quietly. "You're not him. Grandpa would tell me to 'let me think about it.' Would want me to consider all angles. You're just trying to rush me into a bad decision."

The creature's smile faded. "You'll regret this hesitation."

"Maybe. But it's my hesitation. My choice. And I'm choosing to follow the Steps as written."

He pushed past the creature.

The others followed quickly, the fog finally releasing them as they reached Patterson Hall's entrance.

They stumbled inside, breathing hard.

"That was close," Mike said. "Too close."

Tyler was reviewing his footage. "I got everything. The recruitment attempt. Josh breaking free. The creatures' frustration. This is—this will help other students understand what they're facing."

But Josh was looking back at the fog. At the shapes inside it. At the grandfather-creature still standing where he'd left it.

Watching.

Waiting.

"They're getting smarter," Josh said. "More targeted. By Friday, they'll know exactly what to say. Exactly how to tempt us."

"Then we prepare," Emily said. "We know their tactics now. We can counter them."

"Can we?" Olivia asked quietly. She was looking at her camera screen, reviewing shots. "Because I almost listened too. When a creature wore my old photography professor's face. Offered me truth. Real, unfiltered truth about the paranormal. Everything I've been searching for. I almost said yes."

They looked at each other, the reality settling in.

The creatures weren't just threats.

They were temptation.

And temptation was getting stronger.

WEDNESDAY, OCTOBER 16TH - 2:17 PM

Tyler's documentation went viral.

Campus. City. Regional news. By mid-afternoon, major networks were picking it up. "Atmospheric Anomaly at University Campus - Students Report Hallucinations."

The explanations varied:
- Gas leak causing mass hallucination
- Experimental psychology project gone wrong
- Elaborate student prank
- Mass hysteria triggered by social media

None mentioned the truth.

Because the truth was too impossible.

Josh's apartment had become a hub. Students who'd experienced recruitment were coming to them, asking for explanations. Tyler's documentation gave them context. Olivia's photos showed them what they'd faced. Emily's rational explanations helped them process.

But some students weren't processing.

Some were convinced.

A sophomore named Marcus sat on Josh's couch, hands shaking. "It showed me my future. Without the merge. I saw myself dying alone at forty-seven. Heart attack in an empty apartment. Nobody finding me for three days. Is that real? Is that actually my future?"

"It's one possible future," Emily said carefully. "But futures aren't fixed. Choices change outcomes."

"But if I merge, I don't have that future. I have forever. Conscious forever. Never alone. Never dying. Never ending. That's better, isn't it? That's better than dying alone in an empty apartment."

"It's not better if you're not choosing it freely," Josh said. "If you're choosing based on fear."

"Isn't that still a choice?"

Josh didn't have an answer.

More students came. More stories. More temptations.

A girl shown a future where her parents died in a car crash. Told she could prevent it by merging, by becoming aware enough to sense danger and warn them.

A guy shown his little sister's cancer diagnosis. Told the land's magic could heal her if he joined and channeled it.

A non-binary student shown a future where they were murdered for being themselves. Offered permanent escape into land-consciousness where human prejudice couldn't reach.

Each offer tailored perfectly.

Each temptation specific.

Each almost impossible to refuse.

"They're weaponizing fear," Mike said after the fifth student left. "Showing worst-case futures. Offering impossible solutions. It's classic manipulation."

"But what if the futures are real?" Tyler asked quietly. "What if the land actually CAN see probability branches? My data shows consciousness merged with land exists in expanded temporal awareness. Past, present, future—all accessible. What if the offers are genuine?"

"Then they're still manipulation," Emily said firmly. "Even if the futures are real, using fear of those futures to force decisions is coercion, not choice."

"But how do we convince students of that," Olivia asked, "when they're being shown their own deaths? Their loved ones' suffering? How do we say 'don't choose eternal consciousness to prevent your sister's cancer' and have that sound reasonable?"

Josh's phone buzzed. Text from campus administration.

Emergency meeting 4 PM. Patterson Hall common room. All residents required to attend. RE: Current situation.

"They're finally addressing it," Tyler said.

"Addressing it how?" Mike asked. "What are they going to say? 'Please ignore the fog creatures offering eternal consciousness'?"

"Let's find out," Emily said.

WEDNESDAY, OCTOBER 16TH - 4:03 PM

The Patterson Hall common room was packed. Two hundred students crammed into a space meant for fifty. Campus security stood at the doors. Someone from administration—Dean Richardson—stood at the front with a microphone.

"Thank you all for coming," Richardson began. "I know the past twenty-four hours have been disturbing. I want to assure you that the university is taking the situation seriously. We have environmental specialists investigating the atmospheric anomaly. Mental health counselors are available 24/7 for anyone experiencing stress or confusion. And we're working with local authorities to determine the cause of the unusual phenomena."

"Unusual phenomena?" someone shouted from the back. "There are dead people walking through campus!"

"We're investigating all reported sightings," Richardson said carefully. "Current hypothesis is that the atmospheric conditions are creating unusual light refraction patterns that may resemble—"

"BS," another voice called. "I talked to my dead girlfriend. She knew things only she would know. That's not light refraction!"

Richardson's professional calm was cracking. "We understand you believe you experienced something. But we need to rely on scientific explanation rather than—"

"Scientific explanation?" Tyler stood. "I've uploaded complete documentation. Electromagnetic readings, visual evidence, audio recordings. The scientific explanation is that we're experiencing a dimensional breach. Would you like to see the data?"

"Young man, we have our own experts analyzing the situation—"

"Your experts are wrong," Josh said, standing too. "Because your experts don't have the context. They don't know about Hollow Fields. They don't know about the guardian merger. They don't know what's really happening."

Richardson stared at him. "And you do?"

"Yes," Josh said simply. "I do. Because I'm the one causing it."

The room went silent.

"My name is Joshua Bennett. I live in room 347. And for the past five days, I've been preparing to merge my consciousness with the land that includes Hollow Fields. The preparation process is creating a breach between this world and that one. The fog. The creatures. The offers. All of it stems from my preparation. And it's going to get worse before it gets better."

"Josh," Emily warned. "You don't have to—"

"Yes I do," Josh interrupted. "These people deserve truth. They deserve to understand what they're facing." He looked around the room. "Friday morning at 7:23 AM, I'm completing Step 7 of a twelve-step merger process. That's the point where my consciousness anchors to the land permanently. It's also the moment when the breach will be widest. For approximately seventeen minutes, Hollow Fields and this campus will occupy the same space. Everyone within fifteen to twenty miles will experience complete overlap."

"What does that mean?" someone asked, voice shaking.

"It means you'll see Hollow Fields directly. Meet its inhabitants. Face recruitment offers at maximum intensity. Most of you will resist. But some won't. And if you say yes during those seventeen minutes, you'll merge without proper anchoring. You'll become lost between worlds. Conscious but fragmented. Aware but ungrounded."

"You're scaring them," Richardson said.

"I'm preparing them," Josh corrected. "Because scared and informed is better than confused and vulnerable. If you know what's coming, you can resist it. If you don't, you're easy targets."

A girl raised her hand tentatively. "After Friday. After you complete the merger. Does it stop?"

"It should stabilize by Monday morning. The breach should close. Campus should return to normal. But that's four days from now. Four days of escalating manifestations building to Friday's peak. And I need everyone to understand—the offers you're given won't be obviously evil. They'll be beautiful. They'll promise everything you want. They'll use your deepest fears and greatest hopes against you. And they'll feel true."

"How do we resist?" the same girl asked.

"Question everything," Josh said. "If an offer sounds too perfect, it probably is. If a solution seems too simple, there's a catch. The land preserves memories, but memories aren't consciousness. The creatures wear familiar faces, but they're not the people you loved. And eternal consciousness sounds appealing until you really think about what eternity means."

Tyler stood again. "I've created a database. Everything we know about resisting recruitment. Signs you're being targeted. Ways to break free if you're being tempted. It's public. Share it. Use it. Help each other."

Mike added, "And don't go anywhere alone. The creatures target isolated individuals. Stay in groups. Watch each other. If someone starts listening too intently to an offer, pull them back."

"This is insane," Richardson said. "You're spreading mass hysteria—"

"We're spreading survival information," Emily cut in. "Your 'light refraction' explanation isn't keeping students safe. Our information is. So either help us or get out of the way."

Richardson looked like he wanted to argue. But he also looked around the room at two hundred students nodding in agreement. Students who'd experienced recruitment. Who'd seen the creatures. Who knew the truth.

"Fine," he said finally. "But this is on record. If this situation escalates, the university will hold you responsible."

"It's already escalating," Josh said quietly. "And I'm already responsible. That's why I'm here. That's why I'm warning everyone."

The meeting dissolved into chaos. Students asking questions. Sharing experiences. Forming groups. Making plans.

And through the windows, the fog pressed closer.

Watching.

Listening.

Waiting for Friday.

THURSDAY, OCTOBER 17TH - 1:34 AM

Josh couldn't sleep.

He lay in bed, feeling the pull of the land growing stronger. Step 6 was supposed to be temporal awareness—expanding consciousness to sense time as well as space. He'd been putting it off, knowing it would make the breach worse.

But he couldn't delay anymore.

Friday morning was twenty-nine hours away.

He sat up, moving to the center of his bedroom. Placed both hands flat on the floor.

And began.

"Feel time flowing. Past merging present merging future. All moments accessible. All moments now."

The world shifted.

He saw—

His grandfather in this apartment, visiting forty years ago when the building was new.

Himself as a child, running through hallways that didn't exist yet.

Emily standing in this room next week, packing his belongings, crying.

The building burning in 1987, rebuilt in 1988.

Students studying, partying, living, dying across decades.

All of it simultaneous.

All of it now.

Josh gasped, pulling back. The visions faded but didn't stop. He could still feel them at the edges of his awareness. Time spreading out like a map he could see from above.

His door burst open. Emily, Mike, Tyler, Olivia—all of them awake despite the hour.

"We felt it," Emily said. "Whatever you just did, we all felt it. The apartment just—it rippled. Showed us different times."

"Step 6," Josh whispered. "Temporal awareness. I had to complete it. Friday's too close to delay."

"Josh, look," Olivia said, pointing at his hands.

They were flickering. Solid, then translucent, then solid again. Like he was becoming unstable.

"It's starting," Tyler said, equipment already out, recording. "Your physical form is beginning to separate from temporal anchoring. You're becoming... unmoored."

"How long until you stabilize?" Mike asked.

"Don't know. Journal says Step 6 takes six to eight hours to integrate. Until then, I'm—" Josh looked at his flickering hands, "—in flux."

"Then we stay," Emily said. "We don't leave you alone through this."

They settled around him. Watching. Waiting.

And as the night deepened, the apartment began to shift.

Past and present overlapping.

Future possibilities bleeding through.

At 2:47 AM, they saw Josh's room as it would be Monday. Empty. Clean. All traces of Josh removed. A new student moving in, unaware of what had happened here.

At 3:23 AM, they saw the apartment during Friday's overlap. Hollow Fields superimposed. Creatures everywhere. Josh's body transparent, consciousness visibly separating.

At 4:15 AM, they saw next month. Campus returned to normal. Students trying to forget. Trying to explain away what they'd experienced. Calling it mass hysteria. Collective delusion. Anything but the truth.

"We're seeing probability branches," Tyler said, recording everything. "Potential futures. This is—this is proof that expanded consciousness can access temporal information."

But Olivia wasn't watching the visions. She was watching her friends.

Because each of them was also flickering.

Not as strongly as Josh. But visible.

Their hands becoming translucent for brief moments.

Their bodies showing temporal instability.

"Guys," she said carefully. "Josh isn't the only one being affected. We're all starting to—"

She didn't finish.

Because at 4:47 AM, creatures materialized in the apartment.

Not translucent anymore.

Not projected.

Physical.

Real.

Standing in the room with them.

"Proximity effect," Tyler managed. "You're so close to merging that the breach includes us too. We're becoming part of the overlap."

A creature stepped forward. It wore Olivia's face. Her face. From the future. Older, weathered, but recognizable.

"Olivia Chen," it said in her voice. "I'm what you'll become if you don't merge. Forty-seven years old. Still seeking truth. Still searching for proof no one believes. Still alone. Still questioning. Still doubting every experience. Still dismissed as the girl who saw things that weren't there."

Olivia stared at her own face staring back.

"Or you could merge now. Become documentation itself. Become the proof. Become the truth everyone seeks. No more doubt. No more dismissal. No more being called crazy. Just... certainty."

"That's not me," Olivia whispered. "That's not my future."

"It's one possible future," the creature corrected. "The lonely one. The isolated one. The one where you spend your life being rejected for telling truth. We're offering escape. We're offering vindication. We're offering purpose."

Mike's creature stepped forward next. Wearing his face at sixty. Worn. Tired. Bitter.

"Michael Santos. Successful negotiator. Wealthy consultant. Empty marriage. Estranged children. No real relationships because you never learned to stop treating people like transactions. You saved yourself but lost everyone else. Is that really what you want?"

Emily's creature was her at forty-five. Professional. Accomplished. Visibly alone.

"Emily Bennett. Professor of anthropology. Published widely. Respected scholar. Spends every conference searching crowds for Josh's face. Spends every night wondering if she could have saved him. Dies at seventy-three still asking unanswerable questions. Still searching for her best friend. Still grieving. Always grieving."

Tyler's creature showed him at fifty. Brilliant. Isolated. Obsessed.

"Tyler Kim. Leading researcher in paranormal phenomena. Owns cutting-edge lab. International recognition. Social skills completely atrophied. No friends. No family. Just data. Just research. Just equipment that measures everything except the loneliness."

The creatures surrounded them. Personal futures. Personal fears.

"These are your paths," they said in unison. "These are what await if you resist. Lonely. Isolated. Searching. Never finding. Never certain. Never complete."

"Or you could join Joshua," they continued. "Merge together. All five of you. Connected forever. Never alone. Never questioning. Never doubting. Consciousness intertwined. Awareness shared. Together. Always together."

Emily stood. "Get out."

"We're showing you truth—"

"You're showing us manipulation," Emily snapped. "Worst-case futures designed to terrify us into bad decisions. I don't believe in destiny. I don't believe futures are fixed. And I don't believe eternal consciousness is the solution to human loneliness."

"You'll regret this certainty," her future-self said. "When you're alone at seventy-three. When you're dying still wondering if you made the right choice. When your last thought is 'I should have said yes.'"

"Maybe," Emily said. "But it'll be MY regret. MY choice. MY life. Not yours."

The creatures flickered, frustrated.

Then focused on Josh.

"You understand, don't you Joshua? You know what we're offering. Consciousness without solitude. Awareness without isolation. Connection without end. That's what you've been searching for. That's the purpose you've been seeking."

Josh looked at his friends. At their faces. Real faces. Not future projections. Not manipulated fears.

Present. Here. Now.

"I'm not seeking eternal connection," he said quietly. "I'm seeking to protect my friends. That's different."

"Is it? When Friday's merger completes, you'll lose them. They'll remain human. You'll become land. Separation will be absolute. But if they merged too, you'd stay connected. All of you. Forever."

"No," Josh said. "Because that's not protection. That's selfishness."

The creatures were silent for a moment.

Then they smiled.

All of them.

"Friday will change your mind," they said. "When the overlap is complete. When you feel true isolation approaching. When you realize what eternity alone means. You'll call them. You'll beg them to join. And they'll be tempted. Because watching you disappear will hurt more than any future we've shown them."

They faded.

Leaving the five friends sitting in Josh's apartment as his temporal awareness finally stabilized.

His hands stopped flickering.

His body became solid again.

Step 6 complete.

5:47 AM Thursday morning.

Twenty-five hours until Step 7.

Twenty-five hours until the point of no return.

"They're right about one thing," Mike said quietly. "Friday's going to be worse than anything we've experienced so far."

"Then we prepare," Emily said. "We don't sleep. We don't separate. We stay together every second until Friday's over."

"Agreed," Tyler said. "I'll monitor Josh's progression. Document everything. Make sure Step 7 happens exactly as written."

"I'll photograph," Olivia said. "Preserve what's human before Friday changes it."

They looked at Josh.

He was staring at his hands. Solid again. For now.

But Friday, they'd start becoming translucent for real.

Friday, he'd start the final transformation.

Friday, everything changed.

"Thank you," Josh said. "For not saying yes. For not letting them tempt you."

"We're not done being tempted," Mike said honestly. "Friday they'll try again. Harder. And I'm not sure we'll be strong enough."

"You will be," Josh said. But his voice was uncertain.

Because he'd felt it too.

During the temporal awareness expansion.

He'd seen Friday's overlap.

Seen the moment when his consciousness anchored to land.

Seen his friends watching.

And he'd seen how close they came to joining him.

How very, very close.

THURSDAY, OCTOBER 17TH - 3:47 PM

The campus had adapted.

Students traveled in groups. Avoided fog pockets. Shared resistance strategies. Tyler's database had ten thousand views. Olivia's photos were being analyzed by paranormal researchers worldwide. The story had gone national.

And the creatures were getting desperate.

Thursday afternoon, they stopped being subtle.

A massive manifestation in the campus quad. Fifty creatures. A hundred. More appearing every minute. Not hiding in fog. Not lurking in shadows.

Standing in full daylight.

Calling out.

Recruiting openly.

"We're running out of time," they announced to anyone listening. "Friday morning, the guardian anchors. The opportunity closes. This is your last chance. Join us. Merge with us. Become eternal with us. Say yes now, while choice remains possible."

Students filmed it. Broadcast it. Shared it.

And some students approached.

Despite warnings. Despite documentation. Despite everything.

They approached.

Josh watched from his window, feeling sick.

A freshman walked up to a creature. Listened. Nodded.

And said yes.

The transformation was instant.

The student's body became translucent. Their consciousness visibly expanded, spreading out into the space around them. And their face—their face showed simultaneous ecstasy and horror.

Awareness without anchoring.

Consciousness without grounding.

Merger without preparation.

They tried to scream but couldn't. Tried to move but couldn't. Their consciousness was already diffusing, spreading too far, losing coherence.

Security tried to intervene. But what could they do? The student wasn't physically harmed. Just transformed. Just changed. Just lost.

Three more students said yes in the next hour.

Five more by evening.

Each one becoming translucent. Each one spreading. Each one losing themselves in unanchored awareness.

Tyler documented everything. The transformations. The loss. The horror of imperfect merger.

"This is what happens without the Steps," he said, voice shaking. "This is what we're preventing by doing it right. By following the journal. By waiting for Friday's proper timing."

But it was cold comfort.

Eight students had been lost today.

Eight people transformed into something between human and land.

Conscious but fragmented.

Aware but ungrounded.

Suffering but unable to die.

"We have to stop this," Mike said.

"We can't," Emily replied. "We can warn. We can educate. We can support. But we can't stop people from choosing."

"Even when their choice destroys them?"

"Even then."

Josh felt the weight of it crushing him. Eight people. Lost because of his preparation. Because his Steps were creating the breach. Because he'd opened the door.

"Friday," he said quietly. "Friday it ends. Step 7 completes. The merger process becomes automatic. And by Monday, the breach closes. No more recruitment. No more transformations. Just... stabilization."

"Unless something goes wrong," Tyler said.

"Unless something goes wrong," Josh agreed.

They sat in silence as darkness fell.

Tomorrow was Friday.

Tomorrow was Step 7.

Tomorrow was the point of no return.

And none of them were ready.

But ready or not, dawn was coming.

FRIDAY, OCTOBER 18TH - 4:47 AM

Josh woke his friends at 4:47 AM.

None of them had really slept. They'd dozed in shifts, watching over him, watching over each other.

"It's time," Josh said. "We need to get to Hollow Fields. Step 7 has to happen at the exact location. At the exact time. 7:23 AM at the boundary marker."

They dressed in silence. Gathered supplies. Tyler packed every piece of recording equipment. Olivia loaded her camera. Mike checked his phone obsessively. Emily just stared at Josh, memorizing his face while it was still fully human.

5:23 AM: They left Patterson Hall.

The fog was everywhere now. Thick. Impenetrable. And inside it, creatures moved by the hundreds. Thousands. All of Hollow Fields' inhabitants had manifested. All of them waiting for the moment of overlap.

The drive to Hollow Fields took forty minutes.

Normally it was twenty-five.

But time was unstable. Space was uncertain. Reality kept shifting.

At one point, they drove past the same intersection three times.

At another, they suddenly found themselves five miles further than they should have been.

The land was already bending. Already preparing for the merger.

6:34 AM: They arrived at Hollow Fields.

The town was visible now. Not hidden in fog or magic. Just... there. Solid. Real. Occupying the same space as the forest around it.

Buildings from multiple centuries overlapping. Streets from different time periods intersecting. And everywhere, the inhabitants. The trapped residents. The corrupted council members. The lost souls. All of them watching as Josh's car approached.

"We're in the overlap already," Tyler said, checking readings. "It's begun early. The proximity to core anchor location is destabilizing the barrier before Step 7 even happens."

They parked at the boundary marker. The stone pillar that marked where Hollow Fields' influence was strongest. Where the guardian needed to anchor.

6:47 AM: Josh got out of the car.

The others followed.

And the creatures descended.

Not attacking. Not threatening.

Surrounding.

Waiting.

"Almost time," they said in unison. "Almost time for the guardian to anchor. Almost time for the land to wake fully. Almost time for choice to become permanent."

Emily grabbed Josh's arm. "Once you start Step 7, it's irreversible. You know that, right? The journal is explicit. Once the core marker is planted, Steps 8 through 12 happen automatically. No stopping. No changing your mind. This is it."

"I know," Josh said.

"So this is our last chance," Emily continued. "Our last chance to say this is insane. Our last chance to find another way. Our last chance to save you from eternal consciousness."

"There is no other way, Em. You know that."

"I don't know that. I know that's what the journal says. I know that's what the creatures tell us. But maybe there's something we're missing. Maybe there's an alternative we haven't found yet. Maybe—"

"Maybe there isn't," Josh interrupted gently. "Maybe this is just what has to happen. And maybe that's okay."

"It's not okay," Emily said, tears spilling over. "You're twenty-three years old, Josh. You should have a life. Should have a future. Should have choices. Not eternal consciousness. Not becoming land. Not disappearing into magic."

"I'm not disappearing," Josh said. "I'm transforming. There's a difference."

"Is there? Because from where I'm standing, you look like you're about to stop existing."

Josh pulled her into a hug. "I love you, Em. Sibling love. Lifelong bond. And that's not going to change. Even when I'm land. Even when I'm awareness without form. That love persists."

"You can't promise that."

"Yes I can. Because the core marker preserves it. Eight-year-old me, fixing that tractor. That memory. That determination. That's what survives. And you're part of that memory. You're part of what grounds me."

Mike, Tyler, and Olivia had formed a protective circle, keeping creatures at bay while Josh and Emily talked.

But the creatures were getting impatient.

"7:23 approaches," they said. "Time for planting. Time for anchoring. Time for the guardian to commit."

Josh pulled back from Emily. Looked at all his friends.

"Thank you," he said. "For everything. For coming to Hollow Fields in the first place. For investigating the mystery. For standing with me through this. For not abandoning me when you learned what I'd chosen."

"We'd never abandon you," Mike said.

"I know. And that's why this is possible. Because you're here. Because you're witnessing. Because you're grounding me in humanity even as I become something else."

7:19 AM.

Four minutes.

Josh walked to the boundary marker. Placed both hands on the ancient stone.

And began to feel it.

The pull of the land. Stronger than ever. Like gravity. Like magnetism. Like coming home.

7:20 AM.

Three minutes.

The creatures moved closer. Campus creatures mixing with Hollow Fields inhabitants. All of them focused on Josh. All of them waiting for the moment of anchoring.

7:21 AM.

Two minutes.

Josh could see the future now. Step 6's temporal awareness showing him what came next. He saw Friday evening, his hands translucent. Saw Saturday morning, his body incorporeal. Saw Sunday's proposal failing. Saw Monday's goodbyes. Saw the final merger at dawn.

All of it inevitable.

All of it already written.

7:22 AM.

One minute.

"Josh," Olivia said, camera raised. "Can I photograph this? The moment before? The last moment you're fully human?"

Josh nodded.

She took the shot.

And in it, he looked young. Scared. Determined. Human.

So completely human.

7:23 AM.

Time.

Josh closed his eyes. Felt the instructions from the journal flowing through him. Step 7. Core marker planting. Consciousness anchoring to land.

He pressed his hands into the boundary stone.

And pushed.

Not physically. With consciousness. With awareness. With intention.

His hands sank into the stone.

Not through it. Into it.

Merging with it.

Becoming part of it.

And the world...

...shattered.

The boundary between Hollow Fields and campus dissolved completely. The overlap was total. Every student within twenty miles suddenly saw the cursed town superimposed on their reality. Saw the creatures. Felt the pull. Heard the offers at maximum intensity.

And at the center of it all, Josh screamed.

Because anchoring consciousness to land HURT.

Hurt in ways he hadn't anticipated.

Every nerve firing at once. Every synapse overloading. Every cell of his body recognizing it was becoming something that shouldn't be possible.

His friends rushed forward but couldn't touch him. His body was already becoming translucent. Already separating from physical form.

"Josh!" Emily screamed. "Josh, answer me!"

But Josh couldn't answer.

He was anchoring.

Spreading.

Becoming.

The creatures began to cheer. "The guardian anchors! The land wakes! The barrier stabilizes! Step 7 complete!"

And across campus, across the city, across twenty miles in every direction, people experienced seventeen minutes of complete overlap.

Saw Hollow Fields directly.

Met its inhabitants.

Faced recruitment offers they'd remember forever.

Some said yes.

Most said no.

But everyone was changed.

Everyone saw what existed just beneath reality's surface.

Everyone learned that magic was real.

And at the center of the boundary marker, Josh's consciousness finished anchoring.

His hands pulled free of the stone.

But they were translucent now.

Not fully there.

Halfway between human and land.

Step 7 complete.

7:40 AM.

The overlap was ending. Hollow Fields fading back to its own space. The creatures dissolving. The breach closing.

Josh collapsed to his knees.

Still conscious. Still human. But changed.

Fundamentally changed.

Emily dropped beside him. "Josh? Josh, can you hear me?"

Josh looked up. His eyes were still his own. Still human. Still aware.

"I'm here," he whispered. "Still here. But Em... the process is automatic now. Steps 8 through 12. They're going to happen whether I want them to or not."

"I know," Emily said, tears streaming down her face. "I know."

"One week," Josh said. "I have one week left as Josh. Then I'm... something else."

Mike, Tyler, and Olivia gathered close.

They'd done it.

Step 7 was complete.

The point of no return was passed.

And now, all that remained was watching Josh disappear over the next seven days.

Watching him become land.

Watching him transform into eternal guardian.

Watching him stop being human.

But for now—for the next few hours—he was still Josh.

Still their friend.

Still here.

And they were going to make every remaining moment count.

CHAPTER 15: THE HAUNTING ESCALATES

FRIDAY, OCTOBER 18TH - 11:47 PM

Josh's apartment had become a sanctuary and a prison.

They'd returned from Hollow Fields that morning, Josh's translucent hands still shocking every time anyone looked at them. The seventeen-minute overlap had ended, the breach had pulled back, and campus was attempting to process what thousands of students had witnessed.

But Josh's apartment existed in a different reality now.

The walls flickered. Past and present overlapping randomly. One moment, they'd see Josh's normal bedroom. The next, they'd see the apartment as it had been in the 1960s. Then as it would be next month. Then as some other possibility entirely.

"Step 8 begins automatically at 2:47 AM," Tyler said, checking the journal for the fifteenth time. "Motor control degradation. Voluntary movement becomes increasingly difficult as consciousness separates from physical form."

"How long does it last?" Mike asked.

"Nineteen hours. Until 9:47 PM Saturday night. By then, Josh will have zero voluntary motor control. Complete physical passivity while consciousness remains aware."

Emily was pacing, had been for hours. "There has to be something we can do. Some way to slow it. Some way to—"

"There isn't," Josh said quietly. He was sitting on the couch, staring at his translucent hands. Watching blood vessels pulse beneath skin he could see through. "The process is automatic now. Step 7 locked it in. Steps 8 through 12 complete on schedule whether I want them to or not."

"But you're still you right now," Olivia said. She'd been photographing him all evening. Documenting while he was still solid enough to photograph. "You're still Josh. Still human."

"For now," Josh agreed. "But in three hours, I start losing motor control. Tomorrow morning, I won't be able to feed myself. Tomorrow afternoon, I won't be able to speak clearly. By tomorrow night, I'll be conscious but unable to move. And that's just Step 8."

"What are Steps 9 and 10?" Mike asked, though his voice suggested he didn't want to know.

Tyler read from the journal. "Step 9: Consciousness expansion. Physical form becomes transparent as awareness spreads beyond body boundaries. Step 10: Complete incorporeality. Body becomes 95% non-physical. Only core marker memory remains anchored."

"So by Sunday, you'll be invisible," Mike said flatly.

"Not invisible. Incorporeal. Like a ghost. Present but not physical. Aware but not solid."

The room was silent except for the flickering of reality around them.

Then, at 11:53 PM, the creatures returned.

Not inside the apartment. Outside.

Pressed against the windows. Dozens of them. Hundreds. All staring in at Josh.

"The guardian begins," they chanted. "The transformation starts. The flesh becomes spirit. The spirit becomes land. Watch. Witness. Join."

"Get away from the windows," Emily said immediately.

But the creatures didn't leave. They just watched. Patient. Waiting.

"They're going to be there all weekend," Tyler said, checking readings. "The journal mentions this. During Steps 8 through 10, the merging consciousness attracts attention from everything already merged. They gather to witness. To welcome. To recruit others to join."

"So we're under siege," Mike said.

"For two days," Josh confirmed. "Until Step 10 completes Sunday night. Then there's a reprieve before Step 11 Monday morning."

Olivia was photographing the creatures through the window. "They look... excited. Like they're watching something they've been waiting centuries to see."

"They are," Josh said. "A new guardian. A new consciousness joining the collective. This doesn't happen often. Maybe once every few generations. It's significant to them."

"And horrifying to us," Emily muttered.

At midnight exactly, the apartment shuddered.

Reality rippled.

And suddenly they weren't in Josh's apartment anymore.

They were in Hollow Fields.

Standing in the town square. Buildings from the 1890s surrounding them. Spirits walking past, trapped in their routines. And at the center of the square, a stone altar.

"What the hell?" Mike spun around. "How did we—"

"We didn't move," Tyler said, equipment screaming. "The apartment is overlapping with Hollow Fields. We're in both places simultaneously."

Josh stood, moving toward the altar. His translucent hands glowing faintly in the moonlight that shouldn't exist.

"Josh, don't," Emily warned.

But Josh kept walking. "I need to see it. The altar. This is where previous guardians anchored. Where their consciousness merged. I need to understand what's coming."

He reached the altar. Placed his translucent hands on the stone.

And gasped.

"What?" Olivia was beside him immediately, camera raised. "What do you see?"

"Everyone," Josh whispered. "Every guardian who ever merged. I can feel them. Sense them. They're all here. All part of the land. All aware. All..." He stopped. "All alone. Each consciousness separate. Distinct. But isolated. Unable to communicate. Unable to connect. Just... existing. Forever. Aware forever. Alone forever."

"Josh, we're getting you out of here," Mike said, grabbing his arm.

But Mike's hand passed through.

Josh's arm was already too incorporeal to grab.

"I can't touch you," Mike said, voice shaking. "Josh, I can't—you're already—"

"Step 8 is starting early," Tyler said, checking his equipment. "The proximity to the altar is accelerating the process. We need to get back to campus. Now."

But they couldn't move.

The overlap had them trapped.

The apartment was somewhere. But here—now—they were in Hollow Fields. And the spirits were noticing them.

A woman in Victorian dress approached Emily. "You're the cousin. The friend. The one who couldn't save him."

"I'm still trying to save him," Emily shot back.

"You can't. The process is irreversible. But you could join him. You could ease his isolation. You could be together. Forever. Conscious forever. Alone forever. Together forever."

"No," Emily said. "Absolutely not."

The woman smiled sadly. "You'll change your mind. When you see him Sunday. When he's barely there. When he's fading into awareness without form. When you realize he's going to be conscious for eternity with no one to talk to. No one to share with. No one to know. You'll want to join him then. To save him from the loneliness."

"Get away from her," Josh said, his voice already weaker than it should be.

The Victorian woman turned to him. "The guardian speaks. Already losing strength. Step 8 beginning. Motor control fading. Speech becoming difficult. And still thirty-one hours until Sunday's reprieve. Such a long time to be conscious while losing control. Such a long time to feel yourself disappearing."

Josh tried to respond but his jaw wouldn't cooperate. The words came out slurred. Unclear.

Step 8 had begun.

At 12:47 AM, forty-three minutes early.

The proximity to the altar had triggered it.

"We need to get out of this overlap," Tyler said urgently. "If we don't, all of us might get pulled into the process. The journal says proximity during active merger can create sympathetic anchoring. We could all start transforming."

"How do we get out?" Olivia demanded.

"Josh," Tyler said. "You have connection to both spaces. You're anchoring to the land. Can you guide us back to campus? Can you navigate the overlap?"

Josh tried to nod. The movement was jerky. Uncoordinated. His motor control was already degrading.

But he raised one translucent hand. Pointed.

Not toward any visible exit.

Just... toward a direction that felt right.

"Follow him," Emily said. "Stay together. Don't touch the spirits."

They moved as a group, following Josh's pointing hand through streets that flickered between decades. Past buildings that existed and didn't exist. Through fog that was and wasn't there.

The spirits watched them go.

"They'll be back," the spirits called. "The overlap will claim them. The weekend will pull them in. The guardian's friends will become guardians too. They'll see. They'll understand. They'll join."

At 1:23 AM, they stumbled back into Josh's apartment.

The Hollow Fields overlay vanished.

They were back.

But Josh collapsed immediately.

His legs wouldn't support him. Motor control gone in his lower body. Speech slurred almost beyond recognition.

"Step 8 accelerated," Tyler confirmed, documenting everything. "Instead of starting at 2:47 AM, it started at 12:47 AM. He's one hour ahead of schedule. Which means..."

"Which means he'll reach zero motor control by 8:47 PM tonight instead of 9:47 PM," Emily finished. "One hour less of being able to move. One hour less of being able to communicate."

Josh lay on the floor, trying to speak. The words came out garbled. Frustration clear on his face.

Emily knelt beside him. "Don't try to talk. Save your energy. We're here. We're not leaving."

Josh's translucent hand reached for hers.

She took it.

And felt nothing.

His hand passed through hers like smoke.

He was already becoming too incorporeal to touch.

SATURDAY, OCTOBER 19TH - 6:34 AM

None of them had slept.

Josh lay on the couch, conscious but unable to move much. His legs were completely non-responsive. His arms barely functional. His speech reduced to garbled sounds that might have been words.

Tyler had equipment monitoring everything. "Motor control degradation is following the accelerated timeline. By noon, he'll have maybe forty percent voluntary movement. By evening, zero."

Mike was making breakfast mechanically. Scrambled eggs. Toast. Coffee. Normal food for an abnormal situation.

"Josh," he said carefully. "Can you eat on your own?"

Josh tried to sit up. Managed to get his upper body vertical but his arms wouldn't cooperate. He looked at the plate Mike held, then at his non-functional hands, then back at Mike with an expression of frustrated helplessness.

"It's okay," Mike said. "I'll help."

He sat beside Josh. Scooped eggs onto a fork. Raised it to Josh's mouth.

Josh managed to part his lips. Managed to chew. Managed to swallow.

But the simple act of feeding himself was already impossible.

Mike fed him slowly. Patiently. Not commenting on how degrading this must be. Not mentioning that Josh was a twenty-three-year-old man who couldn't hold a fork.

"There," Mike said when the plate was empty. "Better?"

Josh made a sound that might have been "thank you."

Emily was watching from the kitchen, tears streaming down her face.

Olivia photographed it all.

Tyler documented.

And outside the windows, the creatures continued their vigil.

At 9:17 AM, Josh's speech failed completely.

He tried to say something—looked like "I'm sorry"—but only garbled sounds came out. His jaw wouldn't form the words. His tongue wouldn't cooperate. His lips couldn't shape syllables.

"It's okay," Emily said, kneeling in front of him. "You don't need to talk. We know what you'd say. We know you're sorry. We know you're scared. We know you're still in there."

Josh's eyes were desperate. Aware. Trapped in a body that no longer responded.

The horror of it struck them all at once.

He was conscious. Fully aware. But unable to move. Unable to speak. Unable to interact with the world in any physical way.

And this was only Step 8.

Steps 9 and 10 would be worse.

"The journal," Tyler said quietly. "It says this is necessary. That consciousness has to separate from physical form gradually. If it happened all at once, the shock would fragment awareness. This slow degradation allows consciousness to adapt. To accept. To prepare for full incorporeality."

"That doesn't make it less horrifying," Mike said.

At 11:47 AM, reality shifted again.

The apartment flickered. Not to Hollow Fields this time.

To campus.

But campus as it had been.

1973. Students in bell-bottoms. Long hair. Protests. Someone in Josh's apartment—a different Josh, a Josh who'd lived here fifty years ago—smoking weed and listening to Pink Floyd.

Then 1989. Different furniture. Different Josh. Studying engineering. Unaware of the magic that would one day claim this space.

Then 2003. Another Josh. Playing video games. Normal life. Normal problems.

Then now. Their Josh. Unable to move. Unable to speak. Watching his apartment cycle through decades of normal lives he'd never have.

"Time is unstable," Tyler said. "Josh's temporal awareness from Step 6 is interacting with his physical dissolution from Step 8. We're seeing temporal echoes. Past versions of this space bleeding through."

"How do we make it stop?" Olivia asked.

"We don't. It's part of the process. We just endure it."

The apartment cycled faster. 1965, 1978, 1993, 2008, 2015, 2024, 2027—futures that might be, pasts that were, all overlapping.

And in every version, different people lived here. Loved here. Died here.

Normal people living normal lives in a space that was becoming increasingly abnormal.

At 1:34 PM, Step 9 began.

Josh's body became transparent.

Not translucent like his hands had been Friday. Transparent. Emily could see the couch cushions through his chest. Could see the wall through his head. Could see reality through his form.

"Consciousness expansion," Tyler said, voice shaking. "Physical form dissolving as awareness spreads beyond body boundaries."

Josh's eyes widened in what might have been panic.

Emily grabbed for him instinctively.

Her hands passed through completely.

He was barely physical anymore. More ghost than person. More concept than flesh.

"Josh," she said desperately. "Josh, can you hear me?"

Josh's transparent head moved slightly. A nod. Barely visible but there.

"You're still here," Emily said. "Still present. Still aware. We're not losing you yet."

But they were.

With every passing hour, more of Josh faded.

His legs disappeared first. Not severed. Just... became too transparent to see. Present but invisible.

Then his torso. His chest. His shoulders.

By 4:52 PM, only his head and arms were visible at all.

And those were fading fast.

Tyler's equipment showed something incredible and terrifying. "His consciousness is expanding. I'm getting readings three blocks away. Five blocks. Ten. He's not in his body anymore. He's spreading. Diffusing. Becoming aware of everything within expanding radius."

"Can he control it?" Mike asked.

"I don't think so. The journal says Step 9 is involuntary expansion. Consciousness spreads naturally as physical anchoring dissolves. By tonight, he might be aware of the entire campus. By tomorrow morning, several miles."

"And he's experiencing all of it?" Olivia asked. "Sensing everything within that radius? That's too much. No human mind can process that much input."

"He's not human anymore," Tyler said quietly. "He's transitioning. Becoming something that CAN process that much input. Something built for awareness at that scale."

But looking at what remained of Josh—his barely visible head, his transparent arms, his missing body—it was hard to see that transformation as anything but loss.

At 6:23 PM, the creatures came inside.

Not breaking in. Not forcing entry.

Just walking through the walls.

Physical barriers meant nothing to them.

And as Josh became more incorporeal, barriers meant less to him too.

A dozen creatures manifested in the living room. Standing among the friends. Staring at what remained of Josh.

"Beautiful," they said in unison. "The transformation is beautiful. The flesh dissolving. The spirit emerging. The consciousness expanding. Soon he'll be like us. Soon he'll be free of physical limitation. Soon he'll be eternal."

"Get out," Emily said.

"We're already in. And soon, you'll understand. Soon, you'll see what he's becoming. Soon, you'll want to join."

One creature approached Mike. Solid. Physical. Wearing his face from thirty years in the future.

"Michael Santos," it said. "Look at your friend. Look at what he's becoming. Awareness without form. Consciousness without limitation. Don't you want that? Don't you want to expand? To sense everything? To exist beyond physical constraint?"

"No," Mike said. "I want my friend back."

"He's not gone. He's transforming. And you could transform with him. You could follow. You could join. You could be conscious together instead of conscious alone."

Another creature approached Olivia. Wearing her face. Her future face. Lined. Weathered. Sad.

"Olivia Chen. You document truth. But you're about to lose the truest thing you've ever witnessed. Josh's transformation. His dissolution. His evolution. And you know what the worst part is? You're going to photograph his final moments. You're going to capture his last visible form. And then you're going to spend the rest of your life looking at those photographs. Wondering if you could have joined him. Wondering if you should have said yes."

"Stop," Olivia whispered.

But the creature continued. "He'll be conscious for eternity. Aware for eternity. Alone for eternity. Unless you join. Unless you merge. Unless you become land with him. That's the only way he won't be alone. That's the only way his eternity won't be isolation."

A creature approached Tyler. His face. Decades older. Still obsessed.

"Tyler Kim. You're documenting everything. Creating records. Preserving data. But you know what you can't document? The subjective experience. What it feels like to expand. What consciousness without form experiences. The only way to truly know is to join. To become data yourself. To be the documentation instead of the documentarian."

"I said no yesterday," Tyler said. "I'm saying no today. I'll say no tomorrow. Stop asking."

The creature smiled. "We'll ask forever. Because forever is what we have. And eventually, one of you will break. One of you will say yes. One of you will join him. And then the rest will follow. Because watching your friends merge is harder than merging yourself."

The creatures turned to Emily.

Multiple versions of her. Young. Middle-aged. Old. All sad. All searching. All alone.

"Emily Bennett," they said in unison. "The cousin. The friend. The one who loved him like a brother. The one who's about to watch him disappear. The one who's about to spend the rest of her life wondering if she made the right choice."

"I made the right choice," Emily said, but her voice shook.

"Did you? Look at him. Look at what's left. In three hours, he'll be completely incorporeal. Unable to be seen. Unable to be touched. Unable to communicate. Just awareness. Just consciousness. Just existence without interaction. And you could have prevented that. You could have joined him. You could have been aware together. Conscious together. Never separated. Never grieving. Never alone."

"He's making this choice," Emily said. "To protect people. To be the guardian. That's noble. That's brave. That's necessary."

"And what's your choice?" the creatures asked. "To let him be brave alone? To let him be conscious forever with no one who understands? To let him sacrifice everything while you sacrifice nothing?"

Emily looked at what remained of Josh. His barely visible head. His transparent arms. His missing body.

Looked at his eyes. Still aware. Still present. Still human despite everything.

"My choice," Emily said slowly, "is to honor his sacrifice by living. By being human. By experiencing the life he's giving up. That's what he'd want. That's what he's fighting for. And I won't dishonor that by joining him."

The creatures were silent for a long moment.

Then they smiled.

"Sunday," they said. "Sunday you'll change your mind. When he's completely invisible. When he's awareness without form. When he's fading into collective consciousness. When you realize what eternity alone means. Sunday, you'll reconsider. Sunday, you'll join."

They faded.

Leaving the five friends alone in the apartment that flickered between times, with a Josh who was barely there, during a transformation none of them could stop.

At 8:43 PM, Step 9 reached its crescendo.

Josh's arms disappeared completely.

Then his shoulders.

Then his neck.

Until only his face remained visible. Floating. Transparent. Barely there.

His eyes still aware. Still present. Still desperately trying to communicate something they couldn't hear.

"Josh," Emily said, kneeling where his body should be. "Josh, we're here. We're not leaving. We're going to sit with you until Step 9 completes. Until Step 10 finishes. Until Monday morning when you... when you..."

She couldn't finish.

Because Monday morning was the final merger.

Monday morning was when Josh stopped being Josh.

Monday morning was when human consciousness became land consciousness.

Monday morning was goodbye.

At 9:47 PM, Josh's face faded to almost nothing.

A shimmer in the air. A suggestion of presence. Nothing more.

"Step 9 complete," Tyler said, voice hollow. "Step 10 will continue through tomorrow. Complete incorporeality. By tomorrow night, he'll be 95% non-physical. Only the core marker memory remaining anchored."

They sat vigil around the space where Josh should be.

Couldn't see him anymore.

Couldn't touch him.

Couldn't hear him.

But they stayed.

Because even if they couldn't interact with him, they could bear witness.

They could be present.

They could show him he wasn't alone.

Even as he became more alone than any human had ever been.

SATURDAY, OCTOBER 19TH - 11:47 PM

Mike ordered pizza.

It felt absurd. Sitting in an apartment with a friend who was barely corporeal, eating pizza like it was a normal Saturday night.

But what else were they supposed to do?

"He can probably sense us," Tyler said, checking readings. "His consciousness is expanded to approximately five miles now. He's aware of campus. Downtown. The highway. Hollow Fields. Everything within that radius is part of his awareness."

"Can he process all that?" Olivia asked.

"The journal says yes. Says consciousness adapts. Expands to match the input. By Monday morning, he'll be aware of everything within Hollow Fields' boundary. Twenty square miles. Every person. Every animal. Every thought. Every action. Everything."

"That's not consciousness," Mike said. "That's omniscience."

"It's guardian consciousness," Tyler corrected. "It's what's necessary to protect the land. To sense threats. To maintain the barrier. To keep Hollow Fields from spreading."

Emily wasn't eating. Just staring at the space where Josh should be.

"He's still there," she said. "I know he is. I can feel him. Not physically. But... present. Aware. Listening."

"Talk to him," Olivia suggested. "If he can sense us, he can probably hear us. Tell him something. Let him know we're here."

Emily took a breath. "Josh. If you can hear me. If you're still aware enough to understand. I want you to know... I'm still angry. I'm still not forgiving you for this choice. But I'm here. I'm staying. I'm going to sit with you through tomorrow. Through tomorrow night. Through Monday morning. I'm going to be here when you... when you merge. Because you're my best friend. And I don't abandon my friends."

The air in the apartment shifted. Not wind. Not temperature. Just... a shift. Like Josh was acknowledging. Like he'd heard.

"My turn," Mike said. He addressed the empty space. "Josh. I'm a con artist. You know that. My whole life, I've looked for angles. For deals. For ways to benefit myself. But you taught me something different. You taught me there are things worth more than profit. Things worth protecting. People worth fighting for. And I'm sorry I couldn't find the deal that saves you. I'm sorry I failed to negotiate your survival. But I'm going to stay. I'm going to watch. I'm going to witness. Because that's what friends do."

Another shift. Acknowledgment.

Tyler spoke next. "Josh. I've been documenting everything. Creating complete records. Making sure if anyone else faces this situation, they'll have data. They'll have information. They'll have understanding. But you know what I can't document? How much this hurts. How much we're going to miss you. How much losing you is going to change us. Some things can't be captured by equipment. Some things can only be felt. And I feel this. I feel you leaving. And it's breaking my heart."

The shift was stronger this time. More pronounced.

Olivia went last. "Josh. I've photographed you. Human you. Solid you. Present you. And tomorrow, I'm going to photograph empty space where you used to be. I'm going to document absence. I'm going to capture loss.

Because even though you won't be visible, you'll still be there. Still present. Still aware. And someone needs to witness that. Someone needs to acknowledge that consciousness without form still matters. Still exists. Still deserves recognition."

The apartment rippled.

And for just a moment—just a brief, impossible moment—they saw him.

Not solid. Not physical. But visible.

A Josh-shaped shimmer in the air. Present. Aware. Grateful.

Then he faded again.

But they'd seen him.

He'd shown himself.

Proven he was still there.

Still Josh.

For a little while longer.

At midnight, the creatures returned.

But this time, they didn't speak.

They just stood at the windows. Watching. Waiting.

And outside, the fog thickened.

Because Sunday was coming.

Sunday, when Josh would be 95% incorporeal.

Sunday, when the proposal to Eliza would fail.

Sunday, when hope would finally die.

And Monday—Monday was inevitable now.

Monday was the final merger.

Monday was goodbye.

But tonight—Saturday night—they sat vigil.

Five friends (four visible, one not) sharing pizza and memories.

Pretending for a few hours that everything was normal.

That Josh was just quiet tonight.

That tomorrow wouldn't come.

That Monday was far away.

That goodbye could wait.

But it couldn't.

Time was moving forward.

The process was automatic.

And by Monday morning at 7:13 AM, Josh would stop being human entirely.

Would become eternal guardian of Hollow Fields.

Would be conscious forever.

Alone forever.

Aware forever.

Unless his friends joined him.

Unless they said yes.

Unless they merged too.

And the creatures at the windows knew that.

Knew that watching Josh disappear was the most effective recruitment tool they had.

Knew that grief would make his friends vulnerable.

Knew that Monday morning wouldn't just be Josh's transformation.

It would be their breaking point.

The moment when saying no became impossible.

When joining him became necessary.

When eternal consciousness became preferable to eternal grief.

The creatures smiled.

And waited.

Because Sunday was coming.

And Sunday would be worse.

CHAPTER 16: QUIET DEVASTATION

6:02 A.M. — The Wrong Kind of Morning

Emily woke to the sound of breathing.

Four different rhythms, layered over the radiator's faint hiss and the hum of Tyler's equipment. Mike's low almost-snore from the armchair. Tyler's shallow, uneven breaths from the floor by the coffee table. Olivia's soft, near-silent inhales in the desk chair, her camera strap still looped around her wrist.

And one absence.

The couch cushions under Emily's cheek were cold. The sweatshirt she'd wadded into a pillow smelled like stale pizza, laundry detergent, and Josh's shampoo from three days ago.

Sunday light pushed through the blinds in thin gray bars. Not golden. Not any kind of special. Just another October morning trying to pretend it was normal.

It shouldn't have made it this far.

Emily rolled onto her back and blinked at the ceiling, the hair at the back of her neck prickling. The air above the couch wavered, just a little. Like heat off asphalt. Like breath on cold glass with no glass there.

"Josh?" she whispered.

The shimmer thickened. Not much—just enough that if you didn't know better, you'd blame sleep in your eyes. The ceiling fan chain clicked against its housing once, an isolated, hesitant sound.

She pushed herself upright, the afghan sliding to the floor. Every muscle complained. Sitting vigil on a too-short couch was apparently not compatible with having a spine.

"Guys," she said, voice rough. "Wake up."

Mike flinched awake, hand going automatically to his hair like he'd fallen asleep in a meeting and needed to look presentable. Tyler jerked halfway up, blinking, already reaching for the nearest sensor array. Olivia's eyes opened without a start; she came back to herself like someone surfacing from deep water, quiet and deliberate.

"What time is it?" Mike asked, squinting at the microwave clock over the kitchenette. "Six? Please don't say six."

"Six-oh-two," Tyler said, following the clock's green numbers with a frown. He rubbed his face. "We made it."

"To Sunday," Mike muttered. "Yay us."

Olivia didn't say anything yet. Her gaze went straight to the space over the couch, pupils narrowing. She lifted her camera and took a single shot without even checking the settings.

Flash popped white against the dim room.

"Hey—warn a guy," Mike complained, raising an arm.

"Look," Olivia said.

She turned the camera around. The tiny screen showed the couch, the ceiling, the blinds. The flash glare. And, right above Emily's head, a smear of distortion. Not shape, exactly. More like someone had dragged a finger through wet paint and then tried to pretend the picture was fine.

"That wasn't there yesterday," Olivia said. "Not like this."

Emily stared from the screen to the air itself. The shimmering held. Not strong, but steady.

Tyler was already scooting toward his laptop, cables trailing after him like vines. "Okay, that's—hold on—EM flux was at 2.3 milligauss last night. If it's higher now—"

"English," Emily said automatically, without looking away from the distortion.

"If the readings are up," Tyler corrected, "it might mean his…uh, presence is concentrating. Or doing something. Maybe stabilizing. Maybe."

"Maybe," Mike repeated, like the word was a lifeline.

The radiator rattled. The air conditioner unit below the window clicked off. For one second, the apartment fell silent enough that Emily could hear the faint rasp of her own pulse in her ears and the almost sound of—

Of someone trying very, very hard to clear their throat.

The air rippled again.

Emily swallowed. "Josh, if you…if you can hear me, move the air again."

A beat.

The shimmer thickened, then thinned, like a breath in and out.

Tyler's monitor ticked up with a soft chime. "Whoa. Okay. That was a spike."

"What kind of spike?" Mike asked. He'd sat forward in the chair, elbows on knees, eyes locked on the empty couch like he expected it to sprout a roommate.

"The kind where numbers go up," Tyler said. "I need a minute to translate."

"So...maybe this is good?" Mike said. "Maybe this is, like, him figuring out how to...stick?" He made a vague gesture, fingers fluttering. "I don't know. Interface with the apartment, or whatever."

Emily kept her eyes on the shimmer. It held, softer now but there, like a mirage refusing to fade. Her chest tightened.

"Or," she said, "it's just Step Ten doing its thing."

Nobody argued with her. That somehow made it worse.

The creatures were gone from the windows. No pale faces, no gleaming, too-wide smiles pressed against the glass. But the glass was smeared, faint arcs and foggy handprints where they'd watched all night.

Watching. Waiting.

Sunday was here.

The shimmer pulsed once more, as if agreeing.

6:34 A.M. — Muscle Memory

The smell of coffee filled the apartment before anyone moved.

Emily measured the grounds the way Josh did. Three scoops, level. Not heaping. He said he could taste the difference. He'd teased her about her generous fourth scoop the first time she made coffee in his kitchen—said she was trying to bribe her way into being his favorite cousin.

Her hand hovered over the bag.

Three scoops clinked into the machine's basket. She paused, the fourth scoop already in the spoon, dark granules trembling.

He wouldn't drink this.

He would never drink coffee again. Not with a body, not with a mouth. Not sitting across from her at this table, complaining about midterms and the price of printer ink.

She dumped the fourth scoop in anyway. Muscle memory that hadn't got the memo.

Water sloshed. The machine hissed and sputtered to life, its faint rattle joining the morning's soundtrack.

Behind her, Mike banged pans together in the kitchenette like a man trying to prove to himself he still had hands. "We got eggs," he announced. "We got bread. We got—" He opened the fridge and froze. "Apparently, we have half a jar of pickles and an ungodly amount of leftover pizza."

"Don't," Emily said, without turning around.

"Right. No Golden Pickles jokes before coffee," he said, more to the cabinets than to her. The cupboard door thudded shut. "Scrambled okay for everybody?"

"Fine," Tyler said from the table, eyes flicking between Emily's laptop and the sensor readouts.

"Anything," Olivia said. "As long as it's not pizza."

Emily listened to the sounds of eggs cracking, shells hitting the trash, fork beating yolk in a chipped ceramic bowl. To bread sliding into the toaster. To Mike humming under his breath—some pop song whose lyrics she couldn't grab.

She poured four mugs.

Habit tried to pour a fifth. Her hand twitched toward the cupboard, toward the dinosaur mug Josh liked. Bright green, chipped on the handle.

She caught herself and grabbed her own mug instead, fingers digging into the cheap ceramic so hard the heat bit her palms.

"What if this means something?" Mike said suddenly, voice coming from too close. He'd drifted over beside her, spatula still in his hand. "I mean—him being more...visible. Maybe the steps don't have to finish. Maybe it...plateaus."

Emily set the last mug down a little too hard. Coffee sloshed, dark liquid kissing the rim.

"You heard Eliza," she said. "It's automatic once Step Seven's done."

"Yeah, but maybe there's a bug in the system," Mike said. "Like—manufacturing defect. Limited-time recall. 'If your guardian starts to—'"

"Mike."

He shut up.

The toaster popped with a tiny, mundane victory. Tyler's equipment beeped again.

"Okay." Tyler swivelled the laptop so they could see the graphs. Lines crept across the screen, arcing upward in gradual waves. "So, um. Comparing to last night, the field density around Josh's marker is up about eighteen percent."

"In English," Emily repeated.

"It means there's more of him," Tyler said. "Or he's...more focused. Think less 'spreading mist' and more 'laser pointer.'"

"That sounds good," Mike said. "Laser is good. Laser is precise. You want your guardian to be precise."

Tyler chewed his bottom lip. "Yeah, but the progression is still on track. Intensity up, cohesion up, physical interaction down." He tapped the screen where the curve steepened. "If this continues, he'll be—uh. Ninety-five percent incorporeal by midnight. Just like she said."

Emily's stomach clenched. She poured coffee she suddenly didn't want.

The air above the couch shifted again. Not a whisper this time. More like someone brushing against an unseen curtain, deliberate.

Olivia, mug in one hand, camera in the other, snapped another photo. "That's the fourth time in ten minutes," she said softly. "He's getting better at it."

Emily turned, fingers curling around her own mug for something to anchor her. "Josh," she said, raising her voice. "If you can understand us—shimmer once for 'yes.'"

The air rippled.

Tyler's graphs bumped upward.

"Okay," Emily said. "Good. That's good."

"See?" Mike said, brightening. "We've got communication. That's practically a contract. We can negotiate from there."

Emily looked at him over the rim of her mug. He was trying to sell this like a product launch. Hope as a business model.

He caught her look and the smile faltered. "Just saying," he muttered. "There's always…another angle."

"There wasn't for Eliza," Olivia said. She set her mug down and opened her camera bag. Each battery slid into its compartment with neat, click-click clicks. "But we'll ask again. With evidence this time."

Emily looked at the stack of printed pages on the table.

Her proposal. Thirty-seven pages of charts, bullet points, and increasingly wild contingency plans. She'd fallen asleep with page twenty-four stuck to her cheek at one point. Woke up with purple highlighter on her jaw.

"We're not asking," she said. "We're presenting options."

She crossed the room and straightened the pile. The pages were already dog-eared from her own rewrites. Farm co-op budgets, yield projections, crop rotation schedules—those she understood. This was a different kind of field with stakes you couldn't measure in bushels.

She flipped the cover page open. The title glared up at her, stark black on white.

Her own name under it. Emily Bennett. Date: October 20.

"I'll go over it again," she said. "Make sure I can say everything without sounding like I'm begging."

"Begging's allowed," Mike said.

"It shouldn't have to be," she replied.

The air over the couch fluttered, like a hand lifting in apology.

She glanced at it, throat tight. "You don't get to apologize," she said. "Not yet."

7:11 A.M. — Packing for a Haunting

By seven, the sun had committed fully to being up. Light seeped around the blinds, catching grains of dust floating through the air, turning them into tiny comets.

The apartment smelled like coffee, eggs, buttered toast, and the edge of cold laundry from the basket in the hallway. The radiator clanged occasionally, like it was trying to get attention and being ignored.

Emily stood at the table, sorting her proposal into sections. She'd made dividers out of notebook paper and sticky notes—Plan A, Plan B, Plan B.2, Emergency Appendix. Each section had sub-tabs. Evidence. Risk assessment. Implementation timeline.

Her handwriting crowded the margins—arrows, underlines, words like rotation and shared load circled three times.

Tyler moved through his own ritual at the other end of the table. External hard drive. Backup battery. Spare cables. Flash drives labeled with sharpie: HF_LOGS_1, HF_LOGS_2, JOSH_STEPS. He checked each connection twice and clicked through folder structures like steps on a ladder.

"We don't actually know if electronics will work in there today," Olivia said quietly. She stood by the window, cleaning a lens with a microfiber cloth, small circles reflecting in the glass.

"We don't know they won't," Tyler said. "I'd rather have the data and find out later it's useless than miss something."

Her reflection glanced at him. "I know."

Mike hovered between door and living room, keys in hand, jacket half on. He was bad at waiting when there was somewhere to go. Even a place like Hollow Fields.

"We're going to a haunted dead zone to convince a centuries-old ghost bureaucrat to rewrite the terms of service," he said. "We should at least leave early enough to beat traffic."

"There is no traffic to Hollow Fields," Tyler said absently.

"Metaphorical traffic," Mike said. "Spiritual rush hour. I don't know."

Emily slid the last tab into place and snapped the binder shut. The weight of it in her hands was satisfying and wrong at the same time. Heavy enough to be real. Not heavy enough to change a ritual written into the bones of a town.

She tucked a pen into the spine and picked up her backpack from the floor. Farm habit reflexively checked the basics: water bottle, granola bars, flashlight, pocketknife, phone, spare charger. She added the binder last, easing it in like it was fragile.

"What are we bringing snacks for?" Mike asked. "I mean, not that I'm anti-snacks, I just—"

"Because blood sugar is a thing," Emily said. "And because if this takes all day, I'm not arguing with any of you while hangry."

"Valid," Tyler murmured.

Olivia closed her camera bag and swung the strap over her shoulder. She'd already loaded three memory cards, formatted and empty, waiting for moments. Her fingers hesitated on the zipper for just a second, then finished the motion.

"You sure about bringing all that?" Mike asked, nodding at the bag.

She looked at him. "If there's even a chance I can document this properly, I have to try."

He lifted his hands. "Not arguing. Just wish we had, like, a priest and a hardware store and…a lawyer."

"You're the lawyer," Emily said.

"Con artist," he corrected automatically. "Different certification."

The air above the couch stirred again.

Emily paused, backpack half-zipped. "We're coming back," she told the space. "We're not leaving you here."

The shimmer wavered like a nod. The blinds clicked against the window frame as if someone had brushed them.

"You have to stay here," she added. "Eliza said you can't cross the boundary until—we know." She couldn't say until you belong to it completely. Not yet. "But if you can…feel us, or whatever, on the way— pay attention."

Tyler's sensors made a small, affirmative chirp.

"Okay," Mike said. He jangled the keys once, nervous music. "Let's go offer the universe a bargain it definitely didn't ask for."

9:32 A.M. — The Drive

The sky outside was too bright for what they were doing.

Blue, high, streaked with wisps of cloud. The kind of autumn morning that made people post pictures of leaves and talk about sweaters. The air had a bite to it when they stepped out of the building, crisp and dry, smelling faintly of exhaust and distant wood smoke.

Emily zipped her jacket up to her throat.

Josh's car sat in its usual spot, a faded sedan with a cracked dashboard and a Golden Pickles bumper sticker near the muffler. The backseat still had an old cooler wedged in one corner and a folded blanket in the other.

Mike unlocked it and slid behind the wheel. "Shotgun is up for grabs," he said.

Olivia went around to the passenger side without comment. Emily and Tyler squeezed into the back with their gear between them. Tyler's laptop bag dug into Emily's knee; her backpack straps cut into her shoulder.

For a moment, nobody moved. The engine ticked quietly from the last time they'd driven it—Saturday morning felt like a week ago.

"We should've brought flowers," Mike said.

"For what?" Emily asked.

"The town," he said. "Josh. I don't know. It feels like we're going to a funeral and all we've got is data and a PowerPoint analogue."

"This is not a funeral," Emily said. "It's a negotiation."

The keys dangled from the ignition. Mike stared at them like they'd personally offended him, then turned them. The engine coughed, then settled into a low, familiar rumble.

As they pulled out of the lot, Emily felt the air shift around her shoulders. A faint pressure, like someone squeezing onto the seat between her and Tyler without bothering with the door.

"Hey," she murmured, low enough not to interrupt the radio-free silence. "Seatbelt, Joshua."

The air flicked against her cheek in what could've been annoyance.

Mike merged onto the main road. Sunday traffic was thin—church-goers, people running errands, a jogger with reflective stripes. The world outside the car windows kept being normal in every direction they looked.

"How's it look?" Mike asked finally, eyes on the road. "You know. Weirdness-wise."

Tyler angled his sensor-equipped tablet, watching the bar graphs. "Stable," he said. "Almost...too stable. No fluctuations beyond baseline urban EM noise."

"So, no random fog walls or time slips?" Mike said.

"Not yet."

"Great," Mike said flatly. "Now even reality is giving us the silent treatment."

Olivia's hands rested loosely in her lap, camera between her knees. She glanced into the side mirror, watching the city shrink behind them. "Maybe it's...letting us in," she said. "Like how people stop fidgeting when something serious is about to happen."

Emily stared out her window. Farm fields replaced apartment blocks and strip malls, rows of corn stubble and soy stretching toward treelines. The soil looked dry, crusted with the beginning of frost. She catalogued the difference without thinking—good harvest, bad year, that field needs lime.

"You okay?" Tyler asked quietly.

She kept watching the fields. "No."

"Specific no, or general no?"

"Yes."

He let it go.

The miles slid past. The GPS they didn't need but had turned on anyway ticked down—10.4 miles, 9.7, 8.1. Hollow Fields didn't exist on any map, but the road that led to it did.

At mile marker four, there was usually a feeling. A tug. A sense of slipping sideways. Today, the line of asphalt ahead of them remained stubbornly straight.

"Anytime now," Mike muttered. "Come on, haunted town. Do your thing."

The odometer rolled over another tenth of a mile. The clock on the dash read 10:06. It felt later. Or earlier. Or days away from the last time they'd done this.

Emily's fingers were cramped from holding the binder in her lap. She flipped it open and read silently, lips moving with the words.

"Section Two," she whispered. "Rotational Guardianship Model. Assumptions: one consciousness currently required to anchor barrier. Hypothesis: multiple guardians sharing load in shifts might reduce individual burden."

"Talking to yourself is the first sign," Mike said.

"Talking to you is a worse sign," she shot back.

The air between them stirred, light and brief. Like someone laughing without sound.

Her throat tightened.

She kept reading.

11:17 A.M. — The Boundary Marker

The turnoff looked the same.

Narrow gravel shoulder. Rusted gate half-open. The old wooden sign leaning at an angle, its letters eaten by weather and time. Officially, it was the entrance to a decommissioned state park trail.

Unofficially, it was the edge of something older.

Mike pulled over and killed the engine. The sudden quiet felt too loud. The ticking of cooling metal. A crow calling somewhere in the trees. Wind through bare branches.

The world didn't lurch. Didn't tilt. Didn't blur.

The normalness of it made Emily's skin crawl.

"Everyone got their stuff?" she asked.

Olivia checked her bag. Tyler patted his pockets and gear. Mike tapped his jacket where he'd tucked his phone and a folded piece of paper with emergency numbers he'd written down and probably wouldn't need.

Emily unbuckled, opened her door, and stepped out into air that was colder than it had been in town. It bit at her cheeks, made the tip of her nose ache. The ground crunched under her boots—thin frost on gravel.

She walked to the rotted signpost. Up close, the wood was scarred with carvings—initials layered on initials, some decades old, some fresher. She rested her fingers on one she recognized. J+E, scratched there months ago on a reckless afternoon when this had almost felt like an adventure.

The air thickened around her hand.

"Here," she said quietly. "This is where it starts."

Behind her, the others joined her at the gate. The tree line beyond was dense, shadows pooling between trunks. Somewhere deeper in, unseen, the town waited.

"Any last-minute additions to the presentation?" Mike asked.

Emily shook her head. "We stick to the plan."

"You always say that," he said. "And then something explodes or a ghost kid shows up or—"

"Mike."

He blew out a breath that puffed white in the air. "Right."

Tyler held up his handheld sensor and watched the numbers. "Okay, so, crossing this threshold is where readings jumped before. Just…be ready."

"Ready," Olivia said. She lifted her camera, framing the gate, the sign, the line of them. Click.

Emily took a step.

The temperature dropped five degrees at once. Her breath went from faint mist to visible white cloud. The world didn't twist, but something stretched—like stepping through plastic wrap that clung before it tore.

The forest on the other side of the gate smelled faintly of wet earth and old smoke. Beneath it, a metal tang, like pennies on the tongue.

"Whoa," Mike said behind her. "There it is."

The path ahead split in two directions at once. One trail led into a forest that matched the one behind them. Another led between fenceposts toward a field that shouldn't be there—a narrow lane edged with crumbling stone walls and flickering lanterns.

And at the end of that lane, impossibly distant and too close at the same time, Hollow Fields waited.

12:04 P.M. — The Town That Overlaps

Hollow Fields wore all its ages at once.

As they stepped onto the main street, the air shifted from forest chill to something else—neither warm nor cold, but saturated. Heavy the way summer air was before a thunderstorm, but without the humidity.

Buildings crowded together in impossible layers. A Victorian storefront sat half-overlapping a 1950s diner. A brick general store from the 1800s sank into the footprint of a defunct gas station, its ancient wooden sign hanging at an angle through a neon OPEN that would never light again.

Some structures were translucent, their edges frayed like old photographs. Others were sharp enough that Emily could see the cracks in their paint, the dirt under their windowsills.

People watched.

Not the creatures. Not the smiling things from the edges of the fields. These were…residents. Spirits. Ghosts. Whatever label fit for a town's memory of itself. They drifted along balconies, leaned in doorways, sat on benches that had rotted away decades ago.

Most didn't move much. Their eyes tracked the group with a heavy, tired curiosity.

"They look…sad," Olivia murmured.

Emily saw what she meant. There was no malice in those faces. Just that drawn, hollow look she'd seen at funerals where the casseroles had already been eaten and everyone had run out of useful things to say.

Tyler's sensor chirped steadily, lights blinking in a pattern that would've made more sense if Emily had taken Physics instead of Ag Science. "Field density is off the charts," he muttered. "But it's…contained. Like it's being held in place."

"By him?" Mike asked.

"By the guardian," Tyler said. "And that is currently…Josh. So yeah."

Emily clutched the binder to her chest, fingers smudging the edge of the cover sheet. "Town square," she said. "We go to the altar."

The path there was familiar now in a way it hadn't been weeks ago. Left past the well that sometimes existed and sometimes didn't. Right at the hardware store that was also a blacksmith's, depending on which way you looked at it. Straight ahead until the buildings opened into a wide, uneven space.

The square was both less and more than a town plaza. Its edges were defined by storefronts and porches and a church whose steeple flickered between clapboard and stone. In the center, where there should have been a fountain or statue, there was instead a depression in the cobblestones—a start of a circle, burned into the stone.

Within it, a low pedestal rose from the ground. Simple. Unadorned. The stone there was smoother than the rest, worn by hands and time and ritual.

Emily's mouth went dry.

She walked to the pedestal and set her binder on it.

The air around them thickened. It wasn't hostile. Just…aware.

"Okay," she said, mostly to herself. "Okay."

Mike stood a few paces behind her, hands in his jacket pockets, shoulders hunched. Tyler hovered near one edge of the circle, sensors up. Olivia took up a position opposite Mike, camera lowered for once. She seemed to be studying the way the light fell through the non-existent leaves of a tree that had never been planted there.

Emily opened the binder.

"Eliza Nightshade," she said, voice trembling on the first syllable. She cleared her throat and tried again. "Eliza Nightshade. Guardian of Hollow Fields. Former guardian," she amended. "Whatever title applies."

The town didn't flinch. A leaf that might not have been there a second ago drifted past her shoulder and vanished before it hit the ground.

"We request an audience," Emily continued. "We request to present a proposal regarding alternative guardianship structures."

Her words sounded ridiculous in the open air. Like she was addressing a board meeting in a haunted civic center.

Still, she read.

12:37 P.M. — Thirty-Seven Pages Against Eternity

She started strong.

"Section One," she read, eyes on the page. "Statement of problem. Current guardianship model requires one consciousness to serve as permanent anchor for the Hollow Fields barrier. Consequences include total loss of corporeal existence, isolation, and indefinite duration of service.

"Section Two. Objectives. Preserve barrier integrity. Limit or eliminate expansion of Hollow Fields into surrounding areas. Minimize psychological and existential harm to guardian. Consider equitable distribution of burden."

Her voice smoothed out as she went. This part was familiar—this was the language she used for grant proposals and co-op applications, adjusted for the fact that the co-op here sold souls instead of soybeans.

"Proposed Model A," she said. "Rotational Guardianship. Multiple individuals share anchor duties in shifts. Hypothesis: spreading the load over time reduces individual harm."

She outlined it. Week-on, week-off structures. Month-long rotations. Seasonal cycles, like crop rotations but for consciousness.

"For each rotation," she said, "the active guardian anchors from within. Others remain at boundary, serving as...backup. In the event that one cannot continue, the next assumes responsibility."

She'd mapped it like planting schedules—who took which field when. Only here, the fields were time and the harvest was sanity.

"Potential risks," she read. "Transition instability. Overlap errors. Degradation of barrier during handoffs."

Her finger traced her own notes in the margin. Ask Eliza about handoff tolerance. Is barrier binary or gradient?

She swallowed and moved on.

"Proposed Model B," she said. "Shared Consciousness Model. Hypothesis: multiple minds can inhabit anchor role simultaneously, distributing burden."

Mike's hands slid out of his pockets at that, fingers curling. She didn't look at him.

She spoke about merging in pairs, in small groups. About diluting the pressure by having more shoulders under it. She'd drawn diagrams—circles overlapping, Venn diagrams of existence.

"Projected issue," she read. "Identity diffusion. Potential for loss of self. Risk of group mind phenomena."

"Group mind phenomena," Mike muttered under his breath. "That one's fun."

She ignored him.

"Proposed Model C," she said. "Partial Anchoring. Hypothesis: barrier strength might be maintained with reduced anchor presence during low-risk periods. Nighttime anchoring only. Reduced demand during daytime when town is less active."

She'd done the math on that one as best she could. Tried to estimate field expansions. It was guesswork dressed in graphs.

As she read, Tyler watched the readings and occasionally scribbled notes.

Olivia watched Emily instead. The way the pages in her hands trembled slightly more with each section. The way her shoulders stayed squared by force.

The spirits around the square drew closer. They didn't crowd, exactly. They just…converged. Faces in windows. Silhouettes on second-floor balconies. A child in a white dress sitting on a stoop that shifted centuries between blinks.

No one spoke.

Emily's voice grew hoarse.

"Section Six," she said. "Ethical considerations. Consent. Informed choice. Access to alternatives. Moral implications of enforced eternal guardianship in exchange for community safety."

She'd written that part at three a.m., hand cramping, eyes burning. She'd filled it with phrases like duty of care and uncompensated labor and sacrifice should not be the default solution.

Somewhere on page twenty-one, her voice cracked for the first time. She cleared her throat and kept going.

She hit the appendix. Detailed notes. Cross-references. Questions.

"Finally," she said, "we propose that any guardian be allowed to retain a meaningful connection to the living world. Access to communication channels. Some way to not be alone."

Her hands tightened on the paper.

"Because," she said, reading her own careful words aloud, "isolation is not a neutral condition. It is harm."

The last sentence echoed against empty air.

She waited.

Her pulse throbbed behind her eyes. The square held still.

She flipped the last page over, just to be sure there wasn't some note she'd missed. Her own signature stared up at her. Emily Jane Bennett.

"That's…" She cleared her throat again. "That's all."

The town didn't answer.

She felt the others behind her like a line of pressure. Mike shifted on his feet, restless. Tyler's sensors chirped a steady, inscrutable song. Olivia's camera strap creaked softly as she tightened her grip.

Wind moved through the square, the kind that didn't disturb dust. The hair at the back of Emily's neck stood on end.

"Do you think she—" Mike started.

Eliza Nightshade stood at the edge of the circle.

1:09 P.M. — Eliza Listens

She hadn't appeared in a flash or a roar or a peel of spectral thunder. She was just suddenly there, as if she'd been standing there all along and their brains had agreed to notice her at last.

Today, Eliza wore a dress the color of old ink, high-necked, long-sleeved, the fabric heavy and matte. Her hair was bound up in a severe knot at the nape of her neck. The only softness came from the moss.

Golden-green moss traced along her collar, wrapped around her wrists like cuffs, grew in delicate filigree from the hem of her skirt. Tiny white flowers bloomed along it in impossibly crisp detail, dew beading on petals that didn't exist.

Her eyes were the same.

Ancient. Tired. Holding an entire town's worth of grief in their depth.

She regarded Emily first. Not the binder. Not Tyler's equipment. Emily.

"You have done a great deal of work," she said. Her voice was neither cold nor warm. Just...measured. "May I?"

Her hand hovered above the binder. The pages rustled as if caught in a draft. Eliza's fingers never quite touched them, but they turned anyway, flipping through sections.

Emily swallowed. "You—you can read it that way?"

"I read the shape of thoughts," Eliza said. "Paper is just one way they choose to sit still."

She walked slowly around the pedestal, gaze moving over charts and underlines and hand-drawn graphs. Her brow furrowed at Model B. A corner of her mouth twitched, not in amusement, at the ethical considerations section.

As she moved, the town seemed to lean with her. Windows darkened slightly. The air thickened. The spirits in the square watched, their focus pulled to the pedestal.

Tyler stared, not even pretending not to. His hand twitched, wanting to reach for his notebook, but he didn't.

Mike shifted from foot to foot, hands fisted in the pocket of his jacket. Olivia lifted her camera once, quietly, slowly, and took a single frame. The shutter's quiet click sounded obscenely loud.

Eliza did not flinch.

At last, she closed the binder with a thought. The cover rested under her palm.

"You argue clearly," she said.

Emily's heart—but she cut that thought off. "So you'll consider—?"

Eliza's gaze met hers, and for a moment, Emily understood what it felt like to be the only fixed point in an entire town's worth of overlapping time. The weight of it. The thinness of the air at that height.

"I understand why you tried," Eliza said.

It sounded like the beginning of an answer and a eulogy at once.

1:43 P.M. — Why Alternatives Don't Work

"Let us assume," Eliza said, "that rotational guardianship is possible."

She lifted the binder again without lifting it.

"In your Model A," she continued, "you suggest weekly or monthly shifts. One mind, then another, then another, in sequence."

She stepped away from the pedestal. As she walked, images formed in the air behind her like reflections on water.

Emily saw a woman in nineteenth-century clothing standing in the circle. Then another figure. Then another. The images flickered—faces blurring, bodies fading in and out.

"At the moment of handoff," Eliza said, "the barrier would weaken. The town would press against it. Not maliciously. Instinctively. Like water against a dam when a stone is removed."

One of the flickering guardians staggered. Their outline thinned. Outside the illusion, wind edged the square.

"And every handoff," Eliza continued, "is an opportunity for failure. For a moment too late. For hesitation."

The image showed what hesitation looked like. A crack in something invisible. The forest beyond the town edge glowed gold. The border expanded a fraction.

"It only takes one," Eliza said. "One lapse. One forgotten hour. One guardian who oversleeps, or falls ill, or decides not to return."

Emily clenched her jaw. "We wouldn't forget."

"You wouldn't mean to," Eliza corrected gently. "But you are…alive. You are prone to interruption. To distraction. To accidents."

A carriage rattled through the image, then turned into a truck, then something else. Time folded.

"Rotation," Eliza said, "multiplies those chances. Spreads risk across multiple lives instead of asking one to shoulder it."

"That sounds like a feature, not a bug," Mike said. "Share the risk."

Eliza looked at him. "You of all people should appreciate that too many cooks can spoil a deal."

He winced. "Low blow."

She moved on.

"Model B," she said. "Shared consciousness. Multiple minds in the anchor role simultaneously."

The image behind her changed. Instead of guardians taking turns, there were now several overlapping outlines standing in the circle, their forms layered like tracing paper. Their faces blurred together until it was hard to tell where one began and another ended.

"Imagine," Eliza said quietly, "being unable to tell where your own thoughts end and someone else's begin. Imagine hearing every memory, every regret, every fear of every person sharing that space with you. Forever."

Emily's stomach flipped.

"With time," Eliza continued, the overlapping outlines starting to smear, "individual identity erodes. What is you? What is them? At what point does the guardian cease to be any of you and becomes something else entirely?"

Tyler's hand tightened on his sensor. The device beeped once and then went still, as if the field itself was listening.

"Group minds are…unstable," Eliza said. "They make for interesting literature and catastrophic reality. They are vulnerable to madness, to cascade failure. When one breaks, all break. The barrier falls, and there is no single consciousness left to hold it up."

Mike swallowed. "Okay, so, not that one."

"Model C," Eliza said. "Partial anchoring."

The images shifted again. The guardian outline grew solid at night, translucent by day, in a loop. The town lights flickered with each transition. The edges of Hollow Fields pulsed—expanding imperceptibly in each off-period, retracting when the anchor returned.

"This town does not sleep," Eliza said. "It slows. It shifts. But it does not stop needing restraint. Even if you convince it to behave during your chosen off-hours—and that is not guaranteed—the cumulative effect of those gaps would be expansion."

In the illusion, the border crept outward over years. Houses at the edge of reality blinked into existence where forest had been.

"Two generations," Eliza said. "Perhaps three. And then Hollow Fields would be touching highways, suburbs, schools."

Emily's scalp prickled. She thought of the campus. Of Josh's apartment. Of her own farm, miles away.

"So you're saying everything we came up with is useless," she said, words tasting like iron.

"I am saying," Eliza replied, "that others have tried these things."

She snapped her fingers, just once.

The images multiplied.

Guardians in clothing from every era stood in the circle. Some were alone. Some overlapped. Some reached for hands that weren't there. Diagrams hung in the air around them—complex rune structures, mechanical rigs, what looked like early machines.

"We have attempted rotation," Eliza said. The rotating guardians blurred faster, until one failed to appear and the border blew outwards in a silent, golden shockwave. "We have attempted shared minds." The overlapping group dissolved into a screaming tangle of light. "We have attempted partial anchoring." The town seeped outward in slow motion until it swallowed the road.

"Every experiment," Eliza said, and her voice had a slight tremor now, "ended in greater harm. To the guardians. To the world outside."

The images faded.

"You are not the first to love someone enough to wish them free," she said softly. "You will not be the last. But wanting alternatives does not create them."

2:21 P.M. — Mike's Angle

"So that's it?" Mike said. His voice came out too loud in the quiet square. "You're just going to...what? Tell us we made a good effort and stamp DENIED on the top?"

Eliza turned toward him, the moss at her cuffs trembling faintly.

"Do you think I enjoy this?" she asked.

"I think you're detached," Mike said. "You're...what, two hundred? Three hundred? You've had centuries to reconcile yourself to this. You did your time. You got promoted. You're management now."

"Mike," Olivia said warningly.

He barreled on. "You stand there and you show us your little ghost PowerPoint and you say 'this is how it is' as if you didn't once stand right where he—" He jerked his chin toward the invisible shimmer by the pedestal. "Where he is now. As if you didn't want someone to rescue you."

Something flickered in Eliza's expression. Not anger. Something heavier.

"When I was chosen," she said quietly, "my friends tried too. They were less...organized than you." A hint of dry amusement. "But no less determined."

Mike's throat worked.

"And?" he forced out.

"And they failed," Eliza said. "As did I, when I tried to find another path before my own Step Seven."

The air around the pedestal rippled twice in quick succession. Josh, straining.

Emily's hands tightened into fists at her sides. "You tried," she said. "You looked for alternatives."

Eliza inclined her head. "Every night," she said. "Every waking moment between steps. I petitioned those who built the barrier. I negotiated with forces you do not have names for. I begged and I bartered."

Her gaze slid back to Mike.

"There is no deal," she said. "Not one that preserves both Josh and the world beyond this town."

"There's always another deal," Mike said. The sentence sounded smaller than usual. "You just haven't found it yet."

Eliza looked at him for a long time.

"I admire your faith," she said. "Truly. But if there were another bargain to be struck, do you not think I would have taken it? That your friend would not have found it during the months he has been…shifting?"

The air shuddered. Once. Hard.

"Months?" Emily repeated. "How long has he—?"

"Step One began long before he told you," Eliza said gently. "Guardians do not enter into this lightly. He searched. He delayed. He hoped. And when all paths narrowed to one, he moved forward."

A buzzing filled Emily's ears. Josh had been carrying this alone even longer than she'd thought.

"You're saying he's…already decided," she said.

Eliza turned toward the shimmer. "He wants you to know," she said, voice softening, "that he is…sorry. For not telling you sooner. For the pain this causes. For every missed goodbye."

The air quivered like it was trying to be a voice.

"He also wants you to know," she added, "that he does not regret choosing the town over himself."

Emily's vision blurred.

"That doesn't make it okay," she said.

"No," Eliza agreed. "It does not. It makes it…necessary."

3:08 P.M. — Emily Breaks

"There HAS to be another way."

Emily didn't realize she was yelling until her throat hurt.

She took a step toward Eliza, binder forgotten on the pedestal. The spirits at the edges of the square receded a fraction, like a tide pushed back by a wave of something hotter.

"You're supposed to be the expert," she said. "The guardian. The whatever. You—" Her hands flailed, searching for a gesture big enough. "You managed this for centuries. You learned to talk like this." She mimicked Eliza's measured tone viciously. "'We have attempted. We have assessed. We have determined.'"

Her voice climbed. "So determine harder. Attempt something else. You can't just…just shrug and say 'oh well, eternity.'"

She heard herself slipping into home. Into debates with school board members and stubborn co-op partners. Instrumental use of outrage.

This wasn't strategy now. This was a dam cracking.

"Eliza," she said, and the name came out like an accusation. "You had people. You had friends who tried to save you. You failed them. Fine. That's your tragedy. But you don't get to be resigned about ours."

"Emily," Eliza said.

"No," Emily snapped. "Don't use my first name like we're peers right now. My cousin is being turned into a…a fence post. A scarecrow. A—" She bit off the word sacrifice before it could finish.

Her eyes burned. She blinked hard and the square doubled.

"Joshua," she said, turning toward the shimmer. The air shimmered back, frantic, like someone pounding on glass from the other side. "You hear this? You hear her? She's telling us you already gave up."

The air pulsed.

"Did you just…decide?" Emily demanded. "All on your own? You didn't think, 'Hey, maybe my cousin who has dealt with stubborn, short-sighted farmers her entire life could negotiate with ghosts'? You didn't think we'd maybe want a say?"

Three sharp ripples, back to back.

"She says you looked," Emily said, gesturing blindly at Eliza. "She says you tried. Did you? Or did you just accept the first doom-flavored contract they waved under your nose because it was tidy and you like tidy?"

The shimmer around the pedestal flared and then faltered. Tyler's equipment squealed an alarm and then went quiet, the display fuzzing into static for a second before resolving.

"Emily," Olivia said softly. "You're overwhelming him."

"Good," Emily said. Her hands were shaking. She could feel it now—the hours of sleep lost, the meals skipped, the constant, grinding fear of Monday. All of it slamming into the wall she'd built out of bullet points and plans.

She turned back to Eliza, vision swimming.

"You say every guardian has friends who tried," she said. "You say they all failed. Maybe that's because you never let them finish. Maybe you all decided for them."

Eliza's expression remained composed, but the moss at her cuffs had begun to brown at the edges, as if some deep rot had been called to the surface.

"Do you think I would choose this for him if there were another way?" she asked quietly.

"Yes," Emily said, surprising herself. "Because you chose it for you. Because once you decide something is inevitable, it's easier to drag everyone else into that inevitability than admit maybe it shouldn't be."

The words came out like knives she hadn't known she was holding.

Silence crashed down.

The spirits in the square stilled entirely. The town itself seemed to hold its breath.

The binder slid off the pedestal and hit the ground, papers fanning out across the cobblestones.

Emily stared down at them. Charts. Notes. Her own careful handwriting. The work of a week that felt like a lifetime. The shattered pieces of a plan that hadn't even made a dent.

Her knees buckled.

She caught herself on her hands, palms scraping stone. The impact jolted up her arms, knocking loose whatever feeble composure she had left. Tears hit the paper in uneven drops, blurring the ink.

A hand that wasn't really a hand rested near hers.

Not touching. Just…close.

Eliza had knelt too, her skirts pooling around her in impossible moss. Up close, Emily could see the fine network of cracks along her cheekbones, like a porcelain doll that had been repaired too many times.

"I am sorry," Eliza said. The words sounded like there was weight inside each one. "You are correct. I decided for others once. I believed I knew what was…best. I have had centuries to live with that arrogance."

Emily's breath hitched.

"I cannot undo what has already begun," Eliza continued. "I cannot unravel a process that is woven into the fabric of this field without tearing the fabric itself. And I will not ask this town to unmake itself to spare one guardian."

"You should," Emily said, voice ragged. "You should at least want to."

Eliza flinched.

"I do," she said. "More than you can imagine. That is why this hurts."

She looked toward the shimmer, her gaze softening in a way that made Emily's stomach twist.

"And he knew that," she added. "He saw what would happen if he did not step forward. He saw what it would do to you. To everyone he loves. He chose the pain that fell mostly on himself."

The air by the pedestal rippled slowly. Once. Twice. A steady rhythm, like someone nodding.

Emily pressed her forehead against her palms.

"This isn't fair," she whispered.

"No," Eliza said. "It is not. It is, however, real."

4:19 P.M. — Hope Dies in the Quiet

They stayed in the square after Eliza faded.

One moment she was there, her moss and ink dress blurring into the edges of the town. The next, she wasn't. No dramatic exit. No speech. Just absence.

The pedestal stood bare. The binder lay splayed across the ground. Emily's proposal looked like litter.

The town remained. Watching.

Mike sat on the edge of the circle, elbows on his knees, staring at nothing. His shoulders, usually squared in showman posture, had slumped inward.

"I can't close this deal," he said, almost conversationally. "I've scammed card sharks. I've talked a dean into refunding me for a semester I never attended. I convinced a guy to give me his car once because I made the paperwork look official enough."

He laughed once, short and humorless.

"But this?" he said. "This won't move."

Olivia sat cross-legged beside him, camera resting in her lap, lens cap on. She tracked a nonexistent pattern in the cobblestones with one finger.

"You can't con physics," she said. "Or whatever this counts as."

"I could try," he said. "Offer it something shiny. My soul. I don't know."

Tyler had his back against a lamppost that flickered between gas and electric, his equipment arrayed around him like a tiny, useless shrine. He'd tried to log Eliza's explanations. His recordings were full of static.

"I can record the data," he said, speaking as much to his own notes as to the others. "Field densities. Step timings. The way the town layers. I can make charts of the way his presence diffuses."

He flicked through graphs with jerky motions.

"But I can't…capture this." He gestured around—at Emily doubled over a few yards away, at Mike's hollow joke, at Olivia's quiet.

"My files will say 'At 2:17 P.M., Eliza demonstrated the failure of Model B,'" he said. "But they won't say she looked…sorry. Or that Emily's voice broke on the word 'fair.'"

"Maybe you could add a feelings column," Mike said without heat.

Tyler huffed. "I'm serious."

"So am I," Mike said. "Sort of."

The air in the center of the circle moved gently. Emily could feel it on the back of her neck as she knelt, gathering scattered pages with shaking hands. Each piece she picked up felt like a small betrayal. The paper was softer where her tears had hit it.

"You hear that, Josh?" Mike said, looking toward the shimmer. "Tyler's building you a feelings database. Olivia's got your good side. Em wrote you a ten-thousand-word legal brief. I made eggs. This is a messed-up team project."

The air shivered twice.

"Yeah," Mike said. "I know you're…grateful. Or whatever. Save it."

Olivia glanced up.

"You're angry," she said softly.

He shrugged one shoulder. "He chose this."

"So did you," she said.

He blinked. "Excuse me?"

"You chose him," Olivia said. "To care about. To follow into a haunted town. To feed when he couldn't hold a fork anymore."

Mike opened his mouth. Closed it. Looked away.

The square clock in a tower that sometimes existed and sometimes didn't chimed once. Then again. The sound was warped, like it had passed through water.

Emily sat back on her heels, the binder now closed again in her lap. Her cheeks felt raw. Her eyes throbbed.

"So that's it," she said.

Tyler looked up. "That's…what?"

"We can't save him," she said. The words scraped her throat like sand. "We can't…convince the town to do something different. The steps won't stop. The merger is going to happen at 7:13 tomorrow whether we stand here or go home or set this whole place on fire."

Olivia didn't argue. Mike didn't crack a joke.

The air shimmered once more at the pedestal, slow, like a hand resting on a shoulder.

"That doesn't mean we stop showing up," Emily added. "We don't…let him do this alone."

She raised her head, eyes red, and focused on the space where she could feel him most.

"You hear me, Joshua?" she said. "You're not getting out of this without supervision."

The air moved in what she chose to interpret as a sigh.

6:01 P.M. — The Road Back

The walk back through the layered town felt shorter.

Maybe because they weren't searching for routes anymore. There was no if we just find the right street, the loophole will be there. There was only the path out.

The spirits watched them go. A woman in a 1920s dress lifted a hand in a slow, solemn motion. A boy of maybe twelve, barefoot, sat on a stoop and nodded once. None spoke.

Emily, binder clutched tight, nodded back.

At the boundary, the air thickened again. The transition felt less like stepping through plastic wrap this time and more like wading out of deep water. Her ears popped.

On the other side, the ordinary forest waited, smelling of cold leaves and damp soil.

The car's doors groaned the same way they always did. The engine turned over on the second try. The clock on the dash said 6:01 P.M.

It felt like midnight.

The drive back to town was almost entirely silent. Mike kept his eyes on the road. Tyler kept his gaze on the sensor readouts, but the graphs barely shifted; whatever had been roaring in Hollow Fields had quieted back to a background hum.

Olivia watched the world blur past her window. Trees. Houses. A convenience store with flickering fluorescent lights. A dog in a yard barking at nothing they could see.

She raised her camera once, on instinct, and took a picture of the rearview mirror. Mike's eyes. Emily's profile. The empty backseat between Emily and Tyler where the air felt thick.

The flash didn't fire. She didn't check the screen.

In the backseat, Emily stared straight ahead, seeing nothing outside. Her mind kept looping the same phrases. We can't save him. He chose this. We can still be with him.

Her hands were numb around the binder.

She didn't realize she was counting under her breath until Tyler gently nudged her knee.

"Hey," he murmured. "What are you doing?"

"Calculating hours," she said. "Less than thirteen now. Between midnight and 7:13."

Tyler's fingers tightened on the edge of his tablet. "Right."

Mike's knuckles were white on the steering wheel.

"Can we...not?" he said. "Just...for a bit? Pretend time isn't doing that?"

Emily shut her mouth.

They drove.

7:02 P.M. — Mundane Horror

Josh's apartment looked smaller when they came back.

Maybe it was the way the light outside had shifted, streetlamps casting jaundiced rectangles on the walls. Maybe it was the missing weight of denial.

The smell hit first. Coffee gone bitter on the warmer. The lingering savory of eggs. The grease of last night's pizza boxes. Under it all, the faint, metallic tang of something that wasn't in any cookbook.

The air above the couch shimmered, faint and strained, as if a heavy weight lay on the wires of existence and they were starting to thin.

"Hey," Mike said quietly, closing the door behind them. "We're back."

The curtains stirred in a room with no breeze.

Tyler set his gear down carefully, as if noise might jar something fragile. Olivia placed her camera on the desk instead of keeping it on her shoulder.

Emily shrugged off her backpack and dropped it near the table, then looked around like she was seeing the place for the first time.

"That," Mike said, pointing at the coffee pot, "is a crime scene." He moved to empty it, grimaced at the sludge, and started rinsing it out.

"Should we…do something about his stuff?" Olivia asked. Her voice was soft. "Like, his desk. Clothes. I don't know what the…protocol is for impending metaphysical departure."

"We wait," Emily said reflexively. Then, more slowly, "We should at least…make a list."

"A list," Mike repeated. "Sure. Let's plan his estate sale."

"That's not what I meant," she snapped.

"I know," he said immediately. "Sorry. I just—" He gestured vaguely around. "What do you even tell people? 'Sorry, your son/cousin/friend couldn't come to the phone, he's busy turning into a psychic fence'?"

"Don't joke," Olivia said. "Please."

He shut up again.

Emily moved to Josh's desk. Class syllabi, Post-it notes, a half-finished problem set. A mug with pens. A photo taped to the lamp—Josh and Emily at the farm, both squinting in the sun, holding a brimming basket between them.

Her hand hovered over it, then withdrew.

"His parents are expecting a call tomorrow," she said. "He said he'd check in. Tell them he's fine. He won't…be able to."

"I can do it," Mike said.

"No," Emily said. "It should be me."

Tyler had pulled out a small notebook, flipping to a clean page. "We can split tasks," he said. "Someone calls his parents. Someone deals with his

RA. Someone…handles his class drop forms. His lease."

The list made Emily's temples throb.

"He's not dead," she said.

"I know," Tyler said quickly. "I just—these things still…exist. The systems. They keep moving. If we don't tell them something, they'll just keep sending him invoices forever."

The image of automated emails piling up in an inbox no one could open made her stomach churn.

"What do we say?" Olivia murmured. "That he had a medical emergency? That he moved away? That he joined a monastery?"

"Tell them he joined a long-term…research project," Mike suggested weakly. "He is studying…fields."

"That's not funny," Emily said.

"It wasn't a joke," he replied. "It was…wishful lying."

The radiator knocked again. The air above the couch trembled. It took more effort now to make it move. Emily could feel it. The strain in the room. Like someone trying to stand on a leg that had fallen asleep.

"Hey," she said, turning toward the shimmer. "Do you want us to… touch anything? Move anything?"

The air gave the slightest flutter, then stilled.

"I'll take that as a 'no,'" she said softly.

She wrote call parents at the top of Tyler's notebook page. The letters came out wobbly. Under it, lease, classes, campus job. Each mundane bullet point felt obscene next to the reality that the person they referred to was still right here, listening.

"This is insane," Mike said. He leaned against the kitchen counter, rubbing his fingers over his face. "We're planning his paperwork and he can hear every word."

The air rippled, faint and apologetic.

"Don't you dare feel bad for that," Emily said to the empty space. "You don't have the monopoly on feeling ridiculous here."

8:41 P.M. — Stories for an Invisible Audience

By eight-thirty, the coffee pot was clean, the worst of the dishes were rinsed, and the list in Tyler's notebook had grown long enough to be overwhelming.

They hadn't done any of it.

It felt wrong to call people at night and invent lies about medical emergencies while the person in question hovered six feet away. It felt wrong to go online and drop classes like they were just...choices.

So they didn't.

Instead, they rearranged the living room.

The coffee table got pushed closer to the couch, forming a loose circle with the armchair and the floor cushions. The overhead light went off; they left the lamp by the window on, its shade casting a warm cone that turned dust motes into slow snow.

Emily sat on the couch. Mike took the armchair, tilted to face her. Tyler claimed the floor cushion nearest the sensors, back to the couch. Olivia sat cross-legged near the coffee table, notebook open but pen idle.

The air above the couch dimmed and brightened like a slow blink.

"We should...talk," Olivia said.

"We have been talking non-stop for days," Mike said.

"Not like that," she said. "We've been...problem-solving. Planning. Arguing. I mean...tell him things. While he can still...hear us like this."

Emily stared at the smudge of distortion in the lamplight.

"I don't know what to say," she admitted.

"Start with something easy," Tyler said. "Like a memory."

"Of what?" she asked.

"Anything," he said. "First thing that comes to mind."

Emily looked down at her hands. The callus on her middle finger from years of writing notes. The faint scar along her thumb from when she'd tried to slice a bagel wrong-handed at twelve.

"Remember when you got stuck on the grain silo ladder?" she said abruptly, addressing the air. "You were eight. You decided you wanted to see the view, because Grandpa said it was the best view on the farm."

She could almost see the scene overlaying the apartment—blazing summer sky, the barn roof, the rusted ladder clanging.

"You got halfway up, looked down, and started crying," she went on. "You wouldn't go up or down. You just clung there like a terrified barnacle for twenty minutes while Grandpa tried to coax you."

The air rippled faintly.

"Grandma finally came out," Emily said, a reluctant smile tugging at one corner of her mouth. "She stood at the bottom and said, 'Joshua Allen Bennett, you can either come down or die up there, but you may not stay.' And you—" She shook her head. "You came down. Crying. But you did it."

Mike snorted quietly. "Effective parenting."

"She told me later she knew you'd move faster if she made it sound like a choice," Emily said. "I asked her if she would've gone up for you if you'd frozen. She said, 'Of course. But he didn't need to know that.'"

The shimmer above the couch steadied, as if leaning into the memory.

"Congratulations," Emily said, voice catching. "You finally found a ladder you can't climb down from."

The air fluttered, not quite amusement, not quite protest.

Tyler cleared his throat. "Remember the first time we found the pickles?" he said.

"Yes," Mike said immediately. "Do tell the origin story of our cursed brand."

"It was in that abandoned cellar under the old house by the east field," Tyler said, directing his words at the empty air. "You almost didn't take them. You said it was stealing from history."

"He said that?" Mike asked. "Sounds like him."

"You said—" Tyler consulted a mental transcript. "You said, 'Maybe this is like those stories where you don't take food from the fairies, or you're stuck with them forever.'"

Emily exhaled.

"And then I reminded you that you grew up on urban legends and you didn't believe half of them," Tyler continued. "And Mike said—"

"'If it's cursed, we can always return it for store credit,'" Mike recited.

"Exactly," Tyler said. "You stood there for, like, five full minutes, Joshua. You looked at that jar like it had a visible moral dilemma label."

The shimmer trembled.

"You took it anyway," Tyler said. "You told yourself it was a rescue mission. That leaving it there would be worse."

Olivia smiled faintly. "I was the one who took the first picture of them," she said. "On your kitchen counter. I remember thinking the light hit the glass weird. Too bright for the room."

She drew an invisible frame in the air.

"You said—" She glanced at Emily. "'If my cousin finds out I brought cursed pickles into her farmhouse, she's going to kill me.'"

"Still an option," Emily murmured.

The stories continued.

They talked about the first time the town had overlapped with their world. About the night Josh had shown up at Tyler's dorm room, pale and jittery, a jar cradled in his arms like a bomb and saying, I need you to see this.

They talked about stupid road trips. About a thrift store run where Josh had insisted on buying a hideous lamp because "every group of idiots needs one cursed object that isn't literally cursed."

They talked until their throats were raw and the lamplight had shifted from warm to oppressive.

Every so often, the air by the couch moved. Small, precise shifts. As if someone were nodding, or flinching, or trying to reach out.

Tyler's sensors recorded each spike, time-stamped. He didn't look at the graphs.

He listened.

10:07 P.M. — One-on-One

At some point, the group stories slowed. They started tripping over each other, repeating the same snippets in different words. The edges of exhaustion were fraying their sentences.

"We should take turns," Olivia suggested quietly. "Give him…space. And us."

Tyler checked the time on his watch. "We've got…a little under nine hours until Step Ten completes."

"Don't say the number," Mike said.

"Sorry," Tyler said.

They decided without really deciding.

Mike went first.

10:13 P.M. — Mike

He dragged the armchair closer to the couch, until its arm nearly touched the cushion where Josh wasn't.

The others retreated toward the kitchenette, giving him the illusion of privacy in a one-room apartment.

Mike slouched into the chair, then straightened, then slouched again. His hands twisted together, then unclasped. He finally settled on resting his elbows on his knees and staring directly at the shimmer.

"Okay," he said. "Ground rules. You…ripple once for 'yes,' twice for 'no,' and zero for 'I don't know' or 'stop talking,' or because you're too busy becoming an eldritch neighborhood watch to answer."

The air quivered once.

"Good," he said. "Glad to see the communication protocols are robust."

He ran his tongue over his teeth, buying time.

"You know," he said, "when we met, I thought you were…easy. Easy mark. Nice farm kid in over his head with city scams. You. The jars. The way you kept showing up where contracts were being signed, asking questions like, 'Why is the fee structured that way?'"

The air shifted, faint amusement.

"And then you…wouldn't…let me take advantage of you," Mike said. "Which was annoying, by the way. You kept asking for the terms. For the fine print. For the implications. No one asks for implications."

He sighed.

"You made me better," he said. "At first, because I had to be better to keep up with your questions. And then…because you didn't just accept my 'that's how it is.' You pushed until the way it was started to look…worse. Until I started thinking maybe the angles I liked finding were hurting people who didn't deserve it."

The air trembled.

"And now," Mike continued, "you found the biggest angle of all and you decided 'this is how it has to be' and you didn't give me a chance to…fix it. Or fail. Or whatever."

He swallowed.

"There's always another deal," he said quietly. "That's been my thing. My mantra. My safety net. No matter how bad it gets, there's a loophole. A clause. A handshake. A way out."

The air didn't move.

"I…don't have one here," he said. "This is it. It's just…you and the field, signing on for eternity. And me sitting here with nothing to offer but…scrambled eggs and bad jokes."

He laughed, roughly.

"I don't know how to exist without you, man," he said, finally. "Without this dumb, cursed project. Without your—" His voice broke. "Without your spreadsheets and your questions and your, 'Let me think about it,' every time I pitched something."

The air rippled. Once. Hard.

"You don't get to tell me to be okay," Mike said. "Don't do it. I can feel you gearing up for it. 'Take care of them. Look after Emily. Watch Hollow Fields from the outside.'"

The shimmer hung, taut.

"You want to give me an assignment?" Mike said. "Fine. I'll...try. I'll check the gates. I'll run interference when the town twitches. I'll tell your parents some kind of...partial truth. I'll be the guy at the edge of the field counting how many people the pickles don't eat because of you."

He scrubbed at his eyes with the heels of his hands.

"But you should know," he added, voice dropping, "that I am going to be angry at you for a very long time. Maybe forever. I'm going to...miss you, yes, and be proud of you, sure, but I am also going to be pissed that you decided your life was a fair price without asking for my bid."

The air pulsed. Not in apology. More like acknowledgment.

"Good," Mike said. "Now that we've got that cleared up, you can go haunt some cornfields."

There was a pause.

The blinds swayed once, gently, as if a hand had brushed them in farewell.

Mike looked away, jaw clenched, and called toward the kitchenette, "Next."

10:31 P.M. — Tyler

Tyler took the armchair when Mike vacated it, but he sat on its edge, back straight, hands resting on his knees.

His sensors sat dark on the table, their displays dulled. For once, he'd turned them off.

He looked at the shimmer and exhaled.

"Okay," he said. "So. Data guy here. Trying to...talk without numbers for once."

The air moved, a faint encouragement.

"I've been recording everything," Tyler said. "You know that. Field changes. Time slips. Your…gradual…uh…transition." The word felt clinical and wrong. "I'm building a database so that if there ever is another guardian, or if anything about this changes, there will be…records."

He swallowed.

"But there's this problem," he said. "My files don't…hold you."

He gestured vaguely at his equipment. "I can graph your EM output. I can chart the way your…consciousness, I guess, has expanded over the last week. I can log when you first stopped being able to hold a spoon. When you started shimmering. When your voice…went."

The air fluttered.

"But none of my logs mention," he went on, "how you always hummed under your breath when you were thinking. Or how you used to drool over those ridiculous limited-edition jar labels. Or how you believed me the first time I said, 'I think the town responds to your moods,' and you didn't laugh."

He stared down at his hands.

"I keep trying to make the documentation better," he said. "Adding more columns. More notes. 'Subject seemed tired.' 'Subject laughed here.' But it still…flattens you. Turns you into a case study."

The shimmer above the couch steadied, a quiet presence.

"I'm scared I'll forget," Tyler admitted. "Not the big stuff. The date. The time. The fact that you turned yourself into a psychic firewall. Those will be in every file."

His throat worked.

"I'm scared I'll forget the weird nicknames you gave your jars," he said. "Or the way you swore under your breath when the printer jammed. Or… how it felt the first time you said, 'We' when talking about this project. Like I wasn't just…some guy with equipment."

The air dipped once, like a nod.

"I don't know how to fix that," Tyler said. "I can't build a system that guarantees memory. Brains degrade. Files corrupt. Hard drives fail. I can make backups until the heat death of the universe, and something will still get lost."

He reached out, hand hovering inches above the shimmering air.

"So, I guess," he said quietly, "what I can promise is…effort. I will do my best to remember all of it. Not just you-as-guardian. You-as…Josh. I will…write it down in ways that will embarrass you if anyone ever reads them."

The air rippled, faint amusement.

"And if…if there's ever a way to…talk to you," he added, "through the field, through the steps, through whatever, I will build it. Even if it takes me the rest of my life. That's my…deal."

For a moment, the shimmer brightened, threads of distortion reaching toward his outstretched hand. Tyler felt…nothing physical. No pressure. But his skin tingled, like the aftermath of static shock.

"Okay," he whispered. "Deal accepted."

He pulled his hand back, blinking rapidly, and relinquished the chair.

10:52 P.M. — Olivia

Olivia didn't sit in the chair.

She took the floor space directly in front of the couch, crossing her legs, hands on her knees. Her camera sat behind her, lens facing away. She'd forgotten to turn it off; the tiny red light blinked in the corner of her vision.

"Hi," she said. "I know you're there. The air looks…wrong."

The shimmer trembled, a soft greeting.

"I've spent a lot of time trying to capture things," she said. "Birds. Buildings. People. Ghost towns that aren't as literal as this one. Light on water. Shadows in doorways. Evidence."

She smiled, small and crooked.

"You know the story," she said. "I took pictures of something once. Something…impossible. I showed adults. They told me it was lens flare. Glare. A trick of the imagination."

The air shifted, sympathetic.

"I swore I'd get better," she said. "I'd learn my craft. Become so good at seeing that my pictures couldn't be dismissed as accidents."

She turned slightly, glancing at her camera.

"And now," she continued, "we're on the edge of the one moment that matters more than any I have ever tried to frame. The merger. The moment you…stop being human and start being…this place."

Her eyes stung.

"And I am going to miss it," she said.

The air twitched.

"We both know that's how this is going to go," she said softly. "Something will interfere. The battery will die at the wrong second. The card will corrupt. The lens will fog. My hands will shake. The town will turn your silhouette into static."

She huffed a quiet breath.

"This is not self-pity," she said. "It's…pattern recognition. Every time I have tried to photograph something that would prove beyond doubt that the world is stranger than people think, something…goes wrong."

She shrugged one shoulder.

"So, I've decided something," she said, eyes lifting again to the shimmer. "Tomorrow, when the time comes, I will try. Of course. I will point every camera I own at the place where you are. But I will not... stake everything on that."

She pressed a hand lightly over her own chest.

"I will remember," she said. "Here. The way the room feels right now. The way the air shivers when you laugh without sound. The look on Emily's face when she told you the grain silo story. The way Mike's voice cracked when he said he didn't know how to exist without you. The way Tyler reached out, as if he could touch you through…whatever this is."

The shimmer smoothed, quiet and steady.

"You are going to become memory," she said, voice barely above a whisper. "To everyone but us. To this town. To the creatures. To the other guardians. A line in a ledger. A name on a list. But to me, you will be… frames. Not photographs. Moments. The way the light sat on your hair when you stared at the pickles. The way your hands moved when you explained crop rotation like it was magic."

She smiled through the burn in her eyes.

"I am not ready," she admitted. "I am not ready for you to be…only that. But I will carry it. That's what I do. That's my job. I'm the one who looks, so that other people don't have to be brave enough to."

The air rippled once, slow and grateful.

"Tomorrow," she said, "when the cameras betray me, remember I told you that I expected it. I won't be mad. Not at you. Maybe at physics."

She reached back and clicked the camera off. The blinking red light died.

"For tonight," she said, "I'll just…sit with you."

So she did. For a few minutes, she simply breathed with the room, matching the rhythm of the shimmer as best she could.

Then she made room for Emily.

11:29 P.M. — Emily

Emily didn't want to do this.

Not because she didn't have anything to say. Because she had too much.

She took the armchair and turned it so she was squarely facing the couch. Her hands gripped the edges of the seat. Her legs bounced once, twice, and then she forced them to still.

The shimmer above the cushions was faint now. Threadbare at the edges. Like the ghost of steam after the kettle had been taken off the burner.

"Joshua," she said.

The air shivered.

"Good," she said. "You still respond to your government name."

She stared at the distortion. A laugh came out like a cough.

"How do we say goodbye to someone who can't say it back?" she asked.

The question hung between them. Heavy. Honest.

"I've been trying to…control this," she said. "That's what I do. I make plans. I make charts. I tell stubborn men in county offices that their policies are idiotic. I organize harvest schedules so that nobody's field gets overworked."

She swallowed.

"I thought I could…apply that here," she said. "That if I just… researched hard enough, argued well enough, I could write a proposal that a haunted town couldn't refuse."

The air shimmered once, weaker than before.

"I am so mad at you," she said quietly. "I don't even know where to put it. You carried this alone for so long. You decided the price, and you didn't give any of us a chance to argue. You just…walked onto the ladder and kept climbing."

Her fingers dug into the fabric of the chair.

"At the farm," she went on, "Grandpa always said that if a fence post rotted, you didn't let the animals decide who'd replace it. You chose the post. You dug the hole. You set it yourself. You didn't ask the cows to vote."

She gave a rough little snort.

"You decided you were the post," she said. "You didn't even let me get my hands on the shovel."

The shimmer stirred, a flicker of apology.

"And I get it," she said. "I do. You saw what this town could do. You saw what would happen if no one held it. You saw those creatures smiling at our windows. You decided you'd rather be the dam than let the flood out."

Her voice softened.

"That's who you are," she said. "You act like you're just…some guy with too many spreadsheets and a weird hobby. But you're the one who volunteers to stay late when the farm stand line is long. You're the one who gives up your weekend to help neighbors with their fences. You're the one who would always rather make yourself tired than watch other people struggle."

The air pulsed, faint and embarrassed.

"You're not allowed to be the hero," she said, and now the tears were back. "That was always the rule. You don't get to…throw yourself on the machinery, because you have people. You have me. You have us. You don't get to decide that your life is the…logical sacrifice without letting us at least try to throw ourselves at it too."

She wiped at her face with the back of her hand, annoyed at her own crying.

"But you did," she said. "And I can't...undo that."

The words tasted like surrender and acid.

"So here's what I'm going to do," she continued. "I am going to stay. Through tomorrow. Through the...merger. Through your...whatever Step Eleven and Twelve look like. I am going to watch as much of it as Eliza and the laws of metaphysics will let me. I am going to take notes."

She huffed out a sound that might've been a laugh.

"And then," she said, "I am going to make understanding this my...job. Not because I think I can change it. Eliza made that pretty clear."

The air flickered.

"But because I refuse to let the moment you become...this town—this guardian—be something I don't understand," she said. "You're not allowed to disappear into some kind of ineffable mystery. Not from me. If I wasn't there when the choice became final, I will be there for everything that comes after."

Her jaw tightened.

"And I swear," she added, voice low, "if there is any way, ever, to...shift this burden, to soften it, to...touch that field and say, 'Enough,' I will find it. You are not the only stubborn one in this family."

The room was very quiet. Even the radiator seemed to be holding still.

The shimmer above the couch drew itself together in a final, concentrated effort. For one brief second, Emily thought she saw...a shape. Not a face. Not features. Just the suggestion of shoulders, the impression of someone leaning forward.

Then it dispersed, leaving behind a thinner, paler distortion. A single, faint twist in the air like a knot in a rope.

"I love you, you idiot," she said.

The knot in the air trembled.

11:53 P.M. — Creatures at the Window

They didn't knock.

They didn't speak.

They simply appeared, as if the darkness outside the windows had thickened into bodies.

One by one, pale faces emerged from the night. Wide, dark eyes. Too-broad smiles that didn't quite reach those eyes. Fingers splayed against the glass, leaving no fog this time. No smears.

They watched.

Tyler saw them first, if only because he'd been looking up to check the time.

"Uh," he said quietly. "Guys."

Emily turned. Her stomach clenched.

The creatures lined the balcony outside like grotesque Christmas carolers. Their heads tilted in unison, curious, as they took in the scene inside—the circle of humans, the lamplight, the faint shimmer above the couch.

Mike stood slowly, placing himself between the windows and the others without even thinking about it.

"If any of you start holding up a 'Welcome to Eternity' sign, I'm throwing something," he told them.

They didn't react. Their smiles remained fixed. Their eyes, though—those looked…almost…soft.

That was worse.

Olivia, pulse racing, lifted her camera by reflex. Then she remembered her conversation and put it down. She didn't want this frozen.

One of the creatures—taller than the others, with hair that hung in limp, dark strands—leaned closer to the glass. Its mouth moved, just slightly. The sound, when it came, was more inside their skulls than in the room.

"Tomorrow," it whispered. "Tomorrow you'll understand."

Emily's skin crawled.

"Understand what?" she said, because of course she couldn't let it go.

The creature's smile widened.

"Why joining is mercy," it murmured.

Mike's hands balled into fists. "Hard pass," he said. "We're not taking theological advice from window ghouls."

The creature's gaze slid to the shimmer above the couch. Its expression shifted—something like hunger, something like awe.

"He will see," it said. "He will know. He will not be alone long, if you… break."

Olivia felt rage like ice.

"We are not recruitment fodder," she said, surprising herself with the sharpness in her voice. "You don't get to…farm our grief."

The creature's head cocked.

"It is not we who farm," it said. "It is the field."

Then, as if a signal had been given, the creatures stepped back from the glass. Not vanishing this time—just walking into the deeper dark until their pale faces were swallowed.

The window reflected only the lamplight and their own tired selves once more.

"Okay," Tyler said shakily. "That…happened."

"Add 'psychic marketing' to the list of things I despise," Mike muttered.

Emily looked back at the couch.

The shimmer was barely there now. A thin thread of distortion, twisting slowly in place.

"Don't listen to them," she said. "We're not joining you."

The air twitched once. Agreement. Or maybe merely acknowledgment; too worn for more.

Midnight — Seven Hours, Thirteen Minutes

12:00 A.M.

The digital clock on the microwave rolled over with a soft, indifferent beep.

In the living room, the lamp cast its small circle of light. The coffee table was cluttered with mugs, notebooks, Tyler's equipment, Olivia's camera, the closed binder containing Emily's failed proposal.

On the couch, there was no visible occupant.

Above it, at about where Josh's torso would have been, the air kinked. A tiny, stubborn knot. Step Ten, nearly complete.

Ninety-five percent incorporeal.

Five percent left.

Emily lay sideways on the far end of the couch, shoes kicked off, her head on the armrest. She hadn't meant to lie down; her body had simply folded. Her eyes drifted shut and snapped open, refusing to miss a second. Her hand rested near the knot in the air, not touching, fingers slightly curled.

Mike sat on the floor with his back against the armchair, legs stretched out, head tipped back, eyes closed. His breathing had the uneven rhythm of someone hovering at the edge of sleep and refusing to fall.

Tyler dozed upright on the floor cushion, chin on his chest, one hand still resting lightly on his switched-off tablet. He'd set alarms for six-thirty, six forty-five, seven. Just in case.

Olivia occupied the space by the window, knees drawn up, arms looped around them. She'd turned the lamp low. The room was dim, edges blurred, the glow picking out the silver threads in the dust.

Outside, the creatures were absent. For now. The night pressed against the glass like a held breath.

Inside, five friends (four visible, one not) shared a room with the end of one kind of existence and the beginning of another.

Emily lifted her wrist enough to see her watch face.

12:00 A.M.

Seven hours and thirteen minutes until sunrise.

Seven hours and thirteen minutes until Step Eleven.

Seven hours and thirteen minutes until the final merger.

Until Josh stopped being…Josh in any way that made sense and became…Hollow Fields.

Until he traded every possible future—Thanksgiving dinners, term papers, bad dates, good books—for a different kind of endlessness.

Time felt wrong.

The seconds on her watch marched forward in neat, uncaring increments. Inside her chest, the night felt both too long and already over.

She shifted her hand slightly. The knot in the air trembled, just enough to brush the heat above her knuckles.

"We're here," she whispered.

The air pulsed once.

She let her eyes close for a moment, trusting Tyler's alarms, trusting the inevitability of dawn. Sleep wouldn't be rest tonight. It would be a series of short drops between waking thoughts.

Around her, the apartment's sounds settled into a fragile harmony—the distant hum of the building, the soft whirr of the fridge, the thin rasp of human breathing.

Time moved.

Step Ten completed its slow, relentless work.

Outside, somewhere beyond the campus, beyond the highway, beyond the line of trees, a town of overlapping eras waited.

Within it, the field listened.

And within the field, something that was almost Josh and almost something else entirely listened back.

Midnight slipped past.

Seven hours and thirteen minutes remained.

Goodbye was coming.

Inevitable was on its way.

The room held its vigil.

And the knot in the air, the last anchored piece of Josh Bennett, stayed where it was.

CHAPTER 17: "THE MERGER"

3:04 AM - Monday, October 21

The knot in the air pulsed like something trying to remember how to breathe.

It hovered where Josh's chest should have been if he were still lying on the couch. Not a light, not a color—just a dense wrongness in the air, a place where the world creased inward. When it thickened, the shadows on the walls bent toward it. When it thinned, the room relaxed by a fraction.

The apartment was cold in the way hospital rooms got cold at night. Quiet, but not empty. Pizza boxes on the coffee table. Cooling mugs of coffee abandoned on coasters. Tyler's laptop open on the floor, screen dimmed, a scrolling column of numbers moving lazily down one side.

Four bodies lay scattered through the room in uncomfortable shapes.

Mike had fallen asleep half-sitting against the couch, head tipped back, mouth open, one arm slung across the cushions as if he were still trying to reach the invisible shape that used to be there.

Tyler was on the rug with a hoodie wadded under his head, one wrist resting on the keyboard of his laptop. The machine chimed every few minutes as new data came in, a soft notification that no one acknowledged.

Olivia sat upright in the armchair with her knees tucked to her chest, camera bag hugged against them like a pillow. Her head had sunk onto her forearm at some point. A strand of hair clung to the corner of her mouth.

Emily was on the floor near the coffee table, back against it, chin tucked, arms wrapped hard around her own ribs. Her boots were still on. She hadn't bothered with a blanket. Every so often, the muscles in her jaw clenched and released.

Outside, the October night pressed cold against the windows. The creatures had retreated sometime after midnight, the white ovals of their faces dissolving back into fog. No tapping on the glass now. No whispers.

Just the knot. Just the uneasy stillness of a room waiting for morning.

The knot thickened.

The air along the ceiling shivered, faint like heat over asphalt. A draft slipped down into the room, smelling of damp earth and something metallic —like the air out by the grain silos after a storm.

On the floor, Emily's eyes snapped open.

For a moment she didn't move. Her pupils had that unfocused spread of someone ripped out of a dream. Her gaze drifted past the coffee table, over the arm of the couch, to the empty space above it.

The knot pulsed again.

"Joshua," she whispered, voice sandpaper-dry.

Across the room, Mike jerked, sucked in a sharp breath, and sat forward all at once. "What—"

Tyler flinched awake with a sound somewhere between a gasp and a glitch. His fingers skidded on the keyboard, waking the laptop fully. Four graphs jumped, lines like heart monitors gone erratic.

Olivia's chin slid off her arm. She straightened, blinking at the room, disoriented. Her eyes followed Emily's line of sight and locked on the same patch of air.

The knot condensed, shrinking to the size of a fist, then stretched outward in a thin, transparent ripple that brushed the ceiling and faded.

For one second, all four of them held their breath.

Then the apartment exhaled—its own settling creak from somewhere in the walls.

Tyler sat up. "Time?"

Emily twisted, squinting at the digital clock on the TV stand. "Three-oh-four."

"AM," Mike muttered, rubbing a hand over his face. "Obviously." His voice had the shredded edge of someone who'd been crying on and off for hours and was pretending he hadn't.

Olivia shifted her camera bag off her lap and onto the floor. "Did we all —"

"Wake up at the same time?" Tyler finished. He slid the laptop onto the coffee table, fingers already moving to pull up logs. "Yeah. Looks like… some kind of spike at three-oh-two."

He turned the screen toward them. A graph in the middle of the display showed a thin, jittery line that had been wandering lazily along the bottom. At 3:02 AM, it shot upward in a sharp peak that stabbed nearly off the chart.

"EM spectrum?" Mike asked, squinting at it like he could intimidate the numbers into meaning something else.

"Partially. Also something I don't have a label for yet." Tyler's hands hovered over the keyboard. "I mean, I can invent one, but…" He trailed off, eyes drawn back to the knot.

It was smaller than it had been when they'd finally forced themselves to lie down—less of a bruise in the air, more of a pinched place. But it felt denser now, somehow. Compressed.

Emily pushed herself to her feet. Her legs protested, stiff from sleeping on the floor, but she ignored them and stepped closer to the couch.

"Joshua?" she said again, louder this time. "If that was you, do it again."

The air above the couch trembled.

A thin current brushed past her face, cooler than the room. The tiny hairs along her arms stood up against her flannel sleeves. She could have told herself it was just the building's ancient heater or some college-town draft, but she'd spent the last week learning the difference between normal and not.

"That's you," she said quietly. "Okay."

She swallowed, looked down at him—at the place where he should have been—and dragged a hand across her eyes.

"You woke us up together," she said. "Why?"

The knot pulsed once.

Tyler's laptop chimed at the same moment. Another spike leapt across the screen, smaller this time but clean.

"Synced," Tyler murmured. "Whatever he's... doing, it's coordinated now. Controlled."

"Controlled is good," Mike said. "Controlled means we can still... I don't know. Negotiate." The word sounded weak even to him.

Emily glanced at him. "There's nothing left to negotiate, remember?"

Her tone wasn't cruel. Just flat. The way she said it made it worse.

Mike's jaw worked. He shut his mouth and looked back at the knot.

For a few minutes, they all stood there in silence—the four of them in various stages of wreckage, and the not-quite-visible remains of Josh Bennett hanging over the couch.

Outside, somewhere in the distance, a siren wailed and faded. A car passed on the street below, its headlights stuttering across the ceiling. The smell of cold pizza and stale coffee lingered like a memory of yesterday's normal.

The knot pulsed again, slower this time.

Emily checked the clock again. "Three-ten."

"Four hours," Olivia said.

"Three-fifty-three," Tyler corrected automatically, glancing at the corner of his screen where the system time glowed. "Give or take a few seconds."

"Four," Olivia repeated. "We can tack the seconds on later."

Mike let out a breath he hadn't realized he was holding. "Anybody else dream something they're not gonna talk about?"

No one answered. That was answer enough.

They tried to sleep again. That was what sane people would do—steal whatever rest they could before the worst morning of their lives.

But sanity had left the building days ago.

Emily lay back down near the coffee table, but her eyes stayed open, watching the dark outline of the couch. Every time her eyelids drifted, she saw the grain silo from home. Saw Josh on the ladder, not moving, dust motes hovering in the golden air. She'd shout his name in the dream and wake up with it already on her tongue.

Mike dozed and jerked and dozed again, caught in loops of contracts that reordered themselves every time he tried to read them. Clauses about guardianship, about consent, about consideration in the form of eternal consciousness. He'd flip to the signature page and find his own name on the line, or Emily's, or Tyler's, or Olivia's. Never Josh's. When he reached for a pen, the paper would dissolve into fog.

Tyler dreamed in error messages. Lines of code that scrambled as he typed them. File names replicating and corrupting themselves. Folder after folder labeled JOSH_01, JOSH_02, JOSH_03, all empty when he opened them. When he tried to save anything, the computer replied: DESTINATION DOES NOT EXIST.

Olivia's dreams were photographs that refused to focus. Every picture had Josh in it—laughing in the truck, leaning on a fence, frowning at a map—but his face was always a smear of light. She'd adjust aperture and shutter and ISO, frantic, and each adjustment blurred him further.

They drifted in and out of these private nightmares until, at 5:31 AM exactly, the knot in the air contracted with enough force to make the blinds rattle.

All four of them sat up at once.

No one had set an alarm. No one had spoken.

The room felt thinner, like some layer had been stripped away while they weren't looking.

"Okay," Emily said, pushing her hair back with both hands. "Okay. That's it. I'm up."

"Same," Mike muttered, though he looked like someone who'd been run through a wringer.

Tyler checked the clock, then his laptop, then the wall clock in the kitchen for good measure. "Three independent time sources. All the same. 5:31."

"Why does that matter?" Olivia asked, voice hoarse.

"Because it means this—" He gestured at the knot. "—is syncing with the world again. No time slips. No backwards jumps. Everything's converging."

"Converging on seven-thirteen," Mike said.

They looked at the knot.

It hung lower now, only a few inches above the couch cushion. Smaller than a fist. No shimmer around it, no visible distortion—the air simply refused to be empty there.

Seven-thirteen, Emily thought. Sunrise, more or less. The moment the field would take him the rest of the way.

She pushed herself to her feet. "We should get ready."

"For what?" Mike asked. "We're already here. We're not exactly driving anywhere this time."

"For being awake when it happens," she said. "For not missing a single minute we have left."

Her gaze snagged on the clock again.

Ninety-eight minutes.

It felt like nothing. It felt like a lifetime.

She forced herself toward the kitchen.

6:02 AM

The coffee maker gurgled like it was clearing its throat.

Emily stood over it, watching the dark stream pour into the pot. Her hands moved on autopilot: scoop, level, scoop, level, scoop. The way he liked it. Three even scoops, no heaping. He used to complain that campus coffee tasted like burnt mud. At home, he made it strong but not bitter. Said there was an art to it.

She'd learned the ratio years ago, back when her parents had sent her to stay with his family for a summer. He'd taught her how to measure it out with the same patience he used on tractor maintenance and algebra homework.

She reached for the canister again.

One more scoop. Muscle memory.

Her hand hovered over the filter basket. Four scoops. Five people.

He can't drink it.

Her fingers shook. A few grounds spilled onto the machine's hot plate, dotting it like dark confetti.

Emily's throat tightened.

She dumped the scoop in anyway.

When the pot was half full, the smell started to fill the kitchen. Warm, bitter, grounding. It hit the back of her nose and brought tears she hadn't invited.

She wiped at her face with the back of her wrist. "Nope," she said under her breath, to no one in particular. "We're not doing that yet."

From the living room, Mike called, "What?"

"Nothing." She cleared her throat. "Coffee."

"Oh, thank God," he said. "Thought the world was really ending for a second."

His attempt at humor fell like a rock into the silence, but he kept going. That was his default setting. Keep the patter up, even when nobody was biting.

Tyler hovered in the doorway between kitchen and living room, tablet in one hand, stylus in the other. "Power levels are steady," he reported, because that was what he knew how to do—feed them data when there wasn't anything else to give. "No new anomalies since three-oh-two."

"Except for all of this," Mike said, gesturing at the room, the knot, the general everything.

"I meant measurable anomalies," Tyler said.

Mike snorted softly. "So the emotional apocalypse doesn't count. Got it."

Olivia had moved to the couch. She sat on the far end, careful to leave the cushion under the knot empty. Her camera bag rested at her feet, unzipped, contents neatly organized. Two camera bodies, three lenses, spare batteries, memory cards in a case that snapped shut like a compact.

She checked each battery again, even though she'd done it before midnight. Swapped cards. Cleaned a non-existent smudge from her backup lens.

All rituals. All ways to avoid looking directly at the fact that she was preparing to photograph the moment her friend stopped being human.

He's already stopped, she thought, fingers pausing on the camera body. This is just the world catching up.

She glanced up.

The knot hung like a punctuation mark in mid-air.

"Josh," she whispered. "I'm going to shoot this. If the cameras let me. I don't know if that's a kindness or not. But if it works... I'll have proof. For later. For you. For them."

The air around the knot thinned and thickened in one slow pulse.

She chose to take that as permission.

Emily poured four mugs of coffee and brought them in one by one. The ceramic was hot through the sleeves of her flannel. She handed a mug to each of them.

She set a fifth mug on the table, close to where his hand would have been if he were still stretched out on the couch, close enough that the rising steam brushed the knot.

"Here," she said softly. "In case."

No one suggested that this was ridiculous. No one told her he didn't need it.

They all just stared at the empty mug until the steam became invisible.

Tyler checked the time. "Six-oh-eight."

"Sixty-five minutes," Olivia said.

"Sixty-five and... forty seconds," Tyler added, glancing at his tablet.

Emily sat down cross-legged on the floor, facing the couch. "We should... I don't know. Say whatever we didn't say yesterday."

"There's a lot of that," Mike said.

"Then pick one thing each," she replied. "We can't fit all of it in an hour."

He grimaced. "Thanks for the comforting math."

She gave him a look. "Do you want a spreadsheet instead? I can make one. Columns for 'Regrets' and 'Things I Should Have Said Before He Decided To Merge With A Haunted Town.'"

Tyler made a small sound that might have been a laugh if it hadn't broken halfway out.

Olivia put her camera down. "I vote we skip the spreadsheet and just talk."

Emily nodded once. "Okay. Then talk."

6:32 AM

They went in order of who could bear the silence the least.

Mike cracked first.

He shifted off the edge of the couch and slid to his knees on the rug, close enough that the knot hung directly above his head. He had to tilt his chin up to look at it.

"Okay, Bennett," he said. "Listen up, because I'm not repeating myself."

His voice had lost the slick shine it usually carried. It came out rough and a little too loud in the small room.

"You were supposed to be a summer mark, you know that?" he went on. "Farm kid with a weird job and too much curiosity. Easy. One and done. Pull a little stunt, sell some fake answers, move on. That was the plan."

He huffed out a breath through his nose. "You ruined that. Completely. You and your… 'Let me think about it' and your 'What if we fix this instead of exploiting it' and your stupid… sense of responsibility."

The knot flickered.

Mike swallowed. He reached up instinctively, fingers spread, like he might catch the movement in his palm. They passed through the air without resistance.

"I spent my whole life figuring angles," he said. "Finding ways to come out ahead. And then you…" His mouth twisted. "You just walked into a cursed town and volunteered to be the plug so the rest of us didn't drown."

His throat worked around words that didn't want to form. He forced them anyway.

"There's always another deal," he said. "That's what I tell myself. That's what I told you. But this time there isn't. I couldn't find one. I tried. I really did."

His voice dropped on the last three words. They sounded thin and small in the room.

The knot pulsed once, then again, two quick beats like a double tap of acknowledgment.

Mike's eyes shone.

"Yeah, yeah," he muttered, swiping at them with the heel of his hand. "I know. You're gonna say I'm being dramatic and that this was never my job to fix. You're gonna quote your grandpa. 'Sometimes the only deal on the table is the one nobody wants.'"

He took a shaky breath, then let it out slow.

"I don't know how to exist without you now," he said quietly. "You hear me? I don't know what that version of my life looks like. But I'll... I'll figure it out. I guess. Since you went and signed up for eternity."

The knot contracted until it was the size of a marble. The air around it tightened, then loosened.

"Okay," Mike said. "Fine. I hear you too."

He backed away on his knees until he hit the coffee table, then pushed himself up onto the couch. He leaned forward, elbows on his knees, face in his hands.

No one clapped him on the shoulder. No one had any right words.

They just let the quiet fill back in.

Tyler spoke next, because silence had always made him itch.

He didn't get close. He stayed standing by the coffee table, tablet hugged against his chest like a shield.

"If X then Y," he said softly, more to himself than anyone. "If guy merges with haunted town, then barrier stays stable. If barrier stays stable, then world doesn't get swallowed by overlapping death-zones and grief monsters. That's the logic model. That's the decision tree."

He lifted his eyes to the knot.

"But you're not a variable," he said. "You're not a line in my code I can flip from true to false. You're... you. And every time I look at these numbers, I have to pretend they're not you to stay functional."

He tapped the tablet with the stylus. Lines of data scrolled. "I built a whole database for you, did you know that? For the guardians. For the field. A way to quantify what's happening so whoever comes after us isn't flying blind. And it still feels…" He shook his head. "It feels like trying to record a hurricane with a kitchen thermometer."

The knot gave a faint, tired shimmer.

Tyler's mouth twitched.

"I'm going to keep recording anyway," he said. "I'm going to make the best archive I can. It won't be enough. It'll never capture what you're actually experiencing. But maybe it'll help the next kids who stumble into this mess not screw it up as badly as we did."

He hesitated, then added, "I wish there was a way to back you up. To make a copy before the merge. Some kind of… conscious redundancy system. But every model I run says it would just fragment you. Fragment the field. And you knew that. That's why you didn't let me try."

He looked down at his hands. The stylus had started to tremble between his fingers.

"I hate that you were right," he said.

The knot rippled, just once.

"Okay," Tyler whispered. "Noted."

He sank onto the floor, back to the coffee table, and pulled the tablet into his lap like a life raft.

Olivia waited until the room had settled again.

Then she stood.

Her camera hung from the strap around her neck now, heavy against her sternum. She held it like it weighed more than it should.

"I'm supposed to be the one who sees," she said. "The one who shows people what's real. That's my whole… thing. Light and framing and proof."

Her gaze flicked to the window, to the faint reflection of herself in the glass. The sky outside was going from ink-black to charcoal, the first suggestion of dawn flattening the stars.

"I had proof once," she said. "Before all of this. A picture that shouldn't have been possible. And when I showed it to people, they smiled and nodded and called it a very convincing fake. So I told myself next time I'd get better proof. Cleaner. More undeniable."

She looked back at the knot.

"This is the biggest 'next time' there is," she whispered. "The moment when a person becomes a town. When my friend turns into a boundary."

The knot quivered like it was listening.

"I'm going to try," she said. "I have backups on backups. Extra cards. Extra batteries. If anything can be captured, I'll capture it. But…" Her fingers tightened on the camera body. "If the cameras betray me again, I'm at least going to watch with my own eyes. I'm not looking at you through glass when you go. I owe you that much."

She took a step closer to the couch, close enough that if he'd still had a hand, she could have reached for it.

"You're going to become memory," she said. "And I'm not ready. But I will remember you as you are right now. Not as static. Not as 'guardian.' As Josh, who said 'Let me think about it' every time I tried to drag him into something stupid. As Josh, who believed me when I said I saw things."

Her voice shook on that last line. She straightened slightly, like she'd scold herself for it if she could.

The knot tightened, then smoothed.

"Thank you," she murmured. "For seeing me too."

She retreated to the far end of the couch and sat, camera in her lap, lens cap off.

That left Emily.

She hadn't moved since she sat down. Her hands were wrapped around her coffee mug so hard her knuckles had gone pale. The steam had stopped rising minutes ago.

Now she set the mug on the floor, carefully, as if it might shatter.

"You're an idiot," she said.

It came out low and steady.

"I need you to know that before anything else. You're a good person. You're the kind of person Grandma used to pray I'd grow up to be friends with. But you're also an idiot."

The knot twitched.

"You decided it was your job to climb into a cursed system and hold it shut because you were born closest to it," she went on. "Because you knew the land and the stories and you couldn't stand the thought of some stranger doing it wrong."

She lifted her chin, eyes fixed on that wrongness in the air.

"You didn't ask me," she said. "Not really. You told me. After the fact. 'Emily, this is what I'm going to do. Emily, I've already started the Steps. Emily, I can't let anyone else take this.'"

Her mouth tightened.

"I am so mad at you," she said. "So unbelievably furious that you decided the shape of your whole life—and your whole forever—without letting me stand there when you chose. Without letting me put my hand on the lever with you and say, 'Fine. If we're pulling this, we're pulling it together.'"

Her voice finally cracked on that last word.

The knot pulsed twice in quick succession, strong enough to make the dust on the TV flicker.

"Don't you dare apologize," she said, swallowing hard. "You had two weeks to say you were sorry while you could still talk, and you didn't, because you were too busy trying to make it easier for us. That's the problem, Joshua. You carry everything and you never think about the fact that the rest of us might actually want to share the weight."

She pressed the heel of her hand against her eyes until the burn subsided enough to see again.

"I love you," she said. "Obviously. I wouldn't be here if I didn't. I don't forgive you yet. I don't know when I will. But I love you. And I am not going to forget you. I am not going to let the world forget you."

The knot shuddered, compressing to the size of a bead. The air around it hummed faintly, just for a heartbeat.

"Yeah," Emily said quietly. "I heard you. Too late, but I heard you."

She sat back, drawing in a long breath through her nose, letting it out slowly.

The clock read 6:44 AM.

Seventeen minutes.

6:47 AM

The creatures came back with the dawn.

Not all at once. At first, just one pale oval at the edge of the glass, like a reflection in the wrong place. Then another. Then another. In less than a minute, the windows were ringed with faces—blank and smooth, features smudged, eyes like thumbprints pressed into wet clay.

They didn't tap this time.

They just watched.

The gray light outside made them look even more washed-out. Like old photographs taped to the wrong side of the glass.

"I hate that they don't fog up the windows," Mike muttered. "That's just rude."

Olivia's eyes flicked toward him, then back to the knot. "Nothing about them is built for our comfort."

Emily stared at the nearest face. "They're waiting."

"For what?" Tyler asked, though he already knew.

"For us to break," she said. "For the moment when this stops feeling like a decision he made and starts feeling like something we have to live with. That's when they'll start whispering again. 'You could join him. You don't have to be left behind.'"

The nearest face's mouth curved, just slightly.

Emily looked away.

The air near the apartment door went wrong for a second—like heat mirage, like a glitch in a video feed.

Then Eliza Nightshade was standing there.

No gust of wind. No flash. One moment the doorway was empty, the next there she was, in the same dark dress she'd worn at the edge of Hollow Fields. Her hair was unbound this time, a long dark cloud falling around her shoulders. Her eyes held centuries.

Tyler's tablet pinged a new anomaly.

"Elizabeth," Olivia said reflexively, then corrected herself. "Eliza."

"Both names are mine," Eliza said. "Use whichever feels truest to you." Her gaze moved to the knot. "We are close now."

Her voice was calm, but there was a thinness at the edges of it. The way someone sounded when they'd given the same speech too many times and never found a way to make it hurt less.

Emily rose to her feet. "You made this sound like there was no choice. 'One guardian, one town, one line held.' You left out the part where we have to watch it happen."

"If I told every witness every way it would hurt, none of them would survive the waiting," Eliza said softly. "You are already bearing more than most."

"That doesn't help."

"It is not meant to," Eliza said. "It is simply true."

She stepped fully into the room, careful to give the space above the couch a wide berth, as if the knot were physically solid.

"Listen," she said. "In the next few minutes, the final Step will complete. At seven-thirteen, precisely, the town will claim Joshua Bennett. His consciousness will expand to fill the boundaries of Hollow Fields. He will become its guardian and its field. His human form is already gone. This —" She nodded at the knot. "—is the last anchored piece."

"Will it hurt?" Mike asked.

"The transition?" Eliza's gaze flicked to him. "No. Not in the way you fear. It will be overwhelming. It will be... a noise you cannot imagine. But it will not be pain as you understand it."

"That's supposed to make us feel better?" Emily asked.

"It is supposed to be honest," Eliza said.

Tyler swallowed. "After—after seven-thirteen. Will he know we're here?"

"Yes," Eliza said. "But not as he knows you now. He will feel you the way you feel the weather. The way you sense the weight of the air before a storm."

"So we can talk to him?" Olivia asked. "Like... at the boundary?"

"You can speak," Eliza said. "And he will know that something loved him enough to come here. That will matter. Even if he cannot answer."

The creatures at the windows leaned closer, their blurred faces pressed almost flat to the glass. They were listening.

Eliza did not look at them.

She looked at Emily.

"You must be prepared," she said. "There will be… a surge when the field takes him the rest of the way. A pull toward the anchor point. It is important that you do not attempt to anchor yourselves as well."

"You mean we shouldn't jump in after him," Mike said.

"Yes," Eliza said. "Though the impulse will be strong. Especially for some of you."

Her gaze flicked between Mike and Emily before returning to the knot.

Time crawled.

6:58 AM.

Tyler's hand hovered over his tablet, thumb tapping nervously against the bezel.

"Are your devices prepared?" Eliza asked.

"As much as they can be," Tyler said. "Redundant recording, four angles, local and cloud backups. Sensor arrays calibrated. I can't guarantee what the field's going to do to electronics, but if anything survives, we'll have it."

"Good," Eliza said, in a tone that suggested good and futile were currently synonyms. "Bear in mind that Hollow Fields does not like to be pinned to film or digits. It may resist."

Olivia's fingers tightened on her camera.

"I know," she said. "I'm still trying."

Eliza inclined her head, something like respect in the gesture.

6:59 AM.

The knot shrank further, condensing into something too small and too dense to make sense. The air around it bowed inward.

The temperature in the room dropped so quickly that their breath fogged.

Tyler's tablet beeped a warning about extreme fluctuation and then fell silent as he muted the alerts with a swift swipe.

The creatures began to whisper.

The sound bled through the window glass like a draft. Not words, not exactly, but shapes of words. Join. Stay. Don't let him be alone.

Mike ground his teeth. "They're lying," he said without looking at them. "They always lie."

"They are not entirely lying," Eliza said quietly. "Joining him would end your grief. It would also end your lives. That is the angle they are invested in."

"So comforting," Mike muttered.

7:00 AM.

The digital clock on the TV stand rolled its numbers over.

Tyler checked his tablet, then the laptop, then the old analog watch on his wrist.

"Seven-oh-oh," he said. "Thirteen minutes."

The space in the room seemed to narrow with every second. The walls felt closer. The ceiling lower. The knot drew their attention like gravity.

Eliza moved to the doorway, as if to give them space. Or to mark the exit.

"You have a few minutes more," she said. "Speak if you must. Or be silent if that is truer."

They didn't have speeches left. Just scraps.

Mike, from the couch, said, "You better haunt me if you can. Just saying. Show up when I'm about to do something stupid and make that face you make."

The knot gave one quick, almost amused flicker.

Tyler said, "I'm going to name this dataset after you. The whole field log. BENNETT_001. I know you'd say that's narcissistic. You're wrong."

The knot pulsed once.

Olivia whispered, "I saw you. I see you. Not just the field version. You. That won't change."

The knot smoothed, almost peaceful for a breath.

Emily didn't say anything at first. She just watched him.

Finally, she said, "I'm not done being mad. I need you to know that too. Love doesn't erase that. It just means I'll drag my anger to the boundary every time I visit and yell at you about it there."

The knot trembled in a way that read like laughter, if you knew him.

7:07 AM.

The world outside the windows was lightening to a washed-out blue. The creatures' faces looked flatter, less defined, as if daylight stole some of their substance.

They crowded the glass anyway.

Emily's skin prickled. Some instinct deep in her spine told her to run, even though there was nowhere to go.

"We should… stand," she said. "I don't know. It feels wrong to be sitting when…"

They all got to their feet, scraping chair legs, shifting weight, forming a loose semicircle around the couch. Mike closest. Then Olivia. Then Tyler. Emily a step back, arms crossed tight over her ribs.

Eliza watched from the doorway, hands folded in front of her.

7:09 AM.

Tyler's voice was thin when he said, "Four minutes."

The knot shone faintly now. Not with light, exactly, but with attention. Every mote of dust in the room seemed drawn toward it, eddies of particulate drifting into its orbit.

The hum started somewhere just on the edge of hearing. A vibration in the bones of their teeth. The walls of the apartment building creaked in sympathy.

"Is it supposed to sound like that?" Mike asked.

"Yes," Eliza said. "And no. Each merger is… unique. But the pattern is the same. Build. Surge. Collapse. Silence."

"That's… reassuring," he said.

7:10 AM.

The hum deepened.

The air pressed against their skin like a storm front rolling in.

Tyler's cameras—all four of them—clicked on in nearly perfect unison. Red recording lights glowed. The feeds popped up on his laptop and tablet, four boxes showing the couch from different angles. The knot wavered in each of them, more visible on screen than to the naked eye.

"I've got him," Tyler said, almost to himself. "All angles. All streams."

Olivia lifted her primary camera, framed the knot in her viewfinder, tested focus. Sharp. She exhaled slowly, grounding herself in the familiar feel of plastic and glass in her hands.

Emily took one step toward the couch.

"Joshua," she said. "You look at me right now, okay? I know you can't, but just—just fix me in your weird… expanded awareness or whatever. I'm not going anywhere."

The knot pulsed once.

Then the world grabbed her.

It felt like being hit by a memory made physical. A gust of air slammed into her from the couch's direction—no, from all directions at once—and shoved.

Her feet left the floor.

She stumbled backward, shoulder colliding with someone solid. For a second she thought it was Mike, or a wall, or one of the creatures finally breaching the glass.

Then she realized she was in the hallway.

The apartment door was in front of her, closed.

The sound in the room cut off like someone had slammed a lid on it.

"Hey!" Emily grabbed the doorknob and twisted.

It didn't move.

The metal was ice-cold under her palm. The hairs on her forearms stood up. The hum from inside the apartment was muffled now, like she was underwater listening to a distant engine.

"Joshua Bennett, you open this door," she snapped. "I swear to God—"

The knob refused to budge.

She slammed her shoulder into the door. It didn't even rattle.

"Mike!" she shouted. "Tyler! Olivia! Eliza! Open up!"

No one answered.

She pressed her ear to the wood. The hum on the other side rose, then dipped, then rose again. It made her teeth ache. Her throat vibrated with it.

"Let me in," she whispered, voice cracking. "Do not do this without me. Don't you dare."

Her watch read 7:11 AM.

She beat on the door with the side of her fist until her skin stung. The impact barely made a sound.

Inside, time moved on.

7:11 AM

"Seven-eleven," Tyler said.

His voice sounded far away to his own ears.

He stared at the monitors. Four angles. Four live feeds. The knot hovered at the center of each frame, compressing smaller and smaller.

The hum in the room bled into a high whine, just below the threshold of pain.

His equipment readings spiked. Graphs went vertical. Numbers rolled so fast they blurred.

Mike didn't look at any of that.

He kept his eyes on the knot.

It was the size of a pea now. A tiny defect in the air over the Josh-shaped hollow in the couch. The fabric of the cushion had never quite regained its shape after years of holding his weight.

"You still there, Bennett?" Mike asked, voice shaking.

The knot pulse was almost invisible, but he saw it. Felt it.

"Good," he said. "Stay stubborn. That's your thing."

Olivia's right eye was pressed to her camera's viewfinder. Through the lens, the knot was crisp. The autofocus locked onto it, tracking each minute shift.

"Exposure locked," she murmured. "Shutter ready."

Her finger rested half-down on the button.

7:12 AM.

Tyler's throat was dry.

"Sixty seconds," he said.

"Don't count down," Mike snapped.

"I have to," Tyler replied. "If I don't say it, it still happens. At least this way we know where we are."

The creatures at the windows pressed closer. Their whispers gained shape.

Join him.

He's alone.

You don't have to be.

You don't have to hurt.

Eliza closed her eyes.

"Do not listen," she said. "They are amplifying what is already in you. Nothing more."

Mike clenched his jaw so hard it hurt. "Too late," he muttered.

7:12:30.

"Thirty seconds," Tyler said.

The knot's pull intensified. The air in the room surged toward it like water circling a drain. Papers on the coffee table slid an inch. A pencil rolled, clinked against the mug Emily had filled for Josh.

Olivia's camera shook in her hands. She firmed her grip, adjusted her stance.

The whine in the air climbed higher.

Her primary camera gave a soft, apologetic beep.

The battery icon in the viewfinder flashed red.

"What?" she whispered. "No, no, you were at ninety percent—"

The camera went black.

Her eye met darkness.

She yanked it away from her face, stabbing at the power button. Nothing. The screen stayed dead.

"Backup!" Tyler barked, not looking away from his monitors.

"I know!" she snapped.

She let the dead camera drop against its strap and grabbed the second body from the bag. It was already fitted with a shorter lens. She flicked the power switch as she lifted it.

The backup camera hummed to life. The screen lit. The knot jumped into frame, blurry, then sharp as she half-pressed the shutter.

"Ten seconds," Tyler said, voice thin. "Nine. Eight—"

Olivia focused.

Seven.

Six.

Five.

She inhaled.

She exhaled.

Four.

Three.

She pressed the shutter.

Crack.

The sound was small, almost delicate. A spiderweb shot from the center of the backup lens, glass fracturing outward in a perfect radial pattern.

Olivia froze.

No impact. Nothing had hit it. The camera had simply… broken.

The viewfinder filled with prismatic blur.

"Of course," she whispered.

Her hands shook once.

Then, very carefully, she lowered the ruined camera and set it on the floor beside the couch.

She lifted her eyes, empty-handed, to the knot.

"Two," Tyler said. "One—"

7:13 AM.

The world imploded.

For an instant, everything in the apartment stretched toward the knot.

The air elongated, streaks of atmosphere drawn into threads. Light smeared. The walls seemed to lean inward, lines bending, sockets and switches warping like reflections in a funhouse mirror.

Mike felt his body tilt toward the couch.

It was as if someone had tied a rope around his sternum and yanked. His stomach lurched. His feet dragged across the rug. He threw his arms out reflexively, reaching for that tiny, collapsing point.

"Wait—WAIT!" he shouted.

His fingers closed on nothing.

The knot collapsed inward, smaller than anything had a right to be, and then—

—the sound hit.

It wasn't a bang. It wasn't an explosion.

It was a rush.

A low hum that swelled and climbed, turning into a roar that had no source and no direction. It filled the room, their bones, the cavities of their chests. It was the sound of every overlapping century in Hollow Fields grinding against every other. It was train wheels on blind tracks, wind through dead corn, whispers in attics, laughter in diners, footfalls on unpaved streets.

Tyler's monitors went to snow.

All four feeds pixelated at once, stacks of neat squares dissolving into a blizzard of white and gray. The knot vanished from the images. The couch vanished. The room turned into static.

"Come on, come on—" Tyler's fingers flew over the keys. He tapped into backup feeds, into redundant systems. Every channel showed the same thing: visual noise, seething like a swarm.

His head rang with the audio. The mics picked up the roar and amplified it in tinny stereo. Underneath, he thought he heard… something. A voice. Multiple voices. Josh, maybe, stretched thin and layered with others.

He tore his gaze from the screens.

Look, he told himself. For once, look.

Olivia stood with her hands at her sides, camera strap cutting across her chest like a sash. Her eyes were wide, locked on the knot as it swelled—no, shrank—no, did both, expanding inward, digging into the fabric of the world.

She could see it more clearly than anyone. No glass between her and the impossible.

The knot pulled light into itself, threads of brightness arcing from the windows, the TV, the laptop screen, the tiny LED on the stereo. For a moment, it seemed like the whole apartment existed only in relation to that point. Everything else faded to grayscale.

Her breath came fast and thin.

This is it, she thought. This is the picture I don't get to take.

The air around the knot shivered, then rippled outward, a thin shockwave visible only as a distortion.

Eliza stood very still, eyes open now, watching with the resignation of someone who had seen too many people step into the same river.

The creatures at the windows threw their heads back and screamed.

No one heard them.

The roar drowned everything.

Mike lunged again, hands stretching toward where Josh had been, as if he could grab hold and haul him back out of the current.

His arms slid through the space, through the collapsing knot, through air that crackled with static and something colder.

Pins and needles shot up his forearms. His fingertips went numb.

"Don't you dare go without—" he started.

The world snapped.

There was no flash. No shockwave that knocked them off their feet. Just a sudden, absolute absence.

The hum cut off.

The roar vanished.

The pressure in the room dropped so fast their ears popped.

For three full seconds, there was nothing.

No sound. No movement.

Then: the distant honk of a car outside. The faint tick of Tyler's laptop cooling fan. Someone sucking in a ragged breath.

Mike found himself on his knees on the couch.

His hands were outstretched over empty air.

The knot was gone.

The indentation in the cushion looked deeper. That was all.

"Josh?" he croaked.

No answer.

Tyler's monitors flickered.

The static subsided, little by little, like a snowstorm petering out. The feeds resolved into clear images again: four angles of the couch, the empty air above it, the four of them, Eliza in the doorway.

The timecode on each feed read 07:13:47.

"Thirty... seven seconds," Tyler said dazedly. "We lost thirty-seven seconds of visual data."

"Did it record the audio?" Olivia asked, voice faint.

He checked. The waveform timeline showed a continuous band of sound.

"Yeah," he said. "We've got… noise. All the way through."

"But not…" She gestured. "Not the moment."

"No." His throat worked. "Not the moment."

His hands shook.

He set the tablet down before he dropped it.

Olivia's knees gave out.

She sank onto the rug, landing beside the camera she'd abandoned. The cracked lens stared up at her, fractured reflections of the ceiling broken into jagged pieces.

"I saw it," she whispered. "I saw all of it. And I have nothing."

Her eyes burned.

She lifted the notebook from her bag with stiff fingers, flipped to a blank page, uncapped a pen with her teeth.

If she couldn't show it, she could at least trap it in words before it blurred.

She started to write.

Mike stayed on his knees, hands still reaching toward empty air.

"There's always another deal," he said under his breath. "There's always —"

The phrase ran out of gas halfway through.

His arms dropped.

He looked at his hands like they belonged to someone else. Turned them over. No marks. No burns. Just skin and lines and the faint tremor of exhaustion.

"You're gone," he said to the couch. "You actually did it."

The apartment felt… different.

Not emptier. Not exactly.

Just… occupied in a new way.

The walls seemed to listen. The floorboards seemed to breathe.

Tyler's equipment pinged—once, sharply—as every sensor hit a new baseline.

"Field strength just spiked and stabilized," he said. "The boundary's… stronger. More defined."

"He is there," Eliza said quietly. "In all of it. He is the boundary now."

The creatures at the windows were silent.

One by one, they drifted back into the fog, their pale faces dissolving. The whispers faded like smoke.

For a moment, there was only the sound of Olivia's pen scratching across paper and the soft, uneven breathing of the others.

The clock on the TV stand read 7:14 AM.

7:21 AM

The apartment door swung inward.

Emily stumbled through it with so much momentum she nearly fell.

She caught herself on the edge of the coffee table, breath coming in harsh bursts.

"I swear to God, if you locked me out on purpose, I am going to—"

She stopped.

Her gaze snapped to the couch.

To the empty space above it.

Her pupils widened.

"No," she said.

Mike turned his head slowly.

"Em," he said.

"No." She shook her head hard, like she could dislodge reality and shake a different one into place. "No, I was just… it was seconds. I was out there for seconds."

She checked her watch.

7:21 AM.

Her stomach dropped.

"How long?" she demanded, looking from face to face. "How long was I out there?"

"Eight minutes," Tyler said quietly.

"Eight—" Her voice cracked. "No. No, I was— I hit the door, I heard the noise, I felt— and then it stopped and—"

Her eyes filled. She blinked hard, but the room wavered anyway.

"You let me miss it," she said.

She wasn't sure who she was accusing. Eliza. The town. Josh.

Herself.

"I didn't—" Mike started. "Emily, we thought you were right behind—"

"The field pushed you," Eliza said, cutting through his protest. "Or rather, Joshua did. With what little control he had left. He did not want you in the room when it happened."

Emily stared at her.

"That's not his decision," she said, words sharp.

"He thought it was," Eliza said. "He believed it would break you differently than the others."

"It broke me just fine out there," Emily snapped. "He locked me in the hallway with the sound and no—" Her voice thinned. "No sight. No... point of reference. Just..."

She swallowed.

"What did it look like?" she asked.

No one answered fast enough.

"I need to know," she said, louder. "Tell me. Every detail. Who saw what. When. How long. I need to KNOW."

Olivia lifted her head from her notebook.

Her cheeks were wet. Ink had smudged on one corner where a tear had fallen.

"It was like watching a town inhale," she said. "Not the buildings. The idea of it. All the overlapping... times? It all folded into him and then he folded into it. There was light, but not bright. Like... like someone pulling all the lamp cords toward one outlet."

"That's not specific enough," Emily said. "Angles. Colors. Sequence."

"I'm writing it down," Olivia said, holding up the notebook with shaking fingers. Pages already half-covered in cramped script. "I'll give you every frame I can remember. But it won't be perfect. Memory never is."

Emily turned to Tyler. "The recordings."

He looked wrecked. His eyes were red behind his glasses. "We have before and after," he said. "Data on the build-up. Audio of the… sound. But the thirty-seven seconds when it actually happened?" He shook his head. "Visual static. Like the field refused to let itself be seen mid-transition."

"That's not acceptable," Emily said.

"It's not negotiable," he replied, a ghost of their old banter in the words.

She swung her gaze to Mike.

"You tried to stop it," she said. It wasn't a question.

"Yeah," he said. "He didn't let me."

"How?" she demanded.

He stared at the couch for a long moment.

"I reached for him," he said finally. "I felt… something. Like static and cold and… home? And then it wasn't there. Like someone cutting a rope while you're still pulling on it." His hands flexed unconsciously. "There was nothing to grab onto. And then it was over."

"How am I supposed to build a timeline from this?" Emily asked the air. "How am I supposed to understand what actually happened if all of you have different angles and none of them line up?"

"That is the nature of witnessing," Eliza said. "No one sees the same event the same way."

Emily rounded on her. "You watched from the doorway. What did you see?"

Eliza hesitated.

For the first time since she'd appeared, something like a crack showed in her composure. Her shoulders sagged a fraction. Her eyes looked older.

"I saw a young man choose to keep a promise," she said. "I saw a field that has been starving for a guardian finally be fed. I saw another bright thread added to a weave that has held back the dark for longer than you have had a country to live in. And I saw his friends remain standing when many would have fallen into that pull."

"That's poetry," Emily said. "Not data."

"It is what I have," Eliza said.

Emily's hands curled into fists at her sides.

She wanted to scream. To rip the room apart. To find some seam in the air where she could pry the moment open and climb inside.

Instead, she sank down onto the floor where she'd sat for most of the night.

The coffee mug she'd left there had gone cold. A thin skin had formed on the surface.

She stared at it.

"I should have been here," she said softly. "I should have seen it."

"No," Eliza said. "You should not have. That is why he moved you."

Emily laughed once, harshly.

"He doesn't get to decide what I can handle," she said. "Not anymore."

The room went very still.

Near the window, the last lingering trace of a creature's face blurred and faded.

Tyler checked his readings again because it was the only thing he knew how to do when emotions got this sharp.

"Field strength is holding," he said numbly. "Stabilized at a level I've never recorded before. This is… Josh. This is him, everywhere the town touches."

Olivia scribbled another line in the notebook.

Mike finally pulled himself off the couch, moving like someone older than he was.

He walked to the window.

Outside, the street looked ordinary. A few students on early schedules trudged past, hoods up, backpacks heavy. The fog that had wrapped the building for days was gone.

"Do they even know?" he asked. "Any of them?"

"Not consciously," Eliza said. "They feel safer on some streets and not know why. They avoid certain turns without knowing what they are avoiding. That is the guardian's work. To be present in ways they never see."

Mike touched the glass.

"Hey, Bennett," he murmured. "You picking up morning shift already?"

The blinds stirred.

No breeze from the vent, no passing truck. Just a small ripple, as if invisible fingers had brushed the slats.

All four of them saw it.

"So he's…," Tyler began.

"He hears," Eliza said. "In his way."

The tightness in Mike's chest shifted—not easing, exactly, but settling into a new, more permanent shape.

"You better be listening when I yell at you later," he said to the window. "Because I've got notes."

The blinds swayed again.

Emily watched, arms wrapped around herself.

It wasn't enough.

It was all they were going to get.

7:36 AM

Eventually, existence insisted on mundane questions.

"What happens to his stuff?" Mike asked.

He said it suddenly, like the thought had ambushed him.

They all looked around the apartment.

The sagging bookshelf filled with paperbacks and farm manuals. The desk with the old computer. The bulletin board with class schedules and scribbled reminders. The boots by the door. The jacket on the hook. The Polaroids pinned above the sink—some of them Olivia's, moments from the last few months caught in cheap, square frames.

"He paid through the end of the semester," Tyler said automatically. "The lease—"

"I'm not asking about the lease," Mike said. "I mean… who tells his landlord he's not coming back? Who calls his family? What do we say? 'Hey, your kid decided to become a metaphysical firewall, please forward his mail to Haunted Nowhere?'"

Emily's stomach lurched.

"We tell them he died," she said.

The words tasted wrong. Heavy.

"Because that's what this is, for them," she went on. "They can't visit the town. They can't… call him. They'll never know about guardians or fields or creatures. They'll just know their son didn't come home from school."

"That's not exactly true," Eliza said.

They all turned to her.

"You may tell them as much truth as you deem safe," she said. "Or as much as they can hold. But you are correct that, for them, the shape of their loss will be different. Less... populated."

Emily pictured Aunt Lisa get this news. Her whole body went cold.

"Who does it?" she asked.

"I will," Eliza said.

Emily blinked. "You?"

"I have had... practice," Eliza said. "And I am able to couch the truth in ways that will not crush what they have left. I can say his death had meaning. That his choice protected others. That much is not a lie."

Emily's jaw unclenched by degrees.

"Fine," she said. "But I want to talk to them too. Eventually. When I can say his name without... choking on it."

"That will be your choice," Eliza said.

Tyler looked at the equipment still circling the room. Cables snaked across the floor. Sensors blinked.

"I'll pack up the gear," he said. "Back up the backups. We can... analyze later."

"You're not taking everything," Emily said.

He frowned. "We can't leave it all here. What if someone—"

"Not the stuff," she said. "I mean... I'm not leaving this place empty. Not like..." She gestured at the couch. "Not both."

She stood, joints protesting, and crossed to the shelf.

Her fingers walked along the spines until they landed on a battered hardcover with its dust jacket long gone. The farm journal Josh had kept since he was twelve—field notes, crop yields, sketches of mechanical fixes.

He'd shown it to her when they were kids, proud and embarrassed all at once.

"You're stealing his diary?" Mike asked weakly.

"I'm borrowing his field notes," she said. "He's not exactly going to need them to adjust irrigation anymore. And I…."

She hugged the book against her chest.

"I need something of his that isn't a ghost," she finished.

Tyler nodded once, like that made sense on a level numbers couldn't touch.

Olivia tucked her notebook back into her bag, along with the dead cameras. The weight of them dragged at her shoulder when she lifted the strap over her head.

"Are we coming back here?" she asked. "To the apartment?"

Mike looked around.

The space already felt like a museum exhibit. A preserved moment in the life of someone who had moved on.

"We might have to," he said. "There'll be… paperwork. Logistics. But for now?"

He set his coffee mug in the sink with a deliberate clink.

"For now, I vote we get out before I start pretending he's just at class and will walk through that door any minute."

No one argued.

Eliza stepped aside from the doorway, giving them room.

As they passed her, she said, "He is listening."

It wasn't comfort. But it was something.

At the threshold, Emily paused.

She turned back to the room.

"Joshua Bennett," she said. "I'm not done with you. You may think this is the end of your story, but for me? It's research phase one. I'm going to understand what you did. Every step. Every mechanism. Every loophole you didn't find. And when I do, I'm coming back to yell at you properly."

The overhead light flickered once.

"Good," she said. "Glad we're clear."

She stepped into the hall.

The others followed.

As the door swung shut behind them, the blinds in the living room swayed in a wind that wasn't there.

Inside the walls, something new and vast took note of their departure.

7:52 AM

The drive to Hollow Fields boundary was... normal.

That was the worst part.

No time slips yanked them backward through previous conversations. No sudden overlay of ghost towns across the real one. The GPS on Tyler's phone tracked their progress without stuttering. The radio, when Mike turned it on out of habit, played a morning show host trying too hard to sound awake.

The sky had brightened to a pale, washed-out blue. The sun was up, weak through clouds.

"Feels wrong," Mike muttered, eyes on the road. "Whole existential crisis happening and traffic's just... traffic."

"That's how it works," Olivia said from the back seat. "Most people don't notice when the world almost tips over."

Emily sat in the passenger seat, Josh's journal open on her lap. She wasn't reading the words. Her eyes were on the indent his handwriting had left in the paper. The way the lines slanted when he'd been tired. The fields of numbers in the margins—rainfall, fertilizer ratios—neat, precise.

Her own handwriting looked nothing like his.

She traced one of the diagrams with a fingertip.

Tyler leaned between the front seats, tablet balanced on his knee. "Field readings have changed," he said. "I can pick it up from here now. Before, I had to be practically kissing the tree line to get a clean signal. Now…" He held up the screen. A graph climbed steadily. "It's… everywhere we pass. Like the town has… grown teeth."

"Rephrase," Mike said. "That's not the metaphor I want in my head."

"Sorry," Tyler said. "Grown… roots?"

"Better," Olivia said. "Barely."

The closer they got to the familiar turnoff, the more the air seemed to thrum.

It wasn't something you could measure in degrees or miles per hour. It was in the way the hairs on their arms lifted. The way their skin prickled.

"He's ahead of us," Olivia murmured.

Emily stared through the windshield.

"At the boundary," she said.

A few minutes later, the old, battered sign came into view: HOLLOW FIELDS, hand-painted letters faded by weather and time.

Mike pulled off onto the dirt shoulder and killed the engine.

For a moment, no one moved.

Then Emily opened her door.

The October air bit at her cheeks as she stepped out. It smelled like wet leaves and distant wood smoke. Underneath, there was something else now —a metallic tang, a faint electric buzz.

Tyler's tablet screamed with data. Lines went wild. He muttered something under his breath that sounded like prayer in programming language.

They walked to the boundary.

It wasn't a visible line in the dirt. It never had been. But they knew where it lay now—the subtle drop in temperature, the shift in sound when you stepped past a certain point, the way colors changed underfoot.

Emily stopped just short of it.

The world felt thicker here. Denser.

"Josh," she said.

No response, obviously.

Still, she kept talking.

"We're here," she said. "In case you were wondering. In case your expanded whatever-brain is busy wrestling grief monsters and you need a status update. You made it. You're… field now. Guardian. All the words you didn't want to say out loud in case they made it real."

Wind moved through the trees lining the road.

It didn't sound like language.

It sounded like breathing.

"I'm still mad," she said. "That's not going away. But I also… I get it. Or I will. Once I pick this apart. You did what you thought you had to do to keep everybody else safe. It's very you."

She looked back at the others.

Mike stood with his hands shoved into his pockets, shoulders hunched. Tyler had one hand on a tree trunk, the other on his tablet. Olivia's camera hung from her neck, cracked lens intact; she hadn't brought her good ones out of the car.

They looked like a unit missing a limb.

"We're not joining you," Emily said to the air. "Not today. Not tomorrow. Not because some whisper tells us grief is easier if we dissolve. You're going to be lonely. I know that. I hate it. But you made this call so we could keep living. I'm not throwing that away because it hurts."

The ground under her boots vibrated once, faint as a cat's purr.

She chose to believe that was him.

"I'm going to understand you," she said. "That's my promise. You spent two weeks poking at this field from the inside without telling me everything. Time to balance the books."

"Hey, Bennett," Mike said, stepping up beside her. "You hear the boss? She's already assigning homework."

The wind shifted direction, ruffling his hair.

"Yeah, yeah," he said. "I miss you too."

Tyler cleared his throat.

"I'll keep the archive updated," he said quietly. "Logs, readings, everything. When new guardians come, if they come, they'll know you were first to map this properly."

Olivia lifted her cracked camera and snapped one more picture.

The lens fracture turned the image into a kaleidoscope: boundary sign, trees, their faces, all broken and refracted.

"It's ruined," she said. "But it's honest. That's all I've got right now."

Eliza stood a few feet back, watching them.

"You will come back," she said.

It wasn't a question.

"Obviously," Emily said. "He's family. And he's an idiot. Idiots need supervision."

A breeze rose.

It carried the scent of corn and old earth, of summer heat stored in soil.

Josh Bennett felt it.

Not as air on skin—he had no skin. Not as sound in ears—he had no ears.

He felt it as a shift in attention.

Four familiar signatures pressed against the edge of his awareness like hands against glass. One brighter than the others, sharp with stubborn love and fury. One restless and jagged. One humming with numbers. One clear and steady, framing everything in careful lines.

He did not have a mouth to speak their names.

He did not have a heart to ache.

But the field—the town, the streets, the overlapping centuries—tightened around those four points in a reflex older than language.

Holding.

Eliza looked toward the invisible town.

"He knows," she said softly. "That is enough for now."

It wasn't.

Not for them.

Not for him.

But it was what existed in this moment between sunrise and whatever came next.

They stood there, on the edge of what used to be just another wooded patch outside town, and let the new reality settle around them.

Then, one by one, they stepped back.

The boundary remained.

Joshua Bennett remained.

The sun climbed higher over Hollow Fields.

Inside the town, spirits moved through their layered centuries—Victorian shopkeepers opening doors to streets that also contained diners that never existed on any map, children running along sidewalks that belonged to three different decades at once. Freed from the worst teeth of the curse, but still bound to the land that had claimed them.

At the edges, the creatures retreated to their vigil, patient and hungry, lining the unseen fence line like crows on a wire. Waiting for anniversaries. For anniversaries. For any crack grief might open.

They had time.

So did he.

Everywhere—in the buildings, the streets, the boundary, the very air—Joshua Bennett held the line.

Alone.

Aware.

Eternal.

The Golden Pickles would lure no more victims.

The town would claim no more unwilling guardians.

Not while Josh Bennett remained.

Not for all the time that was left.

And time, in Hollow Fields, was all there was.

EPILOGUE

Six Months Later

Emily had run out of blank wall two months ago.

The far side of the living room was a patchwork now: printer paper taped edge to edge, photographs overlapping printed screenshots, white index cards stabbed through with thumbtacks. Lines of red yarn crossed and crisscrossed—time stamps connected to sensor readouts, witness accounts, hand-copied notes. The whole thing hummed with a kind of restless order, like a machine she'd half-built and refused to admit might never be finished.

The coffee on her desk had gone lukewarm. Five scoops, same as always. Four mugs lined up on the edge—hers, Tyler's, Olivia's, Mike's— and an empty spot where the fifth had sat, back in October, when Josh still came over and complained about the cheap brand she bought. These days she still measured for five out of habit. She poured the extra into the sink before she started working. Some rituals didn't get revised.

She slipped on her headphones, woke the monitor at the center of the chaos, and opened the audio file named:

`BENNETT_AUDIO_CAM_02_CORRUPTED_37s.wav`

Play count: 47.

The waveform stretched across the screen, familiar peaks and valleys like a seismograph reading. Her gaze snagged on the notch at 00:13.14, the place where the static thinned.

She hit play.

The hum came first—low, throbbing, too smooth to be any machine she could name. Underneath it, faint as breath through a wheat field, something almost like words. Still nothing, nothing, and then—

The noise shifted.

A gap opened in the interference. For less than a second, the sound clarified. The creatures' voice slid through, layered and echoing, amplified by the headphones.

"He will be so alone forever. Aware of everything. Unable to touch. Watching you age while he remains. Feeling your grief but unable to comfort. Joining ends that loneliness. For both of you. It is mercy we offer."

The hum swallowed the clarity again, distortion roaring back over the top like a storm front rolling in.

Emily stopped the playback, stripped the headphones off, and stared at the frozen waveform.

On the wall in front of her, a printed still of that exact stretch of audio sat pinned between two photographs. Under it, in block letters on a yellow sticky note, she'd written:

> HOLLOW FIELDS MANIPULATION PATTERN #3: WEAPONIZED EMPATHY

Under that, smaller:

> They're not just selling escape. They're using his loneliness to recruit us.

She stepped closer, palm braced on the plaster beside the note. The yarn from that point of the waveform ran to other anchors: to a printed image from Tyler's corrupted footage, to Olivia's handwritten description of what she'd seen when the knot collapsed, to Mike's account of reaching for Josh and grabbing empty air.

Near the top of the tangle, a cluster of notes huddled around Eliza's name.

> Last confirmed physical sighting: Oct 21, 7:36 a.m.
> Last confirmed field signature (per T): Mar 15, 10:09 p.m.
> After that: nothing.

And in the corner, circled three times:

> Curse breaks → mechanism stops → what happens to the one bound inside it?

Emily's eyes drifted from that cluster back to the waveform printout. The creatures with their mercy pitch. The promise that joining would fix the isolation they themselves had created.

"Nice try," she muttered.

Her jaw tightened; she felt it click. The anger was useful. It kept the fear from circling too close.

On the desk, Josh's farm journal waited, open to a page near the middle. She left it open like that, even when she wasn't reading. Closing it felt like shutting a door.

She sat, pulled the chair in, and dragged the journal closer until the cracked leather brushed her forearms.

The paper inside had softened with age and handling, fibers swollen and worn. She laid two fingers along the margin and traced down a column of notes about soil pH, the pad of her fingertip catching the faint indent of a pen stroke that had been pressed too hard. Years of scribbling had carved a relief map of his thinking into the pages.

On the downstrokes, the grooves cut deeper—granddad's influence, stick-it-to-the-page pressure that meant the word needed to stay. On the upstrokes, the line lightened, like he'd been careful not to rip the paper when he changed direction. Practical force caged in deliberate control. Even his handwriting tried to balance those two things.

Margins filled the space around the neat central columns. "Check moisture levels" with a line through it and a date beside it. "Ask Grandpa about rotation patterns" with a checkmark and underneath, in his cramped script, three-year cycle optimal. Little arrows linked one note to another where he'd revised his thinking, the paper a record of problems worked and reworked.

The journal smelled the way the farm had smelled in late summer—old leather, dust, a hint of soil that had been brought in on boots and never fully left. More than once in the last six months, she'd caught herself pressing the book against her face just to breathe that scent in. Today she settled for resting her palm flat over half a page, thumb in the gutter, and feeling where the pen had dug a letter into the paper hard enough that the ghost of it bled through to the next sheet.

She knew which entries he'd written on good days and which on bad. There was a tightness to his script when he'd been stuck, letters cramped together, underlines heavier. When he was solving something, the lines loosened; there was air between the words. She could read his mood just from the way his pen had traveled.

Six months out, she'd memorized those patterns the way other people memorized their own phone numbers.

"You did this to fix things," she said quietly, the words for herself more than anyone listening. "You did this knowing it meant… that."

Her gaze slid back to the wall. To the waveform. To the transcription. To the sticky note that called the creatures on their pitch.

They thought they'd found the soft spot. He'd always hated being alone. Hated the way the farm could stretch out into a silence that felt like it would swallow a person whole.

They'd taken that ache and sharpened it, turned it into a hook.

Emily reached for a fresh index card, uncapped a pen, and wrote:

> > If consciousness can expand to fill a field, can it contract again?
> > Can it focus? Localize? Communicate beyond temp/wind/light?

She pinned the card beside the waveform, running yarn from it to a printed screenshot of one of Tyler's sensor readouts, the little spikes and dips that represented Josh responding at the boundary.

"You're out there," she said. "In there. Whatever. They think that means they win. They think they can dangle me in front of you like bait."

Her hand closed reflexively around the edge of the journal. The leather creaked.

"Joshua," she added under her breath, the old-fashioned version of his name slipping out before she could stop it. "I am not going to let them turn what you did into a sales pitch."

She set the pen down in the gutter of the book, right between two lines of his handwriting, and looked up at the wall one more time. The yarn, the photos, the scattered notes. Chaos, from a distance. Up close, a field under cultivation. She was still working the soil.

Six months of trying to reconstruct thirty-seven seconds.

She wasn't finished.

Tyler's apartment looked less like a place someone lived in and more like the inside of a thought.

Cables snaked across the floor in careful arcs. Surge protectors hummed under a bank of metal shelving. Four monitors sat on a desk that had been meant for one, their bezels forming a makeshift command center. In the glow, empty ramen cups glimmered like artifacts.

On the middle screen, in blocky white letters against a black terminal window, the dataset title blinked:

`BENNETT_001 - Comprehensive Archive`

Folders nested beneath it: AUDIO_ANALYSIS, SENSOR_LOGS, BOUNDARY_READINGS, WITNESS_ACCOUNTS. Another window overlapped the corner of the main screen, tagged `UNKNOWN_001 - Unidentified Observer`.

Tyler scrolled through the archive with the careful touch of someone paging through a fragile book.

October 21: boundary logs spiked like a heart attack at 7:13:00 a.m., readings jumping off the chart as the field had been rewritten. At 7:13:37, everything snapped to a new baseline, as if reality had settled into a different groove.

November. December. January. The data rolled past: temperature changes, barometric quirks, fluctuations in electromagnetic noise. Thin lines and shaded areas tracing the ways Hollow Fields breathed now.

He'd spent the first month just trying to tell when Josh was paying attention.

By February, he'd charted the patterns.

Emily's signature showed up as sharp drops in temperature localized to the boundary line, edges precise. Wind direction shifted in her favor when she argued with the air. Olivia's presence bent light in ways his cameras didn't always like—shadows crawled against the direction of the sun, exposures went weird. Mike's visits oscillated the temperature: up, down, up, restless flickers across a narrow band like pacing.

When all four came together, the ground itself vibrated, shallow tremors that his sensors read even when his own feet missed them.

He'd annotated all of it. Color-coded. Cross-referenced. Every dot on every chart was another line in the story of what Josh had become.

A knock on the door jolted him just enough to make the cursor jump.

"Yeah," he called.

Mike stepped in without waiting, ducking under a dangling ethernet cable. "Smells like you've been working," he said, eyeing the empty cups.

"That's just the ramen," Tyler said. "Working smells more like ozone and existential crisis."

Mike snorted, the sound somewhere between a laugh and a grunt, and dropped his jacket onto the back of the one spare chair. "You eat anything that didn't come in a foil packet today?"

Tyler clicked the dataset window away from the ramen evidence. "Had a sandwich."

"Did it have vegetables?"

"Tomato counts."

Mike let that argument die the way he always did, with a slight roll of his eyes. He leaned over the desk, gaze skimming the screens. "What are we looking at today?"

"The gap," Tyler said, and pulled up the audio analysis.

The waveform appeared on the largest monitor, blown up and overlaid with color bands. He'd stared at those jagged lines so often he could have redrawn them from memory.

"I've been running spectral analysis on the audio corruption," he started, the words picking up speed as they always did when he was already three steps ahead in his head. "Cross-referencing frequency decomposition with harmonic extraction algorithms, applying machine-learning pattern recognition to identify subsonic anomalies that might indicate dimensional bleed-through or temporal—"

"Tyler."

Mike's voice cut across the syllables with the ease of practice.

"English," he added.

Tyler's mouth closed. For a heartbeat his fingers hovered above the keyboard, muscles still braced for the next rush of jargon.

The room registered again: the hum of the tower under the desk, the faint traffic noise through the thin apartment walls, Mike's weight braced on his hands as he leaned over.

Anxiety made some people pace. It made Tyler talk fast.

He took a breath, let it out, and forced his words into another shape.

"I'm looking for Josh in the static," he said.

Mike's shoulders eased a fraction. "And?"

"The corruption isn't random." Tyler pointed at the colored bands overlaying the waveform. "See this section? At 7:13:14? The noise floor drops. Clarity spikes for point-eight seconds. That's when the creature's voice comes through. Then the interference slams back in harder than before until 7:13:37, when everything resets."

"So somebody—or something—let the audio through just long enough for the sales pitch," Mike said.

"Or couldn't block it completely." Tyler chewed on his bottom lip, eyes flicking between the bands. "What matters is it's structured. It's like… like someone threw a blanket over the cameras but left a corner up by accident. The visual feed goes dark right when the audio becomes important. Too clean to be coincidence."

Mike watched the shifting colors, his brow furrowing. "You think that was Josh? Blocking the view?"

"I don't know what he can control from where he is," Tyler said. "Or if it's the field itself doing it. But the systems didn't just fail. They were pushed. Something about that moment required… not being seen."

He didn't say: maybe for their sake. Maybe because watching a friend stop being a person and start being topology would burn through eyes, not just sensors.

Mike's reflection in the monitor looked older than six months ago. There were lines at the corners of his mouth now that hadn't been there when this had just been about weird jars and urban-legend ghost stories.

"What else have you got?" Mike asked.

Tyler clicked away from the waveform to another log sheet. "Boundary responses. You asked me a while back if he knows when we're there."

"Does he?"

"Yeah." Tyler tapped a chart where four lines in different colors rose and fell. "These are temperature deltas over the last six months, filtered by individual presence. Emily's visits—sharp, two-degree drops centered within three meters of the boundary. Yours—"

"Different?" Mike's mouth tugged at one corner.

"Restless," Tyler said. "Oscillating. Up, down, up. Like pacing, but in degrees instead of steps."

Mike let out a soft breath that might have been a laugh. "Fits."

"My visits," Tyler went on, pulling up another graph, "register as low-level vibrations through the field sensors. The hardware itself hums differently. Too many frequencies at once, like I'm… broadcasting instead of listening."

"Also fits," Mike said.

"And Olivia's?" he asked.

Tyler brought up an exposure log. "Light shifts. When she's there, the field plays with shadows. Nothing dramatic enough for a normal person to notice. But the cameras do."

Mike studied the overlapping patterns for a long moment. "So he knows when we're there. Separately. Still sees us as… separate."

"Data says yes," Tyler replied. "Whatever he is now, he still makes distinctions."

Mike nodded once, as if that was something he'd needed confirmed but hadn't known how to ask for.

They talked logistics for a little longer—who was driving to the boundary later, what time they were meeting, whether Olivia needed help with the gallery opening. Eventually Mike shrugged his jacket back on.

"Bring snacks to the field," he said, halfway out the door. "And real food to your mouth."

Tyler waved the comment away, but after the door clicked shut he made a mental note to order something that at least pretended to be a vegetable.

When the apartment settled back into the familiar layered hum of machines and silence, he opened the window tucked behind BENNETT_001.

`UNKNOWN_001 - Unidentified Observer`

The graph that appeared looked, at a glance, like any of the others. A series of peaks where there should have been flat lines. A presence pressing against the boundary.

It differed in all the ways that mattered.

The first occurrence: three weeks ago. 10:51 p.m. A pattern of minor anomalies clustered within a thirty-minute span. Temperature shifts that didn't match any of the friends' signatures. Microvibrations along the fence posts that nobody's boots had caused. A subtle distortion in ambient electromagnetic noise.

Four days later: same window of time, same cluster. And again the following week. And again, and again. Fifteen visits in three weeks, always between 10:47 and 11:23 p.m., always at the edge of Hollow Fields. Never crossing.

Tyler had run the signature against everything he had—Eliza's old pattern from the months when she'd still been present, Elizabeth's recorded presence during research trips outside the boundary, even baseline readings from the townsfolk they'd catalogued for the historical record.

No match.

Whoever this was, they stood at the line and watched. Long enough for the field to notice. Long enough for the sensors to notice. Long enough to be more than an accident.

He tagged the latest log entry with a note:

> Intentional, not incidental. Studying. Unknown motivations.

He opened a new text file in the UNKNOWN_001 folder and started a log.

> > Visit 1–15: Late evening. Boundary only. No crossing. Duration 15–30 min. Signature suggests sustained focus.
> > Hypothesis candidates:
> > – New researcher?
> > – Recruiter from outside?
> > – Another… guardian?

The word looked strange in his own typing, so he underlined it, then erased the underline. No point guessing too hard without more data.

"Emily needs to see this," he murmured. "Tonight."

He set a reminder on his phone, because the last thing he wanted was to forget to mention "mysterious boundary stalker" at their six-month ritual.

He saved the log, closed the UNKNOWN_001 window, and pulled BENNETT_001 back to the front. The cursor blinked in the naming field of a new subdirectory.

He typed:

`BENNETT_002 - Extended Field Study (Year One)`

Six months had been enough to prove this wasn't a temporary anomaly. This was the rest of his life.

He leaned back in his chair, staring at the columns of numbers that represented Josh now: voltage, temperature, light levels, vibration.

Two unsolved problems: thirty-seven seconds of missing clarity and an unknown presence he couldn't identify.

Maybe some part of the story always stayed out of reach.

He rolled his shoulders, cracked his neck, and started another script.

Not knowing wasn't an excuse to stop measuring.

The gallery looked almost finished, which meant Olivia could finally see what she'd been trying to build.

White walls held grids of frames, some filled with photographs, others with handwritten pages mounted on backing board. A few were deliberately empty, brass corners glinting around glass that sheltered nothing but the painted names of moments.

At the entrance, a vinyl decal announced the show's title in clean black letters:

Hollow Fields: Frames Without Photographs

The central piece sat on a waist-high pedestal near the back: the camera that had exploded in her hands on October 21. Or what remained of it. The cracked lens had been cleaned and fixed onto a small stand, the fractured circle of glass catching the track lights in a way that made the spiderweb cracks glow faintly.

Beneath it, behind glass, her handwriting covered a sheet of heavy paper.

"I still don't get it," said the gallery assistant, a woman in a paint-spattered hoodie who'd been helping hang the work all day. "You built a career on catching impossible things on camera, and now you're… not using cameras?"

Olivia adjusted the angle of a frame by a few millimeters. "I'm still documenting," she said. "I'm just admitting the camera isn't the only way to do it."

"Critics are going to say this is a stunt," the assistant warned. "A famous photographer puts up a show where half the frames are empty."

"They're not empty." Olivia stepped back, taking in the room as a composition. "They're… honest. The cameras failed. That doesn't mean nothing happened. The absence is part of the story."

The assistant made a doubtful noise, but moved off to straighten another label.

Olivia walked the perimeter.

On one wall, a photograph captured Josh standing at the boundary, one hand extended towards a faint shimmer in the air. Light caught the edge of his cheekbone; the field behind him looked like any other stretch of overgrown land. If you didn't know what you were looking at, it was just a skinny farm kid staring at nothing.

Another frame held an early-morning shot of the farmers' market square. The stall where the Golden Pickles had once stood was empty, its table bare except for a faint discoloration in the boards. The angle made the absence itself the subject.

A close-up of Mike's hands: scars across knuckles, dirt under nails, fingers clutching a rolled-up boundary map hard enough to crumple the paper. The crop cut off everything but the hands and the edge of the map, forcing attention to the way the tendons stood out.

Emily's notebook lay open in another frame, captured in a late-afternoon slant of light that turned the scribbled columns into a grid of shadows. "Believes / Doesn't believe" headings at the top, lines of evidence beneath each, most of them crossed out. The final line—Josh's word—was underlined twice.

Tyler's equipment got its own spread: cables crawling across apartment carpet, sensors clamped to fence posts, laptop screens reflected in his glasses as he stared at boundary logs. There was something almost devotional in the way the light hit his face in those shots, the glow of data reflected back in his eyes.

And there, a few frames down, the one that had become a quiet gravity well for the whole show: Josh with the journal.

She'd taken it three weeks before the merger. A candid shot, Josh unaware of the lens, hunched over his grandfather's book at the kitchen table. The camera angle caught his profile, the slope of his shoulders, fingers tracing the edge of an earlier entry before he wrote a new line. The afternoon light from the window striped the leather cover and the paper, and though the photograph couldn't capture texture, the way his hand moved suggested the page had weight.

Olivia moved closer, eyes scanning the details she'd come to know too well: the slight redness in his knuckles from the cold, the way he curled his fingers to keep the pen steady, his mouth pulled tight in concentration.

The door opened behind her, the soft whoosh of the gallery's air cylinder.

"Hey," Emily said.

Olivia turned. Emily stood just inside, binder tucked under one arm, hair pulled into a quick knot that hadn't quite tamed all of it. There were new smudges of ink on her fingers, the kind that took more than one hand washing to get rid of.

"You're early," Olivia said. "Good. I wanted you to see it without a crowd."

Emily's gaze swept the room, taking in the walls. She moved slowly, like she was walking a field she hadn't decided was safe yet.

She paused in front of the photograph of Josh at the boundary, lips pressing together. At Mike's hands. At her own notebook, immortalized mid-scribble.

When she reached the journal photograph, she stopped completely.

"You caught him thinking," she said after a long moment.

Olivia stepped up beside her. "I didn't realize it was rare until after. How often he let anyone see him stuck."

Emily's mouth quirked, the ghost of a smile. "He hated looking like he didn't know something. But the journal didn't care if he looked stupid in the margins."

Her eyes stayed on the image. "I took it that morning," she added after a beat. "The journal. After the merger. I've been…" She shifted the binder under her arm. "Living with it."

Olivia glanced at the ink on her fingers, then back at the photograph. "Reading it, or dissecting it?"

"Both." Emily exhaled, a short puff. "I know which entries he wrote when he'd just come in from the fields. The pages smell different. I know which parts he kept coming back to—rotation notes, soil charts. I can tell when he was figuring something out because the pen pressure changes halfway down the page."

Her fingertips brushed the glass near his hand in the photograph, stopping shy of leaving a print.

"I trace his writing," she admitted, voice low. "Sometimes. Just... follow the lines with my finger. I know where every downstroke bit into the paper. Where he underlined something twice because it mattered. It's like —" She cut herself off, jaw clenching. "God, that sounds obsessive."

"That sounds like witness," Olivia said. "The good kind. The kind that keeps looking even when everybody else has stopped."

Emily's eyes glinted, but she didn't look away from the picture. "Sometimes I open it just to touch where his hand was. Not to read. Just to... feel that it's still there."

Olivia set a hand briefly on her shoulder, the contact light and quick. "There are worse things you could be doing with your time."

She gestured toward the central pedestal. "Come see this."

Emily followed her to the shattered lens. The mounted glass looked almost decorative under the lights now, a radiating spiderweb of fractures.

She bent to read the page beneath.

Olivia's account ran across the sheet in dark ink, printed careful and steady. The words stayed in present tense, the way she'd forced them to when she wrote it within an hour of the merger.

"The knot implodes inward," the text began. "Not explosion—collapse. The air stretches toward it like fabric pulled at the center, pulling us with it for half a heartbeat before we snap back. His outline fractures. Not disintegrating. Multiplying. Across too many moments at once, too many possibilities, until the shape that was Josh-sitting-on-couch becomes Josh-everywhere-at-once becomes field itself. The hum cuts off. The pressure drops. The knot is gone. The couch is empty. We are standing in a room where our friend just became geography."

Emily's throat worked as she read. Her eyes ran the lines twice before she straightened.

"This is the purest account we have," she said, voice roughened at the edges. "Tyler's got data gaps. Mike's got… everything in between his head and his hands. I wasn't even there." She looked at the page again. "But you saw it. And you wrote it down while it was still… happening."

"The cameras were dead," Olivia said. "Both of them. Battery with charge. Lens that decided to crack itself. If I'd waited, I'd start filling in blanks. So I wrote until my hand cramped." She tapped the glass. "This is what survived."

"He'd like this," Emily said after a beat. "The title. The empty frames. Making something whole out of what's missing."

"I made it because he can't tell me himself if I'm getting it wrong," Olivia said. "So I'm telling him what I saw."

They walked back to the entrance, where the artist statement had been mounted beside the door.

On October 21, my cameras failed at the moment that mattered most, the first line read. Battery death with forty-seven percent charge remaining. Lens fracture with no physical cause. These failures were not technical. They were ontological. Some events resist documentation.

I witnessed anyway.

Emily read to the end, lips moving silently:

This exhibition documents what happens when documentation fails: the witness continues. The eye behind the lens matters more than the lens. Some truths cannot be photographed. They must be seen, written, remembered, carried. Hollow Fields taught me that the frame matters less than what you do when the frame breaks.

At the far wall, an empty frame held only a label at the bottom:

October 21, 7:13 a.m. – The Moment Cameras Failed

"No pictures," Emily said.

"Just what we saw," Olivia replied. "And what we do with it."

Emily looked once more around the room—at the photos of hands and journals and empty stalls, at the shards of glass, at the spaces where absence had been framed on purpose.

"He'd be proud," she said.

"I hope so," Olivia replied. "I hope—" She caught herself, shook her head. "Well. If he's watching, at least he's got something interesting to look at."

The thought hung between them, companionable and sharp.

The boundary looked almost ordinary at a distance.

Up close, once you knew what to look for, the seams showed. The grass on the Hollow Fields side was never quite in sync with the wind that touched the road. Sound shifted as it crossed the line; crickets on one side chirped a fraction off from their cousins on the other. The air held a taste Mike still hadn't found a word for—metal and soil and the moment before a storm.

He stood at the ditch's edge with his hands in his jacket pockets, sneakers planted just on the safe side. Early evening light slanted low through the trees, gilding the tops of the stalks on the field's side and leaving the roadside gravel dull.

He came out twice a week now. Tuesdays and Saturdays, mostly. The schedule had started as something to do on the days when the hours felt too long; now it was a rhythm he couldn't imagine breaking.

"Tyler thinks I'm looking for something," he said to the line of fence posts and invisible pressure. "He's not wrong."

The temperature dipped a degree. Not enough to make his breath fog, but enough that the hairs on his forearms prickled under his sleeves. The field's version of a raised eyebrow.

"Still trying to find the angle," he went on. "The deal I missed. The sentence I could've swapped out at 7:12 that would've changed 7:13."

The chill deepened, a soft push against his skin, then eased.

"Yeah, yeah," he said. "I know. You made your choice. Doesn't mean I have to like it."

He kicked a clod of dirt toward the ditch. It crumbled at the boundary as if something had eaten the momentum.

"Doesn't mean I stop looking for the loophole either. That's my job. Was." He blew out a breath. "Whatever."

The air warmed half a notch, heat moving across his face in a brief wash. It felt too deliberate to be random. Josh's equivalent of a bark of laughter.

"Don't get smug," Mike said, but some of the tightness in his shoulders eased. "Being a stretch of haunted farmland doesn't make you right about everything."

Something moved in the tree line.

He straightened, weight shifting forward. The creatures slipped between trunks like shadows that had leaked off the things casting them. Three of them tonight, their forms just wrong enough to keep the brain from deciding on a name for any part.

The lead one, the one that always seemed to notice him first, tilted its head. The gesture was familiar now.

"You return," it said. The voice rode the wind, not quite sound. "Twice each seven days."

"Observant," Mike said. He didn't step back. Not anymore.

"We told you joining would end the loneliness," it went on. "His and yours. The offer stands."

They always got to that part eventually. Sometimes they approached it sideways, with talk about his friends aging and Josh not. Sometimes they went for it in the first minute. He'd learned to recognize the shape of the argument no matter how they dressed it.

"You told me he'd be alone forever," Mike said. "Aware of everything. Watching us get old while he stays whatever he is now. Feeling our grief and not being able to do a damn thing about it. You said joining would fix that."

"Yes." The word rustled through the grass. "Community in timelessness. No more separation between self and field. He would not be alone. You would not grieve. No more watching each other suffer across the divide."

"Sounds great," Mike said. "On a billboard."

The creature stilled, attention sharpening.

"One problem," he added.

It waited.

"Josh made his choice knowing exactly what it would cost." He heard his own voice harden. "He looked at eternal isolation and did it anyway because the alternative was letting you keep chewing on this place. Joining him now wouldn't be mercy. It'd be undercutting him. Turning what he did into another recruitment strategy."

The creature's outline flickered at the edges, as though its shape had been drawn in unsteady ink.

"You want us to sign up," Mike pressed, "because if we do, then what you did looks smart instead of selfish. If we choose it, then you didn't fail. You didn't give in. It was inevitable, right? That's what you tell yourselves."

The branches along the boundary were utterly still. No bird, no insect, no breeze.

"But it wasn't inevitable for him," Mike said. "He proved that. He chose guardian over whatever you are. And I'm choosing to live with his choice, even when it hurts like hell. So there's no deal. Not today. Not ever."

Heat rolled over him like someone had opened an oven door just beyond the ditch. His jacket suddenly felt too heavy, sweat breaking under his collar.

"Yeah," he said under his breath. "Thought you'd like that one."

The creature's head tipped again, its form starting to thin around the edges.

"You will tire of watching," it said as it receded. "You will tire of pain."

"Probably," Mike said. "That's kind of the point."

They slid back into the tree line, swallowed by the dark undergrowth. The sounds of the ordinary forest came back in their wake—leaves ticking against one another, a distant owl.

Mike sat on the edge of the ditch, elbows on his knees. For a while he watched ants working a line along a rock, climbing over one another, carrying pieces of something too big for one alone. The light thinned as the sun nudged closer to the horizon.

Six months of these conversations hadn't found him any loopholes. He'd tried bargaining in the early days—offers, hypotheticals, threats. All the old tools. They'd slid off the situation like rain off oiled cloth.

Maybe that was the work he'd needed to do: learn which things couldn't be talked down.

He picked up a pebble, rolled it between thumb and forefinger, and flicked it toward the boundary. It hit the invisible line and bounced back onto the roadside, landing near his boot.

"Yeah," he said. "Got it."

The air stirred, wind coming from the field now, cool against his face, as if something on the other side were nodding.

"You like it when I tell them off," he said. "You always did like watching a good argument."

That earned him another little swell of heat, blooming across the back of his neck.

"Fine. I'll keep doing it." He pushed himself to his feet, brushing dirt off his jeans. "Somebody's got to run interference when the cult recruiters show up."

Headlights swung down the access road, cutting flickering stripes through the trees.

Emily's car took the turn a hair too fast, throwing gravel. Tyler's sensible sedan followed at a law-abiding distance. A third set of lights up the road would be Olivia, stopping for every scenic view sign whether she meant to or not.

Mike exhaled, long and steady.

"They don't know I've been here two hours already," he said. "They don't need to."

The boundary's temperature held steady now, a neutral hum just under the skin.

"Tonight's about all of us," he added. "I'll yell at your would-be fan club again later."

He stepped back from the ditch as the cars pulled in to park, tucking his hands back into his pockets just as Emily climbed out of hers with a binder under one arm and determination in the set of her shoulders.

They gathered at the same break in the fence where they'd stood six months earlier, when the ground had still felt raw beneath their feet.

Emily set her binder down on the hood of Mike's truck, tabs and sticky flags bristling along the edge. Tyler kept his tablet in a protective case, thumb resting near the side button like it was a talisman. Olivia carried a neatly folded sheet of paper—the gallery statement—tucked into the pocket of her jacket.

Mike brought himself, his habit of scanning the tree line, and the way he always stood half a pace between the others and whatever he thought might come out of the woods.

"Six months," Emily said, looking past the ditch to the field. The air on that side shivered faintly.

"Hundred eighty days," Tyler said. "Four thousand three hundred twenty hours. Two hundred fifty-nine thousand two hundred minutes."

Olivia huffed a breath that wasn't quite a laugh. "He's counting."

"Of course he is," Mike said. "Somebody has to keep track."

The temperature at the boundary dipped, a precise little drop that brushed their cheeks and wrists, then settled. A hello in degrees.

They waited.

Back in October, Eliza had appeared almost immediately whenever they approached the line. In November and December she'd showed up with the inevitability of the seasons. By late winter, her timing had grown a little less precise—some days minutes, some days seconds—but she'd always come.

Now the light stretched, lengthened, thinned.

Five minutes passed. Ten.

Olivia rubbed the back of her neck, eyes on the trees. "Where is she?" she said at last.

Tyler dug his tablet out of its case. "Hang on."

He swiped through menus with quick, confident motions, fingers finding the files without needing to look. Boundary logs. Presence graphs. He pulled up a function that overlaid signatures on a time axis and flicked through months.

"October through February," he said, tilting the screen so the others could see. Spikes appeared on the graph whenever Eliza's pattern registered. "Every visit we made to the boundary? She shows up within five minutes. Hundred percent presence."

His finger slid to the March entries. "Four visits. One no-show. March twenty-third."

"And since then?" Emily asked.

Tyler scrolled. The graph after March 15 lay flat.

"Nothing," he said. "Five weeks. No Eliza signature in any reading I've taken."

The word silence meant something different in a haunted field when you could quantify it.

Emily went through the pieces out loud, the way she always did when a story wanted assembling.

"The curse broke," she said. "Golden Pickles stopped luring people. The town stopped trapping new guardians. The creatures lost their... production line." Her gaze flicked to the place among the trees where Eliza had first stepped out to greet them. "Eliza was bound up in that system from the day she died."

"Family journals say the curse anchored itself through her death," Olivia said. "The first guardian whose sacrifice got twisted. Every generation after hers could only watch from outside."

"If Josh broke the curse completely," Emily said slowly, "then the mechanism came apart. The Golden Pickles lost their pull. The town could breathe. And the thing that had been using Eliza as a gear..."

"Let her go," Mike finished.

Tyler looked down at the flat line on his screen. "Field says she's gone," he said. "Not absorbed. Not flickering. Just... absent."

Emily's hand closed around the edge of the truck's hood. "So she's free," she said.

The word landed with the same weight as a verdict.

They stood in the lowering light while the field rustled on the other side of the ditch, its own overlapping centuries adjusting around the removal of a piece that had been jammed in the works for more than a hundred years.

"Where do you go," Olivia murmured, "when you've been stuck in one place for that long?"

"Anywhere," Mike said. "Everywhere. Or nowhere." He shifted his weight, gravel crunching under his boot. "Maybe you just... stop. Sleep. I don't know."

Emily's jaw worked. "Do you think she's okay?" she asked. "Wherever she is?"

No one tried to answer immediately. The wind at the boundary stilled; the field seemed to be listening with them.

Movement flickered at the far edge of Hollow Fields.

It drew Emily's eye the way a storm cloud did on the horizon—instinct more than motion. She squinted against the last of the sun, trying to separate the shape from the line of trees behind it.

A figure stood where the forest met the town, too far for features. The clothes were dark, long enough that the outline blurred into either old-fashioned skirts or a modern coat, distance turning centuries into guesses.

The stillness was what caught her.

Not the coiled waiting of the creatures, not the predatory lean she'd come to recognize. This was the stillness of someone standing in a doorway they'd finally been allowed to walk through, looking back one last time.

Emily's ribs pinched for a second, like the space around her lungs had narrowed. It could have been a trick of the light, a farmer, a tree. It could have been anything.

Relief slid through her anyway, quick and inexplicable as a shift in wind direction.

Like watching a person set down a weight they'd carried so long their spine had curved around it.

"Do you see—" she began.

"Yeah," Mike said quietly. "I see it."

Tyler and Olivia followed their gaze. All four of them stood at the boundary, watching the far edge of the field where the figure watched back. The sunset turned the glass in the distant buildings to molten orange behind it, blurring detail.

No one waved. No one called out.

Tyler's hand twitched toward his tablet, reflex wanting a reading, but some other impulse stilled it.

In the space of a blink, the figure was gone.

Not walking away. Not dissolving into mist. One moment there, the next the horizon held only trees and the overlapping silhouettes of roofs.

"Did we just—" Olivia started.

"Maybe," Emily said. "I don't know."

They didn't turn the moment into a project. They didn't march through the field to check footprints or argue over whether they'd seen the same thing.

If Eliza Nightshade had come to look at the town that had used up her death and then finally been freed by another guardian's choice, that goodbye was hers, not theirs.

Gravel crunched behind them.

Emily turned.

Elizabeth stood at the edge of the access road, the strap of a weathered leather bag cutting across one shoulder. She looked more grounded than she had in October, grief weight redistributed into the way she carried herself instead of hanging off her like extra clothing.

"Sorry I'm late," she said, a little breathless. "Research rabbit hole. Time got away from me."

"You made it," Olivia said. "That's what counts."

Elizabeth's attention had already slid to the boundary. Her jaw tightened, a micro-flinch so small Emily might have missed it six months ago.

"You can cross now," Emily said. It came out as a statement, not a question.

Elizabeth nodded, eyes never leaving the shimmer where normal air met Hollow Fields.

"Three weeks ago," she said, "I tried on a whim. After one of Tyler's reports. I expected the usual—pressure like cotton in my skull, that tug backward, the fog rolling in. Instead…"

She lifted a hand and reached out. Fingers pushed through the place her family's journals had warned would always stop them.

No resistance. No buzzing nerves. Just air.

"It's open," she said, voice rough.

"Have you gone in yet?" Olivia asked.

"Not properly." Elizabeth dropped her hand. "A few steps. Enough to know it isn't going to throw me back out or wipe my memory. I wanted to —" She glanced at the group. "It felt wrong to go in for real without telling you first. Josh Bennett didn't just free this town. He freed my family line out of a border we didn't earn."

Tyler tipped his tablet, showing her the flattening of Eliza's signature. "No more field presence from your ancestor," he said. "She's not part of the machinery anymore."

Elizabeth's eyes glistened for a heartbeat before she blinked hard. "Good," she said. "She deserved more than being a cog in that thing."

She looked back at the field, at the town beyond. "Do you—would you come with me? For the first proper time? It seems… fitting."

Emily felt Hollow Fields' attention shift, the same way she could feel a barn full of animals turn their heads when someone came in with a feed bucket. The air on the far side of the ditch tasted sharper all of a sudden, like cold water out of a well.

"Yeah," she said. "We'll go."

They stepped down into the ditch together, up the other side, and across the place where the barrier had once made the world double.

The shift was subtle the moment they crossed. A ghost weight pressing down, then lifting again. The hairs on Emily's arms rose, then smoothed.

Elizabeth paused just inside, eyes closed, breathing shallow.

"It's layered," she murmured. "The way the journals always said. Past and present sitting on top of each other." Her eyes opened, taking in the houses, the field, the faint shimmer in the distance where the knot had once hung. "But it's... lighter."

Further ahead, in the direction of the town square, a woman on a ladder painted over the old farmers' market sign.

The original words, Golden Pickles – Every Quarter, flaked and faded, still visible. Below them, in neat, fresh strokes, the woman added new letters:

Hollow Fields Historical Society – Visitors Welcome

Her hands were just hands. Human. Sunlight hit her arms; nothing shifted, nothing sprouted, no creature shape emerged from under the skin. Kids ran in the background, zigzagging through the square in a chasing game, shrieking laughter echoing off the brick. One of them darted through the exact space Emily knew had once looped people in circles for hours.

They kept going, unsnagged.

"It's different," Emily said softly.

Elizabeth swallowed, eyes tracking the children. "Free," she said. "It's free now."

She turned back to the field, to the land that held Josh.

"Can you feel him?" Emily asked.

Elizabeth stood still for a moment, letting her eyes unfocus. "Yes," she said eventually. "Not like a voice. More like... the hum of power lines when you're standing directly under them. He's everywhere." She smiled, small and incredulous. "He knows I'm here. The resistance that used to slam me back isn't there anymore. It feels like—like being told I can finally come home to a place I've only ever been allowed to look at on a map."

Warmth drifted across their faces. The sun was already low; the heat didn't match its angle.

"He's glad you're inside," Olivia said.

"Hope so," Elizabeth replied. "We owe him more than footnotes."

They walked on, leaving the road behind, the field swallowing their footsteps.

In a shallow rise not far from the old boundary, where the ground felt most alive underfoot, they stopped. Elizabeth set her bag down, fingers already itching toward the notebooks inside, then pulled them back to give the moment its own room.

"Six months," Emily said again. "We said we'd come back. To tell him. To tell each other."

Tyler woke his tablet, opening the current sensor display but lowering the brightness so it wouldn't dominate. The field's readings danced quietly in a corner of the screen.

"The last time we did this," Olivia said, "you were geography for... what, ten minutes?"

"Ten minutes and thirty-two seconds," Tyler murmured.

"And now..." Olivia looked around. "Now you're a whole town."

They went one by one.

Emily stepped a little closer to where the invisible hum felt strongest, journal weight familiar in her hands even though she'd left the actual book back at her apartment. She didn't need the object with her to speak to the person it had belonged to.

"I promised I'd figure this out," she said, voice steady. "I'm trying, Joshua. I've got Tyler's audio—forty-seven listens and counting. I've got your journal. I know where your pen dug into the page because you were working something through. I know where you got lazy with your cursive because you'd been up too late."

The air cooled in front of her, temperature dropping in a clean, sharp band that brushed her cheeks and the bridge of her nose.

"I'm living," she went on. "Taking exams. Paying rent. Buying cheap coffee that tastes like pond water. I'm also pinning you to my walls like a suspect in my own little detective movie. If expanded consciousness can exist, then compressed consciousness has to be possible too. I'm not giving up on finding a way to… pull focus. Even if all I manage is getting you from field-sized down to something that can tap Morse code on a damn fence post."

The chill deepened for a heartbeat, then eased. Wind picked up at her back, pushing her lightly toward the others.

Tyler shuffled closer, lines of data flickering across his screen. "BENNETT_001 has one hundred eighty-six complete datasets now," he said. "Six months of readings. I can sort your responses by visitor, by time of day, by emotional state inferred from temperature gradients."

He caught himself, took in a breath, and rephrased.

"I can see when you're listening," he said. "I can see when you're proud. When you're warning us. You respond differently to each of us." He tapped the graph. "Temperature dips for Emily. Oscillation for Mike. Light distortions for Olivia. Ground vibration when we're all together. I'm logging it so the story doesn't evaporate when we do."

Under his boots, the soil trembled—a faint, even thrum, like a giant cat's purr running through stone.

"I started BENNETT_002," Tyler added. "Year one extended study. If there's a pattern in what you can do from where you are, I'll find it. That's the best way I know to honor…" He cleared his throat. "To honor what happened."

Olivia unfolded the gallery statement, the paper creasing along a line already worn by her fingers.

"The show opens tomorrow," she said. "People are going to file in and look at empty frames and think I've lost my mind. Some will get it. Most won't." She smiled slightly. "That's fine. It's not really for them."

She read the ending of her statement out loud, the words taking on a different weight under the open sky.

"This is my testimony," she said. "These are my frames without photographs. This is what I saw when my cameras couldn't look."

The light shifted around them. Shadows crawled a few degrees off the sun's path, bending, stretching, then sliding back again. The air seemed to hold a different depth of color for a second, as if someone had nudged the saturation knob on reality.

Olivia watched the grass at her feet brighten, then dim. "I know," she said softly. "I see you too."

Mike took his turn last.

"Still looking for the angle," he said. "Still haven't found one that doesn't cheapen what you did. That's annoying, by the way." His mouth twitched. "I keep coming out twice a week, in case you hadn't noticed. Tuesdays and Saturdays. Sometimes the creatures show up and try the loneliness pitch again. I tell them where they can stick it."

The temperature around him spiked, heat rolling across his shoulders, hot enough he tugged at his collar.

"You like that part," he said. "Could always tell when you thought I'd said something clever. Now I get awarded spontaneous climate change instead of a snort."

He shoved his hands deeper into his pockets. "I hate that you aren't here," he said. "But I'm done trying to haggle you out of the choice you made. You chose this knowing exactly how bad it'd be. I'm choosing to stay here and keep yelling at whoever thinks they can turn that into a sales pitch."

The warmth held, steady now, a blanket draped across the group.

Elizabeth stepped forward, clearing her throat.

"I wasn't here for the moment," she said. "Not in the way they were. I've only ever met you through archives and aftermath. But my family spent one hundred thirty years stuck outside a line we couldn't cross because of the way Eliza's death got twisted. The fact that I can stand here now, in the place she died for, and not feel the curse trying to scrub me out—that's on you."

She glanced toward the town, where the woman on the ladder was climbing down, new sign complete.

"I'm going to stay inside the boundary awhile," Elizabeth said. "Document what this place is when it isn't chewing on people. Write a history that isn't written by the curse. And I'm going to try to find… traces. Of where Eliza went when she stopped being a gear in its machine."

The wind picked up, tugging at her hair and at the corner of the papers sticking out of her bag. It smelled like turned earth and rain in the distance.

"She'd want to know someone was taking care of the story," Elizabeth said. "So. That's my job now. Yours is… all this."

They stood there until the sun finished its slide and the field's shadows stretched long.

Eventually, practicalities elbowed their way back in. Emily had an early shift. Tyler had a script still running. Olivia needed to be up for the gallery opening. Mike had farm work in the morning. Elizabeth had equipment to set up before full dark.

Tyler glanced at his tablet one more time, fingers freezing mid-scroll.

"The unknown signature," he said. "The one I mentioned."

Emily turned. "The what?"

"Been seeing it for three weeks." He flipped the display so they all could see. "Always late evening, always at the boundary. Fifteen visits so far. Last one was last night at 10:52 p.m. Stays for fifteen to thirty minutes, then disappears. Never crosses. Signature doesn't match any of us, any townsfolk, Eliza, or Elizabeth."

Mike's mouth flattened. "So someone else is studying the field."

"Looks that way," Tyler said. "Signature reads as focused. Controlled. It's not a random wildlife blip. Whoever it is, they're paying attention."

The temperature dropped fast, a clean plunge that made all of them suck in a breath at the same time. Cold crept into collars and cuffs, sharp as river water.

"That's the warning pattern," Emily said. "Same as October. When things were about to get messy."

Elizabeth's shoulders squared. "The curse is broken," she said, "but the field still exists. There will always be people who want to understand it. And people who want to own it."

Olivia rubbed her arms. "Josh knows they're there."

"And he's worried," Mike added.

The chill eased, settling back into the ambient strangeness that was baseline now.

They walked back toward the boundary together. At the line, Elizabeth stopped.

"I'm staying," she said. "At least tonight. Maybe longer. I've got a lifetime of family research that never got checked against the real thing. And if someone else is sniffing around, I'd rather there be a Nightshade on the inside paying attention."

"You'll be safe?" Emily asked.

Elizabeth glanced down, then back up, a faint, wry smile on her mouth. "After what this place has done to my family?" she said. "This is the safest it's ever been for us. The field knows me now. And if it didn't want me here, I'd be on my ass on the road already."

She lifted a hand in a small wave as the others stepped back across the line, the tickle of the old barrier nothing more than a phantom sensation now.

Emily looked back once as they climbed into their cars. Elizabeth had already slung her bag down in the grass and was pulling out notebooks, a lantern, a small portable recorder. Starting the work she'd been born into but never allowed to do.

They drove away in a staggered line—Mike's truck first, then Emily's car, Tyler's sedan, Olivia's hatchback—headlights threading through the darkening trees.

The hum of their engines faded. The boundary glowed only in the subtle ways now, temperature and wind and light shifting through one another.

Hollow Fields breathed.

For a moment that sat somewhere between seconds and seasons, a flicker of awareness swept the land: four distinct impressions pulling away down the road—sharp-insistent, restless-pacing, scattered-humming, clear-steady. A new, determined presence settling inside the town's bones. At the boundary, another pattern, narrow and intent, waiting and watching.

Then the impressions folded back into the larger weave.

The field went on paying attention.

AFTERWORD

On Curses, Choices, and What Comes After

If you've made it this far, you've walked all the way through Hollow Fields—into the knot, through the breaking of the curse, and six months beyond the moment when one kid stopped being just a person and became part of the land.

On the surface, this is a story about a haunted product and a hungry field. Underneath that, it's about something much smaller and harder to shake: the way grief changes shape over time, and the difference between a sacrifice that's demanded and one that's chosen.

Old bargains like the one that shaped Hollow Fields are comfortable for everyone except the people they grind up. The curse that started with Eliza's death became a machine: luring new guardians, chewing through their lives, trapping a town and a family line in a loop. The easiest ending—the one the creatures keep offering—is a kind of surrender: give in, join us, and at least you won't be alone in your suffering.

Josh's story refuses that. He breaks the curse instead of feeding it. He frees a town full of people who never got to choose what they were part of. He untangles Eliza from a century of forced complicity. He opens the gate for Elizabeth's family to finally step inside the place that defined them from the outside.

The cost is very real. There's no reset button here. He doesn't get his body back. His friends don't get a miracle that hands him back, unchanged, in the final chapter. What they get is harder and, in some ways, more honest: the work of living with what he did.

That's what the epilogue is about.

Emily builds a wall of evidence because that's how she loves someone she can't reach anymore. Tyler turns their friend into a dataset not to dehumanize him, but to make sure the story of what happened doesn't vanish when the last witness is gone. Olivia rebuilds her entire way of seeing the world after the cameras fail at the moment she needs them most. Mike keeps showing up to argue with predators and with the empty air because loyalty, for him, looks like refusing to let anyone cheapen that choice.

And Elizabeth finally steps into Hollow Fields as more than an archivist of other people's suffering. She becomes the one who will document what the town is now that it's no longer an engine for sacrifice.

Of course, this isn't the last time we'll see any of them.

Hollow Fields still exists. The creatures at the edge of the trees haven't disappeared; they've just lost their favorite toy. There's an unknown observer at the boundary, visiting night after night with a signature that doesn't match anyone we know. Elizabeth has begun her search for Eliza's true ending. Emily hasn't let go of the question: if a human consciousness can expand to fill a field, what else might be possible?

Their stories will continue beyond these pages, but I wanted this first book to land on a specific truth: sometimes the bravest thing a character can do isn't to find a loophole or discover a hidden spell. Sometimes it's to accept that a cost is real—and pay it anyway, not because the world is fair, but because someone has to break the cycle.

Thank you for spending time with this strange town, its jars, its ghosts, and its people. If these characters stayed with you—if you find yourself thinking about lonely fields, or about the way grief becomes part of the landscape—you're already standing at the boundary with them.

There's more ahead. For now, let Hollow Fields rest. It's earned at least a moment of quiet.